THE JEW
AND
THE POPE

SYBIL TERRES GILMAR

INFINITY
PUBLISHING

ISBN 978-0-7414-7633-3 Paperback
ISBN 978-0-7414-7634-0 eBook

Printed in the United States of America

This is a work of fiction. Names, characters, places, and incidents either are the product of the author's imagination or are used fictitiously. Any resemblance to actual events or locales or persons, living or dead, is entirely coincidental.

Published October 2012

INFINITY PUBLISHING
1094 New DeHaven Street, Suite 100
West Conshohocken, PA 19428-2713
Toll-free (877) BUY BOOK
Local Phone (610) 941-9999
Fax (610) 941-9959
Info@buybooksontheweb.com
www.buybooksontheweb.com

To my parents, Rose and Sam Terres, who had the good sense to leave Poland when they did.

Table of Contents

History Timeline — Significant Dates

312 — Constantine conquers Italy and promotes Christianity at its religion and issues edicts against Jews and denounces them as Christ killers.

1215 — Fourth Lateran Council Issues canons: 1) Jews to wear a distinguishing mark on clothing and live in segregated quarters; 2) Jews may not exact interest on loans to Christians, Christians may not do business with Jews who don't obey Church rules; 3) Jews may not hold public office; 4) Converts to Christianity must stop Jewish observances; 5) Jews prohibited from hiring Christian women of child bearing age as servants.

1236 — Pope Gregory IX condemns excesses of the fifth Crusade, in its violence against Jews.

1353 — Boccaccio completes "Decameron," which acknowledges man's power and limitations, setting the stage for the humanism of the Renaissance.

1417–1431 — Pope Martin tries to control the Franciscans' anti-Jewish preaching. Issues a bull in **1429** that protects Jews

1437 — Cosimo de Medici, the Elder, grants the first formal charter to the Jews of Florence for moneylending

1464–1492 — Lorenzo Il Magnifico, becomes the protector of Florentine Jews, supporting Jewish scholarship, Talmudic studies and medicine. Oversees the "Golden Age of Florence," in which there is much interaction between Christians and Jews.

1492 — Sicily and Sardinia, as territories ruled by Spain, expel their Jews. The majority of refugees from the Spanish expulsion head for Portugal and Italy, specifically *Venice, Leghorn* and *Rome*, where they are protected by the Pope

1494 — France invades Italy; Jews of *Florence* and *Tuscany* expelled when the Medici fall from power; they return in **1513**—and bring the Jews back with them

1495 — Charles VIII of France occupies Kingdom of Naples, bringing new persecution against the Jews, many of whom went there as refugees from Spain. Jews will be expelled from Naples in **1510**—and again in **1541**

1508–1512 — Michelangelo paints Sistine Chapel

1517 — Martin Luther posts his theses on the gates of the Wittenberg Church in Germany.

1527 — Rome conquered by Charles V (Holy Roman Emperor) to stop alliance of Pope Julius II with Florence, Milan, and Venice to limit Charles' power.

1536–1541 — Michelangelo paints *The Last Judgment*

1542 — Pope Paul III establishes Inquisition in Rome to ferret out New Christians.

CHAPTER 1

Passion Play Performed

Hordes of people streamed through the narrow entrances to the Colosseum stepping over roosters and chickens that scurried under their feet. Did the artisans, the farmers, the barkeepers, the everyday folk even know that this gigantic amphitheatre once held 50,000 people who cheered sea battles and gladiators who tormented lions? Did they care that a gigiantic earthquake that struck Rome created its fractured structure? An earthquake that left enough stones so that thieves could build fences with them around their simple, impoverished homes? Today, they had come from all corners of Rome to its center to see a spectacle—a spectacle provided by the Papal Palace.

A stooped crone tripped over two quarreling cocks and landed in the mud. She picked herself up, grinning because she knew that today she would be special. She came for a showing of the Passion, and that would mean crying, shouting, praying, and even cursing. What a relief for spirit and body!

Murmurs could be heard among the crowd.

"Not a spit of wind blowing."

"The clouds are waiting to witness the story of our Savior."

"He who died on the cross for our sins."

Some people stepped aside for a herder leading his pigs around the huge oval of the Colosseum to the slop fields where the hogs could gorge on garbage to their hearts' desire. More than the usual amount of discarded fruit, peels, and bread would be available because of the size of the gathering. Pigs and hogs would eat well today. The herder might even pick up scraps for his family.

At the entrance designated for the common folk, tall, short, old, young, and fat Romans arrived. Men wore threadbare tunics and brown leggings. Women wore dyed muslin capes over shapeless dresses patched with care and good sewing skills. Some staggered in, influenced by the wine they had been drinking this morning and perhaps all night. The smell of vomit on their clothes seemed to bother no one, and fellow carousers cheerfully hoisted the inebriated that fell. One woman lifted the cover on her basket to show off her grapes and pears to those nearby. A man with his basket imitated her and guffawed when a passerby reached in and came up with nothing but stones.

A procession of mules entered a narrow side archway pulling carts that carried the sickly clustered so tightly that movement seemed impossible. Some mules carried lone men, women, and children. The papal authorities had set aside this entryway for the infirm—those with shortened arms or legs with twisted and maimed bodies. No one in the crowd averted their eyes from these sorry looking creatures. In fact, people cheered them on as part of the spectacle they were about to see. Maybe a miracle would occur and one of the crippled would suddenly walk again. It had happened before.

The massive gathering of gray clouds dampened not a bit of spirit in the crowd as bottles of home-made wine passed from person to person each taking a swig and wiping his lips with the back of his hand. The person who took the last drink raised the bottle high in the air and flung it against the wall to shatter. A cheer went up as though this was a glorious accomplishment.

At the elaborate and spacious Arch of Constantine entrance members of the clergy in the finest silks and brocades sat astride horses adorned in the papal colors of green and yellow. The crowd cheered as two of the most prominent Cardinals of Rome, Justinian and Carafa entered on their horses. They waved and smiled to the crowd and bowed their heads. Pier Luigi, the Pope's elder son, stayed back several paces to receive cheers from those sober enough to know that he was a military hero just returned from conquering lands in central Italy.

Justinian had spent his boyhood in poverty but had been adopted by an uncle who passed along to him a family name, a coat of arms, and an education in canon law. Once Justinian tasted wealth, he despised those in poverty and expanded his girth and possessions. He never wanted to feel hungry again and he knew every device to maintain power.

Carafa, from early childhood, had visions of leading an ascetic life and sought admission to the Dominican Order. It was his knowledge of Greek and Hebrew that attracted him to Paul. Now it was Carafa who negotiated unpleasantness away from the Pope. He attributed this to his ability to see the world in black and white—good vs. evil. It was all very clear to him.

Cardinal Carafa turned to Justinian.

"We must remember that this was the place where Romans fed Christians to the lions. Look around. Isn't this indeed a victory for our Christian way of life?" Carafa viewed these days with relish.

"We have to be certain that it remains this way."

Justinian waved to the crowd but shuddered at his proximity to the "dirty masses." He would have preferred to be in his own apartment in the Papal Palace eating fried eel cooked in white wine.

As the clergy took their seats, the cheering subsided.

"How about giving us some of that silk?" An old woman stood up and shouted.

"Sit down old woman." A man shouted behind her and slapped her on her back. "We're here to see the play. Maybe we'll even see the Pope but why would he want to come out if he's going to see someone as rude as you?"

The woman raised her arm as though to strike but teetered backwards. Two men caught and placed her upright in her seat. She sniffed and wiped her hand against her nose.

"He's not coming because he's too fancy to come—that's why he's not coming. It has nothing to do with me."

"But there's his son. Now there's a man who knows the right thing to do." This woman seemed proud of her righteousness.

3

Although, the clergy were seated a distance from the poor, it was as though Justinian had heard the words of the women. He turned to Carafa.

"It's a shame that our esteemed Pope could not come today. It would win him favor with the noble families who are here." Carafa knew that Justinian secretly visited families of nobility hoping to gain favor to be considered for the papacy.

"And the others as well." Carafa nodded and waved to the crowd. "He disapproves; he disapproves of the brawling... and Isabella, too, disapproves. She thinks it's unseemly behavior for Christians."

"Isabella, Isabella." Justinian chuckled over her name. "We should write a song about her. It would be about of how much she disapproves of everything going on today."

"And have you noticed that as he's gotten older, he's less interested in spectacles? He really doesn't appreciate how much the people like the play. Isabella's influence? Or, he's getting old?"

"I suspect people like the ducats that their families will receive for being in this play." He was getting tired of talking about Isabella. He wanted to enjoy the day.

The crowd grew silent as three men wearing red and green velvet doublets and white silk leggings rose from the nobility's side of the arena. They blasted three long notes in unison with their golden trumpets signaling the start of the play. Their velvet berets trimmed with gold wobbled slightly with their efforts. The crowd stood as one and cheered—all except the clergy. In the ensuing stillness a tall, gaunt Roman portraying Jesus entered the arena on a donkey. He stopped, slid off the animal, placed his hand tenderly on its mane, and walked to the center of the arena followed by his disciples who kept a respectful distance. Many in the crowd crossed themselves.

It began to drizzle. Some saw this as a sign and stood lifting their hands skyward but quickly returned their eyes to the tableau on the Colosseum floor where an actor held up a banner symbolizing the holy city of Jerusalem.

"I tell you, if they are silent, the stones will cry out," the actor portraying Jesus said.

4

The crowd cheered and threw stones at the actors portraying Roman soldiers and the Pharisees who prevented their Savior from entering the Temple.

The captain of the condottiere looked to the Cardinals who nodded their approval. The guards did not stop the stone throwing. Fortunately, the actors were far away from the reach of the crowd.

Spurred on by the crowd's enthusiasm, the actors led by Jesus moved toward tables laden with coins and with a great show of force, overturned them tossing money into the crowd. Several people ran down the stone steps to scoop up the coins but quickly left when they saw that the coins were fake. The guards deftly used their wooden staffs to give the money grabbers a sharp smack on the backs of their heads, prodding them back to their seats.

Jesus and his ragtag group of thirty followers stopped in front of the nobility and then the clergy. The Cardinals sat perfectly still, knowing that the eyes of the crowd were on them as Jesus chided those in the Temple—the moneychangers and merchants—to give up their ways.

"By what right do you do this?" shouted one of the actor-priests.

"I do not have to inform you." Jesus rose to his full height. "God will give testimony that these coins are idolatrous."

Several actors who portrayed the maimed and blind when they entered, stood and walked and bowed toward Jesus now that they could see.

"Hallelujah! Hallelujah!" They cried out and raised their hands to the skies. Some members of the clergy made the sign of the cross at the miracle. The audience similarly crossed themselves and looked to see if any of the truly crippled and ill among them was cured. No one was. Still they continued to watch the tableau, eagerly waiting for a miracle and a reason to cheer, or weep, or throw stones.

The actors following Jesus, bowed to the clergy and then to the nobility. They moved to the center of the Colosseum where the high priest, Caiaphas, stood. He wore a yellow pointed hat that distinguished him from Pontius Pilate in his white Roman toga. The two actors shouted insults at Jesus.

"Kill the Jews! Kill the Jews!" Members of the audience cried until a Roman soldier approached Jesus.

"Ought we to pay the poll-tax to Caesar or not?" he asked. "Render unto Caesar what is Caesar's and to God what is God's."

Jesus answered.

The crowd included noblemen, their families, and the poor who cheered, jumping on their seats in jubilation. Members of the clergy remained stoic for they knew many were upset with the church's collection and levying of taxes. The actors stopped, faced the crowd, and bowed their heads.

Then twelve men quickly gathered around Jesus to represent the tableau of The Last Supper at a hastily crafted long wooden table. They and Jesus appeared with long dour faces in spite of what should have been the festivity of the Passover dinner celebrating the freedom of the Jews after four hundred years of slavery. Jesus sat next to Peter and lay his head on his chest.

"I have greatly longed to eat this Passover with you before I suffer for I tell you I shall not partake of another until its fulfillment." He paused. "I know one of you will betray me tonight."

He rose and called out, "Judas, Judas."

The crowd stood and roared "Judas! Judas! Traitor! Traitor!"

They watched in silence as an actor draped a red cloak on Jesus, and placed a twisted crown of thorns on his head, handing him an enormous wooden cross shouting, "Here, carry this."

Jesus fell down and several men roughly placed him on the cross. Many in the crowd rended their garments and wailed.

As Jesus was dragged from the cross and placed in his mother Mary's arms, the crowd fell silent. Men, women, and children openly wept as his followers set him in the tomb. When it was sealed, Roman soldiers marched on it in jubilation. The crowd roared "Kill the killers! Kill the Jews! Kill Herod!"

Minutes passed. The trumpeters emitted joyful blasts and suddenly Jesus pushed his way out of the tomb and stood in triumph.

By now men and women were so besotted with drink that they knew not whether to laugh or cry. Many began to throw fruit from their baskets at the soldiers. A stout disheveled man, less inebriated than the others yelled, "Follow me. Come with me to Jew Street." Several staggered behind him to follow a path that circled the Colosseum and led to a cobblestoned street lined with narrow whitewashed stucco homes—some with narrow alleyways between them—others sharing common walls.

"Here it is. Here's the rabbi's house." Drunken revelers fell down and remained in the muddy streets to be ignored or trampled. One woman was so inebriated that she did not move when an old man urinated on her. Another man lifted the woman's skirt to expose her genitalia. A passer-by masturbated, ejaculating onto her face. He then fell over her in a drunken stupor as others ran by.

Shopkeepers and homeowners had prepared for the rampage by removing food stalls from the square and shutting shop doors. The crowd hurled stones at buildings and vomited on door stoops.

*   *   *

As the mob approached Rabbi Hayyim Luzzatti's house on Jew Street, one rotund friar shouted and waved his fist in the air. "Repent, Jew, repent." Many joined in a deafening chorus. "Kill them, Christ killers. Repent, Jew, repent."

The rabbi had been seated at his desk reading in a room that faced the courtyard, away from the street. When he heard the commotion, he moved from the text to put his arm around his wife, Alba, as she sat quietly sewing by his side. She put her needlework down and brought her hands over her ears to keep out the noise and thereby diminish the horror of the disturbance that was taking place outside her home. Her husband kissed her forehead gently and brushed his lips against her cheek. They both jumped as they heard the impact of huge stones hurled at the outside walls of their home. He had been determined when he first built this home to make it strong—walls of concrete painted with talc mixed with tempera, terra cotta tiles instead of dirt floors, and panes of glass for windows.

She went to the window watching the crowd continue their rampage down the street.

"I thought the Pope had promised you this was not going to happen again. No more Passion Plays."

"That's what he told me. He especially told me he didn't like the "rabble" that came after. That was his exact word, "rabble." Come away from the window, please."

As she moved away, a young boy hurled a rock through a window. The shattered glass spilled onto the floor. Alba went to get a broom.

"We'll get that after this dies down."

"You're sure this is going to die down?"

"It will." That's what he had told his congregants when semmingly spontaneous acts of Jew hatred arose. "It will die down. Are we not safe and prosperous here...most of the time?"

"Hayyim, he has an army. He could do something to prevent this."

"Maybe he can. Maybe he can't. Maybe he has to use the army for other...for other big events." He went cautiously to peer out the window. "Look they're going away. There are only a few left in the street—just lying there."

"Half-drunk."

"Completely sotted."

"I can clean up now." She picked up the broom.

"No. I can think of something better to do. Something joyous now that this has past."

"It's getting dark." She took in the power of his arms and shoulders.

"How shall we do this?" He laughed. "The way we always have?"

"No." She loosened her hair and opened the string on her blouse "No, you shall watch me undress first."

"Yes, and then?" He tried not to show his impatience.

'And then you shall promise that you'll go to Pope Paul and ask him to use his army for our protection."

8

He didn't want to tell her that since the Pope appointed Carafa head inqusitior, he was being denied some access to the Pope.

"Light a candle and I will watch you undress."

Slowly and methodically, she lay each piece of clothing on a dresser, and he gasped as the flickering candlelight caught her pale skin and lightened the plum nipples on her breasts.

He turned to look at Alba lying on her side next to him, her white breast revealed through her loosely opened linen nightshirt, and traced his finger around the outline of her breast making concentric circles until he reached her nipple. She stirred but did not wake. He whispered in her ear, "Yes, I'll definitely go to the Pope."

CHAPTER 2

The Pope's Family

At the library of the Papal Palace, Paul searched for a book on the shelves of his vast collection of Greek, Latin, and Hebrew texts. Isabella, the mother of his two sons, Pier Luigi and Ranuncio stared at his back.

"So, my dear, you are enjoying your embroidery?"

"Not quite, Your Holiness, although I'm endeavoring to find satisfaction in perfecting a stitch," she snapped.

As Isabella worked with her head down and close to the needle and thread of the white linen fabric outlined with a unicorn, she would put her embroidery down to read a passage from the open book lying on the table next to her. She would stop occasionally to evaluate the embroidery by holding it up to the light. She watched Paul run his hand carefully over the bindings of gold-embossed. He was getting older, more stooped.

The wooden shelves that housed about one hundred books were elegantly aligned, sanded and varnished to a gleaming ebony perfection. In front of the bookshelves, two chairs stood upholstered in fabric that displayed an intricate floral arrangement of black, green, red, and gold tapestry.

"The design is trying your patience, your eyesight, perhaps?" He turned to look at her, *Cicero's Orations* in his hand. "Or, is it the fact that you're doing an impossible task by trying to read a book at the same time you embroider?" He wanted to get on with his reading but knew that her tone demanded his attention.

"It is neither the design nor my eyesight."

"What then?" He reached for her hand. She noted the blue veins in his hand were more visible than ever. "You've never lost your passion for knowledge." He saw that her gray crown of hair, partially covered by a sheer black headscarf, was like a halo around her heart-shaped face. Beautiful, he thought. She is still beautiful.

"I'm tired of pretending that I'm not reading. Your Cardinals disapprove, don't they, of my desire to learn?" Isabella saw that she had his attention. "And probably my very existence."

He sighed having heard this argument many times before. "The library is yours. Just use it discreetly. Surely you can accept that considering my position as Pope." He opened his book. Avoidance sometimes worked with Isabella who had never lost the strong-headedness and determination of her youth. It was these traits that had made her so interesting to him.

Although she and their children had been favored with apartments at the Vatican, Carafa and Justinian in particular frowned upon her presence. She frequently reminded their sons, Pier Luigi and Ranunccio that most mistresses of Popes had not been so fortunate. Paul valued Isabella's constancy, her friendship, her intellect, and her abiding love and care for their children.

"You're reading Cicero. I remember how easily you used to translate those texts." Isabella's voice rose as she put down her sewing. "I want to read those books as well in Latin, and as long as you have Cardinals who seem to want to eliminate my presence in your library, I cannot."

"You, my dear, think that access to knowledge is all." He did not try to hide the sarcasm. He wanted to get on with his reading. "Translate the texts of Marcus Aurelius and you will have wisdom. The answer to a problem will be in the texts. That's what my Isabella is thinking." She started to reply, but he held up his hand. "I can tell you that you would be better off paying attention to your embroidery. I suspect that there are more solutions in the piece of linen in your hands than there are in the texts."

"I can't study Latin without open access to your library. I want to read when I come here—not pretend to do embroidery." Isabella jabbed the needle into the fabric.

"What you really want..." He pointed his finger at her. "...is access to Papal affairs. You want to tell Charles V how he should fight his wars with the King of France. You want influence."

"Stop sounding so triumphant with your reasoning. You know perfectly well it is you I want to influence." Blushing, she said, "It seems to me that when I had access to your bed, I had access to your thoughts...to your mind."

"You have more access in this court to my library than anyone else. Do you not? While Titian paints me in my chambers, you may sit here and read all you want."

Her eyes captured the lines on the Pope's face, his aquiline nose that bisected piercing blue eyes, the grey-white beard that added authority to his face.

"I hope Titian is doing you justice," she said, tracing the lines on his face. "Titian excels at nudes, but will he capture your deep spiritual quality? I wasn't sure he should be the painter of your portrait."

Isabella knew a great deal about art because of the education provided by her father, Fortunato Martinego Cesaresco. Her father took his name seriously and felt that Roman history and Latin needed to be passed on to his children. In his dealings as an art collector with the Papal Court of Pope Alexander VI, he also had access to great works of art and lovingly shared his expertise with her. Because of her father's work, she had met Paul when he was an acolyte in the palace of the Borgia Pope, Alexander VI. She had also known Giulia, Paul's sister, who was a ravishing beauty and sought by Pope Alexander as a mistress.

"My father educated me and so did you, Alessandro. You taught me so well that I was doing your translations in Latin when you were so busy acquiring your art and your lands as Cardinal. Would you have been happier had I been a dolt? I know you can answer that because you have had more than your share of foolish women in your bed."

"I no longer have women in my bed. You know that." He glared at her.

The library clock chimed the hour and church bells rang in the courtyard. The warm air carried the sound from the outside perimeter of the walls through the enormous windows left wide open to relieve the heat of the summer day in the thickly carpeted and draped room. The noise made conversation difficult, and Isabella wanted to offer words of comfort. She wanted the dissension to abate. She waited until the cacophony died away.

"I know these are difficult times for you as Luther continues his agitation and Henry takes his excommunication lightly. Poor Anne, beheaded. Another Anne divorced. Kathryn Howard executed."

Paul sighed. "Luther and Copernicus nip at the church's heels but Henry nips like a dog in heat at women."

"Henry can 'nip' because the church has lost its way with its indulgences. We have talked before that there must be other ways of getting money to the church."

"Talk. Yes, we have talked," he smiled.

"As for Copernicus 'nipping', the truth may be that the sun is the center of the universe. Why must the church deny science?"

His shoulders sagged. The smile left his eyes. "Since I can't solve all these problems now, let us pay a visit to Pier Luigi. I have good news for him."

He held out his hand to her and she took it. She was always delighted to visit their children together. As they walked through the Hall of Sibyls to arrive at Pier Luigi's apartment, she admired those full-fleshed women. If only she could be as sure of the future as they were, she thought. Isabella shuddered as she remembered that it was a Borgia pope, Alexander VI, who had had all these frescos painted by Pinturicchio. She knew that Borgia popes could be extremely ruthless. They were known for their orgies and mismanagement of papal wealth. She was grateful that Alessandro Farnese who easily became Pope Paul III had not seemed to be that kind of man.

Their son's apartment was apart from his mother's so they hardly ran into one another. This was the way Isabella preferred it. When Pier Luigi had been compared to Cesare Borgia in looks and temperament, she could not believe that he was her child. His morals and behavior were foreign to her.

Pier Luigi's door was open and they entered to find him lying on his huge canopied bed with a fifteen-year-old

13

servant girl, naked from the waist up. She was sucking on his toes.

"I assume she washed those for you before she began eating them," said Isabella.

"Mother, you should knock," Pier Luigi said dismissing the girl with a wave of his hand as she squirmed in a tangle of sheets and rolled to the floor.

Isabella helped her up. The young girl burst into tears, grabbed her smock, and ran from the room.

"You didn't have to do that, Mother. She's a servant girl." Pier Luigi pulled a sheet over his naked body and patted the bed. "Please sit, my esteemed parents. To what do I owe this unannounced visit?" He stretched out his long, muscular frame and placed his hands behind his head.

"Thank you," Isabella said. "I'll sit on the chair. I'd hardly want to fall about as your...your servant girl has done."

Paul sat at the side of the bed and took his son's hand in his. "I've acquired Parma and Piacenza for you."

Pier Luigi hugged his father. "How did you do that when Parma and Piacenza belong to the Papal States?" Isabella glared at Paul.

"That's wonderful. When can I go there? Can I have money to redo the rooms? Bonaventure just brought some lovely damask from Spain."

Isabella stared at Paul waiting for a response, but his eyes fixed on the adoring gaze of his son. Finally, he turned to her.

"I gave Charles what he needed—horses, soldiers, and money to suffocate the brimstone of the German Protestant princes."

"And just where did you get the money?" Isabella's eyes flashed.

"That, my dear, is of no concern to you. Pay attention to your books and sewing, and not to finances or politics."

Pier Luigi interrupted. "Mother, I know you've always been concerned about my spendthrift ways, but I'll not disappoint you. Parma and Piacenza will be ruled well."

"I hope you do it with reverence toward God and the Church."

"Of course, mother." He bowed his head.

"Now that you have the good news, your mother and I will return to the library. I have some reading that I want to finish." Paul took her arm.

"As I have as well." Isabella stood.

Pier Luigi threw his head back and laughed. He had seen this bickering for many years.

As they were leaving, they heard Pier Luigi called out, "Sofia, come back so we may celebrate. Bring wine."

CHAPTER 3

Cardinal Carafa, Inquisitor

Isabella and Paul returned to the library where he eagerly went back to *Cicero's Orations* that lay open on the table. Isabella hesitated before sitting and resuming her reading with her embroidery in hand. Paul looked up from his reading and walked to his bookshelves. He lovingly touched the spines of *Dante's Divine Comedy, The Codex of Virgil,* and *The Vatican Codex of the Bible.*

Isabella looked up. "It was lovely when we used to read these to each other before..."

"Before I became Pope? Yes, it was lovely. Only you had this magical way of making Latin come alive."

"And only you could read Hebrew as though it was coming from the mouth of God."

"That's long gone." He paused to take a book off the shelf. "We have put away childish things."

"Our love was more than childish. We have children now." Isabella tucked a lock of her gray hair into her scarf. "And you spoil our children by giving them land to rule, and they cannot rule their own desires. I can't imagine that Pier Luigi's wife likes his bedtime frolics with little girls. All I ask is they become true Christians."

"Since when can good Christians not acquire property?" Paul smiled. "And I cannot do anything about his healthy appetite." He paused. "She was a beauty, wasn't she?" Paul lay his book on a desk.

"Besides, Parma is done, and I have other things to worry about. Charles pushes for reform in the church, but he has been weak against the German Protestant Princes in spite of the money and arms I gave him. As if that's not enough, the Cardinals argue against Copernicus, and Carafa wants the Jews to become Christians like us. Damn it all."

Isabella started to speak, but he raised his hand to silence her.

"They don't feel it is enough that I issued my Inquisition and placed Cardinal Carafa in charge who likes nothing better to do than find some New Christians who light candles on Friday night."

"Yes," Isabella finally spoke. "The one who knows the New Testament better than Cromwell did. At least he claims that and you seem to listen to everything he claims."

Paul opened his book underlining the words with his finger as her read.

* * *

Cardinal Gian Pietro Carafa paced in a circle outside the door of the library, occasionally stopping to listen but unable to decipher Paul and Isabella's words. He was pleased to hear a vigorous tone to Paul's voice. As his friend aged, he was losing his ability to rule with power.

Gian Pietro Carafa, descended from an ancient Roman family counted as his grandfather the commander in chief of the papal troops under Eugenius IV. Carafa, like Isabella, had encountered Alessandro Farnese in the court of Alexander VI, and although he was ten years younger than Farnese, they had developed a strong bond and remained loyal to each other. Carafa had sensed that Farnese, with his softer intellectual side, had secretly admired the combative nature of his young acolyte. He wasn't so sure how Alessandro felt about him now.

Cardinal Carafa's hair was still black, his skin unblemished and smooth. He watched his food intake to maintain the same girth he had as a twenty-year-old and he carried his tall frame proudly. He usually walked with his thrust slightly forward, making him appear taller than his six feet. His beard, sprinkled with gray, was always neatly trimmed.

He continued listening outside the door but heard only an occasional word emanating from the room. He thought he heard the word "Jew." The Pope occasionally asked him about his role as Inquisitor, but seemed uninterested. Carafa knew that Isabella protested the Inquisition in her talks with the Pope. The Cardinal could not imagine how a woman could be so involved in affairs of state. His father had assured him that women were placed on earth to relieve men's frustrations. Could a woman comprehend the power struggles of the church? Could she understand that it would be nearly impossible to have anyone give up privileges, once their wealth was acquired. He could think of better ways to reform the Church. She told him that Martin Luther was right to rail against the sale of indulgences, but what would substitute for money to pay the army, the upkeep of palaces, the acquisition of art? Carafa knew she pretended to embroider while she was most anxious to convince the Pope of her ideas.

Carafa strained to distinguish their words. How could a woman talk so much? Paul had called on Carafa many times to discuss Papal matters, and he could only hope that the Pope would continue to value him. He must convince Alessandro to be less absorbed by his passion for art and pay more attention to affairs of state. Power, it was about power. Alessandro seemed to have forgotten.

*   *   *

Isabella gathered her sewing, closed the Latin book on the table, and carried it to the library shelf that accommodated the largest books. She knew some of those books had maps that she longed to understand, especially after hearing talk in the Palace of explorers and a place called America. At her urging five years ago, the Pope had ordered that the savages encountered in the New World were not to be enslaved but converted to good Christians.

"At least, you listened to me about the savages in the discovered lands and showed your true self."

Paul gently took the book from her hand and placed it on the shelf.

"It seemed the most humane thing to do as we grow our Christian community. Now, I'm expecting visitors, so you will have to go."

"It's Carafa, isn't it? He's become your closest adviser. You gave in to his insistence on an Inquisition. How can you be the same person who spoke out strongly against the enslavement of people in the New World and allow an Inquisition?"

"We only discuss the Jews because some members of the Church think they have contributed to Luther's crusade. He gains power daily. I must do whatever possible to limit that power. It's a mystery to me why these Jews hang onto their religion. Life would be so much easier for them as Christians."

She started to speak. He raised his hand to silence her.

"Isabella, I'm losing patience." Isabella placed her hand on the rich red silk of the Pope's sleeve as though to soothe him, but Paul gently removed it and guided her to the door. "I appreciate your time here. I must open the door for Cardinal Carafa."

"He sees me as a thorn in the papal palace, doesn't he?"

"Let's just say a rose with thorns." He tried to soften the comment. "I have so many things to deal with, I don't want to add this to the ..."

"You must know that my father would have been appalled by my acquiescence, but because I care for you, I'll leave."

Isabella picked up a length of her dress in one hand and held the embroidery that dangled with many shades of thread in another. She saw that blood had gathered on her finger from where she had pricked herself with a needle, but she said nothing and opened the library door to the hallway. She scowled at Carafa as he entered, gave him a quick nod, and swept out of the room. He bowed deeply.

The cardinal knelt before Paul, and kissed the papal ring on his thumb. He rose.

"I see you are wearing Elijah del Medigo's ring."

"It's magnificent art, isn't it?" Paul held out his hand and on his thin small index finger rested another ring—one of two coiled gold strands embellished with a garnet in the center.

"Del Medigo's a New Christian."

"Yes. It is good that we are increasing our Christian community."

"Are you sure he is not a practicing Jew at night?"

"He is an accomplished artist and I have a lovely ring. You, my dear friend must take time off from searching for your Judaizers." Paul motioned for him to sit down next to him at the library table. He opened a huge book—the writings of St. Augustine of Hippo.

"See Gian. I have the words of Augustine to support me." He pointed to the words as he read them aloud.

We must be strong against paganism. We must destroy that which will destroy us as a faith. The Jews are not pagans. We must not destroy them or immolate them. They are here to bear witness to our salvation. Paul closed the book with a flourish. "That is why I didn't attend the play in the Colosseum."

"But, Your Eminence, Augustine wrote these words hoping they would become Christians."

"Nor did I want members of the Church to support it." Paul suddenly seemed animated. "The Passion Play encourages unseemly behavior and hostile actions against the Jews."

"But there are those that proclaim they accept Christ as their Saviour but still circumcise their babies and refuse to eat pork."

"So I have allowed you an Inquisition."

"A wise decision so we make sure that those who are committed to the Catholic faith are true adherents." Carafa bowed slightly. "I'm indeed humbled that you have seen to make me Inquisitor."

"Who knows?" Paul relaxed. "Some of the nobility may decide to give us more money."

"Or, it may make more people fear you. Another way to get money."

Carafa adjusted his three corner Cardinal's hat. "It is another way to fight against the creeping Protestantism of Luther."

Paul suddenly rose from his chair and went to a huge map on the wall. "Aren't we lucky that we now accept Cristobal Colon's premise that the world is round? I wonder if Copernicus would ever be so fortunate that we accept his scientific information?" Carafa understood that the conversation about the Passion Play and the Inquisition was over. Paul turned to face his friend. He saw a man handsome and regal in his bearing. Paul thought that Carafa was born to be a Cardinal and ambition ran strong in his veins. I should never drink wine with him, he thought.

"Copernicus upsets the order of the church, for you, doesn't he?"

"Many question him. The church must delay acceptance if we are to have our power."

"God and the people will see our strength in Michelangelo's *The Last Judgment* and his rebuilding of St. Peter's." He said nothing about his portrait being painted by Titian. The artist commanded huge payment and the treasury was at an all time low.

"Then there is Henry. What will you do about Henry? Many wish that the Papacy had taken a stronger position than excommunication."

"What will I do about Henry?" The Pope's voice rose. "The church excommunicated him, and he stays excommunicated. But the reality is, I reveal this only to you, that it is *he* who has excommunicated us with his Act of Supremacy. Henry's marriages no longer interest me. A king can never be supreme over the Pope so he is doomed to hell."

"Besides, what would be a stronger position than excommunication?" Paul's face flushed. "Death by burning? By hanging? By torture? You see, Carafa, I can understand what drives people to love—what drives men to be passionate about women and women to desire men. Henry is first of all a man—then a king." Carafa had remained celibate all his life—true to the requirements of the Church. At least with women.

"I beg Your Holiness, please don't let these words be heard beyond this room. Henry may be first a man, but he also has the instincts to protect his position as king, and you...you must protect your position as Pope. I will tell you, you must give up the appearance of supporting heretics, be they Henry or the Jews...or Copernicus."

"I've given you the Church argument about maintaining relations with Jews. They are here to bear witness and if they accept our faith, we are all richer for it. We may just not eliminate them, although you may wish it."

"You live too much in your head, and your books, and if I must say so, your theology."

"There's no theology that says we must present a Passion Play."

"It is a play that lifts people's spirits and commits them to the cross." Carafa rushed his words as he saw the displeasure on Paul's face. "And adds money to your coffers."

Paul could not conceal his annoyance. "I'm getting tired of this discussion."

"I'm just trying to protect you." He turned to leave then added, "You think Isabella has your best interests, don't you?"

Paul sat with shoulders bent and waved his hand slightly in dismissal. "Isabella has a soft heart and she's part of my past and she...she does not influence me."

"I'm just trying to protect you."

"Come back tomorrow. I need some quiet."

Carafa felt the Pope's weariness and bowed toward him. Perhaps the Pope had heard his arguments. Carafa wanted to go out and taste the night air and maybe have an adventure, but he knew he would run into the beggars at the steps of the Palace, and that thought marred the savoring of what he thought of as a small victory.

CHAPTER 4

Rabbi Hayyim Luzzatti Prevails
Upon the Pope

Rabbi Hayyim Luzzatti sat in his library, books strewn about on the table with the Talmud open to the writings of Rabbi Shammai. He read carefully and then turned the pages to read the words of Rabbi Hillel. Back and forth he went with some impatience, comparing the wisdom of these two learned men from Babylonian days. He struggled with managing the conflicting opinions. Shammai warned of too much contact with the Romans. Hillel was more liberal and felt that Jews profited from contact with others. At times, Luzzatti wished there were another rabbi in the city with whom he could discuss such complex ideas. The other five rabbis in Rome said they were too busy with their own congregants, but Hayyim knew the real reason—jealousy and suspicion of his status as the Pope's physician.

Hayyim closed the heavy book, marking the page with an oak leaf, and took an apothecary book off the shelf. He was eager to check the medicinal value of the poultice he had prepared for the Pope. He ran his finger down a list of herbs—comfrey, camphor oil, witch hazel. He then smoothed the wrinkles in his linen shirt with some satisfaction, knowing that he had come up with the right medicine to help the Pope. Mistrustful of the medications procured at apothecaries, Hayyim prepared them in his own workroom.

In the room with the fireplace and large pine table, Alba stopped stirring the kettle, wiped the sweat from her forehead, stirred again, and smiled when she saw Hayyim enter the kitchen with his medical bag in hand. She stuck her finger in the hot mixture and tasted it.

"Alba," he said. "I'm going to the Palace to see the Pope. I'll return in time for dinner."

"You go to visit him on medical issues?"

"And, I hope I can talk to him about the play that evoked such anger against our people." He saw Alba's eyes light up.

"It will depend on his mood," her husband said.

Alba reached for the salt to sprinkle into the soup. "I hadn't wanted to press you, Hayyim, but ever since I heard from my relatives in Venice..."

He interrupted. 'Yes, how are the Gomezes of Venice— beautiful, beautiful Venice."

"That's what I want to talk to you about before you go. I've been wondering if a ghetto could occur here as well. Cousin Alberto says that it is hard doing business being confined to one place, but Cousin Miriam says she practices her Judaism more seriously." She tasted the soup, and this time, she seemed satisfied.

"Sometimes I think a ghetto would be easier for me. They would be right there, all together. Easy to come together and pray and not have to worry about getting caught up in the intrigues of the Gentile world."

"Don't say that. A ghetto here? I like our freedom."

"Alba, you know I shall do my best today to do what you ask." He smiled. "Otherwise, you'll remind about it every day, won't you?"

"Yes, I will." She hugged him, took his face between her hands, and kissed him on both cheeks. "Go and come back safely with good news from the Pope. No more Passion Plays. No ghetto."

Hayyim had met Alba in Rome thirty years ago when she had arrived from Spain with her parents and brother. Hayyim had been an earnest student of medicine at Padua and studied seriously the texts of Joseph Karo when he came to Rome. Alba's father, Abramo Mantino, had been a physician in the court of Ferdinand and Isabella, but he realized it was time to leave Spain when Torquemada became the Inquisitor. Abramo Mantino had known that his daughter led a charmed life at court and worried that she could have entered into its profligate ways. He was indeed happy when he saw that the instruction that she had received in Hebrew, Latin, and Greek helped her see the value of education.

Her mother, Esther, had made sure that Alba was well versed in the laws of *kashrut* and the other unwritten domestic laws of maintaining a Jewish household. These attributes, along with her keen mind, had not been lost on Hayyim, and he fast became a suitor to the dark-eyed Spanish enchantress with lustrous black hair, heavy eyebrows, and an exquisitely shaped mouth that invited passionate kisses. Within the year they were wed, with the blessings of both their parents. A dowry had passed to Hayyim with much amiability.

From the very first time she had set eyes on him when they were still in their teens, she recognized him as someone of extraordinary patience, one who would be slow to enrage, who would love his family, and who received much satisfaction from his books and learning.

"Should I say anything if any of the members of the congregation come to call?" She walked him to the door.

"Tell them to be patient and speak to me at synagogue. Some are so foolish; they cannot work out their own problems."

"No, I will not. I will be courteous to them."

"Yes." He took her in his arms. "God reminds me of the same things you do."

She laughed. "I cannot be in the same category as God, but do you think you could also talk to him about eliminating the law that we have to wear a yellow arm band with the Star of David?"

Hayyim had forgotten that he once thought her stubbornness charming. "The condottieri don't enforce that law."

"He's not going to live forever, my dear husband. Don't you see he's getting older?"

"I don't want to bring up a subject that he is not even thinking about. Awakening a dormant thought can be dangerous."

"You can't ignore the rigid arm of Carafa and his Inquisition." Alba's face clouded.

"It is an Inquisition in name alone. The Pope will not enforce it. And I'm doing everything in my power to keep him alive."

"Perhaps the play in the Colosseum frightened me more than it should have." She embraced him with a light, lingering kiss she said, "Go well," in her musical voice that had become fluent in Italian. "I'm sure you're doing all you can."

Hayyim placed a hand on her head. It was a gesture that he used to perform for their son, Israel, every Friday night and Saturday morning with a special blessing. Israel's departure for Spain and conversion to Christianity had eliminated him as a topic of conversation in their family. The pain was too great for both of them. Hayyim had been furious when he heard the news of the conversion. He had forbidden his name to be mentioned, and he sat shivah*h* for him for ten days instead of the requisite seven. Alba had kept a sketch she had done of her handsome son when he was fifteen and already six feet tall but kept it well hidden.

Hayyim left through the courtyard door debating whether to take his horse, Giacomo who stood patiently in his stall. Hayyim knew that this stall was a modest home for his special horse that seemed to have an uncanny sense of how to respond to his master's needs. Often Hayyim had to ride long distances to tend the sick; Giacomo was always ready and eager, and waited patiently, usually in a courtyard, as the doctor ministered to his patients. The horse could sense if the doctor was too tired to ride at a gallop on the way home, and he would slow his pace. Hayyim blessed this animal as he would bless a member of his family.

He decided not to ride Giacomo to the Papal Palace, but he went out to pet him and offer him some sugar from his hand. Before he left, Hayyim kissed his fingers, then the mezuzah on the door of Giacomo's stall and said, "Be good. Watch my house and my wife." The horse pawed his right foot.

Hayyim walked from his narrow neighborhood street to the broader one filled with stalls and shops. He nodded quietly to passers-by who hurried their children out of his way to the other side. Many knew him as the doctor who helped the sick, but others knew him as the Jew. Esmerelda, the flower woman from whom he bought flowers every Sabbath, waved to him. He knew she appreciated the predictability of money she would receive every Friday night. He took in the irony when he saw people willing to cross a rivulet of slop created by people dumping their chamber pots in order to avoid contact with him.

As Hayyim came to the end of the street, St. Peter's Square was visible with its circle of columns. The sun was too bright for him to see the tip of the obelisk. He took the street to the right that led directly to the Pope's Palace.

There he greeted the Swiss Guards who immediately opened the huge, wooden doors, their helmeted heads barely moving. The guards knew him as a physician who not only brought health to the Pope but healed their families as well.

Inside the Palace, Hayyim walked down the hall to the library, escorted by a guard, eager to see the books that Paul had recently acquired—hand-lettered and hand-painted, with writings from many parts of the world and recently from the German states. At times Hayyim thought about the marvelous wisdom that was written inside those books and wondered if more men would be wiser if they had access to books with their wonderful ideas. Would they then leave behind their superstitions, their amulets, their charms, their talismans?

Hayyim saw Cardinal Carafa leaving the library and nodded to him. He knew this cardinal relished his role as the Inquisitor. Carafa waved a hand to dismiss the guard.

"You come for a medical problem for our friend?"

Hayyim met his eyes with subdued defiance. "Yes, I'm his doctor so, of course, I come for medical reasons, but not necessarily a medical problem."

"You are being evasive...and you do remember that I am head Inquisitior?"

Before Hayyim could response, Pope Paul opened the door of his library and Cardinal Carafa turned and departed.

"Welcome, Dr. Luzzatti. I've been looking forward to our visit." The doctor bent to kiss the feet of the Pope, aware that members of his congregation would disapprove, for it was not in Jewish tradition to bow down before any man—only God Almighty. Mordechai had refused to bow down before Haman in ancient Persia, but Hayyim bowed to Paul out of respect.

"I hope you have good news about my health. Something easily solvable and cured would be a refreshing change for me."

Hayyim had learned to discuss illnesses openly but discreetly. "I'm a doctor—a scientist, but, Your Holiness, your time in the Borgia court did not serve you well."

"I know. I know. And I know you have been a very good doctor for me. What can you do to help me? Come sit here." He motioned him to the opposite side of a large desk.

"I've checked my medical books for your symptoms. You have a disease of your member for which I have brought a special poultice. I would advise you not to have... intercourse." Hayyim hesitated for a brief moment.

"You know I have been celibate for many, many years." Paul leaned forward in his chair with his voice at a near whisper.

"But it is still my business to advise you." Hayyim hoped he was not pushing too hard.

Paul cleared his throat. "May we leave this discussion of my medical problems?"

"Of course," said Hayyim. "It's our conversations of ideas and books that have been so important to me." The doctor was hoping that Paul would share some of the letters that had arrived from the New World. He noticed a new codex that lay on the table, and assumed Paul was going to discuss it with him. Hayyim knew that their closeness had been nurtured because each respected the astute intelligence of the other.

"Wouldn't life be better for you just to accept the Lord, Jesus Christ?"

Hayyim's face turned a pale pink. This subject had never been discussed before. This Pope had let the Jews live in relative openness. Members of his congregation were printers, shoemakers, wool and silk traders, and bankers and thoroughly engaged in the commerce of the community. Many served Christians, although the more religious in both communities frowned upon it. The Pope had seemed to value the Jews for their industriousness, and the rabbi had never heard him utter a negative word about the Jews in Rome.

"After all, the Messiah has arrived. What is wrong with Jesus as your Messiah? Was he not resurrected?"

"Look at the world. It is in disrepair. Wars. Killings. We work to continue to repair the world—take the broken shards from every corner, put them together, and maybe then the Messiah will come." Hayyim was hoping that this made sense to the Pope because it took years of understanding for many to grasp this bit of theology, and he had not come prepared to debate this subject.

"Have I not tried to fix the world? Look at the art we have brought here. Look at Michelangelo repairing St. Peter's."

"We look for perfection in human beings. Those perfect humans will bring us peace."

"That is impossible. We need to go for the possible. Jesus gave us that. Here I will show you in this book." The Pope began flipping pages of the book open on the table.

"It's more than that. We need to all be gathered in the land of Israel." Hayyim was remembering the arguments he had heard from his rabbis.

Hayyim hoped he did not sound anxious to the Pope. He rubbed his hands down the sides of his garments to dry the sweat from his palms. Better theologians than he had argued the case for the peaceful existence of Jews.

"That is a god forsaken land. This could be your Israel." Paul turned slowly studying his friend's face. "You Jews live as you wish here. You pray as you wish. You engage in commerce as you wish." He paused and spoke as though he knew what was on the doctor's mind. "The Passion Play and the tumult that erupted were not of my doing."

"More than any other Pope, Your Holiness, you have let us live as religious and righteous citizens."

"Come, my dear friend. Then what else do you have on your mind? I see that I've upset you with the suggestion of conversion, and I can see that I'm not convincing you."

Hayyim took a deep breath. "You've been very good in not enforcing the laws to wear yellow arm bands as they do in Venice. Some in our community wonder if it's possible to eliminate this law from the books?"

"Why do you worry about this now?" He slammed the book shut. "You worry in foolishness. Taking the law of the yellow armband off the books will cause more of a headache. It is not enforced."

"Laws are important to us. This is a bad law." Hayyim wondered where he got the temerity to continue this argument.

"You need to trust me on this, my friend."

"I have trusted you. But the Passion Play hurts us. As does the yellow armband." Hayyim hesitated. "You have no thoughts of placing us in a ghetto as has been done in Venice."

"Of course, not. I assure you of your own and your community's safety and freedom for now and for the future." His eyes danced a bit. "As long as I'm alive, anyhow. So it is in your best interest to keep me alive, is it not?"

Hayyim arose from his chair and bent again to kiss the feet of the Pope, who placed a gentle hand on Hayyim's skullcap. "I thank you for the care you've given me, and I hope the medicine cures this intolerable itching."

With the good-bye that included much nodding from Hayyim, he backed out of the door and turned into the hallway looking forward to see Raphael's paintings in the Stanza della Stegnatura. He loved their illusions to Greek knowledge and jurisprudence. Cardinal Carafa suddenly appeared and blocked his passing.

Hayyim met his eyes.

"What have you been talking about? His connection with you could put him in a dangerous position." Carafa moved closer to Hayyim.

"I'm his doctor. I'm here to take care of his health. That is all." Hayyim tried to pass Carafa.

"Come, come, my good doctor. Some would suspect you simply because of your blood."

"My blood is the same as your blood. We will bleed the same way if a knife is stuck in our bellies or in our hearts.

Or...in our backs."Hayyim spoke softly but enunciated each word carefully.

Carafa poked his finger in Hayyim's chest. Hayyim gently pushed Carafa's hand away from him.

"Your Talmud gives you lies—a paganism that makes you and your fellow Jews dangerous—truly dangerous."

Carafa was so close to him that he could feel Carafa's breath. Hayyim pictured Alba's face and the faces of his congregants who depended on him not only for his rabbinical wisdom but also for his special connection to the Papal Palace.

"Surely, you don't believe this. Our Talmud gives us ways to live as righteous people."

"Again, why were you talking to the Pope?"

"Because I was asked to." Hayyim knew this would anger Carafa, but he went on. "We've served your Pope well as we have served courts well in many lands. We collect and count your money for you to have fewer sinners in your midst." He tried to walk away again. "It's your indulgence money that we count—not ours."

"I'm not finished with you." This time Carafa put a hand on Hayyim's arm—an arm that did not have an armband. Luzzatti was one of the privileged few who was not required to wear one.

"Why were you here?"

"I'm a doctor. I deal with his health, and I brought him medicine."

"For what?" Carafa dropped his arm.

"That's between the Pope and me."

Carafa raised his voice. "You'll reveal to me what I order you to."

Just then Paul came out to the corridor. "What's this?"

I was looking forward to doing some reading in peace and quiet."

Hayyim answered tersely. "I just told Cardinal Carafa that your digestion had improved." He turned abruptly, hoping that he had not offended the Pope with his sudden departure.

Hayyim walked the long marble corridor, his head bent. In the past he would have lingered to look at the artwork of

Pinturicchio, Fra Angelico, and Raphael. Although he appreciated the talent it took to paint a Madonna and child with such color and imagination, he was glad that there was not so much iconography in Judaism. Idols were smashed during the time of Baal for good reason. One has to speak directly to God. He would go right home to say his prayers.

As he left the palace, Luzzatti acknowledged the Swiss Guards and they nodded back. Hayyim had been able to treat many people and earn their respect. He relished the contact and prayed that the Pope would keep his promise about "no ghetto" for the Jews.

CHAPTER 5

Cardinal Carafa Plots

After watching Luzzatt leave the hallway outside the papal library, Cardinal Carafa hurried through the corridors of the Papal Palace to the Cardinals' library and meeting rooms. He entered a small room off the sacristy and rang for a messenger. He had much to report to the cardinals he considered his most trustworthy associates.

"Take this note to Cardinals Alfonso and Justinian," he said to the young messenger who bowed before Carafa and looked at him with worshipful eyes. Carafa's hand lingered on the luminous cheek of the young acolyte. The Cardinal raised his hand and patted him on his head. "And tell them that I have just come from the Pope."

Carafa paced. Was the aging process softening the Pope's spirit? Had he forsaken his oath to the Catholic Church? Carafa remembered their time in the court of Alexander VI, when Paul had confided in Carafa about his desire to be Pope. Never, at that time, had the younger Carafa seen Paul worry about his profligate life as Cardinal— his life of acquiring property in order to give his lands to members of the family and mistresses. After all, Paul had been emulating the Borgia Pope, Alexander VI, well known for his secular excesses.

Paul's intelligence had been in evidence then as well; his knowledge of Latin, Greek, and Hebrew was formidable. Alessandro Farnese's sharp mind and charm and an ability to ingratiate himself skillfully with political leaders assured his promotion to Pope.

Carafa also understood that Paul was a superb political strategist. At times, he had even managed to outwit Charles V, who had been crowned Holy Roman Emperor over twenty years ago. It was Paul who had convinced Charles to do battle with the Protestant princes of Germany with the help of the armies and money Paul had raised. Of late, Carafa felt that the Pope was increasingly vulnerable to the Isabella's advice and reluctant to use his power. Thank goodness he, Carafa, had convinced Paul that it was a good idea to start an Inquisition. *God will be grateful if I rid this earth of false Christians.*

A knock at the door interrupted Carafa's reverie and announced the Cardinals' arrival. Alfonso followed Justinian, whose size almost hid Alfonso from view. Carafa motioned them to two red-damasked chairs. "We have much to talk about."

Cardinal Justinian's shiny bald dome, softened by a bit of gray fringe around his head, was covered with a round white skullcap. His girth made it difficult for him to walk. He entered the room breathing heavily and collapsed into a chair that started to creak.

Alfonso smiled and said, "I've been telling him to drink less wine."

Carafa brought a larger chair to Justinian and the Cardinal lifted himself out of one chair to collapse into another, drops of sweat running down his brow.

Carafa, who had always been enamored of beautifully sculpted faces, noted that Cardinal Alfonso had not lost the ascetic appearance of his lean frame and smooth-cheeked face. Those traits along with his short stature made him appear almost childlike, an impression that was quickly lost when he started to talk for he had a deep booming voice.

Carafa waited for Cardinal Justinian to speak in deference to his age. Carafa thought *what would it be like if I were Pope now? Where would the loyalty of these two men be? One always had to be careful with friendships.*

"Would you like some water?" asked Carafa, addressing both of them.

"If I may," said Justinian with a glance at Alfonso. "I would prefer wine."

Alfonso frowned but said nothing. Carafa placed a carafe filled with wine in front of Justinian who quickly poured it into a glass and drank as a thirsty man would. Alfonso waved away the glass of water Carafa offered him.

"What are the Pope's plans? His health is good, I assume?" Alfonso asked. "And the coffers must be full. Titian's painting and Michelangelo's latest masterpiece—they cost, don't they?"

"We'll be getting more in taxes from the Jews."

"It's always the Jews for you, Carafa, isn't it?"

"As it is for you." Justinian put down his glass of wine to hear Carafa's response. He never knew exactly how much information Carafa had. "The Jews keep you in the silk and cocoa trade, don't they?"

"The good ones do, but what's important here is whether you've convinced our Pope that his leadeship is in question?"

Justinian belched. "Thinks about his books and his art more than about the need to strengthen us...I mean the Church. And Isabella. Isabella spends too much time with him."

"And who do you spend your time with?" Carafa really wanted to ask him if he had any idea on how to strengthen the Church but thoughtful planning was not within Justinian's grasp.

"Yes, Justinian, just where do you spend your time? I'm as anxious as Carafa to hear your answer." Alfonso smirked. "I hardly ever see you in prayer."

"Nonsense. I pray with the d'Estes, the Guidos daily. They beg for my assistance in prayer."

"I see," Alfonso said. "Yes, they need it definitely more than the ones who are starving in the streets."

"Of course. My people have more time to be sinful. That's why they need more prayer."

Alfonso laughed. "I love your reasoning. We shall be absolved of all sins should you be Pope."

"Gentlemen, this is about our Pope and his leadership." Carafa interrupted. "People want rules—they want to be assured of a way to get to heaven and to avoid Purgatory. We must clarify ideas about Purgatory and remind people that they will suffer if they do not follow the strictures of the

Church...and we must rid the land of heretics. This is what we should be talking about."

Alfonso arched his eyebrow and looked at the overweight Cardinal. "And do you feel the same way, Justinian?"

"It's something to consider. I watched the people at the Passion Play. They were quite moved by Christ on the cross. I doubt if any of them can be taken in by Luther or Calvin after they've seen the suffering of our Lord."

Alfonso smiled. Justinian always knew what to say, but Alfonso doubted if the rotund Cardinal understood them.

"The question is how to bring the Pope along." Alfonso seemed to be speaking to himself. "Is it not? We seem to know how to bring power to the Church, but our Pope wavers. We don't know how much Isabella influences him. It's a miracle that he agreed to an Inquisition." Alfonso chuckled. "Not a real miracle, mind you, but you should feel pleased, Carafa, as Chief Inquisitor, or is it Grand Inquisitor?"

Carafa paced behind the chairs of his friends. "Do you know why the Pope did not attend the Passion Play? Even his son, Pier Luigi, was there. He managed to get to the play that his father hates." Neither of the Cardinals answered. "Do you not wonder how the Jew influences him?" Alfonso and Justinian needed no clarification as to who "the Jew" was.

"The crowd recognized who the real enemy is. 'Kill the Jews,' they screamed. 'Kill the Jews.' "Did you hear them?" Beads of perspiration formed on Carafa's forehead.

"Yes, I heard them." Alfonso said quietly. He knew Carafa was obsessed with the question of the Jews. It was unwise to oppose him openly, but Alfonso had never had problems with them. Bernardo diBelli and Alberto Finzi, in particular, had been helpful and discreet Jewish bankers who lent Alfonso money when he needed it to buy up bolts of silk at a good price. Alfonso knew that they too risked alienation from the Jewish community for allowing him credit when they denied it some of their fellow Jews.

"What do you think we should do?" Justinian said, tilting the carafe. "Do you have any more wine? There's very little here."

"We need to think carefully and act cautiously," Carafa said. Little by little, our Pope will understand what he needs to do. And now, gentlemen, a game of cards with more wine to lighten the mood." Carafa picked up a small table and placed it in front of Cardinal Justinian, then gathered two chairs and placed a new bottle of claret and wine glasses on the table. Alfonso shuffled the cards ready to start. "What shall it be gentlemen? Picquet or Chance?"

"Chance," said Carafa. Alfonso dealt the cards. Justinian raised his glass. "You'll both drink with me, won't you?" Carafa and Alfonso raised their glasses. Alfonso waited until Carafa had sipped from the glass, before he drank. Justinian downed the contents of his sixth glass in one gulp.

CHAPTER 6

Apostate Son, Israel

After his confrontation with Carafa, Hayyim Luzzatti walked quickly down the Palace steps beneath the colonnade of St. Peter's and paused to look up at the scaffolding along the side of the building. From rickety wooden structures, men applied concrete in swift movements to strengthen the sides of the building. Other workmen chiseled heraldic arms, angels with wings, elegant fleur-de-lis designs. Since the Pope's ordination six years ago, rebuilding at the palace was a frantic affair. Hayyim walked carefully to avoid tripping over sharp and heavy tools that lay on the ground.

The Pope had given work to many talented craftsmen who had made their way from Florence to Rome. St. Peter's was definitely in need of repair as some of its walls had begun to lean rather dangerously. The Pope had put Michelangelo in charge of the renovation to assure its magnificence.

Hayyim was in awe of Michelangelo's frescoes on the ceiling of the Sistine Chapel, especially the renderings of Old Testament figures. He was less enamored of *The Last Judgment,* the artist's latest work as Hayyim had found it harsh with its writhing bodies lying in Dante's stages of purgatory. The flayed skin of St. Bartholomew was particularly repugnant to him.

He retraced the path that had taken him to the Palace.. Again, some returned his smile. Some stepped out of the way and looked fearful for they recognized him as a Jew because of his beard and skullcap. He was glad when he arrived at the doorway to his own home, one of the many tan stucco houses on the cobblestone street. The outside wall of his home was awash in bright sunshine. It was his home. With this thought, Luzzatti placed his fingers to his lips and then touched the mezuzah lightly.

He hurried to his study to read his texts hoping to avoid Alba's questions. "Had the Pope been willing to do anything about the armband law? Will he curtail the Passion Play?"

He needed to prepare a sermon. He pulled Rashi's text from a shelf and read quickly from right to left, turning pages rapidly and stopping when he found something he wanted to read carefully. He didn't hear Alba enter.

"Did it go well at the Palace? With the Pope?"

"Not now, Alba. I must prepare a sermon."

"Then I will just sit here and sew while you read." She placed a chair near a mullioned window that looked out over her herb garden.

"I want to say something about Jews and suffering. Something about Abraham needing to sacrifice Isaac, Job and his problems, Moses at Sinai."

"What is it that you want to say? That we have to suffer? Ridiculous." She pointed at her herbs. "See how joyously they grow with sunlight, water, and good earth. Plenty of stories exist in Torah that tell us we can live in joy."

"God gets angry."

"No, you get angry." She picked up her sewing.

Hayyim flipped through more pages, stopped, and began reading silently, his lips mouthing the words.

"So, you don't get angry. Would you like a cup of tea? I made some nice strawberry marmelade and I baked bread today—it's deliciously fresh."

"I said I have to prepare a sermon." He slammed the book closed.

"See, I told you, you get angry. Why is it that I must come after your sermon, your synagogue, and, yes, your Pope?"

"It is an honor to be the Pope's physician—especially for a Jew. It's also an honor to the family when I write an inspiring sermon."

"Maybe Israel would still be with us if you had been as devoted to your family as you are to your Pope and your sermons."

He stood. "Enough, Alba."

Alba had carefully avoided bringing up her son's name whom Hayyim felt had betrayed his religion and brought disgrace on the family with his conversion. Israel had been especially good with accounts. He had kept exquisite records for those who were involved in the silk and spice trade, and although Hayyim wanted him to study to be a rabbi, Israel felt that his calling was elsewhere. Alba remembered when Israel was eight how he questioned his father about praying to a God he could not see. "Will he answer us?" the youngster had asked.

"Only if you're patient," his father had answered.

Israel had turned away from his father, not wanting to show his disappointment, but Alba foresaw that from that moment her son would have a rebellious streak. She wasn't surprised when Israel turned eighteen and set out for Spain making the long trek to Madrid on horseback. His father made him carry the codex of Rashi with him as well as the writings of Marcus Aurelius and Augustine.

Hayyim had worried about his son being caught up in the many battles that he would be sure to encounter along the way, but Israel had arrived safely in the Spain of Charles V, and his skills in accounts were put to work at the court. When Hayyim heard from a friend that his son was successful, he took silent pride in the fact that Israel's perilous journey had been so positive.

The next news had arrived via a short letter from Israel. Alba had read the letter first and reluctantly had given it to her husband to read.

Dear Mother and Father,

An exciting journey to see such mountains and flowing rivers. At first they made me think there might be a God who created this beauty and then I saw people covered with pustules dying in their excrement by the roadside. I know, Father, that if you had been here, you would have helped them. I could do nothing but throw a few coins and ride on.

At court, I keep the accounts for Charles. He strives to limit the work of the German Protestant Princes and that should be helpful to your friend, the Pope, should it not?

In light of world events and my time here, I have decided to accept the sacraments of the Catholic Church.

Hayyim had read no further. He had tossed the letter into the fireplace, had watched it burn and had sat shivah without eating, or bathing for days. Alba had brought him food but would not share in the *shivah* with him. She would not mourn her son as dead.

* * *

"No, it's not enough. We had a son. We have a son." She busied herself with a kettle of boiling water.

"So you want to talk about Israel? To have left this household for Spain is one thing—to have left his faith is another."

"You don't know why he left the faith, and if he truly left the commandments. He can't have discarded all that you taught him. All those times in synagogue. All those studies."

"A mother sometimes finds it hard to accept the truth—even to recognize the truth when it is staring right at her," Hayyim said.

Alba placed a cup of tea and bread and jam in front of him. "Hayyim, please. Please drink a cup of borage tea. It will be easier for us to talk."

"You want me to put Torah aside for a cup of tea to talk about something distasteful? I do love you, my dear wife, but sometimes you exasperate me."

"Your work can wait." Alba wiped her hands on her apron. "Israel is here. He is in this house. We talked. This morning while you were at the Papal Palace."

Hayyim stared at his wife and gripped the edge of the desk to steady himself. "He's here?" His voice quivered with disbelief.

"Yes." Alba took his arm. "He wants to make sure that you want to see him. My dear husband, he's prepared to leave immediately. He doesn't want cause you pain or risk your disapproval. But, I want him here. I want you to see him." She placed a hand on his shoulder. "He is our son."

"I don't know. With all my learning, I don't know."

"First calm yourself. He'll wait for your decision." Alba massaged her husband's back.

"The congregation will consider a *cherem* if I accept him back."

"You are his father. First, will you accept him?"

"I loved that child—that boy—that man—so smart—so good with numbers." He sat head in hands.

"Yes, and apparently, he's still good with numbers. The king calls on him weekly."

"Ah, the court Jews."

"We have had them in the past. Are you not the Papal Court Jew?"

He grabbed her shoulders. "But I am still a Jew."

He let go quickly. "I'm sorry Alba. I'm hurt, I'm torn."

"See him. It doesn't mean you have to accept him. He's not dead."

As she turned to leave, Hayyim lifted his head and spoke barely above a whisper. "Wait. Tell him I do wish to see him. It does not mean acceptance, but I want to look upon his face again."

She left, feeling compassion for both her husband and her son, and hoped that somehow these two men in her life that she loved dearly would be able to see the good in each other. She found her son in the garden. She looked upon her son with his sturdy, solid build and ringlets of dark, curly hair that cascaded over his ruggedly handsome face—a face that now seemed extremely mature for his twenty-three years. Taking his wide, sure hand, she said, "He'll see you, but you must realize that this is quite a shock to him. I understood your rebelliousness and restlessness; your father did not."

Israel hugged his mother. "Not a rebellious streak, mother—an inquisitive one."

Israel went quickly to his father's study, with Alba following a few feet behind, where he saw Hayyim facing the doorway, shoulders bent, head bowed and hands clasped in prayer. When Hayyim raised his head and saw his son, he stood for a moment and stared at him as though he were an apparition. Israel stood locked in place. His father looked tired but healthy with a few gray hairs. Israel raised his arms and approached him. Hayyim shook his head and took a few steps back. Israel hurried to his father and buried his head in his broad chest, and Hayyim could do nothing but place his arms around his sobbing son. After a few moments, Israel turned to hug his mother who seemed momentarily confused between her laughter and her tears.

"Thank you, Mother," he murmured taking her hand in his. "For speaking on my behalf. You made a path for me so I could speak to father."

Hayyim, who had composed himself, said, "I was your father."

"I expect you to be angry with me."

"What does one say? There is nothing written for me in the Talmud about addressing an apostate son."

Israel spoke though not sure if his father was speaking to him or not. "You have to understand. Many do it to have to chance....to have a chance at life. If you're a Christian and you want to work, you can work. If you want to go to University, the door is open for you."

"I cannot understand right now. The shock is too great for me. Perhaps it's best if we start out with you as a visitor...a visitor with news from Spain."

"Perhaps you can talk about Kaballah while I boil some water," said Alba.

"Your mother gives us good advice. What news have you heard about Kaballah? What is the latest interpretation? What is the Grand Rabbi of Spain saying? Does he have any special words of wisdom?"

"No, father." He knew that Rabbi Joseph Karo had been his father's teacher and tried to impart the mystical aspects of Kabbalah to his student. Hayyim had been skeptical yet remained interested.

"Well, perhaps no news exists because no one talked of Kaballah in your court," said his father. "Perhaps you have news about medicines—what the doctors are saying about cures for the crippling of the body and the healing of infections."

"Unfortunately, Father, the court in Spain is not as advanced as we are here. Charles sometimes rules from Germany and, at times, the court is in disarray. Spain is fighting wars on so many fronts now and trying to find wealth in new lands. You may have heard of the Americas?"

Alba returned with cups of tea. Alba interrupted. "I heard you speaking of world affairs but, my son and husband, you're avoiding the subject you need to talk about. You should be talking about matters of faith—matters of acceptance."

"I must explain," Israel began." When I arrived in Spain, chaos ruled because of the words of Luther. I thought the officials of the court would ignore me when I came to work the accounts. But it wasn't to be because the rumors of the court began to swirl talking of Luther as a Judaizer—that's why he wanted to weaken the Church. At least, that's what the clergy were saying."

Hayyim murmured, "Why, even here we know that Luther has true reason to rant against the selling of indulgences."

"But, Papa, I see Luther hardening his heart against the Jews as well as the Catholics. He sees the wrong of the indulgences, lashes out against them, and we're the accountants. Luther knows many Jews weigh and assay the Church's money."

Hayyim folded his hands in his lap. Alba and Israel waited."So far, my son," Hayyim finally spoke, "I do not see the reason for the abandonment of your faith. A faith that is the essence of your soul, your history, our history as Jews."

"I had a friend," Israel began. "Alfredo, who convinced me that I would be better off if I accepted the sacraments. Being so far from home, I did. I was frightened. Perhaps confused. It's that simple. He assured me that no one would know what I did in private." He added, "I read Rashi every night."

"So you did not think what your acceptance of the Catholic faith would do to your family—to your parents—your community here?" He paused. "And—the acceptance of the sacraments—has it really helped your soul?"

"I cannot say about my soul, but I've survived thus far at the court. I was allowed to take this trip here to use the Vatican Library to investigate some legal concerns. You know it holds great volumes."

Alba interrupted. "Thus far?" What is 'thus far'?"

Her son answered quietly. "The gossip at the court is that there is a new Torquemada ready to question anyone with a hint of Jewish blood. Just a drop of blood, mind you. That's all that's needed for possible exile."

"Ah, a Torquemada. There's nothing so devilish as a Jew who rejects his own kind and engages in a form of self-hatred." Alba wiped the sweat off her brow with a piece of muslin and carried the teacups to the kitchen.

Hayyim seemed not to notice the sweat glistening on his brow. "What of the Jews who are left in Spain? Many fled over forty years ago but some stayed. What of those who are there? Is there talk of conversion again?" He didn't wait for an answer. "We must be ready to receive those who are preparing to flee just as our ancestors were received here in Rome."

"Father?"

"This is what we must talk about right now. Nothing else."

"You can't do more than you already have. It's too risky for you—the congregation, your relationship with the Pope. Please, Hayyim, don't ask the synagogue to do more. Israel, you see the danger in this, don't you? Where will we put them? What will happen to us?"

Hayyim answered. "What will happen to us if we don't help? That's the only question that should concern us. You and your parents were helped, weren't they?"

Israel turned slowly to the mullioned window of his father's study, which looked out on the courtyard. Israel felt that he had never seen such a beautiful garden—the reds of the roses were brilliant, he thought. The marjoram, the thyme, and the basil, he knew, made his mother's cooking so delicious. Even when she hung out the laundry to dry, she hung it in such a way that the flora was still evident from the windows. She had that sense of beauty.

"Mother still maintains a beautiful garden."

"Yes, she does. She grows wonderful medicinal plants, as well. She grows rhubarb, myrrah, and cassia to brew for treatment of pain."

He turned away from the window to his father. "Do you accept me as your son after what I have done?"

"I accept that I fathered you—for the moment—this is what I accept."

Alba returned dressed in a brown silk dress with a high bodice adorned with a simple strand of pearls. "Come, we need to go to the synagogue so that our friends can see you."

"This is not the time, Alba. We must prepare them. Let Israel remain here for a while, do his work in the Vatican Library, then we will see. Let the community find out about him slowly."

"No, Hayyim. We have nothing to hide."

"Father, I would like to go. I haven't been in a synagogue in a long time."

Hayyim had kept the news from Alba, that the gobierno—the governing council of Jews that made the decisions regarding annulments, lawsuits, complaints, breach of contract, cherems—had met to discuss a complete banishment for Israel, forbidding him from ever returning to the community.

"It may not be pleasant."

"It is synagogue. How can a place to pray with friends be unpleasant?" Israel said.

CHAPTER 7

Dominican Friar Leo Preaches
at Synagogue

Hayyim, Alba, and Israel approached the family's synagogue. The exterior of its dome, inlaid with turquoise ceramic tile and triangular windows, glistened in the sunlight. The community had been divided during its construction. The crystal-like formation closely resembled the basilica of St. Peter's, and some of the members had objected. Jonas Caravaggio, the builder, had convinced them that the dome would let light pour down on the Torah that was centered on a *tebah*—the place where men stood to recite the prayers of the day. The color, turquoise, would be unique to their synagogue. This particular color had been important to the members here who valued their Sephardic heritage. Many had ancestors in Spain who could recall that brilliant shade used in Moorish buildings. While congregants resisted ornamentation and iconography, they valued color.

Hayyim and Alba, with Israel following, entered through the wooden doors decorated simply in alternating panels of light and dark wood. The deep blue silk on the benches; the swirls of gold paint that intermittently decorated white plaster walls; the modest though beautifully decorated building satisfied his congregants' need for a safe place and a sanctuary for prayer. The Torah scrolls had been hand written by a learned scribe with a quill pen and then inset on rollers that contained no metal or steel because that was material used in war.

As they entered, Israel was tentative. "Do you think I should be here with you now?"

Alba took his arm. "I hope they will remember you as they used to. They loved to see you learn Torah and read your Hebrew without mistakes." Many young women in the congregation had determined that he would be the one to marry. His strong masculine face, dark curly hair, and his determination won a lot of hearts.

"Maybe all they will remember is his apostasy. We will be truthful, if they ask us." Hayyim said.

Alba glared at him.

The Luzzatti family entered to find Dominican Friar Leo, his face choleric, standing on the tebah ranting at the congregation. The Dominican Friar had appeared at some of the other synagogues, but Hayyim assumed that his house of worship would be spared because of his relationship with the Pope.

The friar shouted and raised his fist. "I see a Christ lacerated by thorns when your people placed him on the cross. Your souls are in danger. You must accept Jesus Christ as your Savior and your way to salvation. You are each condemned and you are condemned as a people! You will be damned to a place in hell where you will not be able to count your money and say your mumbled prayers."

He stopped when he saw Rabbi Luzzatti enter with his family. The congregation followed the friar's gaze and turned to see their rabbi and his wife. Many gasped when they saw Israel. Several of the younger women whispered to each other and blushed momentarily torn between terror and delight. Rabbi Luzzatti strode purposefully to the tebah. Alba walked the steps that led to the balcony, and Israel remained at the entrance of the synagogue watching the scene unfold.

"Your Talmud will be of no use to you!" Friar Leo shouted. "To those who thought that Martin Luther would accept you—I know that he published *Jews and Their Lies*. Acceptance of the sacraments will be your only salvation." He screamed, "Accept!"

The synagogue members sat in silence, hands protectively folded on their open prayer books. Rabbi Luzzatti approached the reading table. He spoke in a firm voice as though the Dominican Friar was not there. "It's time to start our morning prayers." He put on his tallit, kissed the corners of his fringes, and climbed the steps of the tebah.

Friar Leo came down from the platform that held the Torah scrolls, and whispered in Rabbi Luzzatti's ear. Then the friar walked up the aisle past the members. "He has done it. He has accepted Jesus," he shouted, pointing to Israel who remained still and grim-faced. He paused before Israel, bowed and swept out of the building his cassock dragging in the dust behind him. Israel moved further inside, but did not take a seat.

Rabbi Luzzatti took the edge of his long linen coat, bent to the floor, and wiped the spot where Friar Leo had been standing.

"Rabbi," Benjaming ben Jehuda stood. A red-headed, beared man of twenty-eight, he towered over his brothers and the rabbi. "We have not been subjected to such harangue for years. It does not take much to start the bloodletting."

"What you have heard is not new."

Ben Viniste stood. "First the Passion Play and now a Dominican Friar proselytizing in our own synagogue."

"It will pass." Rabbi Luzzatti had not opened the Torah scrolls yet. "Soon they will blame us," Di Constantini called out. "Someone will get sick to his stomach and it will be our fault because they imagine we have poisoned their wells."

"They do not enforce the clothing requirement; we do not wear the yellow circle on our clothes. Friar Leo's words mean nothing."

Rabbi Luzzatti held out his hands in supplication. "It's only talk. Not more than talk. The play at the Colosseum? Lets the people frolic in the streets. Yes, I know, at our expense, but it's just a play. We're still reading our books and we're working our trades."

In the upstairs balcony with the women, Alba sat rigid, her hands clasped. He knew how angry the Passion Play made her and how it upset the community. Why was he trying to make light of it?

"You're close to the Pope. Can't you convince him that these diatribes from the Dominicans worry us a great deal?" Ben Jehuda pleaded.

"Of course, he can't convince the Pope," Shimon ben Shimini stood. "Nor does he want to." His voice grew louder. "He couldn't keep his son from being baptized." He sat down gripping the edge of the pew in front of him.

Alba sat forward in the upstairs balcony hoping her husband would be protective of Israel. She saw Israel at the back waiting with arms folded.

"What Israel did in Spain..." the rabbi faltered. "He did what he needed to do; that's all I can say. I can assure you that conditions for the remaining Jews are much worse in Spain than they are here. We've not had a Torquemada here—one who burned people at the stake as he burned books. Israel did what he needed to do save his life. Don't you remember that it's important to save a life—the value of every life?"

Alba sighed. He didn't disown him completely.

"So, Israel, is he still a Jew?" Alberto Finzi who had remained silent until now stood. "Is he still your son? Is he coming back here to practice his accounting skills...at our expense?" Finzi had welcomed Israel's departure so that he could have a near monopoly on the accounting trade in the city.

Rabbi Luzzatti said, "We should get on with our prayers. "Israel is in our house. That's enough to say for now."

Finzi persevered. "But do you welcome him as we should welcome all strangers, or do you welcome him as your son?"

"What is this about welcome?" Bernardo diBelli, Finzi's business partner, spoke. "Someone who has abandoned his faith is not welcome. We should consider a *cherem*. He should no longer be part of this community."

Alba stood up from her balcony seat. "He's our son. He's of our flesh and blood. That's all that matters." Several of the women put their hands to their mouths, but the men ignored her.

"Ask your wife to sit down, Rabbi. She does not constitute a minyan." It was Shimon ben Shimini.

Hayyim looked up at Alba. He glared. She held her gaze steadfast. Israel moved up a few steps down the aisle.

"What is it when a rabbi cannot control his own wife?" Hayyim could not recognize the voice that came from the men's section. Alba sat down, her eyes blazing.

"It's different for us who do not see the Pope," Shimon continued. "We wonder why our rabbi who has access to the Pope can't do more for us." The congregants were silent. "Unless he secretly sympathizes with the Pope. Perhaps we need a Dona Esther to exorcise the demons among us."

"Sit down, old man." Ben Jehuda was impatient. "Rabbi Luzzatti's connection with the Pope has served us well. Some of us here that know better than to believe in a superstitious old woman who claims she can talk to the dead and cure illness with incantations."

"Pope Paul has protected us," said Rabbi Luzzatti. "He's let us live our lives. Forget Friar Leo. Instead worry about our brethren in Spain who still live as conversos. We must open our hearts and our homes to them. Let them come with their belongings and their desire to remain Jews."

"Rabbi, you ask us to take in more people when we are struggling here." Samuel Levitas stood. "Who knows what the Church will do when they see more of us? Perhaps we have been able to manage because we are not so many."

"Yes, and we'll be subjected to more rants from the Dominicans." Hayyim did not try to identify the voice. This was the time to change course for the morning and deliver the sermon he intended to. He caught Alba's eye and her quiet reserve signaled approval to go ahead.

"You," Rabbi Luzzatti said trying to contain his anger, "you've been able to manage because you handle money for the Church. You have your home—your work—your family. These people from Spain will come with nothing, but they still want to be Jewish and observe our laws. All I hear from you is what will the Pope do for us." He raised his hands as though pleading to God to help him. "How can we not afford to take care of suffering people?" He looked grimly from one congregant to another. "It's time to pray. Perhaps in that prayer, we'll gain more wisdom." Rabbi Luzzatti turned to the Torah scrolls open on the table, took the yad in his hand and began to read.

51

Stillness fell upon the synagogue. Dust particles floated in the rays of light of the dome. Israel had finally taken a seat close to the door and sat alone in the pew waiting the words of the Pentantuch. Luzzatti chanted Haftorah, reading from Isaiah in pitch-perfect Sephardic Hebrew.

"But you have burdened me with your sin; you have wearied me with your iniquities. I, yea I, erase your transgressions for my sake, and your sins I will not remember." He hoped that his congregants would find comfort in the words that this God was a forgiving one. The rabbi kissed the ends of his tallit, lifted the Torah scrolls, so that ben Jehuda could replace the velvet gilt -edged cover and gently placed them back in the ark. Hayyim descended the steps of the tebah and without looking or acknowledging any of the synagogue members, left and took the arm of Israel who had been waiting for him at the back of the synagogue near the entrance. Hayyim noted his son's tears but said nothing.

Alba ran down the steps, without the usual hugs and kisses that were shared among the women, to catch up with her husband and son. She hoped her prayers for wisdom and guidance would come to fruition at this most difficult time. She was aware that life at the Papal Palace was becoming more precarious and saw her husband's weariness from shouldering the problem of preserving his relations with the Pope and sustaining his community. Alba wondered how she could help him bear this burden as well as the troubles within their own family. The tirade of Friar Leo and the return of their son from Spain had been a lot to bear in one day.

CHAPTER 8

Isabella and the Library

Cardinal Carafa loved the feeling of grandeur that enveloped him when he entered the hallway leading to the Pope's study. Paul had invested much money in beautifying the halls of the palace by supporting the work of artists. Botticelli and Raphael were two of his favorites along with Michelangelo. The sculptor was working on a rather large, somber, and disturbing painting in the Sistine Chapel. Paul had directed the artist to cover a painting by Pinturicchio, and now *The Last Judgment*, nearly completed, at times both terrified and astonished its viewers.

Of all the Cardinals in the papal court, Carafa, more than others, understood Michelangelo's *Last Judgment*. He knew that the sculptor had been tormented by quarrels within the church as well as the demons within his soul. The burning of Savonarola at the hands of the Borgias in Florence some forty years ago had left the artist particularly scarred.

The Cardinal knocked on the door of the Pope's study as he turned the knob. He was not surprised to find the Pope reading with a magnifying glass in hand. "Please, sit down. I shall be with you in a moment. I'm at an interesting passage of Augustine—such a fascinating mind. I learn something from him every time I decipher a text. It is a wonder I can do it at all since I do not use my Latin as often as I should."

Carafa waited until Paul put down his glass.

"Have you considered that Rabbi Luzzatti should have a different way of addressing you?"

"Truthfully, no. He's a Jew who bows down and kisses my ring, out of respect. At times, he kisses my feet or should

I say, my shoes? Is not that enough? Have you given thought to what would be a better form of address?"

"Perhaps he should kiss the floor where your feet have just been and not kiss your hands nor your feet."

"Tell me, Carafa, what is it that upsets you so about this man?"

"He's a Jew. Your power is precarious." Carafa continued. "We have lost Denmark and Sweden to Luther. It's bad enough that we are fighting Luther, now we must deal with Calvin. Where are the Catholic souls to go if Luther and Calvin have their way?" Carafa became bolder when he saw that he had the Pope's attention. "You may not want to hear this but the influence of the Church is waning and your power is diminishing in the world."

"And what has this to do with our Doctor Luzzatti...the Jew?" Paul slowly closed the book and put the magnifying glass aside.

Paul's emphasis on the word *our* had its effect. The pinkish cast to Carafa's face turned bright red.

"I'll tell you exactly." Carafa shifted from one foot to another. "You have a Jewish doctor. Your appointment of Father Bruno to the court of Archbishop Leonardo at the Cathedral of Toledo was not wise. Your continued relationship with Isabella is suspect."

Paul raised his hand. "Isabella is not part of this discussion."

"You raise considerable taxes on the people to support your acquisitions of art."

"This art is for the church. It adds beauty to the church and demonstrates to God how much we love him."

Carafa was undeterred. "Father Leo makes no progress with the conversion of the Jews or revealing the true practices of the Marranos in spite of your promulgation of the Inquisition."

Paul stared at Carafa.

"While you engage in this struggle with the Protestants you must strengthen your leadership and position of respect in the world." He added, "God is unhappy with us because we are not demonstrating adherence to the Catholic faith...and not adding more Catholics to the faith."

Paul rose from his desk, walked to the huge stained glass window, and turned. "You truly believe this, my friend, I see. Do not worry. We'll strengthen my leadership; we'll choose the way carefully. A teacher of Marcus Aurelius, Apollonius of Chalcedon, said that a man could show both strength and flexibility. We will not disappoint God."

"I am afraid that we are in a situation where your knowledge of Latin and Marcus Aurelius will not be sufficient."

"Neither will your thinking that Father Bruno needs to be recalled because he had a pagan Jewish grandmother who wandered in the desert and supposedly drank the blood of children."

"How do we know that Father Bruno doesn't practice his Judaism in secret?"

"That is why I gave you an Inquistion, isn't it? To ferret out Judaizers. But Father Bruno? Never. He was one of my most loyal students."

"There's Isabella."

"I told you she is not part of this discussion." Paul glanced through the window at the distant cathedral. "She is the mother of my children. Because you never indulged in female flesh, or the possibility of fatherhood, you're limited in your understanding, my friend. Isabella and I have been loyal to one another and are good parents. And our affairs of the flesh are long gone."

Both men stood tall and proud as they faced each other. A knock at the door broke the tense silence.

"Yes, who is it?" asked Paul.

"May I come in? There's something I want to read in one of your manuscripts." Isabella tried the handle, but it was locked.

"Now? Just at this moment?"

"It's important."

"You see, Carafa. It's only books that hold her interest." Paul walked to the door stumbling slightly as his foot caught in a carpet.

Paul opened the door. Carafa replied, "That can be dangerous as..."

"What is it that can be dangerous?" Isabella interrupted. "Surely, not I. An old woman who likes to read books." Her voice was tinged with the keenness of authority and intelligence. Carafa knew better than to answer her, or else he would be entangled in a battle of words.

"My appointment with the Pope is finished," Carafa bowed.

"Stay and continue the discussion. I would like Isabella to hear your thinking about Father Bruno."

"That would be ill-advised. You have my opinion."

"Carafa," Paul sighed. "Isabella has my interests and the interests of the Church uppermost in her heart."

"Was that ever in doubt? How could my love and loyalty for the Church and for you ever be questioned?" She searched around the room and then found a table that held an illuminated manuscript about the stars.

"Let Isabella hear this argument and tell us what she thinks."

Paul walked to the table and closed the book she had been leafing through. "Carafa wants me to recall Father Bruno from Toledo to demonstrate that I mistrust anyone with Jewish blood even if they've accepted the sacraments and dedicate themselves to the Church. He wants to demonstrate that we deal sharply with heretics."

"Why, Father Bruno was one of your best students," she said.

"I reminded him of that."

"Do you know what Father Bruno has been reading?" Carafa looked at both of them with a triumphant smile. "Word has gotten back to me from Toledo that he is reading the Talmud. Do you know what the Talmud preaches?"

"He undoubtedly reads Talmud to improve his Hebrew," Isabella said. "Hebrew, Greek, Latin—they are our languages of wisdom. The Talmud contains the laws of the Jews written in Hebrew. It's a compilation of their laws, their history."

"Do you know what it actually says?" Carafa didn't wait for a response. "It says that God is omnipresent and available to all regardless of their faith—regardless of their lack of belief in our Lord, Jesus. Can we truly accept that? Is that not heresy?" Carafa took a deep breath and added, "Can we believe as well, that the earth is not the center of the universe?"

"Is it faith for you, Carafa, or is it power?" Paul paced. "You await the papacy, do you not? Signs of my death are not imminent enough for you, are they?"

Isabella stared, eyes alert, surprised at the Pope's sudden display of anger and no longer attempting to read.

"Your Holiness. I raise these issues for your good. You cannot question my faith. Have I not been a faithful servant for these past twenty years?" Carafa pleaded.

"Ah," said Paul, "but you want us to question the faith of Father Bruno...and Copernicus."

"It is one thing to believe something yourself and another to be watchful of what you express to others. This is where one understands where power comes from. You could express doubt about Copernicus' theory in order to win more of the Cardinals to your side."

"There," Isabella firmly closed the large book. "I knew he would use Copernicus to draw you into an argument. An argument that has no merit. Copernicus has proven his theories to scientists among us. The Church must recognize this and use this knowledge to its advantage."

"Isabella, I'd ask that you tend to your reading and let me take care of this argument," Paul snapped. "You're a distraction from the argument."

Isabella glowered and reopened the book. She wasn't sure where she left off.

"I am your most loyal servant." Carafa hurried on. I am only anxious for you to understand that there are rumors— the Jews are giving their loyalty to the Protestants. And their money. Our supporters murmur among themselves."

"And what do you think would please our so-called 'supporters' and keep them from murmuring amongst themselves? A Passion Play that permits blood and licentiousness to run in the streets at the same time?"

Isabella almost did not breathe as the men's sentences flew back and forth like lightning.

"More than that, Your Holiness."

"Ah! A hanging, then?"

"Perhaps. Cardinals Justinian and Alfonso have assured me it is warranted."

"Ah! A burning?"

"Perhaps."

"Ah! I was not clear—a burning of books—the Talmud especially?"

"Perhaps."

"A burning of bodies?"

"Perhaps."

"Imprisonment and torture? I have already given you a Papal Inquisition."

"Perhaps."

"Which, which, which? Which do you think will satisfy our faith?" Paul's voice rose. "And our obvious need for power. Trust me. I have not forgotten power."

With the increasing agitation in Paul's voice, Carafa knew he had made his point.

"If we can convince the Jews to convert, we may intimidate the Protestant princes...they might even return to the Church...the one true Church." He waited. "We might even take the property of the Jews as well as their books and that, of course, would give us more money in our treasury. Money that we surely need. I need not explain it to you."

"And that is your sense of the situation?" Paul sat down wearily.

"If we continue to lose princes to Luther and Calvin, we lose money, land and power."

Isabella closed the book sharply, stood, and looked directly at Paul. "I see stupidity and I sense danger—a difficult road ahead for the Church and reform. Agitation against the Jews is not a remedy. We must renew our faith through prayer and good practices, not through denunciations, burnings, inquisitions. We'll have lost our way, should we resort to those...those...those *efforts*."

"Send for Father Bruno," Paul said.

A tiny gasp came from Isabella's lips. Carafa smiled. With a bow of his head, he backed out to leave.

"I shall send a messenger today. It will take about a week, no doubt, but it shall be done. Father Bruno will be here perhaps to face the Inquisition." He shut the door behind him.

Isabella nervously opened the astronomy text again. It was unfathomable to her that the Paul she knew as a lover of books and knowledge, who had denounced book burning and religious persecution, was now agreeing to a recall of Father Bruno. Was the father of her children—the man she loved—getting tired—losing his way?

"It is time for me to go. It is clear to me that my words have had no influence on you." She sighed. "That's not the way it used to be."

"Isabella, these are affairs of state. Sometimes the temporal must be connected with the religious. It's impossible to separate them always. It's not so long ago we fought a war with Spain, Charles sacked Rome and Pope Clement was in hiding"

"Look," she pointed. "You have Raphael's painting of *Pope Leo the Great Meeting Attila* right here to remind you."

"Remind me of what?" he growled.

"That Leo achieved peace and convinced Attila to withdraw from Italy and return to Hungray."

"It's a painting. Real political life is much more complicated."

"I understand the complexity," she stood. "I'm also aware that you are a moral man and a man of reason. I assume I have permission to continue to use the library?"

Paul placed his hand on Isabella's shoulder and swept back a narrow lock of graying hair. "Of course, you have permission to use the library. You need not pretend to embroider."

"Regardless of what Carafa says?"

"Regardless of Carafa. These books are yours as well as mine."

"I suppose the heavens will wait until the next time. I shall go and attend to the ladies of the court. Be well." She knelt to kiss his ring. He accepted the kiss and gently touched the lace that covered her head.

CHAPTER 9

Titian Paints the Pope

Paul rifled the pages of the astronomy book, stopping when he saw an illustration that showed phases of the moon, and walked from the study to his chambers where Titian waited for him to continue his portrait.

In the Stanza Della Segnatura, he stopped to look at *The Judgment of Solomon,* Raphael's ceiling fresco—with wise Solomon sitting on a throne flanked by two distraught yet robust looking women and a well-proportioned, well-muscled man holding a baby by his feet in the air while another infant lay at the feet of this powerful man. Solomon, he thought. Am I like Solomon now needing to make these dreadful decisions?

Paul entered his chambers and saw Titian staring out the window.

The painter turned eagerly when he heard the Pope enter and sit in the chair beside the easel. "Excellent timing, Your Holiness. The light is good, and my bones have not yet begun to creak." Titian liked to complain about his aches and pains.

"Then you will be able to work quickly as I have many important matters to attend to."

The artist had long ago concluded that most people sought out pretensions in their lives. "Can we continue with the same vestments as yesterday? I already have the colors mixed." The clothing was already laid out on the bed.

Paul donned a red velvet cape over his white vestment, and smoothed his grey and white beard over the cape. He sat placing his hands on the side of his chair to indicate that he was ready.

"Don't you want the miter? You wore it yesterday."

"Let's eliminate the heavy hat. I've enough weight on my shoulders."

"As you wish, Your Holiness." As Titian lifted his brush to the palette, a Swiss Guard announced that Doctor Luzzatti was here and wanted to know if he should be sent in.

"Of course, send him in. He must have some medicine for me."

Titian, ever desirous of palace gossip, said, "I can continue to paint while the doctor visits with you."

Hayyim Luzzatti hesitated when he saw that the Pope was sitting for a portrait and realized that Titian was going to continue to paint. Luzzatti carefully unwrapped a small glass vial containing ointment. "Apply this twice a day to the ...to the affected area. It may take several months but with careful application and with..." He hesitated.

"You may speak freely," Paul said. "Titian here is only interested in the outer layer of my being."

"With continued restraint in your physical performance."

"As I've told you, that is all in the past. What I need now is someone to say something interesting to me. Come sit near me, and we'll talk. It'll relieve some of the boredom of simply staring into space."

The artist put his brush down.

"You'll need to limit your movements, Your Holiness."

Hayyim Luzzatti sat opposite Paul on a mahogany chair covered with green damask threaded with gold. He looked around and recognized a painting by Pinturicchio of *The Virgin Mary and the Infant Jesus.*

"You are looking at the Pinturicchio painting, are you not? I hope mine will be of equal beauty," Paul said.

"It will be, Your Holiness," said Titian, ever aware of the Pope's passion for art and flattery. "You're a very handsome subject." He addressed Hayyim. "See how Pinturicchio painted the white folds of the garment so realistically. The Pope's robe will be of equal value."

"I was looking at Mary's face." Mary is always serene, he thought. Luzzatti thought of women of the Old Testament, Deborah, Judith, Ruth, Naomi, Miriam. Were any of them ever serene? Jews always seem to be encountering problems.

"Have you heard my son just returned from the Court in Spain to be with us a while? A difficult trip."

"And what does he report from Spain?"

"He feels that he has been helpful to Charles in his financial matters, although I'm sure you know, he is often away fighting wars." Hayyim knew of the Pope's enmity to the man who insisted on calling himself "The Holy Roman Emperor." Hayyim cleared his throat. "My son has also accepted conversion." It was painful for Hayyim to remember the Pope's question about Hayyim's own desire to remain as a Jew.

"Ah, conversion—a subject that has come up lately with Cardinal Carafa. He is always trying to determine the true convert." He continued. "Are you angry with your son, or the Christians who brought the true faith to him?"

Luzzatti clasped his hands together and kept them on his lap. "We are grateful that we can practice our Judaism freely. We live by the good graces of the Church and your kindness, Your Holiness."

Titian put down his brush and wiped his hand down the side of his smock leaving a stain of magenta oil paint. Whenever the Pope had visitors, especially the doctor, he could not keep still. The painter really loved hearing Vatican gossip and only wished the conversation would turn to something that appealed to his appetite—the lovely ladies of the court.

"Please, Your Holiness. You may converse but I ask you remain as still as possible."

"You're mixing colors, aren't you? I assume I may move a bit while you mix your paints." Paul stretched his right arm and then tried to place it back in the exact same position. "Purity of blood has become important in the court of Spain." The Pope leaned forward with the last comment. "So my cardinals tell me. They also tell me about the torture of those who have accepted baptism, and newer decrees for the *limpieza de sangre.*

Hayyim hoped the Pope could not hear the palpitations of his heart. "We worry but we have hope." He swallowed. "The rabbis of the Talmud encourage us to turn to people of kindness and understanding."

"I've been kind and understanding to your people, and they have contributed much to this Papal court." Hayyim wasn't sure if he detected petulance in the Pope's voice.

"We are *in extremis* as a community—a crisis, if you will. My son tells me that there are Jews who are making their way to Rome from Spain because they are uncertain about their future in that country as Marranos."

"Take them into your homes and feed them. For that you do not need my approval."

"Your Holiness," Titian sighed. "You must not change the expression in your face." He squinted assessing the waning light.

Hayyim knew he needed to be bold. "We're talking about two hundred people. We can't absorb them all. They will need refuge in other parts of the city. Of course, we will pay for whatever lodgings they take. Your blessings and approval will provide protection from members of the community who may want to harm us."

The Pope nodded briefly toward the bust of Socrates, and Luzzatti thought the Pope was going to make some reference to the philosopher's sagacity. Instead Luzzatti heard the voice of Carafa behind him.

"Are there Marranos among those who are coming from Spain?"

"I suspect there are." Hayyim answered him steadily. "They think that Italy will be kinder than Spain or even England, where Luther has begun his verbal assault against the Jews."

"You are naïve, my good doctor friend, if you think I have the power to create space and acceptance for your fellow Jews from Spain," Paul said.

"If not you, then who does?" Hayyim was surprised at his directness.

"God does," Paul answered.

Hayyim should have expected this. In their many theological debates, Paul's frequently turned to God for the solution to problems. Hayyim had heard the words "faith in God" frequently.

"Isn't that true, Carafa?"

"The one true God," said Carafa.

Hayyim stood. "May I tell them that you are considering my request? And remember when I last spoke to you about removing the arm-band law from the books?"

"I'll consider it, along with the other requests that plague me. I've not forgotten about our last meeting when you did ask to have some laws removed. There's much that I need to consider." Paul did not want to reveal that he had recalled Father Bruno from Spain.

Hayyim stood up and started toward the door. Carafa coughed.

Hayyim then turned to kiss the Pope's ring and the floor where the Pope's feet had been. If Hayyim had looked up, he would have seen the frown on Paul's face.

Carafa followed the doctor to the hallway. "You must tell me what you are treating the Holy Father for so I may assure the other cardinals that you are not poisoning him? Many think that your presence is dangerous. Friar Leo returned from your synagogue and reported on the stubbornness of your people."

"You do not trust me? Actually, it is me and my community who must worry about trust. We try to live in peace as good citizens but we are subjected to threats from the rabble and rants of Friar Leo."

"You're indeed a stubborn man."

"I must go. My family is waiting for me." He added, "To go to synagogue."

Luzzatti turned and walked down the long corridor. He sensed that Carafa's eyes were following him. The rabbi left by the massive doors of the Papal Palace and stepped into the Roman sunshine that cast a golden light upon the city and the garbage that rotted in the streets. He decided to take the path of the narrow cobblestone streets directly to the synagogue and not stop by his house. He knew that Alba would go by herself with Israel if he did not arrive home in time. For many years, before Israel left for Spain, mother and son walked to synagogue together knowing that Hayyim would eventually arrive to lead in prayer.

CHAPTER 10

Congregant Finzi Invokes a Cherem

Hayyim arrived at the sweet space of the synagogue anticipating the peacefulness of prayer to find fewer than ten men in the domed light of the sanctuary. Israel was not there, nor were any women in the balcony. The men present were not wearing tallit and some sat with arms folded across their chests as though they were awaiting some news, some discussion. One of the men noticed Hayyim enter and put his finger to his lips. Hayyim walked to the front of the sanctuary and took a seat.

Benjamin ben Jehuda addressed him. "We're extremely worried, Rabbi Luzzatti, about the arrival of Jews who are coming from Spain. We're crowded ourselves in our small homes. Where will we house them? They'll take work from others in the community." As ben Jehuda spoke, some nodded their heads.

Benjamin came to pray every day, as he had since he was a child of six. Now at twenty-eight and the head of a family, he considered it the right thing to do to set an example for Elia, his five-year old. He thought his son would soon need to understand that as a Jew you needed to be vigilant about your place in the world. Acceptance by others was not easily given.

"I'm worried about the Church teachings they will bring with them," said Samuel Levitas, an older, usually quietier member of the congregation. "Some are now Marranos, are they not? I don't want them influencing my children." Hayyim waited for Levitas to say something about Israel but Ben Jehuda interrupted.

"Yes, Rabbi. We do have to worry about our children. The younger members will be susceptible. I'm sure you understand that."

"Look, you even bow to kiss the Pope's ring, do you not?" Levitas snapped. "You are a rabbi so you will not be taken by trappings of Christianity—others do not have your character...or your knowledge."

Hayyim wondered where and when Levitas had heard the news.

"I bow to kiss his ring out of honor to his position."

"We'll have ten Friar Leos here, proselytizing with their anger and hate." Ben Jehuda persisted. "The arrival of more Jews can only encourage the community to be more hostile toward us."

"The Pope will not permit that." Hayyim spoke, hoping that his voice reflected certainty.

"The Pope will do what is practical for the Papacy and the Church," Levitas countered. "If we do not fit into that scheme, he'll permit whatever he deems necessary. We're expendable. Perhaps it is time for a group of us to visit the Pope to impress upon him our feelings." He turned toward his fellow congregants.

"After all, wouldn't that have a greater appeal to the Pope than the appeal of just one person?" Levitas had begun to wonder if their rabbi was losing his way as a Jew. He attends the Pope and his son, Israel, is back in his house. He held his tongue wanting to tell the rabbi that he was being taken in by the Pope's seeming enlightenment.

"When have we been able to trust Christians?" Ben Jehuda continued. "They can turn on us at any moment. The Jews once welcome in Genoa are now being expelled as they were in Spain."

Hayyim knew that Levitas and ben Jehuda just had an arbiter appointed by the gobierno to resolve a financial dispute over the rental of a home. Neither was happy with the decision. Friends and neighbors had discussed it for days and had taken sides. He also knew that others had problems with their dowry payments or apprenticeships. Most members of the gobierno were wise and just, but others ruled by their hearts, not their heads.

"The Pope does not consider us expendable. In our prayers, we need to ask for his health and for our...for our continued survival."

Finzi, who had remained quiet throughout, stood up.

"Rabbi, we are considering a *cherem* against your son— that we want him to leave this community and never be allowed to set foot in our synagogue again." He turned to Levitas. "Why are you not telling him?"

"Finzi, we have not even voted to consider it," said Levitas. "It is serious business to have a *cherem* against a rabbi's son or against anyone for that matter."

"We should pray. Maybe in silence." Hayyim uttered those words almost in a whisper.

Several of the congregants who had remained silent during the arguments looked at him, and uncertainty registered in their eyes.

"Prayer may not be the answer now. We have much to think about." DiBelli spoke. "Besides we don't have a minyan. I'm surprised at you, Luzzatti, suggesting we pray."

Finzi felt emboldened. "An apostate in our midst. A cardinal that insists on an Inquisition, and all you want to do is pray."

"That's all we have right now. That and our justice." Hayyim hoped his voice did not belie his anxiety.

"That's all you have, but it is not all we have. Besides we don't have ten men here. You cannot ask us to pray," said Finzi.

With that the men unwrapped their tallit, kissed the fringes, and placed them in their velvet bags and left. All except Hayyim. He stayed staring through glass in the domed ceiling at the darkening light.

CHAPTER 11

Michelangelo and The Last Judgment

Michelangelo carefully wiped the broad-bristled brush that he had just picked up from Pablo Cordivicci, the only brush maker in Rome, and dipped it into the jar containing a mixture of egg and tempera paint. The stiffness in his back and fingers had diminished during the day. The artist stepped back to look at the canvas that was nearly finished and wondered if the Pope would be happy with the evident pain and unhappiness of so many of his figures. There were those that were clearly ascending to the light of heaven and others descending to the darkness of purgatory. This painting was different from the fully formed and optimistic fleshy figures on the ceiling of the Sistine Chapel, the robust Sibyls, the drunken and lively Noah. He knew that the flayed skin of Saint Bartholomew would be startling to some. In his youth, he had never contemplated painting such harshness. His work was all about bringing an aesthetic of beauty to his art, and he was delighted to be back at the Papal Palace and have a commisision.

He had memories of many arguments with Pope Julius, and he wanted to avoid those with Paul. He was concerned that Pope Paul was falling under the influence of Cardinal Carafa—a man obsessed with restoring power to the Church. The artist took a step back to survey the painting he would call *The Last Judgment*. I hope this proves my love for the Church, he thought. I have much to atone for.

While Michelangelo was lost in thought and considering just what color he would put on his brush, he heard Isabella's voice behind him. She had visited frequently, was one of his ardent admirers, and often asked about his health.

"Michelangelo," she said. "I'm so happy to know that I'll turn a corner in this palace and see your genius at work. It's a distraction from some the unpleasantries around here." She added, "I hope your health is good because Paul is anxious that you start work on St. Peter's."

"This painting has a darker palette than usual." He turned to her. "Does it bother you?"

He had never asked for her opinion before. She took a few steps back to better survey the giant canvas. "No. It reflects the times, I suppose. The wars, the schisms, the scheming for power. I'm tired of having the name of Luther whispered. It should be shouted so people will understand what they need to fear."

The artist looked at her quizzically. "I worry whether a work that reflects the damned among us can be considered a work of beauty." He stared at the painting. "You know, it was Dante's *Inferno* that was part of my dreams for many days before I put the first stroke on this painting."

Isabella noted the dark, almost mangled bodies, cowering together at the lower right hand corner of the painting.

"I'm sure your dominant figure of our Lord will give it light." She wanted to be most supportive of Michelangelo although some of the nudity of the bodies disturbed her.

"May I intrude?" Both started when they heard Paul's voice. "I need a respite from my daily thoughts just to look at something beautiful. And, Isabella, since you are here I am doubly rewarded."

"You're too kind, Your Holiness." Isabella blushed. "It is Michelangelo who indeed tips the scales toward beauty."

The Pope moved closer to examine the huge painting that was covering the wall of the Sistine Chapel. Amazing, he thought. I can hardly remember what had been here before. Is this what people will say after I'm gone? They can hardly remember Alessandro Farnese?

The Pope looked intently at the painting taking a few steps back as though to better appraise it. "I'm not sure this is beautiful." He sighed. "But it will, at least, tell my critics that I understand the difference between heaven and hell.

Luther doesn't think I understand. Well, it is he who doesn't understand."

Isabella started to excuse herself so the two men could be alone, but when she saw Cardinal Carafa coming down the hall, she decided to linger. She would show Carafa she could go where she pleased in the Palace.

Michelangelo looked up when he saw the Cardinal approach, and a cloud fell over the artist's face. He turned his back toward Carafa, picked up his paintbrush, and held it as though he were uncertain of where to start painting.

Carafa broke the silence. "I came to see what Michelangelo was working on—the cardinals are curious and I thought I would report back to them. I see Isabella has already had that privilege. You do not object to so many naked bodies, Isabella? I know Justinian and Alfonso will be unhappy with all this nudity. Well, maybe just Alfonso." He came closer as though to take a better look at the painting, but instead the Cardinal placed a lingering hand on Michelangelo's shoulder. The artist turned so that the Cardinal's hand slipped easily away from his body. "It's a dark world. My misdeeds are many as..." His words hung in the air. "As are yours, Carafa." Then he quickly added, "As are all of ours."

"Do not be worried, my dear friend. Our Pope embraces tolerance." Isabella nodded toward Paul and wondered whether he had seen the intimate gesture between the two men. "He knows the word of God and brings your work and the work of many artists to court." She turned to Carafa and spoke in a slightly mocking tone. "Our Pope does know the way of God. Do you?" Carafa flinched, wondering how much she knew of his past with Michelangelo and a strained silence ensued.

"Michelangelo." The Pope turned abruptly to him.

"Yes, Your Holiness."

"What do you think of my friend, Carafa? And I think he is your friend, too, because he greatly admires your work. He wants me to give my sanction to the Passion Play and present myself at the next one that shows the Jews as killers. He wants me to unleash the wrath of the townspeople upon my friends."

"Cardinal Carafa at times needs to show his streak of cruelty. I've seen that." Michelangelo averted his eyes from both Paul and Carafa.

Carafa's mouth tightened. "I simply want to remind people that the Pope is strong. He has armies, money to pay soldiers. People will obey, and God will show favor upon his people." Carafa added, "Your recall of Father Bruno will certainly help."

"I didn't recall Father Bruno," Paul bristled. "I invited him back from Spain to talk. If that were all that I have to do for a while to quiet the ignorant bloodthirstiness of the masses so they will not turn to Luther, then I would do it. I greatly fear that it will take more than that." He waved his hand dismissively. "I am to see Father Bruno tomorrow in the library."

With a glance at Michelangelo, he said, "Thank you for allowing me to intrude on your work."

Paul swept up a corner of his red robe, gathered it in his hand, and left. His shoulders slightly stooped, he walked with a small shuffle in his gait. Isabella followed immediately behind him and watched with concern. He appeared a bit unsteady on his feet.

She turned momentarily to the artist. "I want to thank you for your work on St. Peter's. The sketches look marvelous."

She hurried to catch up with Paul.

Carafa lingered. "You are getting old, my dear friend. This does not mean I forget the glorious times of our past."

Michelangelo winced. "You must forget because I live now just to repent my past deeds—my past deeds of sinfulness." He looked defiantly at Carafa. "How do you, Cardinal Carafa, want to repent your past misdeeds?" With that question, Michelangelo turned toward his painting, stood back and said, "It's almost finished. *The Last Judgment* is almost finished."

CHAPTER 12

Father Bruno Recalled

Father Bruno sat in the antechamber of the Pope's study holding his Bible, studying Leviticus. He found it easier to carry individual chapters rather than the entire large book as he made his way from parish to parish in Toledo offering prayers and communion to those who came to him. He loved that Spanish city with its green-blue hills and red-tiled roofs and its language so similar to Italian. The Archbishop gave him increasing responsibilities each week at the church of El Transito. Originally a synagogue, El Transito became a church when Ferdinand and Isabella expelled the Jews, and the archbishop saw the worth of maintaining its volumes of books. With all the ministering that he happily did to bring God's word, Father Bruno was most content when he could read at leisure in this wonderful library. Father Bruno had felt blessed to be appointed to his post by this brilliant Pope.

Today in Rome, he delighted to be in the presence of Pope Paul, who shared his love of reading. In the past when Father Bruno was in Rome, Paul called on him to discuss some obscure passage by Aquinas, and they would talk on many different occasions trying to understand what the philosopher meant when he said "well-ordered self-love is right and natural."

Father Bruno knew that the Pope was under considerable pressure for reform now that Luther and Calvin had drawn so many converts, but he still hoped for some theological discussion. He remembered the debates fondly that they last had five years ago.

When the door to the study opened, Father Bruno was startled to see Cardinal Carafa. Father Bruno rose, letting the chapter that had been on his lap slide to the floor.

Should he pick up the book or should he greet Cardinal Carafa?

"You are to kiss his ring and kiss the floor where the soles of his feet have touched."

Father Bruno picked up the small chapter, perplexed by the directions.

"Yes, Cardinal Carafa," and gave a short bow before entering the Pope's study.

Father Bruno was momentarily confused as to how he would get to the Pope's ring as well as the floor where the soles of his feet had been. Paul looked up from his book and extended his hand so that the friar could kiss his ring. When Father Bruno attempted to kneel, Paul signaled him to remain standing. When he extended his right hand, Father Bruno noticed a tremor and saw more gray in his beard than black and more wrinkles surrounding the Pope's eyes.

"Please sit, Father Bruno. I'm happy to see you looking so well. Your time in Spain agreed with you."

Father Bruno took the richly appointed red velvet chair opposite the Pope. Carafa moved to stand at the Pope's right side.

"I'm equally happy to see you." Father Bruno squirmed in his large chair. He wanted to know about the changes that applied to a few. Dare he ask directly? No, I better turn to Abelard, he thought. The Pope became very lively at our talks about this theologian who made history over three hundred years ago.

"Your Holiness, I remember our talks about Abelard."

Carafa sighed. He had heard enough of Heloise and Abelard and could not stand to hear about that god-forsaken woman who gave birth to a child without being married and purified herself by going off to a nunnery.

"You recall what great sermons he gave at Notre Dame?" Paul's eyes brightened.

"I do remember how it was written that his students loved him and made people love the Lord more because of Abelard's words." Father Bruno was glad to hear the liveliness in the Pope's voice.

Carafa interrupted. "That is until Heloise comes into his life and seduces him so that he's destroyed."

Paul glared at him. "We are talking about theology, not about love affairs. Love affairs gone wrong in the church..."

"Yes, theology. May I recite these words to you about the Jews?" Father Bruno worried if his interruption would bear semblance to arrogance.

"What words about the Jews? What did Abelard ever say about the Jews?" Carafa tried to quiet the agitation in his voice.

"These "*...no nation has ever suffered so much for God. Dispersed among all nations, without king or secular rulers, the Jews are oppressed with heavy taxes as if they had to repurchase their lives every day. Heaven is their only place of refuge. If they want to travel to the nearest town, they have to buy protection with high sums of money from the Christian who rules who actually wishes for their death so that they can confiscate their possessions. The Jews cannot own land or vineyards because there is nobody to vouch for their safekeeping. Thus, all that is left to them as a means of livelihood is the business of moneylending and this in turns brings the hatred of Christians upon them.*""

Father Bruno's voice shook as he tried to control his surge of emotions. "You made me memorize those words—words that Abelard wrote to understand more about the world and Jews." His eyes narrowed as he looked directly at Carafa. "Yes, so that I could understand the world of my ancestors. Yes, my ancestors were Jewish. Is that what all this is about? The request to return? My needing to address the Pope differently?"

Carafa wondered what divinity intervened to give Bruno these words at the tip of his tongue. "You and others will know in good time."

"I simply want to advise others who may have an audience with the Pope," Bruno said.

"Later. Now tell me what more do you remember of Abelard?" Paul smiled in anticipation then frowned when Carafa interrupted. "This change of greeting is not true for all."

Father Bruno stared at his beloved mentor, Paul. "Is this true, Your Holiness—that this greeting only applies to a few of us?"

Paul lowered his eyes and replied, "Yes, it doesn't apply to all."

"Then who is it true for?" Father Bruno remained seated and turned to Carafa. He could not display his anger to the Pope, the man he so revered. "Again, is it true for those of us who have Jewish blood? There has been some discussion of this in Toledo—that the Church will not recognize Marranos any more because some do not believe that they have truly accepted the sacraments. They demand proof of purity of blood for generations and generations."

Paul frowned. "Carafa, you can be truly annoying in your quest for so-called purity. I wanted a theological discussion with my brightest student, and you have done your best to interrupt that flow of genuine thought."

Carafa walked from Paul's side and paused in front of a book shelf lined with hand-written manuscripts detailing vigorous polemical arguments. He then stood closely beside Father Bruno. Father Bruno could hear his heavy breathing while Carafa spoke.

"If I may, Your Holiness, you're well aware of what happened to Abelard. Abelard didn't speak for the church then and he doesn't now. It was Bernard, the monk, who opposed him. Remember, he wrote *Against the Errors of Abelard*. Remember, it was Bernard who became the saint and it was Abelard who died in disgrace." Carafa hit his hand against the side of the chair at the word "remember."

Father Bruno stood and moved to the other side of the chair.

"You're right, but there are those among us who still want to do what is just. There are still people who are trying to move in the light and right of God."

"Bah! Words they are. Just words. They will not bring people back to the Church." Carafa looked at Paul wondering if he had gone too far. He could usually tell by the expression in Paul's face, but the Pope was at the window staring into the distance.

"We need to deal with the declining power of the Church. Times are different now." Paul did not turn at Carafa's last statement.

"So you think bringing me back is going to help the power of the Church? Ridiculuous. I have accepted every sacrament, my parents accepted every sacrament, my sisters and brothers have accepted every sacrament? Christ travels with me every day. I bring people to the Church and save souls daily." Bruno watched Paul turn toward him and hold up his hands in a questioning motion.

What is he saying, Bruno wondered? Where is the purpose and love of this man for the church and our God that I used to see when I first became his student?

He sat down, lowered his head and and held it between his hands. "It is not enough?" he repeated. He voice shook with both fear and anger. "I never thought the Inquisition here would have implications for me."

"Cardinal Carafa felt that you should come back. And I...I...I...wanted...well, I thought I could save you from perhaps having to flee in fear. This way you have left Toledo in a state of ...how should I put it... in a state of grace." Paul sat, folded his hands on the desk and pushed aside the open book.

"I can't do any more than I already have to show my allegiance to you and the Church." Bruno wasn't quite sure if this would be acceptable to the Pope or if it would offend him. The Pope's response reflected his ambivalence.

"I haven't decided yet. I'm sure I'll find a place for you in the court. Won't we be able to do that, Carafa?"

More capitulation to Carafa, Bruno thought.

Carafa rubbed his hands together. "We'll find someplace. We'll need you, Father Bruno, to explain to the Jews the danger of their ways. You can be a living example for them. You can convince them to become true *converts*. Don't worry. We'll find a way for you to be useful here."

"Then it's true that I will no longer be in Toledo to serve." Bruno tried to keep his voice from quavering.

"We'll put your persuasive skills to good use." Carafa tried to put a hand on Bruno's shoulder, but he moved away from the Cardinal. Paul rose from his chair to put his hand on his young acolyte's shoulder. This time Bruno did not resist. He still had much love for his mentor.

"I shall see that all goes well for you."

Father Bruno knelt to kiss the Pope's ring.

Cardinal Carafa cleared his throat and coughed into the linen handkerchief he had just taken from the pocket of his surplice.

Paul spoke apologetically. "It would do well if you would kiss the floor where the soles of my shoes have been."

Father Bruno knelt as he had been instructed and remained in this submissive position longer than necessary. The Pope touched his shoulder. "Come, my son. This is not a time for sorrow. Visit with your friends and family while you are in Rome. They will want to hear all about Spain, about Toledo, about great Spanish art. In fact, you must come back so that we can talk about the art of Spain."

Father Bruno stood, made the sign of the cross, folded his hands together as in prayer, and then turned and left.

Carafa's eyes followed him. The Cardinal then bowed solemnly to the Pope.

CHAPTER 13

Cardinal Alfonso, Silk Broker

Cardinal Alfonso left his palace apartment, walked through the town square, and sniffed the fetid air. He lifted the hem of his red cassock to avoid the muddy rivulets coursing over the cobblestones. Women in tattered smocks that barely covered their sagging, pock-marked bosoms cleaned the streets with dirty brooms. Men labored to groom their owners' horses with filthy water and worn out brushes. The odor of horse manure covered by hay permeated the air.

Some women stopped at the stalls to gather potatoes and eggplant for the evening meal. Alfonso smiled slightly as he heard them haggling over the price of the vegetables. They couldn't count to one hundred but they knew how to argue for a cheap price. Alfonso smelled the recently caught fish and shuddered. He touched the scar on the side of his face that reminded him of his brawling youth. This prince of the Church no longer had the constitution for poverty.

Alfonso stopped at two-story, whitewashed, timber framework house crowded by homes on either side. Taking notice of the mezuzah on the right hand side of the lintel, he knocked on the simple wooded door. He had agreed with DiBelli and Finzi that this would be the best place to transact business. Certainly not at the Cardinal's Palace because it was impossible to keep servants and guards quiet. A plump, dark-eyed woman of thirty, her head covered with a shawl, opened the door. A curly haired boy of seven and a girl of ten with hair in long ringlets stood on either side. The mother gripped both their hands and nodded to the Cardinal in the direction of the second floor.

"Ah! They're already upstairs at work. Just like all Jews," Alfonso tried a lightness in his voice. "You do not extend your hand even for a brief brushing of the lips, I see." The woman did not smile.

"What is that man doing here?" the boy asked.

"He's a man of the Church, so why is he here?" his sister asked.

Their mother put her finger to her lips. "They're waiting for you upstairs." She nodded to Alfonso, then quickly cast her eyes away.

The Cardinal climbed the narrow, tilted staircase, entered a room that served as the office for Finzi and diBelli. The Cardinal's eyes took in papers and quills scattered about the room and several locked metal strong boxes.

DiBelli and Finzi leaped up from behind a huge mahogany table when the Cardinal entered.

"Let me find you a chair." Finzi uncovered a seat after dumping a raft of papers onto the floor. The Cardinal sat opposite the two men after blowing the dust off the chair and folding his red silk cassock carefully into his lap.

"I trust your walk to our humble office was pleasant," Finzi said.

"It was most satisfactory. It is good to get out among the people we are trying to save."

Finzi started to speak, but diBelli silenced him.

"Have you thought how you will explain your visit here, Your Eminence? I'm sure that there are some who will inquire," asked diBelli.

Alfonso smiled. "I, too, am becoming an expert at conversion. Ever since Cardinal Carafa pushed the Pope to promulgate an Inquisition, I've become quite good at convincing people to renounce their faith and recognize the one true faith to accept our Lord, Jesus Christ. One could say that I'm even better than the Inquisitor himself, Carafa."

Finzi said, "My wife probably thinks that's why you have come here."

"I've come only for a loan." Alfonso nodded toward the metal boxes. Finzi got up to reach the metal boxes, but diBelli put a hand on his shoulder. "This will be a loan for six months at two percent interest. So we are talking about ten thousand ducats. Am I correct?"

"Are you correct about what?" Alfonso said curtly.

"The interest, the amount, and the period of the loan," diBelli said.

"This is the first time I've been questioned about my word."

"We are here for business—to feed our families, to pay taxes to the Church," Finzi said. "And there are other people who would like to buy up all the silk that will come into the port, to have a monopoly on that product and sell it at a controlled price. People need loans to do that."

"I understand all that. Jews and the world of business."

"But we don't know why the Church forbids men so capable as you to deal in the world of trade. It is a honest way to earn some money," said Finzi.

Alfonso stood and started to walk to the window but his cassock got caught in the arm of the chair. "Damn," he said as he pulled the fabric free and sat down again. "You know perfectly well, we are to be attending to the spiritual needs of our people."

Alfonso stood again and this time approached the desk. "And why, gentlemen, would you be willing to engage in commerce with me when you know that it has recently been forbidden by your gobierno? It is important that we be forthright about this, isn't it? We each need to be...to be honest with one another."

DiBelli looked directly at the Cardinal. "What rules in this world is power. Kings rule because they have power; so do Popes and so do Cardinals. You wouldn't have that power without money to buy soldiers.

It's the same for Finzi and me. But we don't want armies, and we don't want obedient servants."

"It's never been clear to me exactly what you Jews want. If you don't want Jesus Christ, it's very muddled for me."

Finzi grinned. He put a hand on diBelli's shoulder and squeezed it. "We want to have the possibility of escape. Something that you can't understand—the possibility of escape, and that can only come with money." He paused. "We do know that Father Bruno was recalled from Toledo."

"You think I'm naïve, gentlemen. Don't you think I understand that you have your own gobierno to deal with, and money probably speaks to them as it does to my own little army of servants? Enough talk."

Alfonso placed two small sacks in front of the metal boxes.

"Small enough to hide under your garment. Very clever," Finzi said. He studied a piece of paper on his desk. "Oh, I'm sorry. I made an error. The interest is five percent." He pushed the piece of paper toward the Cardinal.

"That is tantamount to robbery."

"You're free to go elsewhere, Cardinal Alfonso." Finzi suddenly turned to the ledger in front of him and rapidly ran his finger down a column of figures. "Again, you are free to go elsewhere."

"Enough Jew bargaining, gentlemen, just give me the money."

Finzi said, "We have your word?"

"Of course, you have my word."

DiBelli said, "We have your word for silence?"

"We have between us only the words of conversion, gentlemen, should anyone ask. Nothing else," Cardinal Alfonso answered.

"What will you say to Carafa?" continued diBelli.

Alfonso said, "I will tell him you are thinking about it."

At those words there came the sound from downstairs of a piece of stoneware that had fallen and shattered.

Finzi looked at DiBelli and said, "My wife undoubtedly dropped something. Sometimes she is clumsy in the kitchen."

DiBelli went over to one of the metal boxes, took a key from beneath the doublet he was wearing, unlocked it, and carefully counted out ten thousand ducats and divided the money between the two bags. The Cardinal took them, turned toward the window, lifted his cassock, and tied the bags to a rope around his waist.

At the bottom of the stairs, he saw the woman sweeping up pieces of broken stoneware while her children assisted her with smaller brooms, their large brown eyes focused on the floor. They stopped when they saw him and ran to cling to their mother's skirt. She wrapped her arms around them as the man left without a hint of acknowledgment.

The woman shook off the clutches of her children and ran up the stairs.

"Well?" she said.

"Well," Finzi said. "We have made a good loan."

"But," said his wife, shaking out the broom out the window to make sure no shards remained, "Did he recommend Jesus to you?"

DiBelli laughed. "No. We made a good deal. In six months, you'll have new porcelain."

CHAPTER 14

Anxious Congregants

Perhaps five hours later, at his home, Luzzatti open the door to Benjamin ben Jehuda and Shimon Shimoni. "I know. I know. Come in."

The wiped their shoes on the hemp mat just outside, touched right hands to their lips and then to the mezuzah on the lintel.

"What do you know?" said Shimoni.

"That people are concerned about Father Bruno's recall." "Alba," he called, "some brandy and glasses in my study."

"Sit," said Luzzatti. "That you want to know if you should think about leaving Rome."

Alba set the glasses and brandy on the table in front of them. "I want to know the same thing, gentlemen, but my husband can't seem to make up his mind."

"This is for the men." Hayyim frowned.

"Oh, really. Won't I be going with you if we leave?"

"Alba," sighed Hayyim. She left. He raised his glass and took a sip of brandy. Benjamin and Shimon both drank the contents of the glass in one gulp. Hayyim twirled the glass and held it up to the window light. "Wisdom fails me at this moment, my friends. I plan to speak to the Pope at my next visit."

"He will be truthful?" Benjamin asked pouring himself another glass of brandy.

Hayyim hesitated. "He usually is. We may start off by talking about manuscripts and philosophers, but often I can approach him on the issues of our community."

The next morning Luzzatti stretched awake to the crowing of the rooster and turned in his bed to see Alba still

83

asleep, her back toward him. She had the cotton sheets drawn up to her chin in spite of the summer heat, but he could see a bit of her shoulder where her gown had slipped. She shivered as he brushed his lips on her bare skin. No time now, he thought.

Hayyim picked up his phylacteries, kissed them, and wound one leather strap above his left elbow so that one square leather box sat on the inside of his forearm and the other box was then wound with the leather strap around his head. He recited the prayers that thanked God for leading the Jews out of Egypt. Where are we going now, he wondered? We fled Spain and Portugal, and the Ottoman Empire before that... and before that Babylon, and before that....

He was so caught up in his thoughts that as he was about to unwind the leather strap, he looked down to see that he had wound the strap around his arm eight times instead of the requisite seven. He quickly rewound the phylactery and hastily repeated his prayer adding a few words of apology to God for not paying sufficient attention. "Trying times, God," he added.

Alba watched him remove his phylacteries. "You're off to the Palace? I shall make you a cup of tea before you go."

"No tea this morning. We'll see each other later." He kissed her on the cheek and started for the door.

"You'll talk to the Pope about the Jews who are coming from Spain?" she called after him. "I was wrong, Hayyim. I know. We must take care and welcome the stranger."

"I've already talked with him. But I'll try again." If the time is right, he thought as he took off for the Palace hoping that a walk in the open air would relieve some of the pressure in his head and his heart.

* * *

After receiving a nod of recognition from the Swiss Guards, Hayyim approached the Pope's bedroom when Cardinal Carafa tapped him on the shoulder. "Remember. You are not only to kiss his ring, but you must kiss the floor where his soles of his shoes have been." Carafa spoke loudly enough for the guards to hear. Two of the guards looked at one another. This was the gossip that their friends loved as they sat down with their pints of beer in the evening. *The Jew was ordered to bow down.*

Luzzatti entered and found the Pope sitting for his portrait. Titian had his paintbrush poised expectantly, waiting for drama to unfold. He watched as Hayyim walked directly to the Pope and bent stiffly to kiss the papal ring and the floor where the Pope had stood. Hayyim's movements were barely perceptible, but it was done.

"I shall leave now, Your Holiness," Carafa said. Should you want anything, I shall be nearby. Simply send your messenger."

"Yes, yes, Carafa. Go, will you. I shall be fine. After all, don't I have a doctor and a painter in the room at the same time?"

When Carafa was out of earshot, the Pope faced Hayyim and took both his hands in his. "It is a silly ritual, but I have not been able to convince Carafa of that."

"You give much to Carafa." Hayyim spoke the words slowly. He thought "much power" but couldn't bring himself to say the words together.

"He is my Inquisitor."

A wave of nausea crept up from Hayyim's stomach. "It was your decision to create the office." He could not believe the words were coming out of his mouth.

The Pope flicked at an invisible piece of cotton on his sleeve. "Yes, it was. Now what is it you want today? The painter awaits so I cannot take the time to discuss the latest manuscripts."

Titian was shaking his head.

"Father Bruno's recall from Toledo."

'Yes, what about it?"

Titian cleared his throat, frowned, obviously annoyed at the Pope's movements. Didn't the Pope recognize that he was dealing with an artist? An artist valued by the nobility with paintings in many palaces?

"I shall be seated before you in absolute stillness in a moment." Paul glared at him, and it seemed to Hayyim that Titian glowered in turn.

"Has he been recalled because of his Jewish roots?"

Paul laced the long elegant fingers of his hands together, placing them smoothly in his lap. He looked at Hayyim gloomily.

"Your Eminence. Do you want that awful expression in this painting? Do you really want gloom to be the face of the Pope?"

Hayyim seemed to take heart at the painter's brazen comments. "And I have been asked to perform a demeaning act. It's groveling, that's what it is." Hayyim didn't want a response from the Pope yet. "My wife asks. I've had visits from my congregants—they are worried." He thinks it is time for a moment of diplomacy. "These are people who have been most grateful to you for how they have been able to live in tranquility...and without fear...until now."

"Father Bruno came back from Toledo for his own good. Life is far harsher in Spain than you can imagine." Hayyim strained to hear him.

"Then his recall has nothing to do with his Jewish grandparents?"

The Pope's jaw muscles tightened. "I'm trying to protect him, believe me."

"What are you saying?" Hayyim asked. "Your Holiness, we must know the truth. We need to plan."

"Plan. Carafa tells me the same thing. Plan for the Council of Trent. Plan to do away with the Protestants." He walked slowly from his chair to his bookshelf and pulled one down to place on his desk.

"You're becoming the most difficult client, I've had," Titian could barely contain himself.

Paul ignored him. "Aristotle would say one needs a plan wouldn't he? The thought of a plan does give one some comfort but no guarantee, right?" He didn't want an answer; he turned to Titian. "A difficult client with ducats, Titian."

Damn him, Luzzatti thought as he watched the Pope adjust himself in his seat so Titian could start painting again. Now he expects me to discuss Aristotle. Hayyim had seen this trait of philosophical debating among many members of his synagogue, who liked nothing better than to read the commentaries of Talmud and then split hairs by adding their own commentaries and thoughts just to avoid dealing with daily problems.

The artist drew back the damask drapes. Light streamed in. The Pope blinked. "Always, there is that appeal to reason. You have read the words of Aristotle, have you not, Luzzatti?"

"I have read them in Hebrew, not in Greek."

"And what else have you read?"

"Your Holiness knows. We have discussed this numerous times. The Talmud, Aristotle, Cicero, Petrarch."

"Maimonides?" The Pope turned toward him, and Titian put his brush down and wiped it clean with a small cloth.

"I've read Maimonides. He's important to my sermons. Why do you ask about him now?"

"He was not necessarily respected and revered by all Jews."

"That is true. We have had as a people disagreements about many things."

"His books were burned by rabbis in France because they were viewed as heretical?"

"An act that has been a great source of pain to me. The rabbis denounced his writings. It was the Dominicans friars who actually burned his books."

"Well, it was a disagreeable act by the rabbis, was it not?"

"It was."

"Then you will understand that there are acts of my Church out of my control that bring me pain."

"One's ability to confront evil and darkness is put to a great test at times. I understand that."

"Have you heard Luther's latest words—That your synagogues should be set on fire and whatever does not burn up should be spread over with dirt?"

"He is a dangerous man."

"Yet, you persist in your faith. Perhaps there was a good reason for your son's conversion."

Hayyim turned gray. He began to cough to rid himself of the phlegm that had backed up in his throat. He withdrew a piece of linen from his doublet and spit into it.

Titian, who had stopped painting to listen intently, looked away.

"I persist in my faith, Your Holiness. It is in my blood, my veins. My son will come back to it, I am sure."

"Father Bruno and I were just discussing Abelard. He spoke nearly the same words to me."

"So we come back to Father Bruno. Can you say why you have recalled him?

"Ask him yourself. I believe he will be at your synagogue soon." Paul waved his hand, and Hayyim realized that he was being dismissed. "Why have you stopped painting? I do not pay you to rest." Titian exhaled, stepped back to view the nearly finished painting, and dipped his brush into the magenta paint.

Luzzatti went over to kiss the Pope's ring, and was prepared to kiss the floor as well, but the Pope was already lost in his portrait sitting. Luzzatti had not brought up the Jews from Spain.

He left and quietly entered the bright light of the courtyard, which was bustling with workmen going about the business of repairing and decorating walls. Women wandered by with loaves of bread that they handed to workers in an exchange for coins. Luzzatti was struck by how the world could go on with its everyday chores while so many crises loomed. He wanted to shout out to the men and women in the courtyard. He also knew that many people in that courtyard were struggling to keep hunger from the bellies of their families and could hardly be interested in his problems and those of his people.

CHAPTER 15

Alba Luzzatti Proposes a Visit

When Hayyim returned home, he found Alba in the largest room of the house with its huge fireplace and dining table. She put her linen embroidery down and searched his face. "Would you like a cup of borage tea now?"

"A cup of tea would be nice." He rarely refused a cup of tea from Alba because he knew it always came accompanied by her bread and marmalade. She had started growing borage as a medicinal herb to help Hayyim's patients and realized its potential as a tea; she set out to master the cultivation of this healthy beverage. She used its pretty blue flowers for decoration, especially on the Sabbath, and the leaves for tea.

Alba took the kettle that had been hanging over the embers and poured hot water into two porcelain cups that were her husband's favorites because Gabrielle di Strasburgo, a celebrated ceramist from Ostia, had made them. The delicate roses that rimmed the fluted edges with its gold inlay were exquisitely drawn and painted. Alba set the cups of tea and bread and jam on the table, and Hayyim took a bite of the bread and sipped his tea.

Alba broke the silence. "Well...?"

Hayyim swirled his cup. "Amazing how this teacup this was crafted to be perfectly centered. The borage leaves lie at the bottom quite contentedly."

"You're doing this deliberately. Just to annoy me," Alba said. "I suppose you didn't like my comment about your ambivalence."

"No, I just need time to tell you what has happened."

"You exclude the women too much. Sometimes you need to ask me if I have an idea." She had wagged a finger. Hayyim raised his eyebrows.

"Where is Israel?" he asked.

"Would you even listen, if I had an idea?"

"Of course. Where is Israel?"

"He's out talking with Senor Calabi about the rendering of his accounts for the silk merchants here. He is worried about running into Finzi and diBelli. They see our son as competition. Actually, I don't know how Finzi's wife stands being married to him. A bully if I ever saw one." She pored some more hot water into his tea cup. "You may have your faults, my dear, but being a bully is not one of them."

"They should be careful. The gobierno will catch up to them—no doubt about that. They dislike anyone having a monopoly on trade."

"I'm waiting for you to tell me about what the Pope said about Father Bruno. You've procrastinated long enough."

Hayyim sipped his tea, leaned back in his chair, and momentarily closed his eyes. She'd want to know the details.

"I have visitors from the congregation asking me what Bruno's return means, and if the Pope will help with the Spanish when they arrive in Rome," Alba said.

"He says Father Bruno will be visiting us in synagogue."

"No." She hit the table with her fist; the teacups clattered.

"There's more. He offered no assistance with the people coming from Spain."

Alba clasped her hand to her chest. "We're in for another harangue. Wasn't Friar Leo enough? I imagine there'll even be book burning." Her voice rose. "It is inconceivable that this man who loves books so much would burn them—would burn our beloved Talmud."

"He did not say he would burn our books." Hayyim scowled.

"Have you thought of approaching anyone else inside the Papal Palace?"

"Who else? I am physician to the Pope. No one else. The childen are off and away, and their mother could not be seen by a male physician."

Hayyim got up to stir the embers in the fire, even though it would create more heat on an already hot day.

"What are you doing?" she said. "It's hot enough." She followed him with her eyes. "This mother, Isabella, have you met her?"

He had taken off the heaviest of his outer clothes and sat in only the lightest of his white linen garments, his head covered with a small round black skullcap. It had slipped to the side when he went to the fire and he immediately adjusted it when he sat down. He patted his head several times as if to make sure that it was going to stay secure.

"I'm doing this because I'm distracted and, no, I have never met Isabella. I know the Pope values her intelligence."

"This is much to lay upon your shoulders as we wait for the people from Spain. They may be heading into a den of lions and tigers—so much uncertainty."

"We must have faith. It is all that we have at this point. God will watch out for us...in some way." His voice belied his words.

"Not without some good thinking on our part. We must have a plan."

"I have spoken the same words to Pope Paul."

"Good," said Alba, "Then you will not be angry with me at what I have done." She swept the table clean of crumbs with her hand, collecting them in her other hand.

"First let me know what you have done."

Alba got up from the table and removed the dirty dishes.

"Those can wait," said Hayyim. "Tell me what you have done." He took her arm and drew her gently back to the table.

Alba stammered," I have invited Isabella to the house to sew with me."

Hayyim could not believe his ears. "The Isabella of Pope Paul? The Isabella of the Papal Court?"

"The very same."

"How did you do that? Let alone, why?" He could not hide the incredulity in his voice.

"I wrote her a note and sent it with a messenger. I thought if you're not successful with the Pope, maybe she would help. Instinct. Woman to woman. Call it what you will."

Hayyim raised his hands upward as though he were beseeching God. "I knew there would be problems because you are able to write. This meeting can only put Isabella in danger and cause problems for the Pope."

"I am the wife of the physician to the Pope. Someone who has been taught to read and write."

"I thought it important so you could also help Israel with his studies. I didn't think of it as a way for you to engage with the mistress of the Pope."

"Do you have any idea what she does all day at the court?"

"Probably she reads books. She sews. She gossips. It's never been of particular interest to me."

"Perhaps it should have been." She turned away and started washing the dishes as though they were the dirtiest dishes in Rome.

"Alba, the congregants are already agitated about Israel and the possibility of more Jews coming to Rome from Spain. You know they discourage contact with Christians. They could call a *cherem* against you. What's more, it could be dangerous for Isabella. Carafa could charge her as a heretic."

A quiet knock at the door ended their discussion. They looked at each other. Again came a knock, and this time it was louder.

Hayyim went to the entranceway and opened the door. There stood a stranger—a man in shabby clothes, clothes that had lost their color, but an attempt had been made to sew the seams anew. The man stood erect, but he was rather thin. He looked exhausted.

Alba called, "Who is it?"

"Yes, may I help you?"

The man spoke almost inaudibly. "I'm Abramo Zefarti." He spoke softly. "I've been traveling for three months in order to get to Rome from Spain. We were told that you are the rabbi in this community."

"Where is the rest of your family?" asked Alba.

"Gone. They are no longer with me.

92

"What?" said Hayyim.

"My wife, Julieta, and my daughter, Raquel, were not well when we started out. We had to sleep in cold, damp caves. I could not keep them alive. Fortunately, Juliet died before Raquel so she did not see her child die."

Hayyim said, "And you have not said *kaddish* for them."

"Only once when I was in a town with a synagogue and could gather a minyan. It's there that they are buried."

"We will take you to synagogue tomorrow where we can say *kaddish* for them. Come," Alba said. He followed her to the courtyard where she gave him a clean basin of water. He splashed water on his face and ran his wet hands through his hair.

"Thank you."

"You must be hungry. Come in to the kitchen. We have some bread and cheese and I will pour you some hot water—perhaps with a bit of lemon." Senor Zefarti bowed to her.

"We carried a special drink with us. Chocolate, it's called." He held out a linen sac to her. "Something that the Spanish tried to keep hidden, but we have been able to smuggle some out."

"Chocolate." Alba's eyes lit up with excitement. "We've heard about this."

"Cristo Colon brought it from the New World." Zefarti laughed. "It grows as a bean."

At the table, after the blessing on the food, he ate the morsels of bread and cheese that Alba had set before them. He was so famished, he could hardly chew the crusty freshly baked white bread that was Alba's specialty. She could always guarantee the quality of her bread because she checked each time she used the flour to make sure that it had not been infested with the mealy bugs that were so troublesome in the heat.

"Thank you for your hospitality. It exceeds your reputation."

"My son told me that the Jews of Spain, particularly of Toledo were having problems. We didn't think that you would arrive so soon. It is such a treacherous, uncertain journey."

"There are more of us coming; at the beginning we were fortunate. My wife and daughter, we were able to take a boat from Barcelona to Genoa. From there, we had enough money to buy three horses and one donkey and they carried us and our possessions for thirty days."

"Where did you sleep?"

"In dank caves filled with bats; in forests on beds of leaves. Sometimes we encountered an inn or a Christian house that would give us lodging for a sum. We always kept Raquel disguised as a boy. I never prayed with my phylacteries—only with my heart."

Abramo lowered his voice. "In Spain, even Protestants were burned at the stake. Some of our fellow Jews received threats from their neighbors—threats that they would be tried for plots against the king and demands for conversion."

"And?" said Alba, who had been listening intently.

"I refused conversion. In my arrogance, I refused."

Alba sighed, "Our son accepted the sacraments of the Church...he said for his safety."

With this, Alba turned to tend to the fire so that her guest would not see the tears that welled up.

Zefarti continued, "We also heard stories of the burning of our Talmud. We decided to leave and we left everything but the diamonds—the diamonds to pay our way. Diamonds sewn into the lining of our coats. Candlesticks so we could light the Sabbath candles...and some clothing."

"Venice would have been a shorter voyage for you," said Hayyim.

"Rome does not have a ghetto. We wanted to be free, to pray, to work." He put his head in his hands. "That's what Juliet and Raquel talked about all the time."

Hayyim and Alba exchanged glances. Alba said, "Until now, we thought we did not need to worry in Rome. Our Pope seems to be wavering."

"But are you not his physician?" Zefarti said.

"I am." Hayyim answered. "And right now it seems to guarantee me of nothing."

Hayyim stood and clasped Abramo's shoulder. "Come I will show you to your room upstairs and tomorrow we will say *kaddish* with you at the synagogue."

Abramo followed him up the narrow staircase just beyond the kitchen. Without removing his clothing, he sank into the bed of down to a deep sleep.

When Hayyim came down, he kissed his wife's cheek.

"So, my dear wife, you are waiting for me. You must be tired. You should have gone to bed."

"I thought this would be a good time to continue our conversation." Alba said. "So, my dear husband, what do you think now about my meeting with Isabella?"

"I say now, we need to consider not only the improbable but the impossible. Invite Isabella to tea. Sew. Chat with her. We will see."

"We will see. We will see if she will accept my invitation."

CHAPTER 16

Father Bruno on a Mission

Israel, who had returned late from his visit to Senor Calabi, met Abramo Zefarti in the morning. Once he got over his surprise, they eagerly discussed the news of Spain over warm bread, tea, and chocolate. Israel had told his parents that there would be refugees from Spain, but he had not expected one so soon. Abramo Zefarti, dressed in his wrinkled clothing, accompanied Hayyim and Israel to synagogue.

"Your time here has been restful?" Abramo was polite in his address to Israel.

Israel turned to see if his father heard. "As restful as possible, considering my conversion in Spain. I'm still feeling my way here."

"Not all are accepting, I'm sure," said Abramo.

"But you understand. You were there in Spain."

Then silence because they had to concentrate on walking single file along the narrow cobblestone streets, careful to avoid bumping into anyone offended by the presence of Jews. Hayyim watched for the horses of nobleman and princes of the court. They easily dominated the narrow streets and expected people to stay out of their way.

At the synagogue, Abramo took a seat, took his prayer book out of blue velvet bag, and chanted openly and fervently with the men, saying the words that professed his awe of God. He could not help but notice the men staring at him. The women stopped gossiping when he entered.

Abramo smiled when he overheard a woman whisper loud enough for him to hear, "We must welcome the stranger."

Israel remained standing at the entrance to the synagogue shifting from foot to foot, unsure if he should take his seat—the seat that he always sat in when he attended synagogue and now was empty. He was annoyed that his father had not made a place for him.

Israel was the first to see Father Bruno enter. Rabbi Luzzatti lifted his head from his prayer book for a moment to catch sight of the friar. *What is he doing here?* He returned to his prayer but realized he lost his place in the text; he tried to recite from memory.

The congregants, too, had halted their prayers and turned to see what had caused the rabbi's sudden silence.

Father Bruno spoke in a clear, forceful voice without breaking his step as he proceeded to walk toward the tebah— the platform in the center of the synagogue. "Please continue. Do not stop on my account."

But the women quieted their chattering. The men did not return to their prayers. After a few seconds, the carillon bells of St. Peter's broke the silence.

When the bells ceased, Rabbi Luzzatti stepped forward. "Since you have not come to pray with us, it would be inappropriate to continue with a guest in our midst."

Some men sitting in their pews nodded in agreement. Others exchanged worried glances. The women sat motionless as they watched with their hands held still in their laps.

"May anyone just not come to sit in your house of worship?" Father Bruno said as he gave a slight bow before Hayyim standing in the raised platform. Hayyim put a hand over his mouth to stem the wave of nausea. *Has he really come here for prayer?*

Benjamin ben Jehuda, the redhead stood. "Please, Father Bruno. We are not accustomed to others coming to pray with us."

Hayyim swallowed the bile that had crept up to his throat. He was grateful he had regained his voice. "Father Leo has already been here to proselytize—and he knows it does no good, for our faith is strong."

Father Bruno towered over them. His face became mottled with the strain of his rant. "Just out of curiosity, do I ever hear Jesus Christ in your prayers?" Hayyim started to answer, but Father Bruno cut him off. "Of course, I do not hear Jesus Christ in your prayers. You have made a mockery of our religion, of our Pope, by not accepting Jesus Christ, by not accepting the sacraments. Are you reading those prayers that denounce our Lord as the Messiah? I wouldn't be surprised if that's what you are reading. Your Torah is the embodiment of evil. Satan lies in those prayers. You will not accept it, but I know it's the truth because I have been there myself. I've read what you've read and it kept me spellbound—but nearly destroyed me. Fortunately, I gave up those readings in time to be saved."

One of the women put her hands over her ears. Father Bruno shook his finger at her. "Put your hands down and listen," he shouted. "If you'll accept Jesus as your savior, you'll have a chance to prove that you may be worthy of his grace and you'll be saved. Not like the person in your midst who lied."

Several men in the congregation moaned; they had heard stories of brutality when their members of their family would not accept conversion. One woman gasped and appeared so pale that two women on either side held her to make sure she would not faint.

Israel took a few steps forward and spoke clearly so that all in the congregation could hear him.

"He's talking about me. Father Bruno is referring to me as the liar. He wants me to confess that I'm not a true believer."

Father Bruno pointed his finger at Israel, his voice somewhat modulated, but still menacing. "Yes, you're the liar. You say that you have accepted Jesus Christ, but here you sit in a synagogue and pray."

"I came to visit friends. I was not praying," Israel said. He felt as though hundreds of disapproving eyes were staring at him.

Rabbi Luzzatti had regained his composure and held out his hands to Bruno imploring him to silence. At the same time, he wanted to silence Israel. He knew how provocative his presence could be here.

"Have you said all that you came to say, Father Bruno? What is it you want from us?" Father Bruno shoulders sagged. "I'm here on orders from Carafa."

"Then this is part of his Inquisition?"

"You're here tearing at the hearts and souls of our synagogue for your own protection. Who had the Jewish blood in your family?" Israel's eyes flashed, his face white with anger. "Who was it? Your grandmother on your mother's side or your grandfather on your father's side? It doesn't make any difference, does it? You have Jewish blood and you want nothing more than to demonstrate your loyalty to the Church by frightening the hearts and souls of people here."

"Israel, please. We will fight the new rules of Carafa our way. With some patience, the Pope can be shown the way and rescind this office." Hayyim wanted to add more, to say something about Israel having got caught in the web of Spanish Inquisition, but Israel interrupted.

"I accepted conversion to have a place in the Spanish court and to stay alive. A part of me is Jewish and will remain so until I die. It was the same for Jesus, was it not?"

Those words reminded Father Bruno of his mission here. "The King of Spain will know of your words, and you will not be permitted in the court. I'll see to that."

"Fortunately, Charles is more tolerant than your Archbishop of Toledo. He recognizes talent and he knows how to use it." Israel was moving closer to Father Bruno.

"Israel, please," Hayyim pleaded.

"Why don't you say 'please' to him instead of to me, father?" Israel said.

The drama unfolding between father and son seemed to give Father Bruno more fuel to address the stunned congregants. "Don't you see that the only way you can save yourselves is by accepting Jesus? Accept the sacraments. Renounce your Jewish God and you will be saved. Become a Christian or die in hell." He raised his fist and waved it in the air as he continued to shout. His naturally pale face had turned pink with his exhortations. "Become a true Christian or die in hell!" Then with his finger pointing directly at Israel, he shouted, "You'll be found out."

With those final words, the tall, angular priest stalked out of the synagogue. The congregants murmured among themselves. Israel walked out behind him. "Why do you do this?"

Bruno looked at him with tears in his eyes. "It is an order and I love the church."

Luzzatti started to chant and pray with fervor. He turned to his congregation. "We will pray and read from today's Torah portion." Hayyim looked to ben Jehuda, Morpurgo, and Bascola to retrieve the Torah from the Ark. Slowly they rose, and the congregation sang softly at first and then with fervor, "*Atah hareyta Lada'at ki hashem hu ha he-lohim ain od milvado.*" (You have been shown to recognize that the Lord is God; there is none besides him.)

As the three men placed the Torah upright in front of Hayyim and took their seats, Hayyim spoke. "Today's Torah portion is about Moses reminding the Israelites of God's promise and presence in the years they spent wandering the wilderness. We must be ever grateful that we have a place in Rome where we have been able to rest and cease our wandering."

He needed Torah right now to begin to quiet the anxiety that came upon him with the scene that just took place in front of him and the congregation.

Finzi abruptly stood without apology and interrupted. "It is not good that Israel is here in our midst. He brings danger to our community."

DiBelli echoed his cohort's sentiments, "Yes. It is not good for many reasons. And who is this stranger? You do not invite strangers without telling us."

Zefarti remained silent.

"Is this true of Israel? Is he still Jewish?"

"We have never had problems here. Is this another beginning of attacks on the Jews?"

"Rabbi Luzzatti is too tolerant. He only wants to please his friend, the Pope."

"The Pope has been our friend."

"Friends can change. Friends are not always with you."

The Saturday morning service of the reading of the Torah portion and *kaddish* never took place. The synagogue filled with the harangues of Father Bruno, a new family from Spain, the rabbi's son and his conversion dilemma—all at the same time—the Passion Play, and the rant of Father Leo.

They knew they would have to go to their homes and sort out these events with family and neighbors to regain any sense of tranquility and order in their lives.

CHAPTER 17

Isabella and Alba

When the summer sun rose, Isabella was already clad in her long dress with its high, unadorned bodice. She chose lightweight beige linen because she thought that would make her less visible as she walked along the streets with their ochre-colored buildings. She dismissed her maid, then left hurriedly by a portal door.

When the messenger had delivered the note to her last week that contained the invitation from Alba, Isabella was surprised and thought about it for a day or two without consulting Alessandro or any other members of the court. She sent a confirming message with her maid who could not read, but yet knew every alley and nook in the city. Maybe she herself could make the Jews a less bothersome subject for him.

She had prized those days with Alessandro when they would discuss the works of Cicero and Marcus Aurelius. His intellect was enormous and helped him become Dean of the Sacred College. During the forty years he had spent as Cardinal before becoming Pope, he had used much of that time to educate himself. He had become fluent in Hebrew and Greek and had frequently quoted Aristotle as a source of wisdom. He prided himself on his openness to ideas and had talked to her frequently about political issues. Now he seemed taken in by Carafa and besotted with art.

She carried a muslin bag filled with linen cloth and sewing supplies and put on a light colored veil to protect her from the flies swarming in the summer heat. It also added to her anonymity, although she doubted that many would recognize her especially with such a simple dress.

No one had seen her leave the palace. She would deal with her return with some sort of a story...possibly that she left her lady-in-waiting at one of the vegetable stalls, or that her horse slipped and had a lame leg. She would think of something. Right now she needed to get to the doctor's house as quickly as possible without being recognized.

Although it was quite early, people were up and about. She was delighted to smell the fresh fruits and vegetables vendors were putting out from their garden with the hope of earning a few ducats; tomatoes, zucchini, and squash were in abundance at this time of the year. She lifted her skirts as men and women were cleaning up the slop of the night before to use for fertilizer for the gardens. She smiled to herself. She had left the palace unnoticed to go someplace of her own choice. An act of defiance at my age is quite wonderful, she thought.

Isabella walked rapidly out of St. Peter's Square, continued four more blocks, passed a narrow alleyway, and stopped at the house with a mezuzah on the door, just as she had been told. Alba opened the door before Isabella even raised her hand to knock. Neither woman saw Alberto Finzi watching from one end of the street. The messenger that Alba had sent to the Palace knew of Finzi's arguments with the rabbi, his dislike of Israel, and immediately went to the banker with the information. The courier knew it would be worth ducats and he was right. Finzi paid him handsomely for the information.

Uncertain of how to greet this woman of the Papal Court, Alba gave a small bow.

"Please, come in. Would you like a cup of hot water and a bit of citrus? I have heard that it is good for the digestive system as well as the skin." Alba had cleaned the house thoroughly in preparation making sure no crumbs or dust were on the floors or furniture, that the mullioned windows sparkled, and there were no weeds in her garden. Even when the house was spotless, she cleaned it again.

Isabella said, "Your garden is lovely. The roses. And I can see the shades of blue, pink, and purple in your hydrangeas." She looked around.

"I think it's best that we sit where the light is good for our sewing. I often sew with the ladies of the court, and we have a special room that is filled with the sun's rays."

"We can go to the courtyard," Alba suggested.

"Wonderful," said Isabella.

Isabella followed Alba out to the courtyard and sat on a simple leather chair. Alba already had her sewing laid out. She poured the boiled water from her kettle into her best porcelain teacup and, though her hand shook, deftly squeezed in the juice of half a lemon.

Isabella accepted the teacup and nodded her thanks. Isabella sipped the drink slowly after letting the liquid cool for a moment and then placed the teacup on a small table at the side of her chair. Who would start the conversation? What would the first words be?

Alba picked up her sewing and sat facing Isabella. It occurred to her that she had never sewn before in the company of other woman.

"Your gold thread...it's exquisitely woven through the bodice. How do you do that?" Isabella said. "Where did the thread come from? I don't believe I've seen anything like it in Rome."

"It came from Florence. We have relatives there."

"Are they happy there?

"They seem to be thriving. The last note we received from them along with the gold thread—they're merchants, you see, and quite successful in getting the thread from China," Alba said. Isabella stopped sewing to hold her piece of linen up to the light.

Alba kept her head very close to the linen while embroidering but spoke with directness. "My family said that the Medicis were more concerned about the Protestants than they were about the Jews."

"I must speak to our purchaser and see if he can acquire such gold thread. Perhaps you will give me their direction before I leave," Isabella said.

"Let me write out their name for you now," said Alba. She went to the desk, scribbled on a piece of paper and handed the note to Isabella.

"You write well," said Isabella.

"My father insisted that I learn to read and write," said Alba.

Silence.

"As did mine," said Isabella.

"It is from letters that I learned about my family in Venice," Alba said.

"Ah, lovely city," Isabella responded. "I loved seeing the gondoliers and happy people on the water."

"That is not what I hear about in the letters."

"And what is your news from Venice?"

"The Jews are not happy about living in their ghetto. They say they cannot leave at night—that they do not have access to the outside world and they need that to exist."

"Being enclosed in their own place with a wall could serve for their protection, could it not?" Isabella deftly worked her needle through the linen stitching back and forth.

"Many are merchants. Many work for the Prince." Alba held her embroidery in her lap without sewing. This is it, she thought. This is where I have to explain it so she understands. "Many need access to libraries. It's connections that are vital for livelihood." Alba paused and added, "Unlike people who have easy access to nobility, we need to work."

Isabella had stopped sewing to hold her linen up to the light. "I do think it's important for people to avoid being exposed only to their own way of thinking. I can see where a ghetto would close them in." She looked beyond Alba at the garden for a moment. "You know, I took a great risk in coming here."

"Oh, yes. I do know that. I hope I have not offended you with anything I've said."

"One cannot be offended by ignorance. I can only assume you do not understand the Pope's dilemmas with the Council of Trent," said Isabella placing the linen in her lap.

"But I do. My husband explained it to me. It weighs heavily on the Pope." Alba stopped sewing and wanted to reach out to Isabella to accompany her words with a gesture of reassurance but instead hit the tea cup which shattered and fell to the ground.

"I'll get the broom," Alba jumped up.

"Just call the servant," Isabella said.

'She's not here, now," Alba lied.

Both women ignored the shards at their feet.

"The Pope hopes to send emissaries to the meeting so that Charles will want to reduce the influence of the Protestants."

"Do you know where that meeting will be?" asked Alba.

"I hear the Pope speak of Trent and of Rome. Right now I don't think they are sure." Several dogs barked. Isabella looked around, but Alba sat still, expectant.

Alba resumed her sewing moving her eyes from the fabric she held in her hands to Isabella's face. Eyes burning, she asked, "Do you think the question of the Jews will be discussed at this meeting you speak of?"

"I'm sure that if Carafa has any influence with the Council of Trent, it will be raised. Paul seems to think that the Jews are quite safe and welcome here." She stopped suddenly. "Is this what you're worried about, my dear? Big decisions about the Jews at the Council of Trent? I think not. Not with Calvin and Luther abounding."

Alba rushed to respond not daring to take a breath. "Isabella, perhaps it is something you cannot understand, but we live in fear. We're at the mercy of the kings, rulers, popes, princes, and so far your Pope Paul has been more than kind to us and we have prospered. He accepts Hayyim as his doctor. He doesn't enforce the wearing of the armband. Yet we know that the Pope asked Father Bruno to return from Toledo and within a day or two of his arrival in Rome, Father Bruno is at our synagogue heaping much abuse on us. We've been accustomed to this kind of treatment from Father Leo, but most of the time we dismissed it by telling ourselves he's a renegade Dominican Friar. But we're afraid that it's very different with Father Bruno...that he came with the Pope's blessings...and his sanction."

Isabella put her hands in her lap. "My, that's a river of words. I wasn't sure what prompted your invitation, but I can see it is fear." She stood and wrapped her linen in a small muslin bag. "I will talk to Alessandro. He has always been appreciative of the Jews in the community. He may not understand how frightened they are." She appraised her embroidery looking closely at the last stitch. "There, I've accomplished quite a bit even with all this talking. Managed to stitch and talk. Quite an achievement. We women can do a lot when we want to." She stood. "I must go. Thank you for the wonderful garden and sharing your talent for sewing with me. And do be careful of the shards when you clean up. Some might still be remaining."

"You're most welcome. I'll see you to the street." Alba was worried that her last comment had alienated this woman who had taken a risk to come to see her. She felt ill with the tension in wanting to ask her if she was going to do anything when she returned to the Palace.

"It's all right. I wish to make a quiet exit and slip out into the street with the hope that no one will see me. It'll be easier if you don't accompany me." She hoped her voice didn't betray the anxiety she was feeling.

"Please be careful upon your return and...and I hope you will come again."

"If it is possible, I will come again. Thank you for inviting me. And...I enjoyed my time with you, and...I am going to talk to Paul about your concerns."

Exactly how she would begin the discussion, she was not sure, but she knew there would be some conversation. She was so engrossed in thought, she did not see the shadowed figure of Alberto Finzi who had moved from his spot at the end of the street so he would not be seen.

CHAPTER 18

Finzi and diBelli Visit Luzzatti

Hayyim galloped through the countryside on Giacomo past groves of olive and fruit trees. The grapes will make wonderful wine, he thought, and I should get back to Alba to see how her time went with Isabella. I was wrong to give permission to such an event. He brought Giacomo to a slow trot when they came to the outskirts of the city along the Tiber River. From there, they walked home.

Dusk was approaching. Hayyim led Giacomo into his stall, gave him water, and lingered over his grooming tasks. He was worried about possible repercussions. What would the members of the Jewish gobierno think? Some frowned on personal relations between Jews and Christians for they felt the contact would contaminate their Judaism. Sometimes business dealings between Christians and Jews were suspect. Hayyim had heard rumblings of a *cherem* for Israel, but thus far nothing had been done.

When he arrived home, he found Alba indoors by a table that held a candle to help her with sewing in the declining light. She greeted her husband tersely.

"Did you have a good ride?"

He bent to kiss her, but she bent to scoop up a piece of imaginary thread on the floor.

"All went well. And your little talk with Isabella?"

"Very well. And it was not a little talk."

"Just an expression, Alba. You know you took a great risk."

"So did she. Her exact words."

"What? Did she risk being brought before the gobierno as you might?"

"Of course not. She's Christian."

"But she will have a place to live. We might not."

"Don't be ridiculous. You're the rabbi and I'm the rabbi's wife."

He sighed. "For heaven's sake. What did you talk about?"

"Would you like some tea?" She saw him frown. "All right. We talked about our sewing. We have much admiration for what each of us is doing. Gold thread and roses and all that."

"Surely that is not all you talked about."

"I very approached her about the subject of the Jews."

And......?

"She seemed surprised."

"And...?"

Alba started to answer, but a loud knocking at the door startled them. Hayyim went to answer it with Alba directly behind him. Alberto Finzi and Bernardo DiBelli stood at the door. These two are up to no good, he thought. They had demonstrated hypocrisy in recent rulings as members of the gobierno by not permitting interest on a loan to a member of the synagogue, yet Hayyim knew they demanded huge interest from members of the Christian community. Hayyim had expressed his objection to this practice at a recent sermon.

"May we enter?" Alberto Finzi bowed slightly.

Bernardo DiBelli wore an elegant velvet doublet and Alberto Finzi looked equally regal in a white linen shirt with dark blue velvet pantaloons. Both wore velvet berets instead of the small skullcap they usually wore at synagogue. Their berets were embroidered with fine gold thread; their beards had been carefully trimmed.

"Of course, come in." Hayyim led them to a small table in the family kitchen and dining room. "Perhaps you would like a cup of wine. Alba will be more than happy to get some for you."

Alba who had not left his side went to the kitchen.

Finzi and diBelli took a seat the table. Finzi spoke first.

"We're not here as your congregants....or your supplicants," he said. He leaned forward. "We are here as members of the gobierno judio."

Luzzatti reflexively adjusted his skull cap. He wondered if either of them had spoken to other members of the gobierno before coming here. Alba brought tea and bread along with a carafe of wine to the table and took a seat next to her husband.

DiBelli looked askance. "Your wife will sit with us?"

"Of course, my wife will sit with us."

"Shall I pour your wine?" Alba asked.

Finzi shrugged and poured a glass of wine for himself and diBelli. Alba picked up her sewing. Finzi cleared his throat. "Perhaps it is best that Alba is here because it is the visit of Isabella that just took place that we need to talk about. You were not present, rabbi. Perhaps you knew nothing of the visit between these two women. It is not good that your wife consorts with a Christian—you know it is contrary to the rules of the gobierno."

Alba's cheeks burned. She stopped sewing with her needle in midair. "My husband treats the Pope and Christians all the time, and I cannot talk with a Christian woman?"

"I know that at times there's such a stipulation by the gobierno," Hayyim said. "But it's never been enforced because we do much business with Christians in the city. I'm sure you do, don't you, Alberto?" Finzi registered no surprise at Hayyim's words. He knew the rabbi would be ready with arguments to defend his wife.

DiBelli drank the entire glass, then pushed it away. "This is terrible. Don't you have anything better?" Alba put down her sewing in her lap. "No. Shall I remove it?"

"No," said diBelli. "Besides it's different for commerce. We make a living when we can when the rules are open for us."

Finzi drank his glass quickly, as well. "You have also brought into our midst your son, Israel, who became a Christian. We can't afford to let our young people be exposed to such heresy."

"Consider what you will," Hayyim said. "He is our son. Besides the entire gobierno has to deal with any thoughts of a cherem."

Finzi hissed. "What your wife has done has never been done before. The wife of a rabbi inviting a Gentile and having tea. Or, maybe they did not have tea. Maybe they drank this vile wine." He shoved his glass aside knocking it over. "Don't you think that information would sway the opinion of the gobierno?"

"Call your gobierno, gentlemen, and make your case. We'll be prepared for whatever consequences. I'll ask you to leave now, for my wife and I are very tired."

DiBelli and Finzi staggered as they went to the door. "This is not the end of it, Rabbi."

"No, this will not be the end of it. Not as long as you continue your business dealings with the Christian community and charge exorbitant interest."

Finzi poked Hayyim in the chest. "You would never bring that up."

"Gentlemen, we will see what is brought up before our community and who will win. Again, I ask you to leave."

DiBelli grabbed Finzi's arm. "Enough for tonight. Let's go."

Hayyim and Alba sat down after the door closed. Alba put her head down on the table near the glass that had toppled. Hayyim reached over and stroked her hair, and kissed her on her neck. She stared at him for a brief moment. "Come," he said. "It is time for some pleasure." She kissed him fully and deeply and followed him upstairs.

CHAPTER 19

Cardinals Reconvene

Cardinal Alfonso paced in his chamber. Justinian and Carafa were late. The heat had invaded the stone walls of the Palace. He stopped to pour water from the pitcher onto his hands and splashed the liquid on his face. What should he do? How could he use the information that Finzi and diBelli had given him without revealing his financial involvement with them? Finzi and diBelli knew about the visit of Isabella to Alba Luzzatti. Alfonso also knew they were annoyed at Israel Luzzatti's return to Rome. If he stayed, he would take their accounts.

Justinian and Carafa arrived within minutes of each other and Alfonso could see that Carafa was annoyed.

"This better be important," Carafa said. "With the upcoming Council of Trent, there is much to be done."

"I need a glass of wine," Justinian said.

"Just seat yourself." Carafa didn't try to hide his irritation. "Alfonso, get on with it."

"Carafa's right. You don't need the wine at this hour of the morning," Alfonso said and poured Justinian a glass of water. He sipped the water and grimaced.

"Just tell us why you've summoned us here at this ungodly hour."

"What would you say if I told you that Isabella visited Alba Luzzatti at her home?" He looked at Justinian.

"That is impossible. It's forbidden—it's even forbidden that women go about by themselves," Justinian sputtered.

"I don't imagine that laws influence Isabella. She does exactly as she pleases and has undue influence over the Pope. She'd like the church to be more 'godly' whatever that means," Carafa snorted.

"How do you know what was at the Luzzatti's?" Justinian asked finishing the water in his glass.

"I think gentlemen, you'll have to trust me. I can tell you my source is reliable."

"May I have more water?" Justinian asked. He smiled. "Actually I would prefer wine." He gulped the water, then said, "Isabella is a thorn in everyone's side."

"You do seem to be full of wise observations today," Alfonso said. "See what happens when you drink water intead of wine."

"How trustworthy are your sources of information?" Carafa asked.

"Yes, how trustworthy?" Justinian echoed.

"They must have a reason for revealing this information to you," Carafa said.

Justinian drew himself up. "You're hiding something from us."

"My sources are more agitated with the Jewess than with Isabella." Alfonso slapped his hand on the table in anger.

Carafa said, "Your silk trade prospers, does it not? I see that you have new damask curtains here as well as mahogany furniture."

"It prospers," Alfonso said, "but my silk trade isn't the reason I have called you together. I'm deeply concerned about Isabella's influence. After all, gentlemen, she may even advise Paul on who should be the next Pope. And what is even worse, he may listen to her. Our Pope is growing old and weak both in spirit and health."

"Would it serve your sources if Isabella weren't here?" Justinian asked.

"They've never discussed that with me," Alfonso sniffed. "I told you they are more concerned about the Jewess...and probably her son."

Justinian spread his hands in front of him as though contemplating their configuration. He was savoring his role. "Are they prepared to do anything about it?" Carafa nodded in agreement.

"Just what exactly do you have in mind?" Alfonso asked. "You, too, Carafa, since you seem to be in agreement with Justinian."

"I'll think about it and let you know," Justinian said. "I must get back to my own chamber." With that he turned and left.

"Well, at least, it's been an interesting morning. This information, if true, could be useful to us, but I would suggest that you don't forget to say your prayers, Alfonso." Carafa said.

"I've already said my prayers and will continue to do so throughout the day. I suggest you do the same."

Carafa said, "I don't have to be reminded."

"Of course."

"Confession might not be a bad idea, either," Carafa murmured.

Alfonso turned to his book of accounts and thought it had been a profitable morning. He had information that no one else had and only he knew the source of that information.

CHAPTER 20

Isabella Confronts the Pope

When Isabella left the Luzzatti home, she walked briskly through Farnesse Square. There she waved away the street vendors peddling their wares, avoiding the fishmongers who sold swordfish and anchovies. Their smell could linger on her clothes. When beggars held out their hands, she fished in her purse for a few coins but threw them to the street rather than putting them directly in filthy hands. She was grateful for the condottieri maintaining some order—sometimes with their horses, sometimes with their staves and spears. Again, she hoped that her ordinary clothing would make her less noticeable. She thought that the square seemed more crowded than usual and, when she looked up, she saw to her surprise that Father Bruno was standing on a platform—the crowd gathering below him. He raised a staff high above his head. She could only catch a few of his words because he was speaking so rapidly.

"You must separate yourself from the Jews. Be mindful of their evil customs. Jewish women will try to beguile you. Do not avail yourself of a Jewish prostitute, no matter what lust is in your heart." Women cheered. Men crossed their arms over their chests.

Isabella couldn't believe her ears. Was this the same Father Bruno who knew the words of Abelard and who had studied at the feet of Paul? Is this what frightened Alba Luzzatti so much? She kept walking and pulled her cloak tightly around her. She saw Jewish merchants standing very still, listening and whispering to one another. They stopped suddenly, for Father Bruno had let out a piercing wail, and the crowd imitated him. Isabella shuddered. "Louder!" shouted Father Bruno. "Louder! Eliminate the devil within you. Wipe out any stain of the Jew, of the Protestant, of Luther, of Calvin. Welcome Christ and give the love of Christ to those who honor him."

"It is they who have allowed women to walk alone in the marketplace." Father Bruno pointed to Isabella who stopped short as she realized that he had selected her from the crowd. Isabella drew herself up tall and pulled down the hood that shaded her face. "They do no such thing to me. I am Isabella Ferrara. I walk alone because I choose to." Her voice rang crystal clear in defiance. The crowd turned to see who this woman was who dared to speak to Father Bruno this way.

"It's Isabella Ferrara—the Pope's mistress." The murmur could be heard through the crowd. The people turned to Father Bruno. Silence reigned. No wind. No bells. Everyone in the crowd seemed to stop breathing to await Father Bruno's reply.

"Of course," he bowed. "You are an excellent woman. I know you, my good lady, could not succumb to the wiles of the Jews. Go well with you, but be cautious, as I can see you are on foot and if you carry money, the Jews may want to take it from you. Go carefully, my lady."

She adjusted her hood so that it covered her hair and watched the spectacle. She heard Father Bruno say, "Now, let us pray. Let us get down on our knees and pray for salvation." Father Bruno knelt on a cushion. The crowd knelt on the cobblestone and bent their heads. The Jews in the back did the same, but no words came from their lips. They simply knelt with their heads bowed.

Isabella hastened back to the Palace and entered through the side door. She went directly to the library. She needed to warn Paul—to warn him of what was happening. She knocked at the door to signal her arrival while the guards stood at attention.

Paul looked up from his desk and scowled. He had been trying to write an agenda for the Cardinals who would be attending the meeting of the Council of Trent in Germany. His frown changed to a smile when he saw her. He was pleased for the distraction.

"Come in, my dear. I shall be finished in just a moment. I am composing my thoughts to be sent with the next nuncio to Trent. It should please you greatly that they're going to be discussing reforms that you've spoken to me about." He looked at her intently. "Your dress appears dusty."

She brushed the dust from the hem of her dress. "This is a great responsibility for you, Alessandro."

"Yes, but with the power of God behind me, it will come it pass. It will bring glory back to the Church. Unfortunately, the cost of this Council will be great, and I must think of levying taxes again."

"That's most unfortunate. You just levied taxes in order to pay for the latest works of Michelangelo and Raphael." She paused, "As well as your portrait by Titian." She paused again waiting for a reaction. "As well as the lands you acquired for Pier Luigi—unnecessarily, I may add."

"Necessary costs - I'll be leaving a great legacy."

"Your meetings with the Cardinals have been going well?"

He turned back to his papers and began to write.

"Well enough. Maybe I can levy more taxes without having the people up in arms, by giving them something of a distraction. I will give them a Passion Play in the courtyard and make it a festival day." He paused momentarily. "I'm expecting Carafa here shortly to discuss some plans."

Isabella stood. "But you promised Dr. Luzzatti that you would not present another Passion Play because it created such havoc and chaos."

"The Jews will happily pay their taxes. They know they live well due to my good graces." It appeared to Isabella that this was an argument he had practiced. "They will not complain, not at all, but the rest....Well, the rest will complain about more taxes, but the Passion Play will lift their spirits. Besides I will have the condottieri out and see that nothing happens to the Jews."

"But then you have to pay the condottieri."

"And they will be happy for the extra ducats and the work I give them. They're warriors, you know. Not everyone can be a scholar...like you."

"Is this what you've gotten from the meetings with the Cardinals?" she retorted.

"Damn the bloody meetings. They take up so much time." When he gathered his papers in some order, he said, "You've been happy with your comfortable lodgings here at the Palace? You do like fine things as well, don't you, Isabella? In fact, weren't you the one who insisted on having an apartment here? All that takes money—lots of money."

"Yes, I like fine things, but not at the expense of doing good deeds." She leaned forward taking the papers and ordering them further. "What of Father Bruno? Must he conduct his harangue again the Jews in the square? Is it not enough that he enters their synagogue and scolds?" She added, "England burns our Catholics. Must you do the same to our Jews?"

The both jumped at the knock on the door.

"That must be Carafa," Paul sighed. "We are not burning people, Isabella."

At that moment, Carafa entered. She was exasperated with Paul. He meandered; he had wandered from his principles, from his ideals. And she was totally unprepared for Carafa's comment.

"I understand, Isabella, that you were able to witness Father Bruno's sermon at work in the square today."

Isabella's blanched but said nothing.

At this, Paul stood and knocked several papers from his desk to the floor. "What is this? You were in the square? Were you alone? Who was with you? Why didn't I know about this? Is this how you know about Father Bruno? Is this why your dress is filthy with dust?"

Carafa answered. "She was alone."

"Is this true? You were there alone as though you were any common woman?"

"I was interested in seeing life outside of the Palace...in order to help you, Paul, with your work," Isabella pleaded. "It's always good to hear what the common people are thinking...not only the Cardinals. Is it not?"

Without waiting for a response from Paul, Carafa said, "Perhaps you were on your way from a visit with a stranger." He emphasized the word *stranger*.

"I don't visit strangers. You know that as well as I do," she snapped.

"I gather then that you do not consider Alba Luzzatti a stranger." He then turned to Paul, who had remained silent throughout the exchange between the mother of his children and loyal cardinal.

"I've tried to tell you that the Luzzatti name is not a good one for you to be associated with," said Carafa. "It is unseemly and dangerous that a woman of the court be visiting with a commoner and a Jew."

"And I've tried to tell you to relieve yourself of your desires for Michelangelo," Isabella retorted sharply. Until now I've remained quiet, she thought, but now I must reassert my influence.

Paul walked between his desk and the shelf of books behind him several times. Then he shuffled around the desk with his hands behind his back, shoulders and head bent. The silence was palpable until he finally spoke again. Isabella jumped at the harshness of his voice.

"You, Isabella, are forbidden to leave the palace on your own and are especially forbidden to have any contact with any of the Luzzattis. Rabbi Luzzatti will no longer be my court physician."

Carafa's face was immobile except for a slight twitching around his mouth.

"And you, Carafa are forbidden to make any visits to Michelangelo. There can be no connections of my cardinals with *men*." Both Carafa and Isabella started to protest, but Paul held up his hand to signal silence from them.

"That is how I wish it to be and that is how it shall be."

He turned swiftly and left the library. Isabella and Carafa stared angrily at one another.

"You must be pleased, Cardinal Carafa." She addressed him with deliberate courtesy but could not hide the disgust in her voice.

He said fiercely, "You do not understand war. I do." He turned sharply and left her standing in wonder at these unexpected ultimatums from the Pope.

CHAPTER 21

Father Bruno

The air in Rome was soaked with humidity that threatened thundershowers. Hayyim sat in the courtyard thinking that he should go inside and bring his books in for protection, but the heaviness of the air and his heart weighed upon him.

He had been reading *The Zohar* struggling to understand the Aramaic, and hoping its mystical thoughts would reveal some wisdom for him. He ran his fingers methodically down the page. *Go deeper,* he read. *Do not let what you see turn your good heart to stone. Repair the world. You must repair the world. Take the tiny pieces that were broken by ill deeds and try to put them back together.*

A thunderclap pulled him out of his reverie, but still he did not move. He turned from *The Zohar* to his book of medicines. What was there besides licorice, comfrey, linden, poultices, bicarbonate of soda to cure gout, the lame, and the syphilitic? He was beginning to doubt the effects of leeches and bleeding his patients. All his studies of anatomy at the University of Padua seemed useless at this point. Why learn about deformities of arms and limbs where there didn't seem to be a cure for those twisted appendages? Where are the cures for the deformities of the soul, he wondered?

The next boom of thunder brought a light sprinkling of rain. Hayyim gathered his books under his plain brown long tunic, touched his head to make sure his skullcap was still in place, and went inside to his study. It never ceased to amaze him how cool the house could be even when the heat outside was stifling. He put the huge book on his desk and returned to the mullioned window to watch the pelting rain as it soaked the earth and showered the flowers and vegetables with needed water. Tall zinniàs bent with the weight of water, but Hayyim knew it wouldn't be for long. With the next ray of sunshine they would be upright. He took that as a metaphor, as a sign for him to lift his spirits, to release himself from the darkness that he felt.

"Hayyim," Alba called, knocking on the door. "Hayyim, you must come quickly. Two men on horseback are headed to our house. They're friars." Hayyim opened the door to his study and went with Alba to the front door. She continued. "It can't be that they're coming to proselytize here. Right here at our house."

He opened the door and peered out. "They may not even stop here."

"No. If they stop anyplace, it will be at this house. Of that I am sure."

"Do you have any tea to offer them or hot citrus drink?"

"I have chocolate from Mexico that Senor Zefarti left, but it has been too hot to keep the fire."

"Kindle it. We must be hospitable if they stop here. No matter what." Alba went back to the kitchen.

He waited. They stopped to give their horses water from the trough near his front door. One of the men jumped from his horse. "Dr. Luzzatti?"

Hayyim was relieved to hear the man's respectful tone. "Yes. How can I help you?"

"Father Bruno. He is very sick and we are here to bring you to the priory. He said you would not deny a sick man."

"But Father Bruno preaches against Jews, and I am no longer the Pope's physician..." The words at the tip of Hayyim's tongue were left unsaid. He was a physician. He would go where he was called.

"We'll take you by horseback. We brought an extra horse for you to ride. I'm Father Leo."

"I'll take my own horse."

"As you wish. Just hurry."

"I'm going to the Dominican Priory to take care of Father Bruno," Hayyim called to Alba. "Please unhitch Giacomo for me."

She stepped out from the kitchen with a piece of cloth in her hand. "But..."

Hayyim held up his hand for silence. "Please unhitch Giacomo."

She tucked the cloth into an apron pocket, averted her eyes, and walked slowly from the kitchen to the barn, wiping door handles on the way. At the barn, she put the reins on Giacomo, and led him out of the stall.

"He's ready," she called. Hayyim came around back.

"No, he's not. Where's his saddle?"

"I wanted to ask you if you know what you're doing going off with these friars?"

"Yes. I'm a physician."

"But..."

"No more 'buts'."

He carefully placed the saddle on Giacomo and tightened the girth. He walked the horse from the stall in the courtyard to the alleyway. Alba watched as her husband put his left foot in the stirrup and swing his other foot over the wide back of his horse.

Hayyim followed the two men and the horse without a rider as they galloped out of Rome and along the dusty road and overgrown forest path that led to the priory. He was grateful for the speed because it forced him to concentrate on the riding and relieved him for the moment of worry.

Hayyim had been riding with such concentration that he did not see the simple stone one-story building appear in the horizon. It was the only building to mark the landscape of forest that surrounded it on all sides. Hayyim dismounted and followed Friar Leo. He heard the prayers of the other Dominican Friars inside—a low hum, a chant, and then some Latin words he could not decipher because they were too soft to hear. It was clear that a gathering of men was praying; he welcomed the soothing tone of their voices.

"They are praying for Father Bruno. They think he is close to death. Please enter here." The friar pointed a third door off the corridor.

He entered the sparse small room that held only a tiny table with a wash basin filled with water, a slop pail covered with a slab of ceramic to keep the flies from gathering, a small window that let in a single ray of light, an undersized three-legged stool, and a narrow bed. On the bed lay Father

Bruno, his feet hanging over the end. Hayyim searched the sick man's gaunt face for some clue to his illness.

The rabbi sat, precariously balanced on the stool. "Father Bruno. May I feel your forehead, and may I examine your stomach?"

Father Bruno nodded and started to speak, "I'm..."

"Please do not talk. Just nod 'yes' or 'no' so you don't exert yourself unnecessarily."

Father Bruno said feebly, "I must say my prayers."

"You may say your prayers silently."

Father Bruno nodded and began to whisper words in Latin.

Hayyim put his hand on Father Bruno's feverish forehead. A very high fever, he thought. Hayyim then placed his ear to Father Bruno's heart moving aside the huge wooden cross that lay on his chest so that he could listen carefully.

Luzzatti was grateful for the anatomical work he had done at the University of Padua; he knew exactly where to place his ear and where to palpate. He also knew the significance of those organs he could feel with his fingers, and he could certainly tell an irregular heart beat.

"Are you in pain?" Hayyim asked.

Father Bruno moved his head indicating "no."

"I'm going to put some pressure on your stomach. Let me know if I'm hurting you."

Father Bruno let out a low moan and pulled himself to a sitting position by latching on to Hayyim Luzzatti's shoulders. He pointed to the slop pail. Hayyim brought it to him and Father Bruno vomited into the pail and then dropped back onto the bed, sweat glistening on his forehead. Hayyim lifted Father Bruno's head and gave him some water. He also dipped a piece of linen in a basin of cool water and placed in on the Friar's forehead.

Hayyim called to the friar who was standing guard outside the room.

"Please call someone to stay with Father Bruno. Hurry, I must return home to get some marshmallow plant."

The friar hesitated for a moment. "Perhaps I should go."

"No. I know exactly where the plant is."

The guard hurried to find help.

Father Gregorio, a portly man, lumbered to Father Bruno's room.

"Jew," he addressed Hayyim. "Have you let him die without the presence of another Catholic soul? You can be hanged for that."

Hayyim ignored the comment. He repeated to Father Gregorio what he had just told the friar. He demonstrated how the cloth was to be dipped in water and wrung out and then placed on Bruno's forehead. "You may need to get cooler water from the stream," Hayyim told the nervous friar.

"What if he should take a turn for the worse while you're gone?" Beads of sweat appeared on Father Gregorio's forehead.

"We are doing everything possible for him."

"He has tertian fever—the parasites are tearing at his bowels now—and we must rid them from his body. The marshmallow plant should help him."

"I will place this holy relic—this cross—in his hands. It comes with its own curative powers," said Father Gregorio.

Hayyim turned to Father Bruno. "Do you understand? I think you're at the beginning stages of your illness and I'm optimistic that we can cure you. I'll be back with some herbs. Father Gregorio will stay with you, keeping you cool until I come back. I'll ride as fast as I can and take one of the young friars with me."

Father Bruno closed his eyes and nodded.

Hayyim unhitched his horse. He and Friar Leo galloped along the forest path then on to the muddy road until they came to his home on Via Angelico. Hayyim frantically searched one of the side cupboards for the newly-dried plant. Alba watched him. "What are you looking for?"

"Help me find the dried marshmallow to take back to Father Bruno." She went to the wide cupboard and handed him several small jars with dried herbs. He looked carefully. "You're sure, now?"

She glared at him. "I'm sure."

"Give Giacomo some sugar because he'll have a hard ride back," Hayyim said.

Alba got the sugar and fed it to the horse from her hand. She whispered in his ear, "Please take care of my husband. Even though he annoys me sometimes, I do love him. See that he comes to no harm." She glanced at Hayyim. He gave no indication that he heard her.

He was busy putting the dried leaves and roots in the saddlebag. The doctor mounted up again and signaled for the friar that he was ready to begin the return journey. As they came to Palazzo Square, Hayyim heard the great roar of a crowd watching a dead man hanging by his neck.

"Who was he?" Hayyim asked Friar Leo once they were out of the square. He tried not to show the horror or fear in his voice. Again, he was glad he had to focus his attention on his riding.

The friar had to shout as the horses' hooves pounded hard on the dry and dusty road. "Giovanni Cardinale. He was an heretic preaching the work of Martin Luther. It is prohibited in this square, but the man persisted. He was warned."

At dusk, they arrived at the priory to an eerie stillness. Hayyim dismounted, tossed Giacomo's reins to the friar, and ran down the corridor to Father Bruno's cell. The tiny room was filled with ten friars holding bowls of water. As he watched, they continued dipping their fingers and sprinkling drops on Father Bruno.

"What are you doing? He cannot breathe with so many of you in here!"

"We're exorcising any demons you might have given him." Father Gregorio spoke for them.

"I don't give demons. I'm a doctor. I try to cure people."

"You're a Jew."

"I want him here. Please leave." Father Bruno moaned.

"If he dies, you'll be responsible for his death." Reluctantly, Father Gregorio led the other friars out of the room leaving only Father Leo.

They left in a solemn procession, chanting a prayer for the health of Father Bruno.

"Bring two bowls—one clean and empty, and one with boiling water," Hayyim ordered Father Leo.

Father Leo returned with the bowl of boiling water. Hayyim swiftly opened the marshmallow root and leaves and placed them in the boiled water. Hayyim let the brew steep for a minute or two then he lifted Father Bruno's head so he could drink.

"Thank you," whispered Father Bruno.

"You're to rest now. I'll give you more in another hour, and when you feel the urge to relieve yourself, I will be here. The parasites need to be flushed out of your system."

And so they continued this way for eight hours, with Hayyim Luzzatti never leaving Father Bruno's bedside, never dozing, being there to receive both his vomit and the brown syrup of his bowels. Each time, Hayyim gave the contents of a slop pail to a young friar who in turn gave it to one of the older friars. Hayyim knew that the pails were a subject of great discussion among the men as they looked for evil signs in Father Bruno's excrement. During the next ten hours, Father Bruno improved.

When Father Bruno woke the next morning, his garments were soaked with sweat. As Hayyim laid a hand upon the sick man's forehead, he sighed with relief, for it was cool.

Father Bruno smiled weakly. "I survived. I'm alive."

"Yes, you survived," Hayyim Luzzatti replied.

Father Bruno stared at him. "I owe much to you."

"Your fellow friars were very anxious that you get well. They did everything possible. I'll call one to help me clean up a bit more." Hayyim started to pick up what was left of the marshmallow plant.

"Wait. Someone will come help clean. First, I want to ask you something." Father Bruno tried to sit up.

"You still need to rest," Hayyim said.

"I want to know if you're angry with me," Father Bruno said.

"More puzzled than angry," Hayyim said. "I cannot understand why you came to heap abuse on us."

"I'm amazed but delighted you came to treat me."

Hayyim debated with himself for a moment. "The harangues at the synagogue—can they stop?"

Again, Father Bruno tried to sit up.

"I must please Carafa in order for this priory to stay open, and I'm sorry for the hurt I've caused you. But, my friend....if there is any other way I can help...."

Hayyim shrugged. "I'm glad you're better. I cannot think of any other way." Hayyim picked up the rest of the marshmallow plant and turned to leave. "I wish you a speedy recovery."

Father Bruno lay down on his bed exhausted.

CHAPTER 22

Isabella and Sons

Isabella sat on a green silk damask sofa with an astronomy text in her hands. Her sons, Pier Luigi and Ranuncio, sat opposite her. Luigi draped his long legs over the side of the chair while Ranuncio sat erect, looking disdainfully at his brother. Isabella wondered how she had given birth to such completely different children; one who constantly sought riches from the Church and gambled too much, hunted with cruelty, and prided himself as a warrior; the other who studied Latin, French, and German and attended mass regularly.

When Pope Paul was Cardinal Farnese, he had been pleased with the birth of his sons, and took some pride in telling the news to his colleagues, though he knew they had clearly taken their vows of celibacy more seriously than he.

Isabella had come to court as a young woman under her father's strong guidance. Her olive skin, waist-length hair, and green almond shaped eyes created a Madonna-like image. Her father, Count Fortunato Martinego Ceasaro Ferrara, had come to the Cardinal to broker the art of Fra Lippo Lippi—a stunning painting of "The Madonna and Child" and he had brought along his daughter, Isabella. Instead of remaining in the background as Farnese and Ferrara discussed the merits and price of the painting, Isabella joined the conversation by pointing out the value of the work of Lippi and compared him to Botticelli. She talked about Botticelli's "Birth of Venus" with familiarity and expounded on the story of Venus.

"Venus was beautiful but this painting of Lippi's has captured the spiritual beauty of a Madonna - a different kind of beauty but beauty, nevertheless." Isabella spoke authoritatively.

"She's as beautiful as you are," Farnese had replied.

Her father had looked askance at this comment from the Cardinal but he said nothing because he did not want to jeopardize the sale of this work.

"You've educated your daughter well, and yes, I'll pay the four thousand ducats for it has been authenticated by your lovely daughter." Isabella indeed had beguiled Farnese. She, in turn, was attracted by this man who wore his cardinal's robe with elegance and had looked at her with obvious longing. "The brilliant eyes said it all," she had revealed to her diary when recounting their first meeting.

Count Ferrara had waited for the Cardinal to count out the four thousand ducats from his desk drawer and had accepted the money with a certain degree of arrogance.

"Come Isabella. We needn't bother the Cardinal any more," said her father who had grown nervous as his daughter's eyes lingered on the Cardinal.

Farnese answered looking directly at Isabella. "It's no bother. I hope your daughter can stay and spend some time looking at other paintings I've acquired. I'd like her opinion."

"I will stay," she said.

Ferrara knew better than to argue with her; she had always been headstrong. Perhaps his daughter's becoming a member of the Cardinal's court could work to his advantage.

Isabella had stayed by the side of Cardinal Farnese until he was elected Pope. The birth of their sons while he was Cardinal had assured her well-being at the Papal Palace.

Throughout that time she would bear the unpleasantness of Alfonso and Carafa, who resented her influence. She had earned an important place in the Pope's world as did her sons.

Today she addressed her sons quietly. "Have you gone to mass this morning?"

"No, mother." Pier Luigi answered. "Too early."

"I've gone, Mother," said Ranuncio.

"I may not go to mass but I do communicate with God daily," Pier Luigi retorted.

She was not placated. "Yes, when you want him to guarantee your winnings at Faro and a steady hand with your sword." She peered at them, her brow furrowed. "Why exactly are you here this morning?"

Pier Luigi looked at his brother. "It's come to our attention that you left the palace to visit the house of Luzzatti's family."

"And just precisely how did you come by this information? You're usually so busy hunting and gambling that I hardly ever see you at the Palace."

"Cardinal Carafa told us," Ranuncio said.

Pier Luigi glanced approvingly at this brother surprised at his eagerness.

"What exactly did Cardinal Carafa tell you?"

In spite of Isabella's conflicts with her sons, they remained dear in her heart, and she suspected at times that Pier Luigi's unruly behavior was due to her extravagances toward her children.

Her voice tinged with annoyance, she said, "That man thought that you'd tell me not to do it again and I'd listen?" Her voice rose. "I visit with this woman to improve my sewing skills. That is all."

"Associating with a commoner and a Jew makes father look weak," said Ranuncio. "Women of the Papal Court do not do that," added Pier Luigi sternly.

"Unlike your women of the Papal Court who think it perfectly all right to equate themselves as whores." She looked steadily at Pier Luigi who blushed. "And since when have you taken an interest in the affairs of the Church?"

"We're looking out for your best interests, Mother," said Ranuncio. He was trying to be the voice of reason in this rather testy exchange.

"My dear sons, you're not aware of my best interests or your own. I am trying to be a good Catholic mother, but you ignore the barest of my attempts. I suggest to you that Cardinal Carafa may not be your best friend or a good ally of your father. I recommend that you go about your business, and I go about mine." She did not try to hide the irritation in her voice. "I'd like to continue with my reading."

"You're our mother and we care about you," said Ranuncio as they moved toward the door.

"I thought I raised you to think for yourselves at least, and to question," she said as they departed. Pier Luigi turned as though to respond, but said nothing.

Isabella, agitated, left the room within a few seconds of their departure. She wanted to go to the Luzzatti household to warn Alba that their visit had become a topic of concern at the Palace. She was especially fearful of this information in Carafa's hands. She walked through the corridor that held the statues of Sophocles, Euripides, and Plato. These statues reminded her of a time when Pope Paul talked of enlightenment, wisdom, and knowledge. Once they had talked the entire night about Plato's idea of civic harmony. Paul had agreed that the object of rule is the good of the people. It seemed a long time ago.

She came to the end of the corridor and found Michelangelo sketching at his desk, with Cardinal Carafa looking over the artist's shoulder. She cleared her throat. When Cardinal Carafa turned and saw her, his eyes flashed in anger.

"You've come to see how Michelangelo is progressing, Isabella?"

"It is my understanding that you're not to be with Michelangelo." She was surprised at her own brazenness and addressed the artist. "Cardinal Carafa seems to have forgotten the Pope's orders."

Carafa exploded, "And you, my dear lady, shouldn't be visiting the homes of Jewesses."

Isabella retorted. "I hoped to be doing some good by visiting the rabbi's wife. What good are you doing by visiting Michelangelo?"

Carafa turned on his heel and stormed out.

Michelangelo fixed his attention on his drawings. He turned to her. "What do you think, Isabella? I'm glad that you have come while there is enough light for you to see the sketches. The dome will be an extraordinary challenge." He paused. "I hope there will be enough money to complete the structure."

"It matters not what I think. But I can tell you that the Pope will admire it, and that is what's important. He will see that a magnificent cathedral will draw people to the Church, and I know that is what he wants—it's what we all want." Isabella peered through the chapel window and saw darkness rapidly descending.

"Have you been receiving your stipend?" she asked.

"No, and I thank you for asking. I have always been able to depend on your concern for my well-being."

"I shall speak to Paul. Affairs of state weigh heavily upon him."

"I do need the money. I cannot live on air."

"Yes, I know. I shall talk to him shortly."

Her father, too, had been supportive of Michelangelo as a young artist and both had watched him grow to a world renowned figure. She had also seen him grow to a man of faith when he had fallen under the tutelage of Vittoria Colonna.

"I'll visit you another day."

He rolled up his sketches. "Please do. Please do. Your presence satisfies me greatly, while Cardinal Carafa's..."

Isabella put a reassuring hand on the artist's sleeve. "It will be all right, Michelangelo. I promise. All will be well."

When Isabella returned to her apartment in the Palace, she was pleased to see that no ladies were present and proceeded to dismiss her maid. Gossip was forever a source of concern for Isabella. Isabella did as she had done before and donned a simple tan muslin cape over her dress. She decided to take off her necklaces and rings to walk to the Luzzatti house. They must be warned of the unrest at the Palace over her visit. She gathered up her embroidery, turned toward the window, and held it up to the waning light. This will be a beautiful piece, she thought. The rose is exquisitely designed. Alba will admire it. To her surprise, she heard the voice of her son, Pier Luigi. "Are you leaving the Palace, mother? You shouldn't be going without an escort."

"My dear son. You should not come creeping into your mother's chambers without knocking. You startled me to death. No, I'm not going anyplace."

"Then why are you wearing that long coat and why have you removed your jewels?"

"I was simply trying this garment on and now I am preparing for some rest. I suggest you leave."

He kissed her on the cheek. "As you wish, Mother. I shall leave, but you must be careful."

"It's you, Pier Luigi, who needs to be careful. Careful of your desires to gather more property and to depend on others than your mother to give you advice."

"I think only of you, Mother," he said. He kissed her on the cheek and left.

Isabella sat on her velvet chair with her coat on. I need to visit this woman, Alba Luzzatti again, she thought. To warn her. This Jewish woman was a woman of substance—not like the ladies of the court.

She waited until she heard no more footsteps along the marble floors of the corridor. She knew that dusk was not the best time to be in the streets of Rome during the summer as beggars and robbers were afoot to say nothing of the plague of mosquitoes. She drew her light cape around her, left through the side entrance of the palace as she had done before, and followed the more circuitous and less traveled route toward the Luzzatti house. It started to pour; the thunder followed by lightning made the path seem all the more treacherous. She turned frequently to see if anyone was following her—at times she thought she heard footsteps along the cobblestone streets, but she knew that at this hour hardly anyone would be out. Many people were at home preparing for the dinner hour, and most did not want to be out in the rain that would leave stagnant pools of water or push the garbage off one street into another. She was glad when the Luzzatti house came into view. Again, she heard footsteps behind her.

She hurried toward the Luzzatti home. She shook the rain off her outer garment and prayed that Alba would hear her knock right away. As she raised her hand to the door, an arm came from behind and squeezed her neck so she could not emit a sound. The knife found its mark and her body slumped to the ground, blood oozing and staining the cobblestones. Her attacker ran with the weapon still in his hand. The killer threw both his knife and cloak in the Tiber River and fled back in the direction of the forest into the darkness.

CHAPTER 23

A Dastardly Deed

Hayyim, Alba, and Israel were seated at the table in the garden to escape the summer heat trapped inside the house. Alba had prepared roasted chicken and zucchini and bread with a hard crust that Hayyim liked so much. Israel had sung the blessing for the meal with a robustness that pleased his mother and father. Alba and Hayyim exchanged glances as they chanted the final "amen" together. The candles flickered in the dark and cast shadows around their faces. Hayyim glanced at his son remembering how easily he had learned his prayers and how he sang them in a lusty voice. Was that going to continue? Was his conversion serious? How could he live in two worlds?

"Yes, mother. I have not forgotten." A loud thud outside the wall of the garden made them look up from their dinner plates.

"Were you expecting visitors?" Hayyim asked of Alba.

"No one. The rain is keeping a lot of people home. Israel, go to the door and see who it is. Or, maybe someone accidentally dropped a sack of flour."

Israel went to the front door. He cautiously opened it and peered out. The street was dark; the rain was now but a drizzle. It was not until his eyes became accustomed to the dark that he saw the blood and a body slumped on the wet cobblestones.

"Father, come quickly. Someone's been hurt." Hayyim hurried outside to where Israel was standing.

"Help me carry her inside," Hayyim said to his son, who seemed unable to move. Hayyim stepped out into the street and lifted her feet. Israel grabbed her shoulders covered with blood; they brought the woman inside and laid her on the floor. Hayyim did not want to risk lifting her to the sofa.

"What is it?" Alba came running.

She then looked down at the body and realized it was Isabella. Alba whispered, "O, God, protect her. Protect us. It's Isabella." She bent down to touch her but Hayyim waved her away.

"Quickly," Hayyim said. "Get some cloth so I can try to stem the bleeding. And boil some water." This was not a usual practice but Hayyim had been experimenting with the notion of "the cleaner the better." After all, wasn't that why Jews had a mikvah? Women cleansing themselves after menstruation continued in Rome; all Hayyim's female congregants participated except those who were pregnant.

Alba fetched clean linen, hurried to put a kettle of water over the fire to boil, and silently thanked God that she had not extinguished the flame. Father and son worked to stem the bleeding by applying cloth after cloth that Hayyim had first dipped in the boiled water and then allowed to cool.

Hayyim said, "She's been stabbed several times."

"She's alive?" Israel asked.

"Yes, thank God. Israel, take Giacomo and ride to the Palace."

"No. I don't think he should go," Alba said. "It could be dangerous for him depending on who is there."

"Then who should go?" Hayyim asked.

"Send a neighbor."

"That's even more dangerous," Israel interceded. "I'll go." He turned to his mother. "And don't worry." He addressed his father. "Who shall I tell?"

"Tell the Swiss Guards. If you can find Giovanni Batiste and Joseph Frech, so much the better. I've helped their families. They'll dispatch the news and alert someone. Then ride back immediately."

Israel left and Alba knelt on the floor cradling Isabella's head in her lap. She dipped her finger in the boiled water, blew on it, and moistened Isabella's lips.

"She's very weak," Hayyim said. "But I think she can withstand the ride back to the Palace."

"She'll live?"

"It depends on how these wounds will heal. I don't know if the knife penetrated any vital organs."

"Perhaps she should remain here," said Alba. Even as Alba offered this advice, she knew it would be impossible for Isabella to stay and recover in their house. The two sat in silence with Alba wiping Isabella's brow and holding the cloth to stem the bleeding. Soon she heard the clattering of a carriage and the hooves of several horses. Hayyim opened the door to four Swiss Guardsmen, strangers to him.

"Where's Israel? Where's my son?"

"See, I told you there would be problems," Alba said grabbing Hayyim's arm.

The guard lowered his eyes. "Carafa ordered him held at the Palace." He shuffled uncomfortably from one foot to the other.

"I'm sure it's only momentary. All this will be straightened out," Hayyim said. This was no time for an argument.

"It's important that Isabella get back to the Palace for care. I'll stop by to see her tomorrow...with permission from the Pope, of course." He motioned for the guardsmen to come in to take Isabella. They gently lifted her into the carriage. Her maid sat, tears streaming down her face and wrapped her arms around her wounded mistress.

"Do you have any words for the maid?"

"Keep the wound clean with cloth that has been dipped in boiled water and see that Isabella drinks little sips of boiled water with lemon."

"Anything else?"

"Pray," said Hayyim.

The Swiss Guard took a huge gold cross from around his neck and said, "I'll rest this on her body."

"Perhaps it is best if you just place it in her hand." He placed his hand on the guard's arm. "Please tell Israel that we will be there to see him as soon as possible, and he shouldn't be afraid."

"I'll do my best, Dr. Luzzatti. He was with Cardinal Carafa when we left." The guard had known and respected Dr. Luzzatti for the care he had given his ten-year-old son who had been sick with blinding headaches. Dr. Luzzatti's ministration of damp cool cloths and herbs had helped his young child considerably.

Hayyim cast a nervous glance at Alba, who had kept her hands clenched in fists at her side.

The carriage with the wounded Isabella clattered away in the night and Hayyim took his wife in his arms.

'We should go now to see that Israel's all right," she said through her sobs.

"No," he said. "Let them take care of Isabella first."

"I cannot believe you're saying that—'Isabella first'."

"Alba," he said clearly frustrated. "She is the Pope's mistress. The mother of his children. She has been stabbed outside our house. Don't you understand?"

"But, our son."

"Our son's an apostate," he said and left to go upstairs. He had lost his patience with her. He couldn't fathom how his son had left the faith, but he had. He couldn't understand why Isabella would be stabbed. He lay in his bed trying to rest his frantic mind.

She joined him but lay there with her clothes on.

"You will go first thing in the morning?" she asked in the darkness of the room. "I'll prepare some food."

"First, I'll go to synagogue and help to say the morning prayers with the men. They're counting on me."

Neither slept and both were up before the rooster crowed at dawn.

"You're going to the Palace to find out about Israel?" Alba said.

"Prayers first and then the Palace.

"You'll speak directly to the Pope?

"To no one else." He did not tell her he had no guarantee.

He washed and quickly donned fresh clothing, left without a morning meal, and scooped up the bag of food that Alba had prepared.

*　*　*

Last night's storm had pushed the previous day's humidity out to the sea. Normally, he took note of the weather on his daily walks to synagogue. He had often thought that clouds or rain could influence the intensity of prayer and he would adjust his chanting to help the worshipers in their daily struggle to connect with God. Today, his mind was on other things. Why had they kept Israel there?

He entered the synagogue to see that someone had opened the windows to let in the fresh air and heard the men praying in strong, clear voices. Each one reciting his own "Amidah." As it should be, Hayyim thought. It's each man's individual reach toward the almighty that is important. Hayyim took his place at the tebah to chant the day's prayers with them and realized he could not bring about his usual vigor. He wanted his voice to resound with the morning prayer, Ma Tovu, "How goodly are your tents, O Jacob, your dwelling places, Israel," but his worries about his son and the events of last night had exhausted him. It was being in God's house and being at one with God and his fellow congregants that allowed him to feel his fatigue for the moment. He was relieved when he heard the final, long AH-men at the end of the prayer. He gathered his wool tallit—still worn in spite of the summer heat—and prayer book, and packed them into the velvet bag that Alba had carefully embroidered with his name. He walked down the steps of the platform to hurry out the door.

Bernardo DiBelli hurried after him. "Rabbi, please, wait a moment. We were hoping that you would stay so that we could talk with you. Members of the gobierno are here, but this will just be an informal talk."

"Not today. I came just to pray. I must hurry to the Papal Palace—a crisis." He paused, undecided exactly what information to reveal. A flush of impatience washed over him. "My son Israel is being held there."

DiBelli remained unmoved. "That is indeed a surprise. Then there is even more reason to talk with you for it is your apostate son that concerns us. We're not even sure that he is part of this community, and yet he sits in our synagogue. We're afraid that your son's presence will bring danger to us. The gentiles will think that all of us should convert for it was that easy for your son to do it. We must make decisions and make them promptly so we think it important to discuss these now. A meeting with us could avoid a meeting with the gobierno." DiBelli could not contain his sarcasm. "Perhaps your son is at the Palace because he is going to have a special court appointment, especially since your wife now sits and sews with the Pope's mistress."

Hayyim was enraged.

"Ridiculous," he said.

He knew from his last meeting with Finzi and DiBelli that the gobierno was considering a *cherem*. The ignorance of the congregants exasperated Hayyim. Yes, some had studied, but most were not interested in philosophy or Greek, or Aristotle, or Plato, or the art of Michelangelo. They did not take halacha—the rules of living as a Jew—seriously. Hayyim also observed that Zefarti was not there. What had happened to Senor Zefarti, who was so thrilled to be able to come to a community where he could worship freely? Where was he?

DiBelli persisted. "So you'll stay for a few minutes?"

The distraught rabbi could hardly contain his anger. He hoped his voice was not trembling. "Yes, but just a few minutes. It is urgent for me to be at the Palace."

The men who had just finished their prayers sat up expectantly in their seats while DiBelli spoke. Hayyim remained standing at his side. DiBelli asked, "Did you see the lightning last night and hear the thunder?"

Hayyim answered. "No, I didn't."

DiBelli continued. "It was so fierce last night that it brought us new weather. We take it as a sign that things must change."

"And what are those things?"

"Zefarti has brought us bad luck since his arrival. We know that the Pope is considering restrictions on us, and the lightning is an omen. We must think carefully what that omen means." DiBelli looked around to see if his words were registering.

Hayyim sighed because he had heard this superstition before. In the past, there had always been enough fellow believers to convince the superstitious ones that these beliefs were just that—superstitions. While one could toss salt over one's shoulder to cast out the evil eye, it was better to accept that as custom rather than truth.

"So that is why Senor Zefarti is not here. He has been told that he is a burden upon the community."

"Why should we want to bring danger into our midst?" Finzi said.

"We cannot neglect our obligation to welcome the stranger in our midst, and if it is a Jew seeking solace in a stressful time, it is even more so our obligation."

"Who is there to bring *us* solace? This is indeed a stressful time for us, brought on by your friendship with the Pope and your son's apostasy, and your wife's arrogance," said Benjamin ben Jehuda.

The resentment in his friend's voice startled Hayyim. Didn't he have any allies in the congregration?

Benjamin continued. "We need someone to cast out the spell that is hovering over this congregation. You should invite Dona Esther to come here with her holy water to cleanse all the evil out of this place."

Hayyim was appalled. "A year ago, I told you that Dona Esther's witchcraft had no place in synagogue life. It is just good deeds, study, and prayer that ward off evil—good deeds, study, and prayer." He slammed one fist into the palm of his other hand. "I must get to the Palace."

"But your prescription hasn't worked," Finzi said. "We are plagued with proselytizing, poor weather, unwanted visitors, and an apostate. Dona Esther can only help."

Hayyim drew his hands up to his temples. "Yes. Yes. When I come back from the palace after seeing Israel, we'll talk about Dona Esther."

A smile flitted over Finzi's face. "We're pleased that you will consider that."

Then Benjamin ben Jehuda spoke, "Go in peace. We shall talk some more. Perhaps after a cleansing from Dona Esther we will have no more Father Leo or Bruno." Hayyim knew that some of the congregants faulted him for the diatribes and harangues of these friars. They had no idea that, whatever Hayyim's influence may have been in the past, his standing with the Pope was now in question. Nor did they grasp that the Pope's own authority was also under constant challenge. Few in the congregation could see the complexity of the times.

CHAPTER 24

Israel Held At Papal Palace

When Israel, out of breath and covered with sour sweat, arrived at the Papal Palace and told the Swiss Guards that Lady Isabella had been hurt, he was taken instantly to Carafa's chambers. The Cardinal immediately ordered a carriage to fetch her. "Make sure her lady-in-waiting accompanies you," he told the guards, "and take Isabella directly to her chambers. Send for Dr. Ludwig as well."

One of the Swiss Guards asked, "Shall this young man return with us to his family? He'll be safer with us at this late hour."

"No," said Carafa. "He'll stay with me."

"But I must go home. My parents are in great distress over what happened and need me there," protested Israel.

"Sit down." Carafa hissed, but Israel remained standing. The guards left and Carafa turned toward Israel. "I told you to sit down." Carafa spit out the words. "You committed this deed and yet you choose to come here?"

"What? What are you saying? I did nothing. I sought only to help the good lady."

At that moment Carafa seemed to catch himself and realized he needed to control his anger. With an effort he said almost in a whisper, "You will stay with us until you tell us the truth."

"I'm telling you the truth." Israel clenched his fists—a trick his father had taught him when he was younger and needed to control his anger.

"I told you to sit down." Carafa pushed him into a chair. "And stay seated."

Carafa pulled the bell cord and a young messenger came running.

"Send for Giarfolo," he commanded. The messenger's eyes darted from Carafa to Israel.

The messenger stammered, "You mean, Giarfolo, the jailer?"

"Of course, I mean Giarfolo, the jailer."

"But he comes up only when you want someone to be taken prisoner."

"Are you questioning me? Do as I say."

"Yes, sir."

The messenger scurried to the dungeon and urged the jailer, who had been dozing, to follow him.

Giarfolo, a hulk of a man with a misshapen nose and back appeared eagerly before Carafa and bent his large awkward frame to kiss the Cardinal's hand.

"Stand," said Carafa as he placed on a finger on his shoulder and pushed him away and then took a piece of linen from his cassock and wiped his hands. "Stop fidgeting and take this Jew to the dungeon."

Giarfolo nodded. "How long will he be there?"

"Take him, I said. He attempted to murder Lady Isabella and is pretending that someone else did the deed. We must all pray that she'll live, but we must know the truth. Take him away."

"That's not the truth," Israel said. He rose up from his chair and started to move toward Carafa.

Giarfolo grabbed Israel, bound his hands and his feet and carried him off over his shoulder through the corridor and down to the dungeon. When Israel shouted that this was "lawless and illegal," Giarfolo smashed Israel's head into the concrete wall. Israel lost consciousness.

When he awoke, his cries of pain could not be heard; the dungeon was deep in the depths of the Palace.

CHAPTER 25

Tragedy

Pope Paul lay in bed, his bedclothes and linen soaked in the perspiration brought on by summer heat. In spite of the high temperature, Paul had wrapped himself in a heavy down comforter and still felt a chill and a peculiar ache in his bones. Of late, he had been overcome with disconsolate feelings—a "dispiritedness" was the way he had described it to Carafa. Even the painting by Titian or the work done by Michelangelo on St. Peter's dome did not lift his spirits. He knew he must reform the Church. We cannot keep losing people to Luther.

"Yes? Yes?" he said when he heard a quiet knock on the door.

"Your morning dress, Your Holiness?" It was his servant, Vincent. "Not just yet. I'll call you when I am ready."

Paul needed time to collect his thoughts and wanted to have some private moments in his bedchamber. But he had an urgent need to relieve himself. He did so in the chamber pot, then pushed it under the bed, and climbed back in bed.

He sat up and put his head in his hands. "I will pray harder—more often. I need to ask God to give me the strength to deal with the world and its intrigues." This time, there was an urgent knock on the door.

"Can I not be left alone with my morning prayers?"

Carafa entered and sniffed the stale air. He also took in the half-finished portrait being painted by Titian.

Paul came down from his bed still in his bedclothes.

"Yes, what is it? What can be more important than my prayers? I have not dressed yet, nor has my servant emptied the chamber pot. What is the crisis?" said Paul.

Carafa placed his right hand to his chest.

"Isabella has been stabbed. We don't know the severity of her wounds. She is in her chamber."

Paul blanched and fumbled with his hands behind his back to find something to steady himself.

"You're not serious. I must see her immediately. Vincent, help me dress. Quickly," he called to the servant waiting outside the door. The Pope stepped behind a screen.

Vincent took the Pope's bedclothes as he removed them, then helped the Pope put on his cassock.

"When? Where? How could this happen right in this court?"

"She wasn't stabbed inside the court." Carafa continued. "She was stabbed in the alleyway outside the home of the Jew, your former physician. She was brought here immediately." He stopped for a breath. "We've been able to stem the bleeding."

"Why wasn't I called sooner? She could have died during the night without last rites." He hastily put on his hat. "Come, let us go."

"I was present all night. We felt that it was best that you have your rest."

"Do not decide for me when I need to rest. I should have been called. And Dr. Luzzatti? Is he in attendance?"

"We thought it best, considering the circumstances to have another physician present. Dr. Ludwig is with her. I also thought that Dr. Luzzatti was no longer welcome here." Paul turned to Vincent.

"Come with me," he said. Vincent followed as Carafa and Paul rushed down the corridor talking.

"Why, he doesn't have nearly the expertise of Dr. Luzzatti. Ludwig didn't study at Padua."

A silence ensued.

"She was stabbed right outside of the Jewish doctor's house. It didn't seem quite fitting that we ask him to tend to her needs," Carafa said.

"How can that be?" said Paul. "I had forbidden her."

"We understand that Dr. Luzzatti and his wife were inside, but we have brought their son, Israel, into our prison."

"Why, Israel Luzzatti?"

"He came to the palace to tell of the stabbing."

"And?"

"And we're not sure of his loyalty to the Church. He's been seen attending synagogue."

As Paul approached Isabella's apartment, he heard wailing from her chamber. "Enough of Israel Luzzatti," he said. He entered and saw her ladies in waiting and maids kneeling by the side of her bed weeping while Cardinal Alfonso read the last rites and placed a large cross on her forehead.

"Leave. Leave, all of you."

"But I've not finished." Cardinal Alfonso protested.

"I'll finish. I surely know what needs to be done to save her soul."

As Paul approached Isabella's beside, he spoke harshly, "Stop. I tell you, stop. Leave and let me be alone with her. That includes you, Carafa." Carafa blanched but backed out quietly. With Cardinal Alfonso in the lead, they others left and the chamber became silent. Paul knelt by Isabella's bedside, took her cold hand in his, and quietly wept. She was clearly slipping away.

He whispered, "I shall miss your wisdom and I shall miss your love of learning and sense of justice. I shall miss your love, yes, your love of our Church. You'll be honored. You'll be honored with a tomb that will bear your likeness and it will be placed in the Belvedere Chapel so that I may view it daily."

Isabella drew her final breath and Paul held her hand kissing it over and over again.

Pier Luigi and Ranuncio had entered quietly not wanting to disturb their father. Vincent put his finger to his lips when he saw them.

"Come, say good-bye to your mother." They both knelt at the bedside, bowed heads, praying together. They helped their father to sit in a chair.

"We knew that she could not survive that deadly assault, Father," said Pier Luigi. "We knew that as soon as she came to the Palace with that demon Jew, Israel, that she would be dead."

"What are you saying? About Israel?"

"We're saying that the man being held in the dungeon of the palace in chains is the killer of our mother," said Ranuncio.

"No, this can't be—not the son of my physician. I told this to Carafa—that it was ridiculous to think that it could be anyone in the Luzzatti family."

"We thought you wouldn't believe us, father," continued Pier Luigi. "We know that you want to believe of the best in people, but to that extent you are naïve."

"Naïve? Naïve? I'm the father to millions of people, not just to you, and I became their father not just because I loved the Church but because I understood when caution was needed and when caution was to be set aside. That is not naivete."

"I'm close to extracting a confession from him," Pier Luigi said. He could no longer contain his annoyance. "Do you want to see him or not?"

"You've already been with him? In the dungeon?" Paul grasped the side of the armchair.

"Yes," said Ranuncio. "You should see him. He should see you in your grief to know what pain he has caused."

"Say your good-byes again to your mother. There can't be too many prayers as she makes her way to heaven."

They both knelt on either side of their mother's bedside. Each took a hand in theirs and pressed it to their lips. All this was done under their father's sorrowful gaze. They did not give up their mother's hand until they peered up and saw a more tranquil expression on their father's face. They hoped this would comfort him.

"Come." The Pope put his hands on his sons' shoulders. "You'll have to lead me to the prison. I have not been down there in years. An abominable place."

"I'll lead the way," Pier Luigi said, and Ranuncio and the Pope followed. "We'll need candles as we approach the lower level."

"Vincent, please bring us some candles," Pier Luigi called. The servant pulled out a dozen candles from an armoire drawer, then went to a room where the fire was constantly lit and came back with two lighted candles and handed them to Pier Luigi.

"Do you wish me to accompany you, Your Holiness?" Vincent said.

"No, you stay. Don't permit anyone to enter my mother's chamber,"Pier Luigi answered.

Vincent nodded and watched as they left the room togther.

As the threesome made their way through corridors and down staircases, ladies-in waiting, guardsmen, and courtiers peered round columns and doors, all awaiting news of the drama that was unfolding.

"Be careful, Father," said Ranuncio. "Place your hand on my shoulder for support. The way is steep."

After they had climbed down countless stairs in what seemed like an interminable amount of time, Pier Luigi opened the door to a room that had only one narrow barred window high on a wall close to the ceiling. When his eyes adjusted to the light, Paul saw a figure of a young man lying on straw, his hands covering his face. He was so still he could have been dead. Pier Luigi walked over to him, kicked him so that Israel rolled over on his side.

"Get up, Jew. Get up, murderer of my mother. Acknowledge the Pope. Kneel before him and kiss his ring." Ranuncio stood behind his brother.

Israel dropped his hands from his face, and Paul stepped back with a shudder. Israel's face was covered with red welts and dried blood. He was lying in his own feces and urine, and his doublet, once of elegant silk, was covered with a combination of blood and vomit. Israel made an attempt to rise to his knees to approach the Pope, but even with an enormous effort, he fell back again onto his own filth.

Pier Luigi pushed him with his foot. "What, you can't rise for the Holy Father? Is it your weakness, your lack of conviction, or your guilt? Why don't you confess? You'll be granted your place in hell for confessors and repenters." Ranuncio put a restraining arm on his brother's shoulder.

Israel tried again shaking his head from side to side.

"What are you saying no to?" Pier Luigi practically shouted. "No, you do not want to rise for the Holy Father? No, to the death of our mother?"

Again Israel dropped back on the filthy straw pallet.

"Please, Pier Luigi. He's too weak to rise," Ranuncio said.

From behind them came the voice of Cardinal Carafa. "Perhaps he is just too weak willed."

"What are you doing here?" asked Ranuncio as he wheeled around.

"Trying to protect and advise your father," Carafa said whispering his response. "He's distraught by the death of Isabella, and cannot possibly think this through correctly to his advantage. I don't think the Jew should be left here to die."

Pier Luigi and Ranuncio looked surprised at Carafa's declaration but kept their eyes on their father's face.

"Someone should see that this man gets cleaned up and has some water and decent food," Paul said.

"Yes, Your Holiness. Of course," said Carafa. The Pope climbed the steps with weariness in his carriage and fatigue showing in his slow measured gait.

CHAPTER 26

Luzzatti Intercedes

Hayyim hurried on the path to the Papal Palace on foot. Alba had given her husband a bag of food with cold chicken, bread, and zucchini that he carried under his cloak. All Hayyim needed to do was to go and talk to Pope Paul, and it would all be explained away. He knew the Pope to be a rational man. He was certain the Pope knew that Israel could not be guilty. Would he be admitted to see if Isabella had improved during the night? Surely they would understand that he did everything humanly possible for her. He was a healer. Yes, his son was an apostate, but he was not a killer.

When Hayyim arrived at the palace gates, he saw Giovanni Batiste stare past him. "I have come to see my son, who is being held in the palace prison."

Joseph Frech acknowledged Hayyim with a nod, but no smile of friendship.

"We have been instructed to inform you that you are to report to the library of the Pope."

"Yes, that is what I must do first. See the Pope. Then my son." He walked down the corridor with the guard towards the Pope's chambers. He was sure that the news of his son's arrest and the alleged assault on Isabella had spread throughout the Vatican. When the guard came to the door of the library, he knocked.

"Yes?" a stern voice emanated from the room.

"I am here with the father of the prisoner," Frech said. Cardinal Carafa opened the door and addressed the guard. "Wait outside the door."

Cardinal Carafa took Hayyim by the elbow and whispered in his ear, "Address the Pope as you should. Pier Luigi and Ranuncio are watching as well."

The Pope moved just slightly to the left before Hayyim bent allowing the rabbi to kiss the floor where the Pope's feet had just been. As Hayyim bent, he saw the two brothers, folded arms across their chests, enigmatic grins on their faces. Where was their sorrow he wondered?

Carafa, right behind Luzzatti, whispered in his ear. "This time the Pope will see you for what you are. Was there ever a Jew who was not deceitful?" Hayyim looked up hoping the Pope would speak, but he was met with sorrow in the Pontiff's eyes.

The Pope seemed smaller and more stopped than usual. Paul barely raised a hand to acknowledge his visitor. Pier Luigi and Ranuncio stood slightly behind the chair on either side of him.

"First, I must ask how is Isabella?" No response. He searched for words that might bring some reaction.

"We had nothing to do with the stabbing of Isabella. I came today not only to find out about my son, but also to see if I can attend to your mother."

Hayyim looked to the Pope for some support, but the cleric remained unresponsive.

"Our mother is dead and we know that your son is the killer," Ranuncio said. Pier Luigi looked startled at his brother's aggressive statement.

Hayyim stared at Ranuncio. "No! She can't be dead! And my son is not the killer. He was in the house with us when the stabbing occurred."

"Do you have any witnesses other than you or your wife who could attest to that?" Ranuncio asked. Pier Luigi nodded.

"Preferably witnesses with *limpieza de sangre*," Ranuncio added.

Hayyim shuddered; he had not heard those words for a long time. They wanted someone without any history of Jewish blood.

"Do *you* have witnesses who saw Israel commit this terrible act?" he asked.

"They do indeed. They've shared that information with me," Carafa answered.

"May I know who it is? My son has the right to address his accuser."

"It's the woman, Esmeralda, who sells flowers at the end of your street," said Carafa.

"Why I buy flowers from an Esmeralda every Sabbath."

"I don't know about your Sabbath or whether you buy flowers from her or not, but she's Esmeralda, the flower woman," Pier Luigi said.

"Exactly, how much did you pay her in order to get her to say this terrible lie?" Hayyim exploded. "Besides, it was nighttime and Esmerela's not out in the evening."

Cardinal Carafa intervened. "You're not going to accuse the Pope's sons of bribing someone, are you? Who's going to believe you?"

Hayyim ignored Carafa's comment and stared directly at the two brothers, rage blazing in his eyes.

"I ask again. How much did you pay her? She has always waited for me every Sabbath to buy flowers, and she knows that I pay her with good coins."

Carafa took a step toward Hayyim and hissed, "It matters not. He confessed. Your son confessed."

Hayyim stared at him. "It can't be. No. It can't be." He looked to the Pope. Hayyim realized at that moment that it was useless to ask about the other witness.

The Pope stared at the floor and appeared to be hearing nothing.

"I want to see my son. I'm entitled to see my son." He added, "I also believe you're required to give him a trial."

"Let him see his son. Take him to the prison," Paul said to Carafa. "I'll take him, father." Ranuncio stepped forward.

Paul said, "No, let Cardinal Carafa take him down. There are things we must discuss in light of your mother's death."

"We'll take care of all the details concerning mother's death," Pier Luigi said.

"I'll decide on the details concerned with her burial," Paul said suddenly appearing attentive. "Now take the doctor to see the prisoner."

Hayyim ignored the smirk that he saw on Carafa's face but reluctantly followed him.

Cardinal Carafa led the way with Hayyim hurrying to keep up. "You'll need candles as it is quite dark down there." The Cardinal handed Luzzatti lit candles as they approached the staircase leading down to the dungeon. They wound their way down one staircase after another. It was hard for Luzzatti to keep Carafa in his sight because they followed the steep winding passage that was barely illuminated by the light of the candles.

"Are we getting close?" Luzzatti asked.

"You'll know when we're getting close." Carafa bristled. Suddenly an overpowering stench made both men cover their noses with their hands. Groans became louder as they drew closer.

"Israel. It's your father. I'm coming." Hayyim hurried passed Carafa.

"I suggest you wait as the door needs to be opened with a key." Carafa dangled the key.

Carafa opened the door to the cell and even with the candle in his hand, Hayyim's eyes needed to adjust to the darkness. In the gloom of the fetid gray dungeon, he saw the body of his son lying on a mat of straw.

Luzzatti bent to touch his son and covered his mouth to stem a cry when he saw his son's face dotted with black and blue welts and dried blood. He saw one of his hands shackled to the wall with a heavy iron chain.

Tears streamed down Luzzatti's face; he made no effort to stem them.

Israel pulled his father's ear down to his mouth. "Father, they've beaten me terribly."

"I know. I know, my son, but I'm here to help you."

"Father, they've beaten me until I confessed."

Hayyim could not grasp all that his son was saying. "What?" He put his head down closer to Israel's mouth. All Israel could manage was a whisper.

"I've confessed to Isabella's death."

"They can't accept a confession from torture. Let me see if you have any broken bones." He touched his son's chest, lifted his arms and legs carefully.

"My chest hurts terribly. It's hard to breathe."

"You probably have some broken ribs." He turned to Carafa. "Is this any way to treat a human being? Torturing a confession out of him?"

Luzzatti ripped a piece of cloth from his tunic and wrapped it around Israel's chest.

"I will secure your release as soon as possible. Are you more comfortable?"

Israel nodded.

"You're certain there will be a release? I think not. I think the Pope has other plans for him," said Carafa.

"I can't imagine that he won't free Israel...after I speak with him *privately*." Luzzatti continued to bind up his son's chest gently, turning him on his side to relieve him of some of the pain.

"Go, father. Speak to the Pope.Tell him I am a good Christian and serve him well. I would not harm anyone."

"You're feverish, my son. You don't know what you're saying." Hayyim turned to the Cardinal. "I must see the Pope."

"We'll first see if he is ready to see you."

"We must hurry. I must get him out of here and get him home for some rest and treatment. He will die here."

"He will not die here," said Carafa. "A killer needs a public death."

"No," shouted Hayyim. "The Pope will not allow it."

The two men retraced their route with the Cardinal leading the way from the depths of the palace to the Papal Library. As Hayyim climbed the steps, he formulated an argument in his mind to present to the Pope. He would tell the Pope that Israel could not have been guilty. He was inside the house with him and Alba all the time. Israel confessed because he was tortured. Hayyim prayed that the Pope would hear him out and recognize the truth.

As they approached the door, Batiste and Frech ignored him. He said, "My son is not guilty." They averted their eyes. "You see," he said to no one in particular. "I will free him."

Hayyim waited until the guards opened the door and entered boldly with Cardinal Carafa following. He did not pause to kiss the Pope's ring, but quickly bent down to kiss the floor where he assumed the Pope had just stood. The Pope was seated on a chair staring vacantly into space.

When Hayyim arose from his kneeling position, he spoke directly to the Pope. "Your Holiness. My son assures you that he is faithful to the Pope and his faith...that is, your faith." Hayyim tried to speak confidently and clenched his fists to keep his hands from trembling. "He could have nothing to do with Isabella's death. He was with Alba and me at the time of the stabbing."

The Pope folded his hands and rested his chin in its valley listening.

Hayyim continued. "There's someone in your court who wishes to lay the blame at the feet of my son, Israel. Is it possible there are those in your court who would gain from the death of Isabella, or who would gain by foisting the murder on a Jew?"

"Who would want her death? It cannot be imagined."

"Your Holiness, please. There are people here who are using my son so that they might gain favor with you."

"Impossible. Your son confessed and must be hanged."

Hayyim stared in disbelief. "But he was tortured. He confessed because he was tortured."

"If it were not true, God would not have allowed him to confess," said Carafa.

The Pope waved his hand imperceptibly.

"See that the hanging is merciful," the Pope said to Carafa.

The Pope sat impassively and Hayyim understood that with this thinking, talking, arguing, and appealing to logic would not work. He simply turned and left formulating plans for a rescue for his son. I can outthink and outplan them, he thought. Israel will be rescued.

CHAPTER 27

Congregation Plans a Rescue

Carafa left the Pope's chamber, glancing at Raphael's *Madonna and Child,* one of his favorite paintings. Michelangelo's latest work with its naked, tormented bodies was troubling for Carafa, but just thinking of Michelangelo and the writhing nudes brought about a memory of desire. He wanted Michelangelo to paint the old way, when he was less worried about salvation and damnation. Was Michelangelo trying to make a place for himself in heaven with this painting, "The Last Judgment?" That was it, wasn't it? Michelangelo was worried about eternal damnation.

Carafa opened the door to the small room off the Chapel, and found Justinian and Alfonso deep in conversation, referring to several open books on a long mahogany table.

"Ah, Carafa," said Justinian, looking up and placing his hand on his portly stomach. "We're just looking at pages of Church doctrine to see what they tell us about a Jew who has committed a murder against a Christian woman."

"The Pope has decreed that Israel will be hanged in the public square," said Carafa.

"We're just making sure that there was no law that could be used against us. The Doctor is as well versed in canon law as he is in Hebrew law," said Justinian. "And we want to make sure we are following the law."

"This is what they mean by reform in the church, isn't it?" asked Alfonso.

"Not necessary to brush up on your theology in this case, Justinian. The only effective weapon Luzzatti would have is proof of someone else killing Isabella," said Carafa.

"And it is Israel who killed her and has confessed," said Alfonso. He paused momentarily, peering over his eyeglasses at Carafa. "Correct? There are no other suspects?"

At that moment Justinian turned the pages of the huge book, stopping at one page and reading intently.

Carafa looked suspiciously at Alfonso. "You know something that should be shared? The Jew confessed."

Justinian looked up holding his finger on a particular paragraph. "We are simply checking. We need to be theologically correct." Justinian paused. "I remember a time when being theologically correct meant being morally correct."

'You can close the book, Justinian." Carafa said. "We're already making plans for the public execution. And it must be well publicized. Everyone must turn out for it. Especially the Jews."

"They'll resist," said Alfonso. "Some strongly. They will not see this as just."

"Our guards are loyal to us. In fact, they are loyal to anyone who has money," said Carafa. "You know that well, don't you Alfonso?"

"I was talking about justice, not loyalty," said Alfonso.

Alfonso took the book to another table. "I want to read now. Maybe I have a different interpretation of the Latin."

"Forget about the law." Carafa rubbed his hands together. "We'll immediately post notices on the door of every Jew's house in the community and notify them when the public hanging will be. We'll have the black hood prepared and the garrote will be of the strongest material."

Alfonso and Carafa exchanged glances, and Alfonso closed the book. "I guess law will come later," Alfonso said.

* * *

Luzzatti rushed home.

As Hayyim approached his front steps, he saw that Alba had washed the blood away. Inside, she was sweeping rapidly even though there wasn't a crumb or speck of dust on the floor. She put the broom against the wall when she saw Hayyim. "Tell me what has happened to Israel."

"Isabella has died. The stab wound was very deep," he said quietly.

"No," she put her hand to her mouth. "Where's Israel? Why isn't he here?"

He hesitated.

"Hayyim, what is it?"

"Israel has confessed to the killing. He was tortured." She sat on the nearest chair.

"They're planning to hang him in the public square," he continued. He paced while she sat with two hands hugging her cheeks.

"The Pope?" she asked.

Hayyim took her hands from her mouth and held them tightly against his chest.

"The Pope himself told me that it would be done."

"How? How could he do that? What's happened to your friendship with him? Your good care?"

"He is getting older and the upcoming Council of Trent weighs heavily on him."

He released her hands.

"Is it his sons?"

"Perhaps. But Carafa more than ever seems to have undue influence over him. But I have a plan to rescue him."

"A plan? What kind of plan?" Alba said.

"Come we must go to the synagogue," Hayyim said. "We'll need help." Alba drew a shawl around her head. "I'll explain when we get there."

He refrained from telling her how tired he was and that he was not sure how the synagogue would greet this news. He had not told her of his encounter with Finzi and DiBelli— a meeting of the gobierno to excommunicate Israel, they told him.

He carefully adjusted his wife's shawl to make sure her hair was covered.

They hurried to the synagogue in silence, carefully stepping on the uneven cobblestone streets to maintain balance and avoid the slop that was left from the day's waste from each household.

At the synagogue, the men were reciting their prayers. When they saw the rabbi enter with his wife, they looked up and stopped.

"What's this?" said Samson di Constantini, a devout Jew, who looked pointedly at Alba. "You know your wife cannot pray with us."

Squeezing Alba's hand to silence her, Hayyim spoke. "I'm not here to pray." He scrutinized di Constantini. 'You've heard nothing?"

David Morpurgo, the butcher in the community who took pride in his precise koshering of meat, replied, "We're here to pray. What is it?"

"I'll be brief," said Hayyim. "Israel is a prisoner at the Palace. They are going to hang him—publicly. Isabella Farnese was stabbed outside our doorway." Several men gasped. "She died this morning and Israel has been accused." Hayyim watched their faces as they tried to grasp the significance of his words.

"Your wife should not have been consorting with gentiles," said di Constantini.

Hayyim took a deep breath. "Israel went to the palace to report the stabbing of Isabella and was arrested, placed in prison, tortured, and...and he confessed." Before Hayyim could continue, Shimon Shimoni said, "I knew it. I knew that apostate would bring disgrace upon us."

"He confessed? How could he confess if he was not guilty?" di Constantini asked.

"They tortured him," said Joseph Flammetta, an older congregant. "We remember stories of our families being tortured in Spain, and then Portugal, just for being Jewish."

"Yes," said Hayyim, "And it's written in the Talmud that a confession to anything under torture cannot be taken for truth."

Some of the men began to recite the Shema. "Hear, O Israel, the Lord our God is One." Others kissed the end of their prayer shawls. Others began to beat their chests and rock back and forth in prayer.

Hayyim waited till it was quiet again. "I have a plan to free our son. We will bribe the guards and the condotierri who are to bring Israel to the public square...for his hanging. There, we'll have a horse waiting for him."

"That is preposterous," said di Constantini. "A plan for an apostate."

"He wasn't removed from our community. He is still one of us," said Morpurgo.

"How do we know, he was not guilty?" argued Constantini.

Hayyim glared at him. Alba started to speak but Hayyim interrupted. "He is not guilty. He is being framed."

"He was in the house," Alba added.

Moses Bascola, a silk trader and wise in financial and military matters, also had a son who was a converso, finally spoke.

"You'll need enough ducats to bribe at least ten men. Then money for a horse. Then money to pay people to hide Israel."

"You're right," said Hayyim. "I will guarantee success, but I can't do it without financial support from this congregation." He waited for someone to say something.

"Some of you have done well in the silk trade, in tailoring, and in banking," he added.

"You'll see." Bascola looked around. "Because of this act of Israel's, they'll tax us more. That has always been their response. *Tax the Jews.*" Bascola looked around to see if anyone accepted his words.

Abramo Zefarti spoke. "It must be done. We must use our money and our ingenuity to prevent this injustice. The courts will not treat us fairly."

"You are new here. You're not in a position to speak," said Flammetta.

"I am a Jew who escaped torture," said Zefarti. "You've all forgotten what it means to be pressured under torture. Go back to the graves of our parents and ask them." Zefarti's face reddened.

Some of the men shifted in their seats embarrassed at Zefarti's scolding. They had not had much contact with Zefarti since his arrival from Spain, and most had been suspicious and unwelcoming.

Di Constantini glared at Zefarti in disbelief. "You'd give your resources to a Jew who has renounced his faith?"

"You have no idea," Zefarti looked at each man, "what it is like to live under the rule of an Inquisitor. Someone who looks to see if your blood is 'tainted' because you had a Jewish great-grandmother and then you lose your right to your land, to your work. What would you do as a man to protect your family?"

Silence met his pointed question.

"You've lived with a Pope who has encouraged your commerce—a Pope that has let you live your lives as Jews. You've not known another kind of life," Zefarti continued.

Alberto Finzi put his prayer book aside. "But Israel is no longer a Jew."

"I agree with Finzi," DiBelli said.

"You are in no position to argue—you and your trading with Cardinal Alfonso," Zefarti said.

Finzi started to protest.

"Never mind. We know," Moses Bascola waved his hand. "I'm convinced. With a contribution from everyone, no one will be giving up everything. We'll have enough to bribe the guards."

Senor Zefarti said, "I can assure you of my financial help."

And so it went on for an hour or more with opinions offered from everyone about the most complicated issue the community had ever dealt with—a public hanging, a rabbi's son who had converted and confessed to a crime, a plot to avoid the execution, bribery, a collection of funds. Who would ever have thought that their little community would have to face problems as complicated as these?

Finally, Hayyim signaled to Alba that she should go to the women's section. As she climbed the stairs to the balcony, he said, "We must pray and read the Torah chapter for the day. We will do it quickly because there is a human life at stake." He moved the *yad*, the pointer, to the appropriate passage in Deuteronomy and intoned the Hebrew rapidly. "When you enter the land your God is giving you, you shall not learn to imitate the abhorrent practices of those nations." The chanting and the swaying continued until a final quiet "Amen," and then Shimon Shimoni asked, "Do we save a soul the only way we can? Do we let a man die who does not deserve to die?"

Alba held her breath as she watched the drama unfold from the small balcony where women sat.

Shimoni continued, "I take the congregation's silence as assent. We shall wait for the Sabbath to end and meet this evening at my house. Until then we are sworn to silence. It's agreed?"

Finzi and DiBelli and said nothing.

The other men carefully folded their tallit and placed them in embroidered velvet bags, placed their prayer books in a slot in front of the pew, and filed out to go to their homes where they would have a meal that had been prepared the day before and kept warm over the hearth.

"Will you all be there to contribute?" Luzzatti asked. "It says in the Torah, we have to save a life."

"They'll be there," Shimoni said.

"I'm not sure," said Zefarti.

"An extra prayer, then, gentlemen," Luzzatti said.

The rest filed out in silence.

CHAPTER 28

Raising Money

That evening, Senor Zefarti was the first to arrive at Shimoni's house and Hayyim embraced him. The other men arrived one by one and sat on long benches in silence. Shimoni's wife entered quietly and placed lit candles around that cast shadows on the men's somber faces. Constantine wrapped his tallis around his shoulders as he sat next to Zefarti. They exchanged no words. Hayyim took a place in the middle of one of the benches.

"I hoped you did not rush through Havdalah, gentlemen," Constantine said. "We could do some singing here."

"No. We need to save a life," Hayyim said. That should take precedence."

Flammenta, Morpurgo, Finzi, and diBelli were not there.

Luzzatti stood and addressed the men. "There are two Swiss Guards to bribe and eight members of the condotierri who will be in charge of taking Israel from prison, putting his shackled body into a horse-drawn wagon, and parading him through the streets to the public square. One will have a horse to take the decapitated body..."

A shudder ran through him at that point.

"...through the streets after the hanging to make sure that everyone in the city of Rome gets to see this terrible deed. But it's not going to happen. That horse is to take the body through the streets that will ultimately take Israel to safety."

Shimoni was the first to speak. "Where is he to go? How far away can he get with a horse?"

Luzzatti hoped his voice conveyed authority. "He's to go to the abbey of Father Bruno." This was the only place he could think of where Israel could possibly be safe until he was well enough to travel. Hayyim remembered Bruno's words "...if there's any other way I can help..."

The men began to murmur among themselves.

"How can you put any faith or trust in Father Bruno?" All eyes were on Moses Bascola. "Are we raising this money to rescue a Jew or to send someone into the clutches of a devil?"

"Father Bruno and his fellow brothers are grateful for my cures. They are willing to take Israel into their care and hide him until he can safely leave for....Well, at this point, I'm not sure where he would be safe, but that will come."

"You are sure they will keep him safe?" Zefarti asked.

"I'm sure," Hayyim lied. He had to say something to get their support and rely on his instinct that Father Bruno would not deny him protection of his son.

"If this is the plan, this is what we must support," Zefarti said.

Bascola shrugged. "I'm not sure, but I gave my word. What do you say to one hundred ducats for each guard?"

"That won't do it." Zefarti rose.

"Two hundred fifty ducats, then," said Bascola.

Luzzatti interjected. "Papal authority can give the guards and condotierri more and will give them more, especially for an event as important as....as this hanging."

"What is it you'll suggest, Rabbi?" asked Moses.

"It's with much heaviness in my heart that I propose an amount that will be a burden for the community, but I am confident that's the amount necessary to save my son. It must be five hundred ducats for each of those involved."

"But that is more than we can afford," protested Shimon Benjamin rather sharply. "Besides it is such a risky business."

"Yes," chimed in Bascola. "How trustworthy will the guards be once they receive their money?"

"And there's more," said Shimoni. "Father Bruno, really?"

"I don't know that we have those resources in the community," continued Benjamin.

Senor Zefarti interjected proudly, "I have the resources to help. I came with diamonds, and if we can get those diamonds sold, they'll translate into large sums of ducats for us."

Shimon, ever the businessman, responded, "Then it's settled. Samuel Gootfreund is here from Holland. He's staying with me and my wife this week for he didn't want to eat where there is no attention paid to kashrut." Shimon gave a meaningful glance to those members that he knew put butter on their table next to their meat.

Hayyim thought that he should intervene before an argument took place that detracted from the important business at hand.

"I'll prepare a sermon on the importance of maintaining a kosher home—next week. I assure you. I'm sure God wants us to concentrate first on this horrible crime being committed against my son. Wasn't the binding up of Isaac the most important business that God thought needed attention? We'll talk of kashrut later. Now we must talk of this man who is here from Holland who can be a savior."

Shimon Shimoni returned to the task at hand. "As I said, my cousin, Samuel is always looking for diamonds. Of good quality, of course. If Zefarti is willing to give up those diamonds, then we'll have the money."

Bascola interjected. "We're all aware that our decision is fraught with many dangers. Many dangers." But then as an afterthought of encouragement, he added, "Still, it won't be the first time that the Jewish people have been in dangerous situations. Martyrdom isn't an option for us. *L'dor v dor.* From generation to generation. We need generations to come to continue our history."

"Now that we have the money issue solved, we must get on with the planning. Who's to talk to the guards? How's the money to be transferred? How are we assured of the loyalty of everyone?" asked Benjamin.

Bascola was energized. "The abbey—the arrangements need to be made at the abbey. And the horse—we must not forget about the horse. It must be one of the fastest horses around."

Hayyim breathed a sigh of relief. "We'll use Giacomo."

It was done. The community would help with the money. Now, it would be up to him to gather those around him who could help with the plan. What should he do first? Go to the abbey? Talk to the guards? Visit Israel to give him hope. Not tell him of the plan. He could be tortured. Just a visit—maybe he could get some good food to him.

Hayyim stood. "I thank you with all my heart for what you are doing. I know it's a sacrifice, but it will be a sacrifice that will show the way of courage for generations to come. Now return to your families and greet them with ardor and joy after the Sabbath."

Hayyim needed to meet with Father Bruno as quickly as possible. He hoped that Father Bruno remembered his promise.

CHAPTER 29

A Ride to the Monastery

Hayyim rose the next morning at dawn and said his morning prayers with extra fervor, taking time to wind the leather phylacteries with precision. He wanted God to especially hear his prayers today. He had not been to the abbey since he had helped Father Bruno. Was he still in good health? Hayyim was trusting his instincts that the man was being truthful when he said he would help. He knew it was a hard thing to explain—that the man who had heaped so much abuse on his synagogue would now come to its aid, but Hayyim had decided to take that leap of faith.

"Well, Giacomo. We're in for a lifesaving ride," said Hayyim as he saddled up his horse. Giacomo whinnied in anticipation.

The horse stood patiently while Hayyim adjusted the tack. As Hayyim mounted the animal, he whispered in his ear, "Take me quickly to the abbey." Hayyim sat tall and urged Giacomo on with his strong legs and sure hands. Never once did he use the whip that was tucked into the side of the saddle. As soon as he got to the edge of the city, he galloped through woods and over streams, not really seeing the luxuriant, abundant flora of the forest, until he and the horse arrived at the courtyard of the abbey. Giacomo, panting hard, was soaked with perspiration. Hayyim led his horse to the water trough, gave him the apple that was in his pocket, and tied him to a post.

He patted the horse's neck. "Thank you, my dear friend. Wish me luck."

Hayyim approached the thick wooden door of the abbey—dignified in its austerity—no figures were carved on the door. Inside Hayyim heard melodious chanting of Latin

168

prayers. He knew others must be copying books; they excelled at the writing of illuminated manuscripts.

Luzzatti rang the bell that hung at the side of the door. When there was no response, Hayyim pulled the chain much harder in order to be heard above the cadenced chanting. Above the singing, Hayyim heard footsteps come toward the door. The door opened slightly and a short, rotund brother, dressed in a long dark-brown robe with a cowl that nearly covered his face, peered at him.

"Ah, Dr. Luzzatti, I'm surprised to see you. No one is sick right now," he said as he opened the door wider.

"I'm pleased that you recognize me, Father Gregorio. I've come here on a very different mission. I hope I can see Father Bruno."

"We're just ending our prayers. If you'll wait here in the anteroom, I'll inform Father Bruno. I'm sure he'll be happy to see you. He talks often of your healing powers."

Hayyim stepped inside, trying not to show his anxiety to the man, trying to quiet the voices of doubt in his head. To lessen the agitation, he paced back and forth from one end of the anteroom to the other. Fortunately, the room was at least four meters long so it gave him enough walking space. He stopped when he realized that the chanting had ended and he heard the sound of shuffling footsteps of friars returning to their cells. Father Bruno opened the door.

He clasped his large hands around Hayyim's. "Ah, Rabbi Luzzatti, I'm happy to see you. Since you have been here, we have expanded our garden to include wood sorrel, snakeroot, garlic, elder bark..."

"I haven't come here to discuss medicine with you, although I'm happy that your garden has expanded to include these herbs. I've come for another reason."

"Then if you haven't come to see the garden, come with me to the library and we can see the latest illuminated manuscript that Brother Adelmo has copied. It should please you for it's being written in Hebrew." He added, "Hebrew has always had a special fascination for me as a way to reach God." He paused. "You really understand that, don't you? I came to your synagogue to save myself and this monastery—not to harm your people."

"Yes, that is why I'm here today. I think you understand compassion reaches God—not hate. I've come here not to discuss manuscripts or medicinal plants." Hayyim had put his hand on Father Bruno's arm. "I've come to discuss the plight of my son, Israel." The friar gazed at the doctor, trying to decipher the agitation he heard in his voice.

"It must trouble you, I imagine, knowing that your son has disavowed his own religion. It's like disowning one's family. Isn't it? It must be terrible pain for you and your wife."

Hayyim interrupted him. "It's apparent that you haven't heard the news."

"News comes to us slowly here. As we are thirty kilometers from Rome, it sometimes takes weeks for us to get information."

"Then you haven't heard that Isabella was stabbed outside the doorway our home."

Father Bruno made the sign of the cross and then bowed his head.

"I pray for her soul."

Father Bruno looked at Hayyim. "But what has this to do with your son, Israel?"

Hayyim bowed his head. He didn't know how to begin to explain what happened for it seemed so painful and so impossible at the same time.

"Come." The friar led Hayyim to a nearby bench. "You can speak honestly with me." Just then one of the brothers ran up breathlessly to Father Bruno, but Bruno waved him away.

Hayyim took a breath and spoke rapidly but steadily. "My son, Israel, is in the papal prison. He rode to the palace to tell them of Isabella's stabbing that took place outside our home. They threw him into a filthy cell. And, what is worse, the torturers extracted a confession from him, and they plan to hang him in the public square." Hayyim inhaled sharply.

Father Bruno furrowed his brow.

"I have a plan and it involves you and your monastery, so I hope it will meet with your approval. We plan to seize Israel as he is being taken to the public square, where it will be crowded. I know that Carafa especially wants as many people as possible to see this event to prove the power of the Church. The Jews are all required to come, and for the first time in a long time, they're to be identified with a yellow circle of fabric."

Hayyim waited, thinking that Father Bruno might want to say something. As Father Bruno remained quiet, Hayyim continued.

"After we free him, we want to bring him here." At those words, Father Bruno looked startled, but Hayyim continued to talk almost afraid to take a breath. "We need you to hide him." Then in an additional rush, Hayyim said, "He can wear the abbey's garments, he knows your prayers. He'll fit in."

Father Bruno finally spoke. "Won't they follow you?"

"We have enough money to bribe the Swiss Guards and I'm sure they will hold back."

"So the loyal Swiss Guards can be bribed?" When Bruno saw Hayyim's questioning look, he added, "Paul always assured me of the loyalty and devotion of the Guards, so I'm a bit surprised."

Hayyim went on. "It's being done with much money from our community. Money that will make us poorer. Some of us will even go hungry for a while...but it's money that'll be used to save a life."

"You know I hold you in high esteem—you saved my life—but this is a very dangerous request you're asking of us. We're still dependent on funds from the Palace to help us with our care of the poor. Should they find your son here, it'll be a matter of great danger." He rose and held out his hands to Hayyim. "I'll have to discuss it with the rest of the brothers here, and I'll give you my answer tomorrow."

"There's not much time," pleaded Hayyim. "We risk danger by having this plan exposed to more people."

"You know, I'm expected to convert the Jews—not take care of their children." When Bruno saw Hayyim's pained expression, he said, "I meant that only with irony. Come back tomorrow and I'll have an answer for you."

"I'll return tomorrow." Hayyim stood. "I'm at your mercy."

"Come, my good doctor. I'll walk you out. I'd like to see your famous horse."

As they walked out, an observer would have seen two figures of approximately equal height and bearing with only the flowing garment of the friar creating an outline of difference to the man at his side who wore a velvet doublet over pantaloons. Two humans engaged in daily struggle of life against the drama of events being played out around them. Because of the warmth of the day, the rabbi only had a small skullcap on his head and Bruno had let the hood of his garment fall to his shoulders as though to capture the last of the sun's rays on his bare head. As they approached Giacomo, the horse snorted and pawed the ground.

"He's anxious to go." As Luzzatti approached the horse, he whispered. "Have you prayed, my good friend, for Israel?

Father Bruno smiled. "I thought you were such a rationalist. I couldn't imagine you asking a horse to pray."

Hayyim shrugged. "I must rely on wit, rationality, and prayer to help my son. Giacomo, as I will, will do anything within his means to help."

"Then we must use him for the escape."

Hayyim turned to Bruno eagerly. "Are you saying then that you will help?"

Father Bruno caught himself. "I must talk to the brothers first. They need to agree. We have come to depend on each other."

"Of course, I understand. If you have news for me, please send a messenger." He suddenly took Bruno's hand in his and bent to kiss it. "Thank you."

"Don't thank me yet," said Father Bruno. His face clouded. "Travel safely, my good friend. Travel safely."

Hayyim mounted his horse and, because he sensed Giacomo was eager to take off, began to gallop immediately. The rabbi did not notice Father Bruno make the sign of the cross then fold his hands in prayer.

CHAPTER 30

The Friars Decide

Father Bruno left the anteroom of the priory, noted the fading sunlight. "Getting close to the evening meal," he thought. "Should I meet with the good brothers now or wait until their stomachs are full?" He decided to convene them later. Let them make the decision after the evening meal. He had been taught by Paul that good decisions are best made on a full, not rumbling stomach aching for food. He thought back to the time when Paul was full of generosity and goodness and always urged him to work for salvation with good deeds. This conversation with the friars was certainly going to be difficult for him and strange for them.

Like most abbeys, the priory was built like a cross, with shorter north and south corridors traversing longer corridors to the east and west. Between each cell a narrow arched opening allowed sunlight and air to enter and was cool during the summer heat but much too cold during the winter. To reach each friar's cell as quickly as possible, Father Bruno walked the north, east, west, and south corridors in that order, knocked at the door of each cell with the message, "We'll be meeting in the great room immediately after the evening meal. Please be prompt."

And they were. All thirty friars arrived to take their seats in the sparsely equipped hall. Its high, vaulted ceiling with internal buttresses added to the dignity of a room furnished only with tables and benches made of pine. Because of the summer heat, the fireplace was empty and dormant.

Father Bruno took his place in front to address the expectant brothers. "We shall begin with prayer, asking for wisdom in a difficult and complex situation." They bowed their heads. *Pater Noster, qui es in caelis, sanctificetur nomen tuum adveniat regnum tuum...sed libera nos a malo.* Several of the brothers glanced at one another wondering what this complex and difficult situation was all about. At the end of the prayer all thirty of them lifted their heads in anticipation. Many of the brothers had asked to come here and work with Father Bruno for he had a reputation for having a generous spirit and a desire to make the world comfortable for the poor and sick. They were glad to have him back from Toledo.

"We need to hide someone for a period of time." Father Bruno's tremulous voice was so low that many had to strain in order to hear him. "We must treat that person as a brother and...and one of you will have to leave. Should anyone come to visit, they'll see that we are still thirty men still living in harmony."

No one moved. Father Bruno continued, his voice growing stronger and surer.

"I'm sure you all remember Rabbi Luzzatti, the good doctor who gave me such attention that he was able to cure me from my wretched bowel problems. His excellent knowledge of herbs was such that we are growing those here now." He frowned. "Some of you were not so pleasant towards him with your commentary and did not treat him as I would have wished. I hope you will pray for more compassion."

"They're wonderful herbs. We've even used some in our cooking and we can see that our digestive systems have improved." Adelmo, who was in charge of the garden, loved every opportunity to speak about what he was doing. "Much less gas. Amazing that it is coming from a Jew."

One or two brothers let out a chuckle but Justin spoke quickly, "Yes, they are not to be trusted to do such good work."

Father Bruno sighed. How hard it is to change bad thoughts. He hated to think that this is what the church promulgated. He had nightmares of his demonic foray into the synagogue to demonstrate his allegiance to the church.

"Are you truly asking one of us to leave? We who have devoted so much time here and are such brothers to one another?" Brother Bart, who had hunched forward, hesitated before he continued, but he saw he had everyone's attention. "How could one of us leave and allow a stranger to be in our midst? The praying, the garden, the care of the sick, our manuscript books. You cannot allow a stranger in just to..." His voice trailed off when Father Bruno raised his hand in a gesture of supplication.

"You know I wouldn't do this unless I felt that our Church was in crisis and that we who are true believers must extend the Church's goodness. The Council of Trent will come around to our way of thinking, but it will take many years." He looked at the brothers' earnest yet skeptical faces. "Lady Isabella was stabbed outside the house of the doctor and died of the stab wounds within the palace. When their son, Israel, went to the Palace to inform them, they imprisoned him, and tortured him to confess. The papal authorities want to hang Israel in the public square this coming week. Dr. Luzzatti is planning a rescue and wants his son to stay here until he can be smuggled out to Spain."

The monks murmured among themselves. "Isabella? Isabella dead? Dr. Luzzatti's son?"

"This is truly complicated," Adelmo spoke. "Not only are you asking us to take someone whose devotion to the faith is uncertain, but you're asking one of us to leave—to go far away from our home."

"It's not the first time we have been asked to leave. How many of us have been asked to go to this land they call the New World where there are people who worship snakes and walk around with barely a cloth to cover their bodies?" Friar Prior had been trained in the rigors of theological debate, and had some knowledge of the outside world. He preened with self-satisfaction as he spoke.

"So are you volunteering to leave?" It was Adelmo.

"I didn't say that," said Father Prior turning a bright shade of red.

"I'll go. I'll go so that Israel may come here and live among us." Father Nicolas, who had been sitting alone on a bench in the back stood up and spoke quietly. All eyes turned toward this man so tall that his giraffine neck had become stooped from the years of bending under all these short doorways. At sixty, he appeared older, with his shock of platinum hair that hung down to his back. His eyes were set deep in the sockets of his elongated face, and his cassock hung limply over his tall, thin frame. His most recent illness had taken its toll. "My time on this earth is not much longer, and I am sure that God will recognize my leave-taking here as an act of piety and scoop me up to heaven."

A smile appeared on the faces of some of the men at the mention of the word "scoop," but those smiles quickly disappeared when Father Agincourt said in a brittle voice, "You need to die among us. The best way to prepare for death is to die among your brethren to be assured of a proper Christian burial."

"No," said Father Nicolas. "I shall return to my family in Portugal. "Besides," he smiled slightly, "you know my background—a converso family when they decided that conversos were no longer welcome in Spain and would be subject to the Inquisition. I, luckily, came to Italy and found my true calling—the care of the sick and unfortunate—and found all of you. But it's time for me to return to my family. They'll welcome me back, I'm sure. It's only right that I leave and that Rabbi Luzzatti's son takes my place. So...it seems that this is the plan that God wants. Why else would he have given me this illness that shortens my time here on earth?"

By this time, the room was almost in complete darkness and two of the friars walked around bringing fire to the candles. Father Bruno saw concern in the expressions of the men as the light flickered across their faces. Finally Adelmo spoke, "It's not his faith I am worried about. It's the trouble that will be heaped upon us should we be found out. Do you realize the danger in this ...in this plot?"

"Aren't we accustomed to danger? The danger of not doing the Lord's wishes and therefore being relegated to the Inferno?" Agincourt spoke that last word with emphasis, for he was in the process of copying Dante's *Divine Comedy*. In spite of its importance and that it had been written nearly two hundred years ago, the abbey did not own the book, and Agincourt was determined that all should read it and be aware of its contents. Dante's tale from Purgatory and Paradise to the Inferno made Agincourt acutely aware of the virtuous acts that needed to be performed on this earth. He continued, "It will be a good deed, perhaps the best deed that we have done, to rescue a man that may have been falsely accused. Now what is it we have to do to prepare?"

No one responded. Father Bruno said, "Shall we pray, and then you offer me your decision?"

Father Nicolas drew a long breath. "I suggest that we return to our individual cells to be silent with our thoughts and our prayers and return to Father Bruno when we first sight the moon."

Father Bruno looked over the serious faces of the men. "I'll wait here for your return and pray and search my soul as well." The brothers stood as one and left in an orderly single file.

Sometimes Father Bruno wondered how this all had come about. Was it a miracle that these men could rise in unison, then proceed to walk out together without an overt signal from anyone? Would another miracle happen? He started to pace. Only he did not do so in a back and forth motion; instead, he walked a circle around each of the six tables that seated five of the friars at mealtime. He did that ten times and in the middle of the eleventh turn, the men started to file back. Father Bruno completed his circuit and took his place at the front of the enormous dining hall. The brothers then took their seats and waited.

Father Nicolas stood. Father Bruno was aware that he was holding his breath.

"We'll accept Brother Israel here on the condition that he truly becomes one of us and lives with us for at least thirty days. In thirty days we feel that we can make a good friar of him and he can then decide if he is to return to Spain. If he returns to Spain, we know that he will be all the more convinced of his Catholic faith." Father Nicolas spoke in a firm voice.

"And you, Father Nicolas? What will you do?" Father Bruno looked with love and sympathy upon this man.

"I'll leave on the same day that Israel is brought here, and he'll become Father Nicolas. I'll be honored. I'll need a horse and some provisions to ride out of here quickly and I'll plan to stop at various abbeys along the way. I know I'll be welcomed and accepted."

"Then, may I report this to Dr. Luzzatti?"

"Yes, please do and if he will accept our conditions, Israel Luzzatti will be more than welcome here."

"I shall be ready to ride to the doctor's house tomorrow. God bless you all."

CHAPTER 31

An Intricate Plot

No longer welcome at the Papal Palace, Hayyim had more time to practice medicine for neighbors. They were coming to see him with boils, distended stomachs, aching feet, bent backs, and a huge variety of coughs—some deep and throaty, some nasal and whiny. They came, both Christian and Jew. Each time he offered herbs and advice, each patient knew they would also be given some borage tea and some of Alba's bread with a cube of cheese. No one came on Friday afternoons and Saturdays because they respected the family's Sabbath.

If he were not treating a patient, his head filled with thoughts of his son in prison and the threat of public hanging. When Alba put homemade bread and tomatoes fresh from the garden in front of him, he hardly noticed.

"Please eat something, Hayyim. You need your energy. Not eating while waiting for a response from Father Bruno does you no good."

He looked at his wife's pinched face and tired eyes. "You aren't sleeping well. This is an ordeal for both of us." He reached out to caress her cheek.

Alba spoke, trying to keep the tears from welling up.

"What we must be concerned about is that Giacomo will be in good condition for the escape, and that we'll raise the money. At times I have dreams that one of the Swiss Guard will betray us." She looked at him. "It's possible. Isn't it?"

He frowned. "Only God knows what is possible and what is not. We simply must do the best we can and have faith. First we must wait for a word from Father Bruno to see what the members of his abbey have said, and then hope that no one among them will betray us."

Alba went and fetched him a cup of water that she had drawn from the bucket. She added a slice of orange. "Drink this."

As she handed him the beverage, he raised the palm of her hand to his mouth and kissed it. She shuddered with pleasure and said, "Drink, please."

They were both startled by the knock at the door. "It could be Father Bruno," said Hayyim.

Alba did not voice what was on her mind. She was worried that her husband had placed his trust in Father Bruno so easily. She knew him from his terrible tirade at the synagogue and what Hayyim had told her of Bruno's gratitude at her husband's care. Could one trust such a person?

Hayyim rushed to the door and slid open the tiny window door that allowed one to see outside. It was Father Bruno. Hayyim quickly opened the door.

"Please come in." Hayyim motioned him in to the vestibule of the house. Alba moved silently to the kitchen. She could not bear to acknowledge this man but wanted to remain within earshot.

The two men exchanged no handshakes. Hayyim knew that Alba would be disturbed if he offered the friar the comfort of a chair so they stood awkwardly in the small space.

"I've come with good news. The friars of the abbey are in agreement that we'll give your son, Israel, a safe haven. Father Nicolas has agreed to leave, and we will make arrangements for him to return to his family in Portugal."

Hayyim tried to control the joy and relief that were making his heart dance.

"Then what will happen when Israel is ready to leave to return to Spain?"

Father Bruno furrowed his brow. "We will cross that bridge when we come to it. In the meantime, we can assure you that your son will be well cared for and, most importantly, well hidden."

"I'm grateful for your kindness." Hayyim bowed.

"We're both about the business of saving lives...and souls," Father Bruno said. "You in your way and me in mine," he added.

Hayyim Luzzatti was impatient. "The public hanging is to take place in two days. I'm permitted one more visit to my son, at which time I'll explain all the details to him and have the money ready for the Swiss Guards. Go and may God be with you."

"And with you," Father Bruno said.

"I'll go immediately to the synagogue to see if all the monies have been gathered."

As Father Bruno was about to leave, Hayyim extended his arms and the men wrapped their arms about each other.

"May the God that is always with you continue to be with you," said Hayyim, as though he were blessing a member of his congregation.

"I'll pray for your success," Father Bruno said.

Hayyim walked to the kitchen where Alba was busy preparing a pot of vegetable soup even though there were already three jars in the cupboard. She looked up at her husband when he came into the room.

"It's done. Israel will have a place to hide after his rescue."

"And you trust Father Bruno and the friars at the abbey?"

"We have no choice, my dear wife. No other alternative. We cannot let Israel stay in that prison and this altogether too risky plan needs much help from many people and God. I'm on my way to the synagogue to collect the money and hand it over to the Swiss Guards."

"I'll go with you."

He took her in his arms and planted kisses all over her face, excited about the plan that would release Israel and delighted with his wife's spirit.

"No," he whispered into her ear. "It's not wise to have a woman there at this meeting. It's a meeting about money—it's not a time for prayer."

She drew away, and he saw her scowl.

"You stay here and advise my patients. Many respect your wisdom about herbs from the garden and will want to discuss that with you while they wait for me. They'll also be able to see your practices of cleanliness, and we all know that is sorely needed in many of these households."

"No one is likely to come and all I will do here is worry," she said. "I should be with you."

"No," he said. "Not this time. I need you here."

After she walked quickly to the kithen, Hayyim could hear her banging the ladle against the sides of the cooking pot.

* * *

Hayyim left with only a ledger book in hand, leaving his tallit and prayer book on the stand in his study, and walked the few blocks to the synagogue. He paused every few minutes to wipe the sweat from his face and then carefully tuck the piece of linen in his doublet. He had never been involved in anything where such danger was possible and lives were in the balance. He acknowledged neighbors in the streets with a brief nod, the blacksmith hitting the anvil to hammer out a horseshoe, the beggars, Esmerelda selling flowers on the street. Normally, he would stop to have a few words with them—but not today. He stepped over the man reeking of urine lying drunk in the street. Sometimes he would stop to drop some coins in the man's hand or murmur some kind words to him, but today his thoughts preoccupied him.

He arrived at the synagogue with its whitewashed walls and blue crenellated window trim. He entered with trepidation and then relief when he saw that all the members who had promised him money were there as well as some others: Abramo Zefarti, Joseph Flammeta, Shimon Shimoni, Moses Bascola, Samuel Gootfreund, David Morpurgo, Samson di Constantini. He sighed with relief. That feeling changed quickly when he saw that Alberto Finzi and Bernardo DiBelli were there as well.

Moses Bascola, the financier, motioned to the rabbi to take a seat. "The people who said they would help have all come with their money today. They see this as critical to the life of our Jewish community. Again we are being persecuted and used as...as..." He could not find the word.

Joseph Flammeta spoke up. "Scapegoats... the word is scapegoats," he said bitterly. "For centuries when things are not going well for the rulers, the Jews become their targets for ridicule, for taxes, even for burnings—and we see that danger arising again here. This Pope had been kind to us, but we understand we cannot always depend on the Pope's kindness. There's a 'terribleness' in the air, and if we don't fight back with whatever resource we have, we'll lose everything and need to start over in another land. We should consider a cessation on the payment of our taxes."

Moses interceded quickly not wanting to get sidetracked into the question of withholding taxes and another long discussion. "We've come with the money for Rabbi Luzzatti's plan."

Luzzatti took out his ledger. "I would like to keep a record and have it certified by the *Notai Ebrei* so that if some day I am in a position to repay, I will know exactly how much I owe each of you."

No one protested. Each man knew that keeping accounts was critical. Many had come from banking families; maintaining meticulous accounts was important to their livelihood. They were also pleased that the rabbi considered this a loan; although given the difficult nature of the times, they were aware they might never see their money again.

Joseph Flammeta said, "Here is one thousand ducats that my family gives with all their heart."

Moses Bascola said, "The silk trade was excellent this year—one thousand from me."

Abramo Zefarti from Spain said, "I was able to make the sale of diamonds—one thouand ducats."

David Morpurgo said, "I have only two hundred fifty ducats but it is offered with much love."

Samson di Constantini placed his money on the table. "I, too, have only two hundred fifty since my farm did not produce all that much this year."

Hayyim wrote down each man's name with the amount they gave and when they were done quickly did the addition.

"We are missing two thousand four hundred ducats. I only have one hundred to contribute, as I am no longer allowed to administer to the Pope. That will mean we need to raise twenty three hundred ducats."

All eyes turned toward Alberto Finzi and Bernardo DiBelli. They had remained quiet throughout the proceedings. Finally Finzi spoke. "You men are foolish—as foolish as women—giving money for a man that you don't know is even true to his Judaism. You sit here willing to give all this money with no questions."

"That money could be used for widows in our community," Di Belli added. He thought it best that he not name any particular widow because he knew it would be a reminder of the frequency of his visits to several of them in the community.

Zefarti sputtered. "It's a man's life."

Finzi retorted. "He's an apostate. We were planning to convene the gobierno to decide if we should call a *cherem* against the very man you are foolishly trying to save."

"You've known nothing but acceptance in Rome. You have no idea what it is to live in a place where you may be persecuted as a Jew at any time." Zefarti's voice rose as he made his argument.

"This isn't a question of faith to you, Finzi," said Hayyim. It's a question of your need to monopolize the accounts trade here. You're frightened because Israel has come back to be competition for you. It's you gentleman who should be brought before the gobierno for your scheming."

At Hayyim's angry statement, some shouted curses and shook their fists at Finzi and Belli. Others yelled approval at the rabbi's comments.

Bascola tried to bring the meeting back to order by shouting, "There are several members here who are part of the gobierno. Not one of them will go along with a calling for a *cherem* against Israel at this time." He looked sternly at all the men. "I'm right, aren't I?" A few shifted in their seats averting his eyes.

Finzi and DiBelli looked at one another. DiBelli stood. "Rome has been good to us. Suddenly there are threats to

our community, and it happened with the arrival of Israel."
He stopped. "And Senor Zefarti."

"No," said Flammetta calmly. "It started before that.
Remember the Passion Play." Several nodded.

Bascola directed his comments to Finzi and DiBelli.
"Since you're not here to contribute money, I suggest you
leave. Also, should our plan for Israel's escape go awry, we'd
look to you two first as the culprits."

As they walked out, Elijah del Medigo waddled into the
synagogue, his girth making it difficult for him to walk
quickly. No one had heard from him since their first meeting
to plan Israel's escape so they were surprised to see him
here. "I'm sorry I'm late, gentlemen, but I was in the process
of getting the repayment of a loan from one of the Pope's
Cardinals. I shall not name him, of course. But now, I have
twenty-five hundred ducats to offer, and they're placed in
your hands with hope for luck. Our finances have prospered
here but we should not grow rich without caring for all in the
community. It is against God's law."

Hayyim couldn't believe it. He raised his face toward the
ceiling of the synagogue and mouthed a silent "thank you."
He stood and didn't bother wiping away the tears in his eyes.
"Gentlemen. I can't thank you enough. I'll take this money
and place it directly in these moneybags." He pulled out two
linen bags tied with string from underneath his doublet.

"They're expecting you?" demanded del Medigo.

"Two of the Swiss Guards will work with the condotierri.
I will meet the two at certain columns of the colonnade. I
will only need to look into the eyes of each of these men as I
hand them the money to verify loyalty."

They remained silent. Finally Flammetta asked, "They
are trustworthy?"

"It's the only thing I have—my knowledge, my intuition,
and my faith. These members of the Swiss Guard will help.
They understand."

"What if they're caught?" asked Bascola.

"They've made arrangements to flee to the North to
Switzerland and find farm lands and shelter. Now, they have
an opportunity to lead a different life." Hayyim tried to

answer with certainty, but the reality was he could not be sure about the final outcome. Risks were involved.

"God be with you. Be safe and be careful. Although it is only a short walk to the Palace, this is a momentous journey that you take," said Flammeta.

"It's a wild, wild scheme," said Morpurgo who had been silent and observant until this point.

"I shall leave the ledger book here to be hidden in the safest place that Moses Bascola can find. Should there be any problems, then I'll be the only one implicated. I want none of you or your families to be threatened. It's enough that you have given me the monies. You needn't take any more risk." The men nodded gravely, some stroking their beards.

Hayyim walked from the synagogue to St. Peter's Square. He saw before him the church under construction atop the site where St. Peter was crucified. He thought for a moment about how powerful stories of martyrdom could be and knew he did not want to be a martyr—he wanted to survive with Alba and he wanted Israel to survive.

He looked at the sun and determined that he was coming close to the time when Giovanni Batiste and Joseph Frech would be passing by. The Guards always marched in twos, so the plot needed to include two men who could be relied upon. Hayyim entered the colonnade and saw that Giovanni and Joseph were making their circuit and would be passing the fifth column soon, the one that held the statue of Saint Cecilia. He moved toward the column and as they approached, he handed each man one of the bags that he had just removed from his waistband. They swiftly reached out a hand. No one blinked. No one nodded. No one turned to the left or to the right. They walked on and Hayyim turned toward the direction of his home praying that his trust in these men was going to be honored—to not reveal the plot and to distribute the money fairly to the condotierri.

He saw Cardinal Carafa coming toward him. "Doctor Luzzatti, have you come to visit your son to say your final farewells? Better today than the day of public execution." Carafa put a hand out to indicate that Luzzatti should proceed no further. "Why do you look frightened? You who have such belief in your faith? It is faith that makes us strong, isn't it?"

Hayyim pushed Carafa's hand away from him surprising himself with his own temerity. "I thought I'd visit, but I've changed my mind as it is too difficult for me to see him in such terrible conditions."

Cardinal Carafa's took a step closer to Hayyim. "If only he hadn't committed that heinous crime against Isabella, then you wouldn't have to see him in these 'terrible conditions' as you say."

Luzzatti drew a long breath but did not move backwards. "He didn't commit that crime, and I believe you know it."

Carafa took another step closer. "I'm aware of no such thing, Rabbi Luzzatti, and I'd suggest that you be careful where and when you say those words."

"God will judge."

"Your God is in no position to judge," snapped Cardinal Carafa and with that he turned to enter the Sistine Chapel while Hayyim Luzzatti went in the direction of his house.

When Hayyim arrived home, he first touched his fingers to his lips and then to the mezuzah. He realized that he was exhausted. He always took the responsibility of saving lives seriously. To have it be his own son—this was incomprehensible to him.

From the garden, Alba had heard the door open and ran to him. "Well? Come sit here with me and tell me." Her voice was urgent as she drew him out to a garden bench.

"Give me a minute." He sat wearily next to Alba. "Well, it's done."

"Oh, my God," Alba said. "We'll have our son back."

"It's easy to say, hard to think about, and harder to accomplish. So many things can go wrong."

"But, the plan is a good one."

It was more of a question than a statement.

He took her hands in his and repeated. "It's done. We wait one day. The money is in the Guards' hands. I have treated their children and families, and they had respect for me then."

"I cannot wait until Israel is back," Alba said bending down to pull a weed from the garden bed. "And that he can see this beautiful garden again."

Hayyim brushed her tears away and took in the sea of roses, and zinnias, marigolds, as well as the silvery green of her herbs, and said, "Soon. He'll see your beautiful garden soon." He hoped his words were convincing.

CHAPTER 32

Pope Paul's Decision

Cardinal Carafa moved from the basilica through the chapel and glanced upward at the piece of fresco that had just been moved from the town of Ferrara to the chapel wall. He wondered when all this indulgence in art would stop. Where would the Church continue to find the money to support all these artists? Even Cardinal Alfonso was obsessed with his Palazzo, and all his energy went to raising the money to build his grand estate.

But what I need to worry right now is about Luzzatti's presence in the colonnade, he thought. Can I believe a Jew about anything?

Carafa looked up and admired the curve of the arches bowing toward each other and ending in a divine space. There must be a God, he continued to reflect, to have given mortal men the ability to create such beauty. It was mortals who created the sculptures of Moses and Marcus Aurelius. His Michelangelo was one of the few—only he was not really his. Now he was even more distant—now that he had been forbidden by the Pope to see him.

When he saw Justinian and Alfonso come sweeping down the corridor to enter the Cardinals' library, Carafa stopped before Bramante's statue of Jesus. He made the sign of the cross for the benefit of Justinian and Alfonso and to atone for his thoughts about Michelangelo. He lingered, wanting the Cardinals to be present and seated when he arrived. Deference meant power. Did it not? They would have to wait for him.

By the time he entered the apartment door, Justinian and Alfonso were seated in red velvet covered chairs, whose backs reached above their heads.

"You're a princely pair, gentlemen," Carafa said. "But there are more important matters than your appearance, are there not? Are all the preparations in order? The Swiss Guards are ready? The extra horse for our prisoner? The scaffolding for the hanging is in place? The Jews have been ordered to come? Or have you been too preoccupied with getting your portions of food, Justinian, and administering to the nobility? And you, Alfonso, have you been obsessed with the selling of your silks?"

"All is in order. There'll be no problems." Justinian picked at the grapes in a bowl and offered some to Alfonso, who brushed them away.

"The prisoner is so weak that we know it won't be difficult to get him to the gallows. He won't be able to cry out his loyalty to Jesus Christ and let the crowd think that we're killing a Christian," Alfonso said, slumping in his chair a bit.

Carafa asked, "You're sure of this?"

Alfonso nodded his head solemnly. "He's barely alive. The Jews will tremble when they see him, but what's more, Luther and his followers will now be more fearful each day of their lives...when they see our power," he said stroking his stubbled chin.

"Hypocrite," muttered Carafa.

"What?" asked Alfonso.

"Nothing," said Carafa.

Justinian seemed oblivious to the tension between Carafa and Alfonso. "This will remind people of the supremacy of our Pope, won't it?"

"Especially when our Pope has forgotten how to be a supreme leader," said Alfonso.

Carafa glared at Alfonso who pretended not to see Carafa's displeasure.

"Shall we visit the Pope now to tell him of the plans for the hanging? At least, he should be informed," said Carafa.

"I'm not sure he's even interested," said Alfonso. "He remains in his room while Titian paints the portrait. Occasionally, he goes out to visit Michelangelo at St. Peter's. He seems apathetic but this is understandable with Isabella gone. His will and spirit no longer seem strong, and if you watch carefully, you will see his walk is slow and unsteady."

Justinian continued popping grapes in his mouth. "We should go to his chamber, where he's being painted. He'll be most relaxed there."

When they reached his chamber, the Pope was posing for Titian with hands folded in his lap and a faraway look in his eyes.

The artist looked up in annoyance when he saw Alfonso and Justinian enter, a step behind Carafa. "Gentlemen. Must you bother the Pope now? I would like to finish the hands before the light fades." Paul looked down at his hands and his eyes remained fixed upon them as though startled by their appearance—prominent blue veins and dark brown age spots. "That's enough for today. We have serious matters to discuss."

"As you wish," Titian bowed slightly, "but I must clean my paintbrushes." Titian hoped that would give him time to eavesdrop on their conversation.

"Take your paintbrushes away to clean them." The Pope waved his hand to dismiss Titian but the artist moved slowly gathering his supplies.

Paul got up from his chair and began to pace.

"I've been thinking about this hanging..." The three cardinals glanced at one another.

"I saw the sorrow in my friend's eyes when I told him that his son would be hanged. How can I do this? I don't want to be a part of this."

"But, Your Holiness, we have a confession," said Justinian.

"Do you think I don't know that the confession was coerced?"

"A confession can't be coerced unless there is some truth to it," said Carafa boldly. "And this is our chance to show our power to the Lutherans and Protestant princes who want to dominate the Council of Trent. They will see that we cannot we trifled with." Silence ensued. "A killing creates fear. Fear underpins power," continued Carafa and then added "And our Lord would wish it to be."

"What about Charles?" snapped the Pope, abruptly alert and attentive.

"You're suddenly so alive, Your Eminence," Titian said. "I want to capture that spirit on canvas."

"I told you to leave," the Pope glowered.

"Yes, I'm going," Titian said and scurried out the door.

"How can this hanging possibly mean a victory of substance over Charles?"

"Charles will see that we are still powerful, and he will not consider supporting the Protestant princes. It's as simple as that," said Carafa.

"Nothing's simple," barked the Pope lowering himself down in the chair again.

For the moment, the Pope had emerged from his melancholia. He knew Charles and politics better than anyone in the room.

"And what is more, do we want war with the Protestants? Do we want another sack of Rome? You do remember it was Charles who came and destroyed this city just fifteen years ago?"

"And look how we rebuilt this great city," said Carafa, a deep blush rising from his neck to his face. The Pope was maddening in his vacillation, in his inability to make a decision. Carafa thought he had convinced Paul that the hanging of Israel was necessary to demonstrate the power and dominance of the Church, yet here he was questioning the decision.

"We have the words of Cardinal Sadoleto, Contarini, and Giberti who have written of the many abuses of the Church," said the Pope. "This is what we need to dwell on. At my advanced age, I don't want to die thinking I've lost to the Protestants because of the selling of indulgences." He paused. "I know Isabella would have thought so as well."

Carafa kept his tongue. He did not want to say that it was the exorbitant gifts of land to the Pope's children and grandchildren that were part of the problem as well as the Pope's extravagances with his art. It was indeed hard to confront the Pope on these matters. Sometimes Isabella had been able to intervene—but now she was dead. Carafa was aware of the irony of his thoughts. Isabella—a force for good—a force for his good?

Carafa said, "I guarantee you that with this hanging we will get people to contribute money to the coffers of the Church and the Jews will gladly pay more in taxes...just for some assurance. We'll have the money we need to pay the army as well...as well as the money that you want for your works of art." He turned to the Cardinals who had remained silent. "Isn't that correct?" They both nodded.

Paul sighed; his shoulders drooped, and he was about to dismiss the Cardinals when Pier Luigi and Ranuncio appeared in the doorway.

Carafa appeared surprised and dismayed. He did not like unanticipated events or appearances. But the Pope looked pleased. "Come in. It gives me great pleasure to see you—especially you, Pier Luigi, because you have the eyes of your mother." Ranuncio stiffened slightly but said nothing. He looked around the room and said pointedly, "Can we be alone, Father?"

"It's important that we talk with you privately," Ranuncio urged.

"Your father is tired. He shouldn't be bothered now," Carafa interected.

"These are my sons. They may speak. But you're to stay as well." Pier Luigi started to protest. "Ranuncio has this crazy idea, and I'm not sure the Cardinals need to hear it."

"No, my sons, they're to stay." He waved for them to be seated behind Pier Luigi and Ranuncio.

Ranuncio spoke first. "Father, we were the ones who brought Israel to you. We were the ones who convinced you to put him in prison and hold him there. We thought that was the right thing to do. But..."

Paul was impatient. "I know all that. I am tired of all this talk about Israel Luzzatti. I want the hanging to be done with so I don't hear his name any more."

Ranuncio continued, "But we...I have read about torture, and it strikes me as it is not something the church should condone."

"Ranuncio has suddenly taken a great interest in the church," Pier Luigi said.

"That's not true," said Ranuncio. "I've always been loyal.... Going to Mass, especially after Mother died. It's what she would have wanted."

"Yes," said Paul. "Your mother would have liked you going to Mass."

"Didn't the flower woman and the fish monger say they saw Israel start to run after they saw Isabella slumped on the street?" questioned Pier Luigi.

"They also said afterwards that they saw a mysterious stranger run towards the river," said Ranuncio. "And then when they heard that Israel was to be hanged, they came to us and said that they had lied." He stopped. "You, my brother, know that as well as I do. Why do you continue to lie?"

Carafa spoke up quickly. "Pier Luigi doesn't lie. They probably lied because the Jews bribed them. They have enough money to convince the good witnesses to change their story."

Pier Luigi said, "That's probably true, Father."

Ranuncio stood. "We're talking here of life and death, which you and Mother taught us to take seriously. Haven't we grown past the Middle Ages, when torture was routine? Don't people come from far and wide to see your works of art—your library of wisdom with its books of Greek, Latin, and Hebrew? It was wrongful torture and you need to acknowledge that, Father."

The Cardinals sat somewhat bemused at these two young men, one with a degree of self-righteousness that they knew existed but seldom had it been expressed—at least, not in their presence. They looked to the Pope unable to decipher his feelings or predict his reaction.

"There are events in the world that are bigger than you, Dr. Luzzatti, his wife, and your mother." Paul looked at the floor and up again at his children his eyes quiet now. "The future of our Church may depend on this. That's all I can say to you."

"But Father," Ranuncio said. His father held up his hand.

"You heard him," said his brother.

"You can see that your father has made up his mind."
Justinian spoke with unusual vigor. "Don't annoy him. He
has much on his shoulders. This public event will bring
money into the coffers, and that is important."

Alfonso turned to Ranuncio. "You're to do nothing to
interfere with this execution. Then he added, "Be present at
the hanging to demonstrate your loyalty to the Church...and
to your father."

With this Ranuncio turned to his father. "Are you
requiring me to be there?"

"Yes. You'll be present with the other members of the
clergy."

"Will you be there, Father?" asked Ranuncio.

Paul rose wearily. "You're all to leave now. I must lie
down. But please fetch Titian for me. He'll be close by, I'm
sure."

As they left, the Pope lay on his bed and covered his face
with his hands. When Titian entered, he coughed slightly.
"You wanted me, Your Holiness? Surely it's too dark to sit
for a portrait."

"I just want you to tell me that the portrait will be
beautiful."

"It will, Your Holiness. It will be beautiful."

Titian added unctuously, "It will also show that you
were a good Pope."

CHAPTER 33

Israel and an Unruly Crowd

Israel lay on his straw mattress, unable to move and barely able to think. Every bone in his body ached. His mind wandered in and out of consciousness. When he was awake, he prayed for immediate death because the image of the public execution that kept coming into his mind terrified him. He would be incontinent; he would curse; he would cry. He had no idea if that hanging was to come today, tomorrow, or the next day, as all sense of time had vanished for him.

Imagine, he thought, I am lying in my own feces. How have I come to this point? Not having the energy to move his lips, he began to pray silently in Hebrew, *Hear, Oh Israel, The Lord Our God the Lord is One.* That prayer blended with an entreaty to "Our Saviour, Jesus Christ" begging forgiveness for his sins.

His father had stopped coming to see him. Torture had ceased abruptly. Was it because he had confessed? Why had he admitted guilt? He confessed because he could not tolerate the pain. He deserved to die because he was such a coward. Christ would not have given in to such a confession. He wanted the words of Rashi; he wanted the words of Marcus Aurelius; and he wanted the words of Augustine. Mostly, he wanted his own father and mother.

In his agitated state, he did not hear the opening of his cell door by two Swiss Guards. Giovanni Batiste put his hand over his mouth and nose to suppress the stench as well as to stifle an outcry at the horror of what he saw. Joseph Frech stared in disbelief. Giovanni took the first step forward to Israel and bent down close to his ear.

"We're here to take you to the public square," Giovanni said.

Israel tried to stifle sobs. The end was fast approaching, and he felt the need to be brave.

Giovanni added words of comfort. "You'll be safe with us. Your father has seen to it that you'll be safe. Do you understand?"

Israel uttered, "My father...?"

Giovanni said still close to his ear, "Yes, your father."

Israel moaned, "Our Father..." and fainted.

Joseph whispered from behind to Giovanni. "They're waiting for us. They'll wonder why it is taking so long to bring him up, so we must hurry." He wiped his sweaty palms on his velvet doublet.

"Come. Help me pick him up. Take his other arm and we'll carry him up the steps to the outside." Giovanni started to raise Israel from the straw when the prisoner let out a low moan.

They bent down on either side and lifted him up. Because he had lost so much weight, they easily carried him through the long dank corridor to the dungeon exit where the execution cart awaited them. It had been specially designed by the condotierri with an enormous coffin-like box with air spaces covered by bars. This way the prisoner was protected from the crowds along the route because it was important that his death be in the public square.

Giovanni and Joseph did not know the details of the escape plot, but Zefarti had plied the drivers with wine in the morning. The two Swiss Guards were surprised to see a rather disheveled man, dismount, and pull down a side of the box. "Slide 'im in there, will ya," he slurred while wobbling to and fro. "This is going to be a grand day with some excitement, isn't it? We haven't had anything like this for a while. I've been down to the public square this morning, and there's already a crowd."

The other driver, who held the reins, slapped his thigh in agreement, "The women are there, too. Some nice-looking ones in their best dresses, only they have blue strips sewn on their shoulders. But I would know the Jews from their nice clothes, anyway. It's going to be a great day to see someone get his comeuppance for murdering Isabella...and for murdering Christ."

Joseph Frech remained silent, but Giovanni Batiste took the cue. "It'll be a wonderful day and we're glad to be a part of it.... aren't we, Joseph? We carried this wretched prisoner all the way because he did not even have the capacity to walk. A weakling."

"It doesn't matter," said the driver as he got back on his seat. "As long as we can get him up to the gallows."

"Oh, we'll get him up on the gallows, all right. You just leave it to us," said Giovanni briskly.

With that he and Joseph moved to either side of Israel and lifted him into the cart and slammed the top down without locking it. Giovanni whispered in Israel's ear although he was not sure the young man could hear him. "Take heart. All will be well. We'll be taking you up to the gallows but no harm will come to you."

The driver took off for the square and the horses' hooves clattered on the cobblestone streets. Giovanni and Joseph rode alongside with another horse following. It was as the driver had said: Everyone was at the public square. As they drew closer, Giovanni could hear the drunken shouts of men in the crowd.

"We're here to see that the right thing is done," one woman said to the stranger standing next to her. The stranger nodded her head and shifted from side to side a bit unsteadily.

"That's why we're here," they confessed to one another. "It's not just to see the gore."

"It's good that the Jews are learning their place."

"It's a shame, isn't it, that they have to wear the yellow circle over such nice clothes?"

"But it'll remind them of their place."

The Jews of the community—all five hundred of them—stood at the back of the crowd, elegantly dressed in spite of the yellow star on the arms of the men and the blue stripe sewn into the women's clothing. The men wore velvet tunics, some of variegated colors over their brown leggings, and the women wore long colorful linen dresses with high bodices embroidered in silk. Some were bedecked with long ropelets of pearls—the fashion of the day for stylish women. The Jews knew that this fancy dress would irritate some in the crowd, but they had agreed to dress in their Sabbath best as an act of pride and and defiance. Rabbi Luzzatti stood tall with Alba at his side.

One drunken man yelled pointing to Hayyim. "He's praying, but he's not praying to our Lord, Jesus Christ. You can bet on that. No, he's not praying to Jesus Christ."

Then the crowd took up the chant, "No, he's not praying to Jesus Christ. No, he's not praying to Jesus Christ." They repeated it over and over again until the first person to see the cart and horses approach stood up on a box, waved his arms, and shouted above the din, "They're coming!" The chanting stopped, and people turned to see the carriage coming, flanked by two Swiss Guards on horseback. And a horse on Giovanni's side.

Only Hayyim knew that it was Giacomo—Giacomo was to carry Israel to the monastery. The cart would give chase and, of course, would not be able to find him or the horse. Hayyim had practiced the route daily with Giacomo, and for the past month, the horse lived at the monastery of Father Bruno. Hayyim was sure the presence of Israel on his back would help his beloved horse follow the route. The horse had been Israel's joy in his youth before he left for Spain, and Israel, like his father had learned to be an expert horseman.

Hayyim knew that after Israel was rescued, this wonderful animal would have to be sent out to the hills because he could inadvertently lead searchers to the monastery. Sometimes Hayyim wondered if he had indulged his son in too many worldly ways. Israel had always wanted to explore what was on the other part of the street, the other part of town, the other side of the mountain and Hayyim had encouraged him to do so.

"Why is that extra horse there?" asked one of the women in the crowd, not as drunk as the others.

"Why, that's to carry him away after he's dead," responded a man knowingly.

"Are you sure?" she asked giving him a flirtacious wink and bending over to make sure that he saw the curve of her bosom.

"You'll see. Mark my words. Just watch that horse."

"I thought they'd let him hang here for a day or two." The woman's eyes narrowed. "You know, like a lesson to everyone. Just the way they let Jesus hang on the cross. They'll see what it's like."

The man continued to speak to her with authority, appreciating her ample bosom at the same time. "Of course, they will. The horse is for later on. It's more efficient this way."

The closed cart drew up to the back of the platform on which stood a long pole with a horizontal wooden extension and a strong rope that hung from it. The stand of tall cedars a few feet behind the platform served as a barrier, as did the condotierri that lined the sides to keep people away. The space behind the platform allowed the cart to ease in.

The lone man who stood on the platform was hooded, and only Hayyim knew that it was Abramo Zefarti. He had bribed the hangman to take his place. The men of the synagogue realized that even with their bribes and intentions, they must maintain control until the last minute—and that meant that the hooded man had to be one of them. Hayyim could only think that Zefarti's act was daring and courageous.

As the cart drew close to the platform and stopped, a cheer went up from the sea of waiting people. Someone could be heard shouting, "Kill the Jew! Kill the Jew! He killed Isabella! He killed Christ!" Joseph Frech, who had been leading Giacomo, stopped on the other side of the carriage. Hayyim held his breath. The top of the cart opened and another roar came from the crowd. They waited, but no one descended. No one had seen what had happened from the other side of the carriage. Giovanni and Joseph had deftly taken Israel out of the cart by lowering a side panel and then quickly tying him to the horse. When Israel cried out in pain, Giovanni quickly grabbed a piece of linen and stuffed it in Israel's mouth. The drivers had been too drunk to be aware of what was happening.

"Where's the Jew?" came another cry from the crowd. The chant was picked up by the rest of the crowd so that no one heard the noise of the horse's hooves racing away with

Israel's body tied to its back. The people crowded and shoved to move closer to the execution site, but the condotierri pushed them back. Suddenly someone cried, "Look" when he saw the horse racing away with a slumped body on its back and the cart chasing after it with its empty box veering from side to side. As bewilderment raced through the crowds, the condotierri continued to hold the crowd back. The police stood firmly with their horses. Several people then turned their attention away from the platform to the Jews in the back. During that split second, the hooded man who stood at the gibbet slipped off his hood and robe and melted into the crowd, wearing the clothes of a peasant.

Again, a lone cry from someone in that multitude set the crowd afire. "The Jews are still here. They did it. They did it."

People were so intent on their rampage that they did not see the Cardinals of the Papal court standing near the platform. If they had taken the time for closer inspection, they would have seen Pier Luigi and Ranuncio with looks of bewilderment on their faces.

The Cardinals' astonishment then turned to anger, and they quickly summoned their horsemen for their animals to return to the Palace.

Because of their disappointment, the crowd threw the fruits and bottles of wine that they were planning to consume, at the Jews who covered their faces and bodies as best as they could and began to run. The crowd pursued them. Fortunately, most of the Jews had come with their horses so they mounted the animals, pulling their wives up behind them. Bottles, apples, and tomatoes flew after them.

Ammunition spent, many dispersed; some lay on the ground so drunk that they could not get up.

Hayyim returned to his house with Alba, careful to lock the door, and prayed that nothing would happen to the synagogue. As soon as they were locked inside, they held each other. Alba was shaking so hard that Hayyim had to hold her and smooth her hair over and over saying, "He'll be all right. He'll be all right."

"What will happen to us?" she asked, her voice quivering.

"Nothing."

"But the Swiss Guards?"

"I'm can only pray for their continued loyalty and their desire to leave the Church."

"They'll accuse us anyhow, just as they accused Israel," she said weeping.

"All that is important now is that Israel is out of the dungeon, on his way to the monastery, and that Giovanni and Joseph and the other guards are on their way back to Switzerland."

She said, "They'll find out about our involvement at the Palace. They do not know yet what has happened, but when they find out, our troubles will begin anew. All those people who helped us will be implicated."

"Is Israel not on his way to safety?" he asked soothing her hair. "Isn't that most important?"

"I hope they'll help him to regain his strength at the monastery, and I hope that he'll be well."

"We'll have a message from them shortly. I can't go out to the priory for a while since we'll be watched. But that will pass in time."

She smiled at him through her tears. "You'll get to him as soon as possible, though?"

He took her hands in his. "As soon as possible," he said.

CHAPTER 34

The Cardinals Question

"How did this happen?" Cardinal Carafa paced the huge papal hall that was so large that it could house all the cardinals within two days of traveling distance from Rome. Panels of frescos lined the walls with scenes depicting scenes of Christ entering Jerusalem, but Carafa took no notice. While he paced, Alfonso and Justinian sat at the end of the huge mahogany table surrounded by intricately carved chairs with seats covered with red damask. Justinian looked over the figs in front of him carefully turning each and sniffing a bit. "Can't be too careful," he said to Alfonso.

A slight smile played around Alfonso's mouth. Alfonso, who cared more about his profit in the silk trade than the righteousness of the Church, secretly admired the capacity of anyone who could use their skills to get the better of a situation. This was something, of course, he could never reveal to Carafa.

"I have a touch of joint pain," said Justinian. "Otherwise, I would be pacing with you. I need to vent this anger I have at the Swiss Guards. They had to be part of the criminal plot. It couldn't have been done without them."

"And yet we cannot find any way to implicate them," said Carafa. Then he added, "You, my dear friend, could avoid such joint pain if you didn't eat as much."

Justinian took no notice of Carafa's last remark. All the figs were gone and he was carefully refilling his wine glass. "We can just condemn them. Much in the same way that we handled...." He did not complete the sentence. The others knew he was talking about Israel. "But I assume the Pope would not give such an order."

"You assume correctly. He's not interested in allowing any monies to pay for soldiers to search for Israel or the Swiss Guards," Carafa answered.

"He's told you this directly?" asked Alfonso.

Carafa put his fingertips together over his mouth as though he needed to contemplate his response. "Yes. And he will not let us use the rack."

Alfonso rose from his seat, walked over to Carafa and touched his shoulder. "I know this must be difficult for you. You think that with Isabella's death, you can convince the Pope that God wants the strictness and rigors of the church you care so deeply about."

"And you don't care?"

"Indeed, I care. I think I'm a bit more practical and recognize that flaws are part of the human condition."

Carafa turned away to hide his disgust with what he regarded as Alfonso's greed. He knew about his connection with the Jews. Alfonso didn't know that Carafa had sent spies to uncover the reasons for his prosperity. Alfonso was buying up parcels of land at an extraordinary rate with money that seemed to be in plentiful supply—at least for Alfonso.

"But these flaws—do they include the possibility that you would give money to pay witnesses?" Carafa put up his hand. "I'll answer that. Absolutely not because it would mean you would have to give up some of your money to pay for church items, and that is not in your character, Alfonso."

Justinian laughed. "He's just like a Jew. Makes money and holds on to it."

Alfonso walked back to Justinian and wanted to splash wine in his face, he was so annoyed. Who was this fat cardinal who did nothing for the Church but toady up to the nobility? "You eat, Justinian, and I'll make the money. Let's be honest and perhaps we'll both secure a good spot in the heaven to come. We need to see that the Pope does not give away his power at the Council of Trent—for the good of the Church."

"Yes, indeed," added Justinian whose head was nodding as he struggled to keep his eyes open. "We must tend to the ills of the Church, otherwise the families of nobility may abandon us."

Carafa sat rigid. His hands in his lap, he kept twisting the ring on his middle finger. In his heart, he knew he did not trust his closest allies to truly bring about the necessary reform for the Church, but what was most disturbing to him was that he could not convince Paul to find the funds that it would take to pursue Israel and the Swiss Guards.

Carafa's silence gave Justinian license to continue. "Luther thinks we'll suppress the evangelical movement, but we're trying to bring Christians together. Several members of the d'Estes family have asked that we do so."

Carafa ignored Justinian. He didn't think him capable of theoogical judgment let alone political decision making. "The Jesuits will insist on the doctrine of justification—to be received only in conjunction with God's power. They've been meeting and preparing their own agenda. If Paul is too tired to exert his leadership, then we will. We must see to it that the bishops from Switzerland and France and even Spain may not vote by proxy at the council. The current bishops from Italy and Germany will be easier to control, and our dominance over them should help us to shape Church doctrine as we want." As an afterthought, Carafa added, "Our Pope doesn't think of these strategies as he should."

"What is it that my father doesn't think of as he should?" Ranuncio entered the room—so silently that he startled the Cardinals.

Alfonso said, "You should announce your entrance. Where's Pier Luigi? You're without your brother?"

"My brother is content visiting his lands in Parma and Piacenza. May I sit at your large table, gentlemen? I have some tarot cards that require space."

Carafa spoke sternly. "This is a Cardinals' room. You know that tarot cards are not permitted here. Your mother would be appalled."

"You're not to be talking to me about the memory of my mother, who would have despised your plot to torture an innocent man for your own gain." Defiantly Ranuncio put the cards on the table and pulled out one card after the other.

Carafa spat, "It wasn't for my own gain—it was for the good of the Church." When Ranuncio did not respond and just stared at Carafa, he continued, "Besides, the Jew confessed."

Alfonso and Justinian remained quiet taken aback by Ranuncio's behavior.

Ranuncio turned to his tarot cards. "Oh, my. I'm to acquire land. How can that be when my father always thought that Pier Luigi should have so much land?"

The Cardinals exchanged glances. Ranuncio continued to turn the cards that he lay out on the table. "Here's one that says searching for someone who has fled will be to no avail." He placed his finger on his chin and an elbow on the table, seeming to be totally engrossed in the tarot cards. "Let me ask you a question, gentlemen. How's your search going for Israel and the two Swiss Guards? Not well, I've heard."

Alfonso said with bluster, "We'll find them."

"May I suggest that you cease your search for them, unless you want me to tell my father of the various meetings that you've been holding unbeknownst to him? May I also suggested that the parcels of land near the Tiber that were set aside for your new homes now be placed in my name."

Alfonso could hardly believe his ears. He started to speak, but Ranuncio cut him short.

"If you don't give up your lands and place them in my name, then my father will not only know of your extracted confession, but he will also know of your fortunes in the silk trade. You're aware that my father disapproves of such extravagant gains by members of the church."

Carafa blanched. Alfonso folded his arms across his chest.

"I'm sure you'll do the right thing, gentlemen." Ranuncio shuffled the cards in succession with little effort. The cardinals kept their eyes fixed on the movement of the cards.

Justinian protested. "That wasn't your father's desire or intention. He has been careful to reward those most loyal to him."

"I think, gentlemen, you don't understand the meaning of the word 'loyal,'" said Ranuncio. "I believe we're finished here. Proceed with your discussion. I'm sure there are many serious issues of religion that weigh heavily on your hearts and minds." With those last words, he made his way down the corridor to his own apartment leaving the tarot cards on the table.

"Can he get away with this?" asked a stunned Justinian who for the moment had stopped eating.

"We'll see," said Carafa. "We'll see what the good brother thinks he can get away with. He does not know that he is playing a game that he can't win. I wonder if Pier Luigi knows of his plans."

He turned on his heel and left the Cardinals Alfonso and Justinian sitting and staring at the tarot cards.

CHAPTER 35

Life at the Monastery

While the Cardinals were listening to the unexpected and sudden claims of Ranuncio, an exhausted Giacomo carried the near lifeless Israel to the priory. The Swiss Guards, Giovanni Batiste and Joseph Frech, had watched the wagon sink to the depths of the Tiber River. They then galloped the route to the monastery to assure Israel's safe arrival. The smell of baked bread wafting from the kitchen's chimney welcomed them as they unhitched their horses in pitch blackness. The waning moon was only a few days old.

Father Bruno as well as Friars Leo, Domingo, and Sebastian had lain on the wooden floor of the anteroom to get some rest and to better hear the arrival of horse and rider. They assumed the horse carrying Israel would be coming at a gallop, and they would hear the pounding of the horses' hooves reverberate through the floor.

Father Nicolas had departed from the monastery just two days ago with the blessings and support of all the brothers. He had left with a horse, some provisions of food and water, his Bible, a copy of the Talmud, and a light heart. The men noted that a particular radiance to him the day of departure. They prayed for his safe arrival in Spain where he could slip into the comforting arms of his family. With his leaving, his room was made ready for Israel.

"He's coming," said Father Bruno, wide awake with anticipation. The others quickly rose from the floor to peer out the window. Their eyes adjusted to the dark as they saw Giacomo go to the exact tree where Hayyim Luzzatti had last stopped. The horse snorted and pawed the ground, as though calling attention to himself and his rider.

"It's a miracle. God must be working all his powers," Father Leo said.

"I believe God is living inside this horse. That's what I believe." Father Domingo crossed himself.

"I think God would want us to get this man inside right away," said Father Bruno. He turned toward the Swiss Guards. "You are most welcome to spend the night with us."

Giovanni turned toward Joseph who shook his head.

"No, we must leave as soon as possible," Giovanni said. "It's too dangerous for us to linger, and you need to tend to Israel."

"We will just give our horses some water and food and be on our way," Joseph added.

It was fortunate that Israel was unconscious; this was the only way his bruised and broken body could have tolerated the long, difficult ride. Out in the dark, each brother carried a small lantern embedded with a candle. When they saw Israel on the horse and held up the light to his body, they gasped—for although he was tied on the horse as though he were one great big saddle bag, one arm was clearly separated from the shoulder, dried blood covered his head and his forehead, and through his ripped clothing, they could see large black and blue welts.

"He's unconscious," Father Leo spoke first.

"He doesn't even look alive," Sebastian said.

"He's breathing," Father Bruno said. "Hold your lanterns up for me. Tie up the horse." He spoke brusquely but took charge in a competent and loving way. He touched Israel lightly on the shoulder, then stroked his face and forehead. Israel did not move.

"I'll carry him, Sebastian. You'll lead the way back. Hold your lantern high."

"But, he's too heavy for you," protested Father Domingo. "Let me help."

"No, I know what to do. I remember how carefully Dr. Luzzatti treated me. He had the kindest hands." Father Bruno carefully placed both hands at Israel's waist, pulled him down slightly, lowered his own shoulders, and slung Israel across his back so that he was perfectly balanced with arms and legs hanging down on either side. Israel emitted a low groan. I don't know how much we can help him, Bruno thought, but if careful attention and prayer will help, then we will spend our days in prayer and tending to his pain.

"Besides, he's not heavy at all; he's almost all skin and bones. We need to make him comfortable before he awakes fully, and send this horse on his way. Untie the horse, Father Leo."

Father Leo approached Giacomo slowly. "You're sure this is going to work?"

"Dr. Luzzatti said that he practiced with him many times. Pray that he heeds his master's wishes."

Sebastian and Leo led the horse in the direction of the forest. Domingo followed and stood watching as the horse ran in the direction of the hills. The brothers took this is as sign of a possible miracle in their midst.

The hooded friars, in their brown robes knotted with simple hemp belts, walked quietly down the corridor in order not to wake the others who worked hard during the day harvesting grain, baking bread, and boiling herbs to prepare medicines. It was important to take care of the crop now because the summer sun would soon be over, and the brothers lived their days by the rhythm of the seasons.

They approached Father Nicolas' empty cell, and Father Bruno laid Israel down on the bed.

"Go get some sleep," Bruno said to Leo and Domingo. "Sebastian will stay with me to help."

"When will *you* get some sleep?" asked Domingo.

"When my body feels the need. Sebastian, go fetch some boiled water from the fireplace and bring it in a basin here with some of the newest linen cloths." Father Bruno carefully removed the filthy, ripped garments from Israel. Israel slipped in and out of consciousness. Sebastian brought the basin of water into the room, clasped his hand over his mouth and nearly dropped the basin when he saw the prominent ribs, bloated stomach, and bruises and welts all over Israel's body. The skin was especially raw around the ankles where he had been shackled.

Father Bruno dipped the cloth in boiled water and cleaned away the dirt. Sebastian wiped away tears with the sleeve of his cassock.

"He's been circumcised," said Sebastian.

"As was our Lord, Jesus Christ...and as was I," said Father Bruno continuing to dip the cloth in water and wipe away the blood and dirt from Israel's body. The water in the basin quickly became dirty.

"Bring me fresh water with a clean cloth." He had seen Dr. Luzzatti emphasize the need for clean linen, but didn't really understand why. He was determined to do his best for this young man and the father whom he had learned to respect.

When Sebastian returned, he saw that Father Bruno had turned Israel on his side to clean the back of his legs and buttocks covered with feces and dirt. Father Bruno washed Israel with the same gentle touch.

Sebastian took away the filthy clothes to be burned, and brought fresh sheets. The two men worked to place new sheets on a bed of straw. They moved him quickly and efficiently. When Israel groaned, Bruno whispered in his ear, "You're safe. You'll be safe." They covered him with a blanket of lambs wool to ward off the chill of the night air.

"You go and get some sleep." Bruno said to Sebastian. "I'll stay with him."

Sebastian returned to his cell worn out from work and anxiety. He slept deeply and dreamed of angels and devils battling in the air above the place where the dirty linen had been burned.

Father Bruno sat next to Israel's bed and periodically checked his breathing. When he could, he lay on the floor to close his eyes a bit and rest. He watched Israel sleep fitfully, sometimes stirring because of the pain. When the morning sun came streaming in to the small window high up in the room, Israel tried to raise his head.

Israel blinked and focused his eyes to see Father Bruno's face. Father Bruno moved so Israel would not have to stare into the light of the window.

"Where am I?" Israel managed to say.

"Do you feel well enough to sit up? Are you hungry? Here, I will help you."

Father Bruno lifted Israel to a sitting position and was amazed how light he was. Israel put his head against Bruno's broad shoulder.

"I'm afraid I can't sit without your support."

"Just lie down. Sebastian is making a special mutton broth. Fresh herbs from the garden." Father Bruno wanted to tell him that he knew all about the medicinal herbs that Hayyim Luzzatti used and Alba Luzzatti grew in her garden, but he knew that this would not a good time to talk about the young man's parents.

Sebastian poked his head in without waiting for a welcome. This was standard practice at the monastery as all goods were shared and every moment of every day had its rules and practices known to all. Privacy was not a value.

"I'll have the mutton broth ready. Is Brother Israel ready to have some?" asked Sebastian.

In the kitchen, Sebastian had supervised the cooking of the stew to make sure it was done with the bones of a freshly killed lamb, and fresh vegetables from the garden. The brothers did not like to waste and were sometimes inclined to use "day-old" greens—an anathema for Sebastian.

The two brothers worked together, one holding Israel's head up slightly and the other putting teaspoons of broth carefully in his mouth. Israel took the broth eagerly, but he had to rest after five spoonfuls. The broth made his stomach growl.

From his supine position, he said weakly, "You called me Brother Israel. Why did you call me Brother Israel?"

"Not now," said Father Bruno. "Now is the time for you to heal your body and when you are stronger we'll talk about your spiritual growth. You'll understand more as you heal."

For the next five days, Israel gave himself over to the care and feeding these two men provided. Surely, he thought, these men know my father and that is why they are treating me so kindly. How did I get here? How did I ever manage to escape a public hanging? Where's my father?

He grew stronger and on the evening of the fifth day, he was able to sit in a chair and gaze out a window. He spoke hesitatingly to Father Bruno, who had come in to check on him.

"I would like to take a walk tomorrow to see the grounds. I should be well enough to take a short walk in the monastery and perhaps outside to see the garden. A bit of air would do me good, don't you think?"

Father Bruno prayed hard during the night hoping for some guidance that would help him find the right words for Israel. Would he understand the agreement that his father had made with the monastery?

The next morning, Father Leo and Father Bruno came in to help Israel dress.

"I don't know you, sir," Israel said to Leo.

"I helped with your rescue," Leo bowed his head.

"Do you know the way back to my home?"

The two brothers exchanged glances.

"How did I get here?"

"Your horse, Giacomo, brought you here."

"And where is Giacomo now?"

"In the hills far away from here."

"You remember nothing of your arrival here?" Father Bruno asked.

"No."

"We sent Giacomo away so that he could not trace his way back to here."

Father Bruno gathered a brown cassock with a hemp belt and handed it to Israel. "Here, wear this for now. Father Sebastian baked his wonderful bread, and made you mutton broth." Then we'll go directly outside to the garden. The morning air will be good for you, and we will be able to answer your questions...and talk about your future." Father Bruno decided not to add the word "here" to the end of the sentence.

Israel glanced at the brown hooded robe with its tie of thick rope on the bed and asked, "Is this what I'm to wear?" In all the things he had done in his lifetime, including being at the King Philiip's court in Spain, he had not encountered Dominican Friars.

"That's all we have here, and you'll be safe in that cassock. If anyone from the outside visits, all you need to do is cover your head with the hood." Father Bruno paused to search Israel's face. "Should anyone outside the monastery arrive here, you'll be Father Nicolas," Father Bruno said.

"Father Nicholas," Israel repeated. "I can be Father Nicholas until I understand what's going on. Does my father know I'm here?"

"Yes, and undoubtedly he's being watched by some from the papal palace."

"Is it that Pope Paul wants him to come to harm?" Israel asked anxiously.

"Not Paul, but Paul is no longer his own, shall we say, his own person. Carafa seems to have extraordinary influence over him." He paused holding the cassock up for Israel. "But I'm sure your father and mother are safe." He hoped his words sounded reassuring to this young man who had been through so much.

Israel stood and donned the garment carefully. Many of the black and blue marks and bruises had faded by now and his ribs were no longer so prominent. Israel put his hand out to steady himself.

"I can walk alone. Lead the way, and I'll follow you to the dining room."

They walked in silence, Israel following Father Bruno with a slow gait. The monastery was elegant in its simplicity and its structure—wide planking on walls and floors and evenly spaced columns surrounded a well-maintained garden filled with herbs and vegetables. Each cell door was equidistant from the next. Israel took in its tranquility.

He entered the dining hall, and sat in the empty seat of an eight-foot long table where six brothers sat supping quietly. One of the men served him a bowl of vegetable soup with a large slab of whole grain bread and some butter. Israel smelled the freshness of the food but could only eat a small amount. He worried that his wrenching diarrhea would start again. He sat quietly and looked at the other men who ate in silence. Some occasionally looked up at him but seemed intent on finishing the soup in front of them. When they bowed their heads at the end of the meal, Israel bowed his head with them. When they left their places to file out to their rooms, he filed out with them and went back to his room and lay exhausted on his bed. I am not ready to leave this place yet, he thought. Clearly he would be staying here a while. He looked upon this as an opportunity to learn and rest but he was also eager to get back to his family and a life at the court in Spain. The rabbi's son had been given a second chance at life, and certainly Spain would be more hospitable than Italy after all this. Perhaps his parents would go with him to Spain although, up till now, they had considered Rome their sanctuary. It was all too much for him to think about now.

CHAPTER 36

The Vatican and the Talmud

Pope Paul sat alone in his library, bent over the pages of the most recent illuminated manuscript created by one of the brothers at the Jesuit monastery. Opened just two years ago, the monastery had been a thorn in his side. Carafa had assured him that he would be pleased by the exacting standards of Ignatius Loyola. His rigid principles that included bringing more religious rigor, though, conflicted with Paul's plans for the Church. He wanted grand art and buildings and some reform; the Jesuits wanted real and grand reform. Paul as Pope had been willing to deal with them because the brothers had a marvelous ability to decorate books. The beauty of the lettering of Gregor of Cyprus' words copied from a Byzantine manuscript delighted him.

Paul turned each page carefully, his head bent close to the text, and read slowly from the Greek writings to find, inspiration, wisdom, and perhaps comfort. *"The glory shall go to those who are just toward all fellow men."*

He turned to the Marcus Aurelius book nearby on the table and opened to the page marked by a dried rose. He had read a particular passage two days ago, and he marked it to read again even though it had made him feel uncomfortable. *"You are an old man. Stop allowing your mind to be a slave, to be jerked about by selfish impulses, to kick against fate and the present, and to mistrust the future."* He wanted to ask Doctor Luzzatti about his restlessness and agitation, but he was no longer his doctor. Could it be due to some imbalance in his bodily humours? His mind was a jumble of the grief he felt over Isabella, the pressure from his

Cardinals, the lack of funds in his treasury, the upcoming Council of Trent.

He walked to the door and spoke to the guard just outside.

"Please ask Cardinal Carafa to meet me in my chambers. I will be there with Titian."

When he entered his chamber and saw the artist waiting for him, Paul smiled; he was genuinely glad to have some distraction from his disquieting thoughts. Titian was busy drawing curtains back to let in more light and fussing with the position of the chair.

"I was hoping you would come on time today, Your Holiness. The light is excellent now."

Carafa hurriedly dressed in his red robe and tri-cornered hat and almost ran to the Pope's chambers. It had been a while since Paul had wanted companionship or to have his portrait painted. They had not yet discussed Israel's escape. If such an outrageous event had occurred two years ago, the Pope would have called all the Cardinals and Bishops near Rome and the commander of his army and demanded an explanation. Heads would roll. Now the Pope brought forth an occasional missive and spent an inordinate amount of time with his books.

When Carafa entered, Paul was seated for his portrait. Titian walked around folding and refolding the Pope's red cassock and repositioning the Pope's hat. He took one hand of the Pope from his lap and placed it on the arm of the mahogany chair.

"You called to speak with me, Your Holiness?" How would he answer the question about Israel's escape?

When Paul motioned for Carafa to sit, Titian said, "Please, Your Eminence. I can only continue if you remain still and if this visitor does not disturb you."

"This is a good time for me to talk with Carafa. I think he has probably been waiting to converse with me for some time. Haven't you, Carafa?" He added, "Titian is quite adept at painting even while I'm talking. Aren't you, my friend?"

"You have needed time to recover from the shock of Isabella's murder," Carafa said.

"Sit, my friend. Yes, Isabella's murder."

"But don't sit where you are blocking the light," said Titian.

Carafa refrained from saying anything about the artist's impunity. Not now, he thought, not now when he appears to be giving some comfort to the Pope. He is making him look distinguished in his old age.

"Heaven awaits, Carafa? What do you think?" The Pope's tone seemed almost benevolent.

"Of course it does. I'm surprised that you even question this."

"With Isabella's death, I have begun to examine and question much—that inner examination that's so necessary to a good life. We all need it, don't we?"

So, thought Carafa, this is about Isabella. He needs to get over her death so he can get on with the work of the Papacy. "We do and we shall do everything we can to recapture the man who murdered Isabella. He cannot be very far away."

"I think he is very far away and at the same time he is very close. This man is somehow very close. Don't you feel it, Carafa?" The Pope's voice was barely audible as he leaned forward.

"Please, you must remain still," Titian interrupted.

Carafa was uncomfortable with the Pope's comment. He needed to refocus him. "The Council of Trent. Now that you have negotiated with Charles to assert your supremacy, do you have an agenda for the next phase of the Council?" He watched for signs of annoyance in Paul's face, but Paul waved his hand dismissively.

"The sacraments, of course."

"Some are saying that we must deal with the handling of sinecures," said Carafa.

"Yes, of course, the sinecures," Paul answered belatedly.

Carafa knew that Paul was reluctant to give up anything of his material world. The Cardinal continued to prod him with practical problems.

"Have you thought of another way to pay for the rebuilding of St. Peter's? Buonarroti will want his money."

"Why are you calling him Buonarotti? He's Michelangelo, and we are lucky to have him. He left Florence to come here."

"He comes where the money is, right, Titian?"

Titian continued going from palette to canvas knowing full well to keep out of the discussion.

"What could be a greater monument to the Church than the reconstruction of the site where Peter was to have been buried?" A defensive tone had crept into the Pope's voice. "This will show God our commitment to him. This edifice will give the people renewed spirit to show that life goes on...there is heaven if you live the right life."

'I don't doubt that," said Carafa. "It's the money. Where is the money to come from to pay for it all? Some are upset about the indulgences." Carafa took a breath. "Perhaps you can impose another tax on the Jews. They've been quite successful with the silk trade and their banking." Carafa had argued with the Pope about this before and always met resistance.

"I must keep the Jewish community content. They have expanded trade here. They're even financing voyages to new lands and we reap benefits from those distant places." He looked directly at Carafa. "Now, you may not think so Carafa, because you do not often partake of wine, nor spices, but many do. Chocolate, have you tasted chocolate?"

"It's not the Jews' happiness that is important here. Some look upon you as being too soft on these people. Wouldn't God be pleased if we were all Christians?" He paused and glanced at Titian who seemed focused on the canvas before him. "Don't you want Titian to receive the monies he has earned? Don't you want to be recognized as the Pope who built up the Church to all its glory and magnificence?"

Given the choice between beautifying a building and buying a work of art, or a display of tolerance, Pope Paul would always choose the building, a monumental sculpture, the beautifully bound manuscript. Carafa thought that the Pope's craving for art was even more apparent since the death of Isabella. Maybe it was a distraction; maybe an attempt to keep a connection with Isabella who shared his passion for art.

The Pope asked testily, "Do you have any suggestions to resolve some of the problems of this particular situation?"

Carafa hesitated. "The problems of which particular situation?"

"You know—the situation with the Jews—with Dr. Luzzatti, his son...the one who managed to escape." Carafa was startled to hear the Pope bring up the subject. He heard his voice mingled with impatience and grief.

Carafa chose his words carefully. "The people are upset that they couldn't see the spectacle of the public hanging. They need to see apostates driven out of the Church. Therein lies their confusion about Luther and his followers. Why is God even allowing them to exist? Why is God even allowing the Jews to continue to exist." He paused. "Let us remember, our people also need some diversion in their lives with spectacles, burnings. They're less likely to turn to Luther for comfort." When the Pope remained silent, Carafa continued, "We could burn...yes, we could burn their Talmud. People like a grand conflagration as much as they like a hanging...and the Talmud has made insulting references to Jesus and Mary."

"How can I, a Pope who loves books, sanction the burning of a book—especially this ancient text?"

"The Talmud. I heard the Talmud is a wicked book. Isn't there a passage that says Jesus shall be boiled in excrement?" Titian spoke softly.

The Pope glared at Titian. "You're a painter, not a scholar. Attend to your painting and I'll attend to the Church."

Paul addressed Carafa. "Dr. Luzzatti and I have discussed the Talmud many times. He and I have both garnered wisdom from it. It reflects eight centuries of thought and work. Of course, there will be thoughts that are unpleasant for the Church, but that is true in all writings...even in ours. Are we not accustomed to controversy ourselves?"

Carafa wondered how much he could push the Pope at this moment. A man ambivalent, unhappy at his loss of

Isabella, perhaps overwhelmed by the needed political decisions.

"Threaten to burn the Jews' books publicly and I can guarantee that you'll have more money from them and more money from the 'good Catholic' landowners and shopkeepers. You'll gain respect from the Protestant princes."

"That's what you think it will take to fill the coffers?"

"Yes."

The Pope turned to Titian and said, "That's enough for today."

"But, Your Holiness. Just a bit more time while there is some light."

"There'll be light tomorrow." Titian took his time leaving paying meticulous attention to the placement of his paints and the cleansing of his brushes. Neither Carafa nor Paul said anything. Paul stood, eased the tension in his back, went from the window to open books on the table, stood reading for a while, then moved a quill pen from one side of the table to the other. He finally dipped the pen, scribbled something and handed the small scrap of paper to Carafa.

Carafa read slowly, trying to decipher the shaky handwriting. "This orders a burning of the Talmud."

"Isn't that what you wanted?" Paul asked Carafa.

As Titian shut the door Paul said, "Go to all the synagogues and collect them. Announce when the burning will be and demand that all the Jews be there...all of them from all the synagogues. Make sure you collect taxes as you collect books—the more books they have, the more taxes they'll have to pay."

"I'm glad that you are taking this course of action," said Carafa.

Paul looked drained and exhausted. "We must preserve the Church by whatever means necessary and it can't be preserved without wealth."

"I'll take care of it, Your Holiness," said Carafa.

* * *

Carafa left and immediately went to his own library and asked the messenger to summon Alfonso and Justinian. The two Cardinals entered together and Carafa wondered how they always seemed to arrive and leave together no matter when.

"The Pope has ordered that all the Talmuds from the Jewish synagogues and homes be confiscated. The most trustworthy of the condotierri will do this - they are to collect taxes as well. For each Talmud found we will collect 25 scudi."

"And?" said Alfonso.

"And they're to be burned."

"Really?" said Justinian. "Does Paul truly mean it?"

"First we will go to homes and synagogues with the orders," said Carafa. "Then we will have the condottieri do the collecting of the books and the monies."

Alfonso said, "Well, apparently you have this all figured out. And if we meet resistance?"

Carafa said, "The condotierri. That will be enough."

"Where is this burning to take place?' Justinian asked. "The nobility will want to know."

"In the public square." Carafa replied. "This time we will succeed because I will hire the guards myself."

Alfonso rubbed his hands together. "And you will order the people to come?"

"The Jews will be ordered to come and the rest will come because it is going to be a grand conflagration....a very grand conflagration. And we will not make the same mistakes."

CHAPTER 37

The Congregation and the Talmud

On arriving at synagogue on Friday evening, every rabbi in Rome found a notice at the entrance door warning of the Church's plans for each Jewish congregation. All knew that they would come together as a Jewish community to deal with this disaster, even though their congregations may have spoken prayers or sung melodies a bit differently. They were not only known as "People of the Book" but also as "People of the Books." Many of them could quote The Talmud from memory with its centuries and centuries of wisdom. *Whoever destroys a single life is as guilty as though he had destroyed the entire world; and whoever rescues a single life earns as much merits as though he had rescued the entire world.* Hayyim knew they felt the same way about their Torah and the Talmud—their sacred texts.

The rabbis had agreed through messengers who hurriedly ran from synagogue to synagogue that they would meet at the Catalan synagogue furthest from the center of Rome. When Hayyim joined them, they greeted him with reserve; he had always been somewhat suspect, even evoking jealousy because of his close relationship with the Pope. But no matter what their opinion had been about Israel leaving the faith, they all understood that the rabbi's son was not the killer of Isabella. Their history had taught them that Jews were often wrongly accused of unspeakable crimes. Indeed, they were silently proud that Israel had escaped a hanging.

"Your son is well?" Rabbi Ben Ezra, the Ashkenazi leader, asked. Rabbi Ben Ezra was at least eighty years old, but he stood erect, and his eyes looked upon the listener with keen interest.

"Yes, for the time being." Hayyim hesitated, then spoke softly. "He suffered terribly and now with this burning of the Talmud, I've been thinking that it is time to leave."

Rabbi Ben Ezra put a comforting hand on Hayyim's arm. "Not yet. Not yet. We can help each other. We need to help one another."

Rabbi Elijah di Sabato was ten when his family came to Italy from Spain at the beginning of the Inquisition. He spoke in a gravelly, harsh voice. "This may all have come about because of your wife's consorting with a Gentile."

"Not now. This is not the time for that," said Rabbi Ben Ezra.

Rabbi Samson di Constantini, born to parents who had ancestors in Italy for hundreds of years, agreed. "The Talmud is at stake. What was done was done, and who knows what gives these Christians the sudden anger to deem our books unfit?"

"So," said Rabbi Ben Ezra. "Do we give them some books to burn to satisfy their demand?"

"What are you thinking?" said Rabbi Abraham diLattes. He was the Catalana leader and developed a following through the delivery of his fiery sermons. Hayyim had disapproved because he felt they delved into areas of the supernatural, and thus, the irrational. With diLattes' voice rising, he addressed the other rabbis. "We know that only one of us has had much contact with the Pope lately." He looked directly at Hayyim, but Hayyim ignored him. "Maybe it is because of him that we are suffering."

In spite of diLattes' comments, Hayyim looked upon all these men with a sense of friendship and sympathy that he had not anticipated. They dealt with the minutiae of the everyday life of their members; gambling problems, fidelity issues, apprenticeships—even the murderers among them. It all came to the rabbis first, who might then have to turn the matter over to the gobierno—the governing body of the Jewish community. But now they were dealing with the very soul of the Jewish people—the burning of the beloved book that had given them so much direction in how to go about their daily lives.

"My friends," said diLattes. "For some reason you are ignoring my concern about Rabbi Luzzatti, or should I say Dr. Luzzatti? Maybe he has brought this upon us? It is something to consider, is it not?"

Hayyim paid no attention to the comment. "I like Ben Ezra's idea." He waited to see if there was any dissent. "We'll hide some books and give them some when they send around the condottierri. They don't know how many we have...they may assume what they want...but they won't have more than ten to burn."

"DiLattes is suggesting something else," said Rabbi Ben Ezra. "We need to listen." Hayyim remained silent.

"I am suggesting that we gather a group of us...rabbis and businessmen from the community, and *we* pay a visit to the Pope. We can do that; we've done it in the past." Rabbi diLattes looked around and saw that he had the attention of the others. He continued. "There's nothing to keep us from going to tell the Pope that we do no wrong with our Talmud. Perhaps he hasn't heard this enough from his doctor."

"I beg you. Don't make such a visit. It's too dangerous and too great a personal risk to anyone of us," Hayyim said. "Don't forget what happened to my son."

"Just because you are no longer appreciated at the Palace, doesn't mean that some of us wouldn't be welcome for a meeting." Rabbi di Sabato seemed excited at the prospect.

"Please," said Hayyim. "Please understand. The Pope is in a very weakened political position and relies on bad advisors."

Rabbi Elijah di Sabato paid no heed. "I think Rabbi diLattes has a point. We have not visited the Pope for a while. I suggest that we gather a delegation and find out for ourselves what has caused this change. Perhaps we can find a way to appease him."

Rabbi Ben Ezra said, "It's too dangerous; it's too dangerous. Give them their books and their burning, and we'll then come up with another plan. And maybe we have to think about leaving." But di Sabato and diLattes ignored the rabbi with the most experience in the community.

Rabbi Ben Ezra persisted. "We have to think about where we are going to hide the books if the Pope does not listen to reason."

Hayyim cast a grateful glance at Ben Ezra. "I know exactly, but perhaps that will be looked upon with suspicion as well if I tell you." By this time, he had lost much of his patience.

"I think it is time for more reasoned judgment." Rabbi diLattes continued. "Perhaps we should withhold our banking services."

"Ridiculous! They'll set up their own Christian lenders. Withhold taxes? You'll wind up in prison." Hayyim's voice quavered. The palms of his hands perspired.

"Do we have agreement, that we'll, at least, go to the Palace to plead our case?" Rabbi diLattes said. "Without Dr. Luzzatti?"

The others slowly nodded one by one in agreement. Rabbi Ben Ezra held back tears and briefly put his hand on Hayyim's shoulder.

"Good," said Rabbi diLattes. "We will meet there tomorrow and ask for an audience. Gather two important men from your synagogue. I'm sure that with such a large delegation, the Pope won't refuse to see us. And if he is busy with prayers or ecclesiastical affairs, we will wait." He turned toward Hayyim. "I suggest you invite Finzi and DiBelli as part of your congregation. They seem to have a different point of view than most of your members." Hayyim started to protest but saw more words would be pointless now.

He sat alone as he watched them leave and saw the filtering sunlight come through the mullioned windows of the synagogue. He said to himself, 'It's in God's hands. It's in God's hands."

* * *

Two days later, twelve men dressed in their finest clothes, most in velvet doublets of red, black, and green and black tights, arrived at the the entrance to the Papal Palace.

The men entered, went to the guard's station, and asked to be admitted to see the Pope. Since the death of Isabella, the Pope had been disinclined to see visitors, but the guard felt it best not to offend these well-dressed men from the community. Indeed, the guard knew one of them who had been good enough to lend him money to pay the rent on his modest home.

Upon the guard's announcement to the Pope's secretary that there was a group of well-dressed men waiting to see him, and that he thought they followed the Hebrew faith, the messenger returned and said that the Pope asked if Dr. Luzzatti were among them. The guard, who knew Dr. Luzzatti well, replied that he was not.

"Please show them to the Pope's library. And ask Cardinal Carafa to be there."

The men followed the guard to the library, took their seats, and placed themselves in a semi-circle facing the Pope's chair. They sat quietly, taking in the red damask drapes, the handsome carved mahogany furniture, the paintings rich with color, and the beautifully bound books. Their eyes lingered on the texts and some noted that the Pope had several copies of The Talmud on one of the shelves. Di Constanini signaled Ben Ezra, and the older rabbi just raised an eyebrow in acknowledgement.

The Pope arrived with Cardinal Carafa. The rabbis and delegates stood together and bowed in acknowledgment and respect.

"You should each come and kiss the ring of the Pope, at least. That's what Dr. Luzzatti has done in the past." Cardinal Carafa's voice was high-pitched.

Rabbi ben Ezra, noting the lassitude in the Pope's eyes and the anger of Carafa, spoke unapologetically but politely. "It's contrary to our religious beliefs to do so. Even during the time of Haman, who by the way, is on the ceiling of your Sistine Chapel, we didn't bow down to idols or people who represent idols." Then as if in the way of explanation, "We bow our heads only to the unseen, all knowing, and all powerful God."

Carafa folded his arms across his chest. "Then perhaps this meeting should not go on."

Pope Paul silenced Carafa. "Let them speak." He then addressed the men directly. "Please be seated."

Moses Bascola, who had been one of the men selected to accompany the rabbis because of his success in financial affairs, stood and said, "We have come to plead with you not to burn the Talmud. We live peacefully, and we pay our taxes to you gladly."

Rabbi diLattes stood, did not wait for the Pope to answer, and asked in a conciliatory manner, "Perhaps you can explain your reason for doing so."

Moses Bascola glared at him because they had agreed there would be just one spokesman.

"There are phrases in your book that are damaging to our image of Jesus and Mary," Cardinal Carafa said. "Shall I read them to you?"

The men all sat in silence looking around to see who would answer. Bascola was not that well versed in the Talmud.

Finally Samson di Constantini answered, "That's just a reflection of our history—of one person's thinking at a time. We don't act on those words. They're not written in hate, and what's more they're of ancient times." He hesitated. "I'm sure that you have words in your documents of ancient times as well as deeds that you question." Rabbi Ben Ezra looked at him questioningly.

Cardinal Carafa's eyes blazed. "It is not for you to tell us what is in our documents."

Carafa had hoped that the Pope would intervene, but he had remained silent and impassive. Suddenly, as though awakened from a reverie, Paul asked, "Where is Dr. Luzzatti?"

Di Constantini looked around and saw that no one was going to say anything. Most sat with eyes downcast. "We thought we could better convince you of our loyalty without him. That there is no need to burn our books."

Carafa's face flared with anger. "And none of you were part of the plot that helped the escape of Israel, the Jew who deserved to be hanged? I'd like each one of you to stand up and swear that you were not part of the plot and that you know no one who was part of the plot."

At this, Moses Bascola said with absolute firmness, "If this is what you want, this is what it will be. I'll be the first to swear." And that is what each member did for they had long been inculcated with the belief that they needed to protect their community. One by one they stood and uttered the words, "I swear I was not part of the scheme that kept Israel Luzzatti from hanging."

"But the Talmud influences you and influences others." Carafa said. "How else would Jacob Maninetto have become a Jew? How could that happen without your proselytizing, without your evil words in your Talmud?" The Pope who had seemed distant and removed throughout Carafa's retorts and questions with the Jews, suddenly appeared interested awaiting Bascola's response. When he was a Cardinal, the case of Jacob Maninetto, a monk becoming a Jew, had been widely and sometimes wildly discussed.

The men remained so still that Moses Bascola's heavy breathing could be heard. No one moved. They had not anticipated that this would be brought up in the conversation. Yes, Mantinetto had become a Jew after being a member of the Dominican order and he had done so after attending the Sacred College and learning Hebrew and reading the Talmud. He had also discovered that his mother's grandmother had been Jewish, and he finally understood why candles were lit in their house when she was alive.

Rabbi ben Ezra spoke, for he knew of this drama that had taken place twenty years ago. "He became a Jew of his own volition. We don't ask for people to join our faith. More people have left our faith than joined it."

The Pope's interest was piqued. "And why do you think that's so?"

"For many reasons." Moses Bascola spoke. "They're tired of living with the threat of persecution. They see opportunities in conversion." He paused and added, "Many are cowards."

Suddenly Rabbi diLattes found his voice and added quickly, "We have many commandments that we have to fulfill and some people don't have the strength to fulfill them. Not many...some." He stood as well. It was painful for him to say this.

"I've heard your arguments, gentlemen." The Pope spoke in a distant voice. The visitors shifted in their seats.

The Pope stood. "You're to give your Talmud to the condottieri when they come to collect them. You're to be present when the books are burned, and since we couldn't have Israel Luzzatti condemned for the murder of Isabella, the books will be his substitute."

The men looked around to see who would challenge the Pope.

"What if we can find Israel for you?" Alberto Finzi spoke from his seat. "Will you give up the burning our Talmuds?"

DiBelli also stood. "Your Holiness," he bowed slightly, "we would like him back so we—we Jews can try him for the crime of conversion. With so much desire, we should be able to find him."

The other men, still in shock over the Pope's decision, stared in disbelief at Finzi and DiBelli.

The Pope looked straight ahead signaling to Carafa that it was time to end the meeting.

After seeing that the Pope was not going to say more, Carafa stammered. "There's that possibility... I mean to save...to save your...sacred texts. Israel would seem a fair exchange." Carafa was imagining another hanging or even a burning—this time with much more security.

When Moses Bascola rose, diLattes was the first to stand with him. Each one rose slowly. Several of the men bowed deferentially while others were determined to leave with their heads held high. They ignored Finzi and DiBelli who remained stiffly in their seats. Carafa called out to them as they were leaving. "Gentlemen, you're leaving without an answer."

DiLattes, the firebrand, apparently spoke for the group. "I believe we know the answer. If we give you Israel, you won't burn our Talmuds. Correct?" He spoke with defiance. "Then, I guess, gentlemen, you'll have to prepare for a book burning."

CHAPTER 38

Home

Alba set a slice of her oat bread along with a dollop of freshly churned butter before her husband. She walked back to the fire, threw a piece of kindling on, and dipped her hand into her apron pocket to pull out a clean piece of linen to wipe her brow. Sitting across from Hayyim, she watched her husband carefully spread the butter along the flat of bread, take a bite, and chew deliberately while drumming his fingers on the table. He slowly got up and threw another twig on the fire.

"There's enough heat for the soup," Alba said.

Hayyim returned to the table and pushed the plate aside. "I was just making sure." In the short trip from table to fireplace and back again, he conjured up the image of the visit of rabbis and congregants with the Pope and shuddered. He imagined them in the Pope's study—a room he had known so well. No one had come to report to him what had happened, and he didn't know whether this meant good news or bad news.

"You may not want to eat, my dear husband, but I want to know what happened." She pushed another piece of bread toward him. "Don't you like the bread? I just made it this morning."

"The bread is fine, and I have no idea of what happened. Did you see anyone coming to report to me?" He wanted to bite his tongue at his shortness of temper, but he could not keep his frustration in check. The Pope had dismissed him; his fellow rabbis had dismissed not only him but his wisdom. And when could he ever say to her that this may never have come about if she hadn't had her visit with Isabella? Not now, he thought.

"I'm going to try to ride to the monastery to see Israel. I want to talk with Father Bruno to see what he thinks about Israel's health."

Alba turned again toward the fire, beads of perspiration poring down her face. This time she added nothing but stirred the soup so rapidly with a large ladle that drops spat from the kettle in every direction.

"I'm riding Hillel," he said. "Would you give me some loaves of bread and jam and I'll take them with me? The brothers will be glad to receive the bread. I think you use more eggs than they do."

Normally she would have smiled at this small piece of knowledge of her husband's. It was part of what had drawn her to him...this paying attention to details of their household and of her world. Only he would know that she made her bread with eggs, but today she took the ladle from the soup and laid it on the table with a loud clatter. She quickly wrapped the bread in parchment paper and put some jam, which had been sitting in a bowl, in a small jar handed both to him, without the usual kiss on the check and "travel safely and look out for robbers." Her usual affection lay someplace under her irritation with him.

"Be careful with the jar. See that it doesn't break on your ride." He took the jar, set it aside on the table, gathered her in his arms, and started to plant kisses all over her face, her neck, her breasts. She pushed him away. "We've no time for this now."

"Later," he said.

"We'll see," she said.

Hayyim was pleased to see that Hillel was as smart as Giacomo and could find his way to the monastery after only a couple of runs. Although, he didn't stop to see Israel—he was afraid he was being watched—he always stopped at the trough to give the horse some rest and water. So when his master gave him slack in the reins, that was the signal to go to the monastery, and Hillel loved that ride because he loped over small streams and up hills just steep enough to challenge him but not big enough to wear him out. Somehow Hillel knew when the rich leaves of the forest covered a hole that he should avoid.

At about three kilometers into their ride, Hillel began acting strangely, suddenly slowing into a trot from a full gallop, turning his head from side to side, and resisting Hayyim's leg commands to move back to a gallop. Hayyim heard dogs barking and the galloping of horses' hooves. This was strange, as this path through the forest was seldom used. Thieves stayed away from the woods, because there would scarely be a traveler worthy to rob.

Hayyim heard the unmistakeable grunting of a boar in the distance as well as men whooping and hollering. As the group came closer, Hayyim recognized them as members of the Papal Court; their hunting garb showed the papal colors of green and yellow. His first thought was to urge Hillel to a gallop and flee in the other direction, but decided it would be safer to acknowledge the group as they sped by.

As they came closer with pikes raised, Hayyim recognized them as Cardinals Alfonso, Justinian, and Carafa, and they clearly knew him for they brought their horses to an abrupt halt and lowered their spears. The boar could still be heard now some distance away although now the grunts were interspersed with squeals.

Hayyim acknowledged the three with a nod while patting Hillel's neck and whispering in his ear that they would be going soon. The horse shifted from side to side for a minute or so, then stopped and remained still. Hayyim relaxed the reins.

"Good day."

Alfonso addressed him icily. "This is a path used mostly by hunters. You're not a hunter, are you?"

"No, I'm not a hunter." Hayyim had considered saying that he thought it cruel to chase animals for sport, but he remained silent.

"Then why are you here? Is it that you have more time now that you are no longer the king's physician?" Justinian wobbled a bit on his saddle as he spoke.

Hayyim realized that he was sweating under his garments although there had been a pleasant cool breeze. "Hillel, this horse, is the reason I am here. He needs his exercise and this is the best place for him to run at full gallop."

Carafa narrowed his eyes. "Isn't this a new horse for you?"

"My horse, Giacomo, died after suffering an illness. He was buried according to our law." Why, thought Hayyim, am I saying this? They cannot be interested in how I bury my horse. Stop prating nonsense.

Carafa's horse reared slightly and whinnied. "I'm sure you'll show us the grave if necessary." Alfonso became impatient. "Not now. We need to be going on. The dogs will lose the scent of the boar if we linger. This can wait."

Carafa raised an eyebrow. Didn't Alfonso sense there might be something here? Wasn't Giacomo the horse that ran off with Israel? No, Alfonso, was more interested in the damn boar. "We can send the condottieri to search within ten kilometer radius of here. Surely we have the resources to do that, do we not, Cardinal Alfonso?"

"Of course, we have the resources. It shall be done as soon as we have killed the boar." With that, Alfonso tipped his hat; it was not the usual cardinal's hat. It was green velvet made in the style of the day for members of the nobility. With another tilt of his hat, they were off.

Hayyim held Hillel back—he wanted to join the other horses for he was eager to run. Hayyim waited a few minutes, then kicked hard with his heels and gave Hillel free rein, saying in a whisper as though he were afraid of being overheard, "To the monastery."

When Hayyim arrived at the priory and tied up the horse, he adjusted his doublet and his hat and wet his face and hands at the water well that served the trough. He saw several of the brothers outside walking in twos or alone, some reading as they walked, others in whispered conversation, and he noticed one alone in quiet contemplation. Hayyim followed close behind his son along the path and nodded to the other brothers who seemed to be walking and praying at the same time. Hayyim was close enough to hear Israel saying prayers—prayers that were associated with rosary beads—and he imagined his son holding the string of beads in his hand. Hayyim did not want to startle him, so he touched Israel gently on the shoulder. He withdraw his hand quickly from the fabric of the friar's robe. Israel turned to see his father and gave him a warm embrace. Tears of joy welled up within Hayyim. "It's been so long. There were nights I could not sleep wondering how you were."

Israel turned away from his father's arms slowly. "It's wonderful to see you. How's Mother? How was your ride out here? We'll sit on the bench here. It's a bit chilly but if we sit in the sun, we can capture some of the warmth of the day. It's a lovely day, isn't it?" A torrent of words flowed from him. They sat on the bench, each feeling tremendous joy in the other's presence. Hayyim took his son's hands in his and said softly, "Let me look at you. It's a miracle that you look so well. Are you completely healed? If so it is indeed a wonder." He leaned closer to him. "And the dungeon. Have you recovered from the dungeon?"

An air of anxiety hung over Hayyim as he watched his son struggle to answer. He wanted to be the protector, the father, but his son was away from him in Spain where he adopted Christianity, then in a dungeon, and now in this monastery. How is he to be a father to this "child"—this person?

"Sometimes my ribs hurt and I still have headaches, but all will get better with time. I've gotten excellent care here." Israel paused as he saw the worry in his father's face. "Father, it's best that I be most direct with you. I know you're interested in my health but..."

"But what? Considering the fact that you were nearly dead, I'm overjoyed. You're almost ready to leave here to be able to go with us. Mother and I are considering leaving Rome."

Israel cleared his throat and took in his father's questions and worried eyes. "No, Father. I've decided to stay here. They took me in, hid me, and cared for me. I can't just leave them as though they were just a fleeting moment in my life. I want to help and repay them. They put themselves at risk for me. How many people do you know would do that for me?"

Hayyim stared at his son and knew he needed to choose his words carefully. "Your mother and I would give our right arms for you."

The sun was quite warm even though it was late afternoon. The rays shone through the giant oak creating shades of light and dark that appeared mystical. Israel looked away in the distance, fingering the rosary beads in his hands in no particular order.

"They're proselytizers, aren't they? They want to make sure that we all become Christians?" Hayyim spit out the word, "all."

Israel took his father's hands in his. "No. They don't want to convert all of you." Hayyim winced at the last phrase. His son was continuing to write himself outside of his religion. "The brothers here are disgusted with the actions of the Papal Court. They simply want to help the poor and want to eradicate the practice of indulgences from the Church. That's their work and that's the mission I want to join. I can't turn away from those who have been good to me."

Hayyim thought back to the day not so long ago when Israel returned from Spain, and he was torn between seeing him back and the anger that he felt at his conversion. He welcomed him, secretly hoping that his son would come back to the faith, but here now was another rebuke. He hesitated. "Did you know they're planning to confiscate the Talmuds from the synagogues and burn them?"

"Why don't you and mother convert? You're knowledgeable in the New Testament. You'll have an easier life. With the rise of Martin Luther we are living in times that are much more dangerous for Jews. Do you always want to live in danger?"

Hayyim swallowed hard and turned his face away from his son, afraid of what it would reveal. He tried to sound reasonable when he put his hands on his son's shoulders.

"If we were not in a place where others could see us and where quiet is the norm, I would scream and shake you at the same time. How can you say those words? Are you forgetting that I'm a rabbi? Your grandfather and great grandfather were rabbis?" Don't you see? Don't you see that we as a people are caught in the middle of a struggle for power, and we have fought that struggle and cannot give in."

"And aren't you tired of being in the middle of that struggle? You could rid yourself of that struggle."

"What I haven't told you my son, is that I ran into the Cardinals when they were out hunting." He paused. "Can you imagine that? They're out hunting while the Church is falling apart. Protestanism creeps up upon them, but it creeps."

Israel spoke as though he had not heard his father's comment. "Father Bruno knows that we will have to deal with the excesses of the church. I'd like to stay and help them. We're planning to send some delegates to the Council of Trent shortly and they will call for a limitation on indulgences."

Dear God, thought Hayyim, he is one of them. Hayyim stood and addressed his son. "The condottieri... they'll be here. When the Cardinals finish their hunt, I'm sure they'll direct a search of a ten kilometer radius and if they do, they'll find you here. You must leave here and find your way to another country. Perhaps back to Spain."

Israel sat, head down, and kept his hands folded in his lap. "No, Father. I'm not going to leave here for I know I'll be protected. I assure you that I'll be sheltered here...in some way....I'll be sheltered and protected. Father Bruno knows of my intentions."

"Father Bruno doesn't know that the Cardinals will have the condottieri searching in this vicinity shortly. He doesn't know that there's to be a burning of the Talmud. These are very dangerous times. I'm afraid for your life and your mother's and others in the community. It may not be safe for Jews here in Rome any longer...even conversos...especially conversos."

It was nearing dusk. The sun's rays had diminished and no longer burned, but the dust still sparkled. Hayyim reached over to his son, and took his son's head in his hands and kissed him on the forehead...a gesture he had done for the first fifteen years of his son's life. It was usually done only on the Sabbath, but Hayyim chose to do it now. Israel kept his head bowed, not resisting his father's love nor the ritual that accompanied it.

"I must go now for there is much to do. I'll come back to see Father Bruno another time. I should return to your mother now." They parted with a quick embrace.

Hayyim walked to where Hillel had been tied up, and the horse nuzzled his master in comfort. Hayyim pushed him away and held the horse's head between his two hands. "Hillel, they're going to burn the Talmud, and my son wants to be one of them. What do you suggest?"

The horse tossed his huge head out of Hayyim's hands. "All right. Are you suggesting that it's in God's hands?"

Hayyim mounted the horse, slapped him on the rear, and said in a loud voice although no one could hear him. "We'll see. We'll see."

CHAPTER 39

Burning

Hayyim arrived at his synagogue where he knew the men would be meeting. The approaching dusk had not diminished the intense heat. After tying up Hillel, he was grateful for the cool interior of the synagogue guaranteed to linger by the thickness of the walls. A few candles cast flickering light in the sanctuary and on the men's somber faces. They were seated around a plain wooden table dressed in simple black garb. It took him a few minutes to recognize the faces of Finzi, DiBelli, ben Veniste, Benjamin, and Bascola. Yes, and Rabbi Ben Ezra.

When he took a seat at the table, they nodded their welcome. The men were discussing whether or not they could accept the ruling of Rabbi Ezekiel that Hannah Margolis' hymen had been broken because of a fall. Hayyim knew that Hannah was only five years old, and his medical training had taught him that it was impossible that a hymen rupture could be caused by a fall, but unless they asked, this was an argument he did not want to enter now. It would come up again.

Rabbi ben Ezra addressed him. "Does the esteemed doctor want to weigh in on this discussion?"

Hayyim shook his head. "Not now."

"Then we will table this for another time and go on with more urgent business." Rabbi Ben Ezra stood and bowed slightly toward him. Hayyim thought that the men were looking at him rather expectantly. So the meeting had not gone well, as he had anticipated. Hayyim hesitated a brief moment before speaking. "You were received by the Pope?"

"Yes, and Cardinal Carafa was present as well," Bascola spoke. "We owe you an apology and ask for your help in this tragedy that's about to occur."

"We say this knowing that you have had enough tragedy in your personal life. Your son ....," Ben Ezra said.

"Right now, my son is no concern of yours." Hayyim blinked to hold back tears. His back was slick with perspiration. "The community deserves utmost protection and we have the responsibility to provide it. Our laws say that, and I hope your hearts say that as well." Finzi and diBelli squirmed in their seats.

"We await, Rabbi, to hear your words of wisdom," Moses Bascola said. Hayyim thought that he heard sincerity in those words and was glad for them.

"Don't blame yourselves for the decision of the Papal Palace. Don't think you were inadequate in any way," Hayyim said. "There are those in power who influence Pope Paul. As always we're at the mercy of rulers and we.... we've yet to be rulers of any land since David, so we must think carefully if we are to remain in Rome." The men murmured to one another.

"Can you honestly be thinking that we need to leave here?"

"We've made our homes here, our children go to school here, universities are open to us; we don't live in a ghetto as do our brothers in Venice," said Rabbi Ben Ezra who had been here the longest—even during the reign of Pope Clement VII.

Hayyim rubbed his eyes and the men, for the first time, could see the redness around the rim of his eyes and the dark half moons underneath. The flickering of the candles cast an eerie shadow on the side of his face, making it appear even more strained.

"You witnessed the attempts to hang my son. Now there is talk of book burning." He waved his right hand for emphasis or to relieve his agitation.

At this,David Benjamin, who had always been somewhat antagonistic toward the rabbi, stood. A tall forbidding man with a hollow-cheeked well-worn face, he always wore the finest of velvet clothes and had succeeded in the spice trade because of his sense of adventure and willingness to take risks. Benjamin had earned the respect of the community. Some were even intimidated by him. Hayyim knew that Alberto Finzi and Bernardo DiBelli looked upon Benjamin with admiration.

"It was your error to send your son to the Palace and your error to allow your wife to invite Isabella to your house. It does us no good to tempt fate like that." Hayyim wondered if Benjamin was sweating under his doublet; although his face glistened, he showed no beads of sweat on his brow or his cheeks.

"By the way," Benjamin added, "Have you heard from your son?"

"No," Hayyim said, thinking he needed to ask God for forgiveness for his lie.

The men watched as Moses Bascola intervened.

"We can't resolve your feelings about Israel Luzzatti and the family, nor can we take on the task of leaving Rome. We must focus on the burning of our Talmud."

Hayyim took Bascola's words as a cue to speak. "I have a plan"

"Our books have been burned before and we've survived," said Benjamin.

Hayyim wondered why this man, who hardly ever attended synagogue and was not a member of the gobierno, was so adamant. Hayyim spoke wearily, "My comment about leaving Rome is only a thought, and we can certainly deal with that later...if at all. I don't wish to impose my will on you."

David Benjamin took a piece of linen from his pocket, and slowly wiped his face. The men watched in anticipation of more words, but he took his seat.

Hayyim continued. "We must each prepare one Talmud to give them when they enter the synagogue. Keep one preserved in a place under the floorboards. The condotierri won't go tearing them up, but they will search through libraries and the ark itself." Rabbi Ben Ezra covered his eyes with his hands.

"What about those in our homes?" asked David ben Veniste. He worried about the five hundred-year-old Talmud in his house; he came from a long line of rabbis.

"You're a printer," said Rabbi Luzzatti. "Hide the valuable one. Print something that looks like a Talmud. They won't know the difference."

"Why don't we give them a list of everyone who has a Talmud?" Benjamin asked. "Possibly, there'll be less destruction."

Bascola countered sharply. "It is the ultimate act of cowardice to comply like that."

"It isn't an act of compliance. It's a ploy to protect the community. Maybe then they'll leave us alone."

Hayyim Luzzatti answered. He could actually hear his heart pounding; he inhaled sharply as he began to speak. "I agree. They wish to demonstrate their power with the Jews in order to show their power to the Protestants. Let them have their demonstration of power. Martin Luther is winning over the indulgences. The Catholic Church needs to win out over something. It might as well be our Talmuds that will never really be lost to us. They can't rip it out of our hearts and minds. Let's give them the books. They will see it as submission."

David ben Veniste stood and spoke in an unsteady voice. "Do you think they'll then let us live in peace? Perhaps we will need to leave Rome. But now, I prefer to defy them by hiding our precious books."

Finzi finally stood, and all eyes turned toward him, tired as they might be. "I must remind you, gentlemen, we wouldn't be here discussing this possibility if you had agreed to my plan. I'm sure that the rabbi knows where his son is. We're sacrificing our religion, our books, ourselves for one man who has disgraced our community."

DiBelli rose beside him, his face flushed. "The rabbi's wife associates with Christians. That's heresy in our community. Perhaps his wife was a practicing Christian."

Finzi put a hand on his friend's shoulder to silence him, but his business partner would not remain quiet.

DiBelli continued. "The rabbi's son returned to take over our accounts, mind you, our accounts that we took care of while he was in Spain practicing Christianity, and the rabbi's wife socializes with Christians. How can you people be taking this man's advice?"

Finzi pushed his friend down and grabbed on to the back of the pew, face bright red. "Jewish women should not consort with Christians," he shouted. "God told me that Isabella should die in order to prevent your wife from continuing to see her." He immediately covered his mouth with his hand in horror, realizing that he had all but confessed to the murder of Isabella.

Pandemonium ensued. Hayyim lunged at him. Ben Veniste pulled him back. Prayer books dropped from laps onto the floor and were quickly picked up and touched with lips. "How could you?" someone shouted.

"It's against Jewish law," ben Ezra practically screamed.

Hayyim slumped in his chair, recognizing the unnecessary abomination that had been wrought upon his family. What malevolent hand of God had come down to cause such evil?

The room grew dark. The night sky was without a moon, and the glowing candles barely shed any light. What were they to do with this confession?

David ben Veniste finally stood. "Gentlemen, I have much work to do for I must create Talmuds that will be thrown on the pyre." He looked at the group and said, "I will need help. I can teach you to set the type. Are you willing?" All raised their hands except Finzi and DiBelli.

"And I," said ben Venesti, "I'll create the list and deliver it to the Cardinals tomorrow. They'll know it is true for I will give them lists of only the wealthiest in our midst."

Hayyim sat in stunned silence. Weren't they going to say anything about Finzi's confession? "Gentlemen," he cried. "We have had a confession. We have a murderer in our midst." The last words he uttered in Hebrew. "Did you not hear, or are you deaf to justice?"

Moses Bascola walked around and stood in front of Hayyim, putting a hand on either shoulder as though he were literally holding him together. "We'll hold court to deal with the murderers in our midst, but for now we must maintain silence. Should the church authorities know, more wrath would be brought upon us. We'll deal with them ourselves."

The rabbi could only stand with the assistance of Bascola. "We must pray," and Hayyim began the ancient prayer used for thousands of years when adversity faced the Jewish people. They did not pray in unison but they arrived at the end together—"How long, O Lord, shall the wicked rejoice?" and they ended with a resounding "amen."

"Then it is agreed," said Moses Bascola. "We'll see each other again in front of that terrible fire. Prepare the children so they know how to behave."

The men left the synagogue in darkness. Some mounted horses. Most walked to their nearby homes and with unsteady voices told their families and trusted Jewish neighbors of the plan. Mothers tried to explain to young children who could not possibly comprehend why this was happening. Why would anyone want to burn books? They had one day to execute their plan because in two days, the condottieri would be at their synagogues and their homes.

The families were so well prepared that when the condottieri arrived, the doors of the Jewish homes were practically thrown open to them. Rather than hand the books directly to the condottieri, the men let the enforcers search their houses, so that the soldiers would think they had discovered a well-hidden Talmud. Some of the condottieri were zealous and cruel as they searched, leaving wanton destruction in their wake. Others were more respectful when they entered the homes of people they recognized from their daily lives as traders, merchants, or bankers.

That night after all the books had been collected, parents and children stayed in their homes. Some fathers read from the Talmud to the children and women in the family who could not read, or who had not been educated in Hebrew. They went to their beds early and some of the men and women made love after the husband had brushed away the wife's tears. Sleep eluded many; perhaps the very youngest ones, who could not begin to fathom their parents' restless thoughts, managed to dream.

Although the next day was the Sabbath, no one prepared for synagogue. They did their morning chores in silence, quietly ate the breakfast meal of bread and jam, and each dressed in their finest garments of velvet and silk. The men reluctantly affixed the yellow circle to the sleeve of their garments and the women wove light blue silk strips of fabric through their hair. It had been required of Jewish women in the past by the Roman clergy; they thought it would be wise to follow a former stipulation. Some rode in carriages and others on horseback while the rest walked solemnly together. They were again prepared to stand together as a community for a horrible event.

When the Jews entered the plaza, a roar arose from the crowd. "Burn the books! Burn the books!" Although a ring of horses of the condottieri held the crowd back, some flung bottles at the Jews, but fortunately they were too far away and the glass shattered on the cobblestones. Immediately five young boys came out with brooms and swept the glass away to avoid problems for the horses as well as the clergy who were to appear there. Which of the clergy would be there, no one was sure. Would the Pope come this time? And if he did, what would that signify?

When Hayyim and Alba Luzzatti arrived on foot, they stood stoically in the part of the plaza that had been set aside for the Jews. They stood next to the family of Moses Bascola, closest to the pyre...more than anyone else except perhaps for the person who was to cast the first torch.

"What is that?" Alba clutched Hayyim's arm as she gazed upward. Hayyim looked and saw a pole affixed in the middle of the pyre with a noose attached to it. As Hayyim's head went up, so did the heads of the others standing there with him, and a shudder went through the crowd. What did this mean?

Before long, trumpets sounded and Cardinals Alfonso, Justinian, and Carafa came out on magnificent white horses decked out in the papal colors of green and yellow. If not for the anguish attached to the scene, it would have been a splendid sight. As the Cardinals rode out, a cheer went up from the crowd. The noise diminished suddenly when they saw a man slumped on the fourth horse with his legs bound, his hands tied behind him, his head covered by a large hood—being led by one of the largest men in the condottieri. The crowd was so still that Cardinal Carafa, who spoke without shouting, could be heard by everyone.

"Behold, an apostate in our midst. Someone who has left his Christianity to return to a Jewish faith and thinks he can flee. His promise to remain true to the Catholic faith was broken; he is like all Jews, not to be trusted." Normally the crowd would have let out a cheer, but they, like the Jews, remained in stunned silence. Who was this hooded man? Carafa resumed his speech. "When we found him, do you think we found the Christian Bible with him? No, we found the Talmud, the heretical book we are burning today. He says he is a Christian man. Do you believe him?"

The crowd recovered from its stunned silence and answered together. "No. No!" And as if someone had cued him, an anonymous voice came from the crowd, "Burn him. Burn him. Burn the books." His voice rang loud and clear and needed to be said only once before the rest of the crowd picked up the chant.

"Burn him! Burn the books!"

The Jews in the crowd held tight to their children's hands. As they started to cry, mothers and fathers clasped their hands over the children's mouths to avoid drawing attention to themselves. "Be brave," they said. "This is the time to be brave like David."

"We found this man on his way to Spain, fleeing from the monastery. Our marvelous condottieri found him hiding in the woods." Although the Cardinal expected a cheer at this last sentence, the crowd remained silent, for many of them had suffered under the ruthlessness of the police of Rome.

"The monastery." Alba clutched at Hayyim's sleeve. "He said, the monastery." Hayyim started forward but was pulled back by Moses Bascola on one side and Alba on the other.

Cardinal Carafa saw the gesture and immediately pounced on it. "Yes, Dr. Luzzatti, you have something to say?"

"This is wrong. You have courts of law if someone has done something wrong. Do you not?"

Alba clutched at his sleeve pulling off the yellow Star of David and they both reached to the ground to pick it up. "It's Israel. They have found him. We must do something," she whispered.

They both stood and Hayyim felt himself supported by the strong arm of Moses Bascola. Alba stared straight ahead still holding the yellow cloth in her hand.

Cardinal Alfonso started to speak, but Cardinal Carafa raised his hand slightly, and Alfonso remained silent. "I suggest you hold on to your yellow star, Dr. Luzzatti." Carafa looked as though he were studying the rabbi's face for some sign of distress. "Religious law is higher than the laws of the state." He then raised his right hand toward the sky and brought it down sharply.

"Let the burning begin."

With that, the huge guardsman who had stood beside the hooded man dragged him down, carried him on his back and placed him on a bench, and a lad of sixteen shaped the noose around the hooded man's neck. A cheer went up and the youth removed the cowl and the crowd could see a gaunt face burning with a feverish glow, eyes turned upwards. Hayyim and Alba both covered their mouths. It wasn't Israel. Hayyim recognized Father Nicholas and hung his head. Another man's death. He was at the center of another death. Was this what God wanted? Hayyim watched, barely able to breath. Alba held back tears.

The guardsman then went to the burning embers in which a long staff had been placed with pitch soaked rag at the end. As he pulled it from the embers, it flamed. By this time, a soft rain began. Someone in the crowd said, "Light a strong fire. It must burn even in the rain."

"The rain will last but a short while, and we'll see a burning that we have been waiting to see for a long time. The Cardinals' presence guarantees that this apostate will burn," answered another with authority as he picked at the lice on his hairy arms.

"I can't bear to see the burning of flesh."

"They crucified Our Lord, didn't they? Now they will see a burning and understand what suffering is."

Before putting the fire to the books, the guardsman tightened the noose around Father Nicolas's neck, the assistant quickly removed the bench and threw it into the pyre. The guardsman patted his assistant on the back because simultaneously as the bench was removed, Nicholas' neck snapped. Hayyim wondered who had bribed the guard to help Father Nicholas avoid death by burning. Who?

Simultaneously, the guard lit his torch to the books and most of the crowd watched in silence as the fire blazed. The books burned quickly as did Father Nicolas' body. The smell of burning flesh permeated the damp air.

Hayyim turned to Alba. "I cannot bear to watch this." He took her elbow and started to walk. Carafa called out, "The Jews are to stay until the end. Until every page has turned to ash and every piece of his flesh is crisp."

"For the good Christians who will stay and stamp out the faggots from the fire, there will be coins for you," added Justinian.

The drunkest among the crowd managed to gather the few coins that surrounded the remains. Children with tears streaming down their faces were silent. The community of Jews remained oddly protected by the condottieri that were nearby.

More of the crowd dispersed. Most had seen what they came for; some wanted to hear shrieks and howls and were disappointed; others spent energy in cursing the Jews and felt satisfied. They were content to have a reason to continue to celebrate in their homes and inns where more brew could be had. Just then, Cardinal Carafa signaled that the trumpets be blown. The fanfare drew the crowd to a halt.

"Let it be known that the Church will deal with all measure of apostasy this way. Go to your homes and pray that you realize the goodness and the power of the Church as your way to salvation. Both young and old shall be thinking about salvation and fulfilling the sacraments of the Catholic Church is the only true way." He raised his voice, "Do you agree?"

With that some in the crowd of onlookers raised their fists and shouted, "Kill the heretics. Murder them all. The Catholic Church is the only salvation." Cardinal Carafa said,

"I do not hear everyone's voice." With that, a roar came from the crowd, "The Catholic Church is our only salvation."

Cardinal Justinian shouted, "It would be louder and have more vigor if the Hebrews joined us." Members on both sides of the crowd looked at one another.

Justinian, seeing Carafa frown, barked, "Not today. The next time." Then he turned to make sure the Jews heard him and repeated, "Not today. The next time." A few in the crowd cheered. Most remained silent and turned to leave. Cardinal Alfonso gave the signal that the trumpeters, the condotierri, should depart now and so they took off on their horses, leaving the Jews in stunned silence.

When the crowd was gone and they were sure that none of the Christians were coming back to taunt them, the Jews went to the smoldering ashes and each man scooped up a pile of in a linen handkerchief.

They walked in twos and threes, in silence—the men leading, women and children following. When they reached the cemetery, Bascola and Benjamin found shovels and dug a hole. Then, each who had a white handkerchief with ashes, dropped it into the hole. Finally, they took up the shovels and threw loamy dirt on top until the linens were completely hidden from view. Then they murmured the Kaddish for the dead.

After the prayer, all eyes turned to Hayyim. "No. Not today. I cannot be your rabbi and console you. With what? With some piece of liturgy that says it's part of God's plan. I cannot. A God who would give me Israel and allow this good man to go to his death in such a horrific manner. Go to your homes and talk with your families. Think about your future in Rome."

He took Alba's hand and started to walk. No one else moved. "Go home," he said. "That is all I can give you now. Go home."

CHAPTER 40

Pope's Illness

Alba and Hayyim returned to their home after the burial of ashes in the cemetery, touched the mezuzah on the frame of the front door, put their fingers to each other's lips, and then held each other in silent sorrow. "What's going to happen to Israel?" asked Alba. "What's going to happen to us?" Her husband tried to console her with an embrace and a kiss on her forehead, but she pulled away. She repeated, "What's going to happen to us? To Israel? You must go to him tonight."

"No. There are too many drunken brawlers on the street—the condottieri are still out. Someone may decide to follow me. No, not tonight," he said tersely. "Tomorrow, I will ride out there and talk to Father Bruno and Israel again. They will be devastated when they hear the news about Father Nicolas and perhaps will not want Israel at the monastery. His presence just means danger for them." He extended his shaking hand to her. "Come, a cup of hot water with lemon juice and some grapes from the garden. We need something to change the taste in our mouths after such a terrible day." He averted his eyes so she would not see his tears.

Alba kindled the fire and put the kettle on the hearth to prepare the hot water. She managed to do all these chores with tears streaming down her face. "I don't think I can bear any more. Isabella, the burning of our Talmud, Nicolas being burned at the stake, and Israel. They will still be searching for him. I can't bear to think what will happen if they find him."

"One minute, one hour, one day," said Hayyim soothingly. "We will deal with it all." Just as they were about to sit down with their drink, they heard a fierce pounding on their door. "Dr. Luzzatti, open up, quickly."

"Please be careful," Alba tugged at the sleeve of his cassock. Hayyim rushed to the door with a long wooden staff in hand. When he opened the door and peered out into the moonlight, he was astonished to see two Swiss Guard from the papal palace—one still on horseback.

"Dr. Luzzatti," said the mounted guard, trying to hold his horse still. "We are here to take you to the palace. The Pope is ill."

"I am no longer the Pope's doctor."

"Nevertheless, these are our orders. We will take you on one of our horses so that we can get there quickly."

Hayyim saw that there was no point in arguing. If they wished, these guardsmen were big enough and could simply sweep him up and place him on a horse. "I will go and get my bag. Give me a moment."

With that he went to the back room to fetch his bag of medicinal herbs and told Alba of his mission. "Don't go." She grabbed his arm. "It is too dangerous."

"There are two Swiss Guards outside. I've been asked by the Pope to see him because he is sick. I'm a doctor. I don't have a choice, do I?"

"Perhaps this is just a ruse."

He saw the Swiss Guards becoming impatient. "If anyone comes for my help while I am away, tell them that I will be back soon, that I'm on a personal errand."

Alba's shoulders slumped. She knew there was no point in arguing with him, and she kissed him on both cheeks. "May the God of Abraham go with you."

Hayyim carried his bag and went to the two guards .who waited for him on the cobblestone streets. The fish monger stopped cutting the innards out of the fish he was working on and the flower woman dropped the bouquet of zinnias upon seeing two Swiss Guards on great white horses with Luzzatti holding onto the back of one of the guards as they cantered off in the direction of the papal palace.

When they arrived, Hayyim dismounted, and the guard said, "William will accompany you to the Pope's bedroom."

With William leading the way, Hayyim walked to the Pope's chamber. Although Hayyim was walking rapidly behind William, he reflected for a moment that he had not been in the palace for a while. A new painting graced the wall outside the chamber. Hayyim looked briefly and saw an elegant woman staring at the viewer, declaring herself nobility. He recognized a younger Isabella and thought, "All this beauty. For what?"

Hayyim arrived at the Pope's bedroom. The completed portrait of the Pope dominated the room. Titian had made him appear powerful and wise in his red robes with his white beard and piercing eyes, in spite of a body bent with age. The Pope lay on his bed. The red-robed, and red-hatted Cardinal Carafa stood at the bedside.

Pier Luigi and Ranuncio, both somber, were seated at the edge of the bed—their eyes, red and bloodshot.

Hayyim bowed slightly to Cardinal Carafa. "I'm surprised that I was called."

"You weren't my choice, but the Pope requested that you be brought in." He looked at the Pope. "He's quite ill, and I don't think your usual bag of tricks will work."

"I'll need to talk with him, and then do an examination. Do you wish to be here while I do that?"

"Of course, I'm to be here."

The Pope's sons remained silent. They apparently had neither the will nor the desire to intervene.

"I'd like to be alone with Dr. Luzzatti. It's been a long time." Pope Paul addressed his sons in a whisper. They leaned forward to hear him. "My sons, you are to leave as well."

The two rose from their seats reluctantly. Ranuncio whispered, "We'll be outside." He then turned to his brother. "Come, Pier Luigi."

Carafa did not move. The Pope waved a tired hand toward him. "Wait outside. Should there be a problem, I'll ring the bell." As Carafa started to protest, the Pope said, "Don't dismiss me yet, Carafa." The Pope picked up the bell at his side and rang it with all the energy he could muster. It rang dully.

"I shall be right outside the door." Carafa reluctantly backed out of the room, bowing to the Pope.

Out in the hallway filled with tapestries and marble busts of past Popes, Carafa sat on a leather-bound chair and held a book in his hands while Pier Luigi and Ranuncio paced. Ranuncio finally stopped before Carafa, towering over him with anger. Ranuncio's voice shook as he spoke. "You know perfectly well that Israel Luzzatti and his family had nothing to do with the murder of my mother. Yet, you do nothing to find the real killer. All you think of is your power and lands. How do I know you're not responsible for the illness of my father?"

Pier Luigi pulled his brother away from Carafa. "You're not thinking clearly, Ranuncio. Your frustration with Carafa will not help to bring back our mother. Dr. Luzzatti will be able to tell if Father has been poisoned."

Upon hearing his brother's words, Ranuncio slumped on the marble floor and sat shaking with sobs. Pier Luigi knelt in order to put his arm around his brother.

Carafa spoke in a restrained whisper. "Whatever you may think, I've always loved your father and wanted nothing but the best for him and the Church. I would never harm him. And the two of you should not be pointing fingers at me regarding the acquisition of lands, considering how much you have within your own domains."

Three men sat in silence—an awkward distance among them.

Inside the Pope's chamber, Hayyim talked to the Pope. "I shall have to press on your stomach and try to listen to your heart, so I'll need to put my ear to your chest."

Hayyim pressed on the Pope's stomach, and he let out a low groan.

"Did that hurt?" asked Hayyim. The Pope nodded. Hayyim pressed again to locate the source of the pain.

"Do you remember we talked about where exactly the soul is located?" Hayyim was prodding and trying to discern any strange formations so he did not answer right away. The Pope with a surprising burst of energy asked, "Do you remember or not?"

"Yes, I do remember," Hayyim answered. Hayyim then put his ear down to the Pope's chest and heard a steady rhythmic heart beat. "Your heart is quite sound. Where is your pain?" He hesitated. "Do you suspect poison?"

"No, but my sons do," he shrugged. But I'm an old man my friend."

Hayyim gave no indication of surprise when he heard the Pope use the words "my friend," but his uncertainty about being there was not diminished.

"I want to know how life has been with you since..." The Pope could not finish his sentence. He lay back on his bed, staring at the white satin canopy that hung above.

"Do you mean since all the troubles began for my community?"

As tired as the Pope was, he seemed to gather strength as he talked. "Yes, they must seem like troubles to you, but you have no idea what my troubles are here in the palace and indeed over the world. We are trying to help heathens come into the fold so that they will achieve salvation. Can you imagine that there are people on the other side of the ocean who lop off the head of someone simply because they've lost a silly game of ball sports?"

Hayyim knew that he was referring to the recent news of short, dark people in lands far across the ocean. After Columbus' voyage, other adventurous men took ships and traveled far to see if they could acquire new trading routes, riches, and converts for kings and popes. Hayyim was not sure of the order of importance of their desires, but he was aware of new discoveries being made and new worlds to conquer. He had heard of a Florentine, named Verrazano, a Cabeza de Vaca of Spain, and a Magellan of Portugal, and he marveled at their courage to travel to such distant places where one was never sure of what danger awaited. He wondered what drove these men. If he were to leave here, it would not be to conquer anything but rather to have a safe place for himself and his family.

The Pope asked him again, "Can you imagine that?"

Hayyim responded wryly. "No, I can't imagine such cruelty....over a game. But please, without offending Your

Holiness, I must ask you to be quiet for a moment for I need to concentrate on my examination."

The Pope did as he was asked and remained still as Hayyim continued to probe him. The Pope turned on his side so that Hayyim could listen to the Pope's lungs through his back.

"I must ask you some questions now, and I hope you'll not be too embarrassed to answer them," said Hayyim.

"I've been feeling too ill to feel any sense of shame. Ask whatever questions you wish," the Pope responded.

"How much food and what kind do you eat during the course of a day and..." Hayyim hesitated. "And how many times do you leave your feces in the pot....and what do they look like?"

The Pope paused. "I'm entirely aware of my fragility and that I'm merely human flesh." The Pope stopped for a moment, for his breathing had become labored. Hayyim was surprised that the conversation had taken this turn for even in their moments of extraordinary discussion and friendship, the Pope had never spoken of himself as a mere mortal and certainly the people around him had never expressed that thought even in a whisper.

"I can only drink a clear chicken broth. My feces? Constantly terrible. I have seen drops of blood in that syrupy stuff."

"How long have you had these symptoms?" Hayyim asked.

"About six months. At first, I thought it was something I ate." The Pope gave a small derisive laugh. "For a moment, I even attributed my lack of good health to Satan. But just for a moment. When you are very sick, you can believe almost anything." He looked up at the canopy of his bed. "What I really want is the truth. Does this illness mean the end? That I need to prepare for a heavenly journey?"

Hayyim said, "I don't know...yet. I must consult with some of my books and I shall have to take a ride to the monastery where they have an extensive collection of books and an herb garden. If I leave now, I can be back tomorrow around the middle of the day." Hayyim thought Alba would be pleased that he had a safe way to get to the monastery where he could see Israel, or, at least, know how he was faring.

"I'll give you a horse and a Swiss Guardsman to accompany you." The Pope tried to sit up and reach for his bell.

"Your Holiness is too kind. There's no need. I can find my way out there."

"Call Cardinal Carafa in. He'll direct one of the guards to help you."

Not the time to argue, thought Hayyim. He opened the heavy wooden door and found Pier Luigi and Ranuncio sitting on the floor. They stood quickly and looked expectantly at Hayyim. Cardinal Carafa sat on a leather chair his head falling on his chest with sleep. Rather than put his hand on the Cardinal's shoulder to awaken him, he cleared his throat as loudly as possible. "The Pope wishes to speak with you."

Carafa gathered himself up. "Is he all right?"

"I'm sure he'll share with you what he wishes."

Carafa approached the bed cautiously and leaned over to hear Paul. "Please give the good doctor a horse and have a Swiss Guard accompany him to the monastery to get some medicines."

Pier Luigi then spoke, "We'll accompany him, Father. Don't call the Swiss Guards away from their duties here. We can be of help in assuring a safe, quick trip out to the monastery." Hayyim started to protest thinking of the danger to Israel, but Carafa silenced him with a wave of his hand. Hayyim followed him to the stable at the back of the palace with Pier Luigi and Ranuncio. Hayyim admired the way the horses were kept. The blacksmith, who lived in a room off to the side of the stable, was ready to shoe any horse when necessary. The dogs that greeted him were well fed.

Carafa moved closer to Hayyim and kept his voice low. "I dare not leave the Pope now but someday I will visit that monastery to get to the bottom of the duplicity that is there. I'm sure there is some chicanery that is involved with Father Bruno and the friars. That monastery is close to where we saw you in the woods when we were out hunting."

Carafa signaled to one of the stable hands. "Bring these three men horses that need some exercise for they have a ten-kilometer ride."

So be it, Hayyim thought as the stable hand saddled up the horses. I will have to be very careful when I go there. He shrugged thinking maybe God will pay a bit of extra attention to this dilemma.

CHAPTER 41

Good Herbs

The men rode out of Rome along the Tiber River to the forest and through the fog. When they entered the woods, the haze turned into a dense mist that covered the leaves of the trees and drenched the riders. The horses, equally soaked, rode through thicket and bramble sure-footed and steady. By the time they came to the monastery, the men were so wet that when Father Leo, a rubicund, robust man with lively eyes, came to greet them and take their horses, he directed them to go to the dining room where they could dry themselves by a fire.

"A cup of boiled water with orange and a bowl of vegetable soup will do you some good," he said. The three men entered the dining room and saw the brothers eating in silence. Hayyim noted a black cloth draped over the doorway.

"This is a strange place," said Pier Luigi as they took their seats with friars who paid them no attention.

"It's not so strange," said Hayyim ignoring the bowl of soup that had been set before him.

"You're not eating," said Ranuncio.

"I'm not hungry," said Hayyim trying to suppress his pleasure when he saw Father Bruno approaching.

"Thank you, Rabbi Luzzatti, for joining us." He acknowledged the Pope's sons with a bow. "Welcome to our humble abode. It's an honor for us to have you here." The brothers bowed stiffly.

Pier Luigi said, "So this is where Father Nicolas lived."

Father Bruno hesitated before replying, but looked directly at the two young men. "You see, we knew he was gone but we thought he would be back. He'd been acting strange of late...he'd been ill with bad stomach problems and I think he was distraught by the thought of death. It's something we work on here but not everyone can easily grasp the idea of leaving this earth. We knew he needed to go...we thought he would be back. We were hoping he would have found his way back here but...other events intervened."

Pier Luigi started to speak, but Hayyim interrupted. "We're here, Father Bruno, so that I can pick up some herbs to boil and give to the Pope for his stomach. I need fresh opium poppy and helleborous niger."

"I'll send Father Leo. It might be interesting for Pier Luigi and Ranuncio to see our medicine garden." Father Bruno rang the bell summoning Father Leo.

Hayyim added, "I'll be with you shortly to choose the best herbs from the garden for your father."

"We can wait for you," said Pier Luigi.

"I want to talk to Father Bruno for a moment about his health," said Hayyim.

Ranuncio grabbed his brother's arm. "He said he'd be along shortly. Father Leo's waiting."

"Listen," Pier Luigi said. "We are with the father of the man accused of murdering our mother. We're in a place that was the home to Father Nicolas—an apostate if there ever was one. It would behoove us not to let Luzzatti out of our sight."

"He will be in our sight," Ranuncio sneered.

"You promise?"

"Don't be silly. Let's go and look at the garden and find the herbs."

"Yes, gentlemen," said Father Leo. "I think that's an excellent idea."

Pier Luigi scowled. "Let's go, then," he said, "and be done with it."

As the three men left the vestibule, several of the brothers watched Father Leo dressed simply in his brown linen cowled cassock walk alongside Pier Luigi and Ranuncio clothed in pantaloons with stripes of red and gold silk and velvet doublets adorned with gold buttons. The brothers towered over the short, portly Father Leo.

When they were out of hearing distance, Father Bruno said, "We've much to talk about. What's the condition of the Pope? Come we'll walk along the path that circles the garden."

"He's quite ill. The truth is I don't have much hope for his recovery. There's something eating away at his body—his stomach, his bowels. The only thing I can try to do is bring him some comfort with some herbs. It's difficult to say what will help."

He paused struggling to find the right words. "I want to suggest that we plan for the escape of my son. In that way, you'll be free of the responsibility of his care."

Father Bruno put his hand on Hayyim's elbow drawing him a bit closer. "Father Leo will see to it that Israel is warned of the presence of Pier Luigi and Ranuncio at the monastery. He won't be found today, but...." His was silent for a moment. "We've never talked about the terrible ordeal of Father Nicolas."

Hayyim kept his eyes fastened on the path as they walked together. "I'm so sorry. I pray to God every day for forgiveness."

"Not your fault, my good doctor. Once Father Nicolas left here, it was in God's hands."

"A sobering experience. Rome is no longer safe for me or my family, and it will get worse with the death of Paul. Israel needs to understand that this cannot be a permanent place for him."

Hayyim paused waiting for Father Bruno's words but he had knelt to inspect the soil around an elderberry bush.

"I've nothing but respect, gratitude, and honor for the work you do and for your help with my son, but I need to know if you will help with his escape? I think it is too dangerous for me to see him now with the Pope's sons here."

"I must see about getting water here, and, yes, we will help with the escape." He hesitated. "His presence is dangerous for us as well."

"Will you tell Israel he's to meet us at the edge of the forest tonight? I'll be coming with a carriage."

Father Bruno continued inspecting foliage—a great oak was beginning to drop its leaves. "At what time?"

"About two hours after darkness falls. Alba and I will bring regular clothes for him to wear."

"Don't worry about the cassock. Find someplace to burn it. Go out to the garden, select the herbs, and I'll talk to your son. What shall I tell him about where you'll be going?"

"Tell him that we will be going to Salonika. The Turks have welcomed Jews there. I believe we can make the trip in about a month and I've made inquiries as to how we can secure help along the way."

As soon as the words were out of his mouth, Hayyim realized how much he trusted this man. Hayyim looked at the sundial and saw that he would have only two hours of daylight left to select the herbs. He shook Father Bruno's hand. "I must get back to the Palace. I thank you with all my heart. Know you'll always be included in my prayers."

Father Bruno said quietly, "As you and your family will be in mine." He faltered. "I regret the pain I caused your community." Hayyim held the friar's eyes for a moment and remained silent.

When Hayyim got to the herb garden, he saw Pier Luigi, Ranuncio, and Father Leo bending over plants and smelling them as they went along.

Hayyim requested a basket from Father Leo to hold the selected poppy and helleborous niger.

As they gathered up the herbs, Hayyim looked up to see Israel approach the garden from the northern end of the path, his head bent, reading a small book. Hayyim quickly bent down to gather more plants.

Israel beamed when he first spotted his father, but as soon as he saw Pier Luigi and Ranuncio his smile faded. The two brothers looked up at the approaching figure quizzically. Pier Luigi was the first to say, "Why this friar looks just like..." Before he could finish the sentence, Ranuncio pulled at his sleeve and said, 'Yes, he does resemble our cousin from Parma. Come, we must finish gathering these herbs for Father." Pier Luigi looked at his brother questioningly but said nothing.

Hayyim watched carefully as this drama unfolded. With guarded eyes, he acknowledged Israel with a nod. Although he could have been polite and made up a name, his fear and uncertainty would not permit him to speak. Neither Ranuncio nor Pier Luigi said anything, but would they reveal their knowledge later on?

Hayyim said nervously, "We must ride back quickly while we still have some daylight. I want to brew these herbs in hot water and then give them to the Pope to see if we can heal the problem in his intestines."

The men said their good-byes to Father Leo, placed the herbs in the saddle bags, mounted their horses, and rode through the forest. Hayyim thought that one of them would say something about Israel or "the cousin from Parma" but neither did. Hayyim was grateful for the new horse's sturdiness. Surely Hillel would be able to take the family with its belongings to Salonika.

When they arrived at the palace, they went immediately to the Pope's bedroom. Cardinal Carafa was seated at the Pope's bedside.

"How is he?" asked Pier Luigi.

"He appears very weak and has taken a turn for the worse. He can't retain even the mildest of broths," said Carafa his voice wavering.

From the bedside, came the Pope's faint voice. "Is the medicine here?"

Hayyim was about to speak, but Cardinal Carafa answered for him. "Luzzatti's here with the herbs."

"Then leave us."

"Your Holiness, the herbs will have to be brewed and steeped in hot water," Luzzatti said.

"Pier Luigi and Ranuncio will take the herbs to the kitchen and, Carafa, you will remain outside."

Ranuncio was about to speak, but Pier Luigi bowed and took his brother's arm and said, "Yes, Father. We'll take care of brewing the herbs."

The Pope lifted a hand from the side of his bed. Hayyim Luzzatti took the Cardinal's seat.

"What have you decided to do?" the Pope whispered.

Hayyim was startled by the question. "I'll have these herbs brewed, and we'll see which ones bring you some comfort."

"That's not what I meant at all. What are you planning to do about your life here?" The Pope's breathing was raspy and heavy.

Hayyim wondered why the Pope was asking this question now. Did he know he was planning to leave Rome with Alba and Israel?

"I'm planning to live my life as usual. I'm happy that the Pope has seen fit to invite me back to the Palace for I truly miss our conversations, but I'm sure that future visits will be up to the Pope and his wishes."

The Pope replied faintly, "Come closer. Again, I ask you what are your plans?"

"My plan is to take care of you and see that you get well. Don't you want to see Michelangelo complete St. Peter's? Don't you want Titian to finish your portrait?"

There was no answer from the Pope's bed. He had closed his eyes and appeared to be in a deep sleep.

Just then, Cardinal Carafa entered with Pier Luigi and Ranuncio who carried trays of cups filled with steaming water in which the various herbs had been brewed.

"You may leave now, Dr. Luzzatti. Dr. Ludwig will be here shortly to take care of the Pope. One of the sons or a guard can accompany you on horseback. I'm sure the Pope would want to see your safe arrival home after all that you've done today."

"But I have special knowledge of these herbs." Hayyim started to protest.

"You are dismissed," said the Cardinal.

Hayyim realized continued protest was futile without the Pope being awake to support him. "Thank you. I prefer to walk. I've arrived at this palace many times on foot and can leave the same way." He bowed to Carafa and the sons.

Before stepping out into the hall, he turned back and said, "You need to see which of these herbs help. There's no certainty. Some of these depend on how well the person can tolerate the liquid. Look for the one that will give him the most comfort." Hayyim then turned to leave - he did not want Carafa to see his tears.

As he reached the end of the long corridor, he heard the footsteps of someone running and turned to see Ranuncio waving at him and yelling, "Stop." What could he want? He faced the young man who resembled his mother more than his father.

"I recognized your son—that is the young man who is said to have killed my mother," said Ranuncio.

"He was in the house with his mother and me all the time."

"I know that—I know that he was tortured to confess, but we could be more helpful to you if we did know who murdered our mother."

"I don't know," Hayyim said.

"I was only hoping that you knew, so we could help Israel live in peace. We think it must have been someone who knew that Mother was going to visit your wife and frowned upon such... such consorting." Ranuncio looked carefully at Hayyim.

"I know of no one who would do that." Hayyim knew in his heart that he could not betray Finzi and DiBelli to Ranuncio, although he considered their act to be an abomination. He knew the gobierno would have to deal with these two men, and he preferred that it be done by his community rather than the Church.

Ranuncio's eyes hardened. "The real killers, Rabbi. Why won't you expose them when it could make life easier for your son?"

This time Hayyim showed no hesitation. "I told you I don't know. I repeat, I don't know." He turned and left the papal palace, leaving Ranuncio staring at him in disbelief. He shouted after Hayyim, "You foolish man."

CHAPTER 42

Michelangelo's Concern

Dr. Ludwig listened carefully as Cardinal Carafa told him of Doctor Luzzatti's recommendations. Ludwig was concerned when he saw the Pope lying immobile, his face ashen. He thought that these might be the Pope's final hours, and he wondered if Carafa understood that because he kept talking about liquids.

"These liquids may or may not be helpful and we'll know only when he can sip them and see if he improves or not. You know, I don't trust Dr. Luzzatti."

"You needn't be so anxious, Carafa. I have faith in the work of this Jewish doctor. He's a good physician who has treated many of my Christian friends. Let me examine the Pope." Dr. Ludwig bent his ear to the man's chest. "That heaviness in his breath is not a good sign. I'll stay with him while you take a rest. I'm sure it's been hard on you assuming so many of the spiritual burdens of the Pope."

Cardinal Carafa nodded. "Your offer is much appreciated." Although he was extremely tired, Carafa knew that time was of the essence. The Pope's death might be imminent, and the man had made no plans for his successor. Paul had never revealed to Carafa his thinking about the next Pope and what his mandate should be. What would be the legacy he was to pass on? Was it his art? His mission to reform the Church? His tolerance toward the peoples of the new world? His library of books? All the land he acquired and his desire to pass it on to members of his family? St. Peter's? What of Justinian and Alfonso? They had been by his side during these days of planning for the Council of Trent. Their ambition was not even disguised. To what lengths would they go? Thus far he had been able to rein them in because he was the one who had most access to the Pope.

When he reached his chamber, he directed the guard to call Justinian to his quarters and asked for some wine to be delivered. Maybe that would help loosen his tongue. When Justinian arrived, the guard brought in a flask of claret and two glasses and set them down at a table where Carafa was already seated with a deck of cards.

Carafa dismissed the guard. "I'm so glad you have come," he said.

Justinian took his seat and arched an eyebrow. "Cards at this time? It feels quite frivolous that we should be playing cards with the Pope being so ill."

"I'm bone weary and need some distraction. The Pope's illness is quite serious." He looked for a reaction from Justinian, but he remained expressionless. Carafa continued, "Dr. Ludwig is with the Pope now. What shall we play, and will you have a glass of wine?"

"Will you have some?" Justinian eyed the crystal claret flask.

Carafa smiled. "It comes from the Pope's own vineyards and you know we've had a good growing season this year. The wine has been fermented perfectly."

With that Carafa poured two glasses of claret from the crystal flask, and started dealing the cards. Justinian knew from the number of cards that they would be playing Picquet. A Spanish visitor had recently brought the game to the papal court.

When they had taken the first sips of wine and played some cards, Justinian said, "Perhaps the Pope will get better."

Carafa took a sip of wine, played a card, and then drew from the deck. "He's quite ill. He even called for Dr. Luzzatti."

"Do you think the Pope knows how sick he is?" Placing a card on the table, Justinian said, "My ace trumps your king."

"Yes, I think he knows he's going to die."

Justinian held a card up to his cheek for a few seconds before putting it out on the table. "He's said nothing about succession?"

"Nothing," said Carafa, again laying down a card and taking another from the deck.

Justinian lifted the glass to his lips but put it down without drinking. "Then it will be up to us...those of us who were closest to him. We should begin to plan now, for it won't go well for us to not have a Pope of our choosing in place as the proceedings for the next meeting of the Council of Trent are taking place."

'I didn't know you had taken such an interest in the Council."

Justinian frowned. "You underestimate me, Carafa. I know enough that the Protestant princes will continue to exert their influence if they know we're without a Pope."

Carafa nodded and threw out a card. "We'll need the Pope's approval to begin the process of succession and an indication from his doctor that his death is imminent."

Justinian played a card and nonchalantly asked, "It is?"

Carafa nodded, and the playing of cards and sipping of claret continued.

"Where's Alfonso?" Justinian questioned. "He's usually here when we are together. I think this is the first time that I'm sitting down with you alone." He shuffled the cards in his hands.

"Alfonso is a bit ill himself and asked to be excused," Carafa lied. "You'll see him when he's feeling better, I presume?" said Justinian.

"Yes, I'll see him when he's feeling better. I think it's time for you to go, for we are both a bit drunk and a bit tired."

"Not too tired to think about the possible selection for the next Pope?" asked Justinian, wobbling a bit as he stood, holding the back of the chair for support.

"That must be the most important thought of our temporal life," said Carafa, a bit steadier on his feet.

When Justinian left, Carafa asked the guard at the door to go to the Pope's chamber to inquire about the Pope's health. The guard came rushing back and uttered just the two words, "Raspy breathing."

"Good," muttered Carafa. "Then there's still time." With that he lay down on his bed and slept for ten hours, dreaming only of smoke rising from a chimney and Michelangelo standing on a scaffold on the outside of that chimney trying to put a brick in place.

The next morning he arose early with a bit of a dull headache, but the dream reminded him that he had not visited Michelangelo for a while. Nor had the great sculptor sought him out. Carafa missed the cheerfulness and joy of Michelangelo's youth. In his old age, he had taken on an extraordinarily ascetic life.

Carafa passed by the Pope's chamber and learned that he was still asleep. According to Dr. Ludwig, there had been no changes during the night, even with the administering of helleborous niger. The Pope was unable to tolerate it. Carafa thought of going to morning mass but decided that Michelangelo would probably be in his best humor at the first part of the day, before the other workmen arrived. Dealing with so many different artisans frequently put the sculptor into a foul temper.

When Carafa arrived, Michelangelo was up on the scaffolding, and when Carafa called up to him, to his surprise, the sculptor shouted, "I'll be right down." Carafa was amazed at the rapidity with which he lowered the scaffolding and alighted. "My God," he thought. "This man has the energy of four twenty year-olds." That thought lit a thirst in Carafa's loins "Still?" he thought. Michelangelo took Carafa's hands in his.

"Tell me, how is the Pope?"

Now Carafa understood why Michelangelo had lowered the scaffolding; normally he did not like to be interrupted in his work. The state of his contract and the money for his work depended on the condition of the Pope.

Carafa knew that Michelangelo and the Pope suffered many arguments about money. Michelangelo felt that the Pope did not understand the extent of rebuilding St. Peter's Cathedral—a project that Bramante, Raphael, Peruzzi, and Antonio da Sangallo all had tried to work on without much success. Endless squabbles had ensued when Michelangelo wanted Sangallo's outer walls demolished. The Pope did not agree until he saw Michelangelo's blueprint of the simple diamond shaped floor plan with four great piers to support the dome. The Pope had liked the majesty of it and its resemblance to the Sistine Chapel.

"He's sleeping. It's difficult to assess his condition." Carafa looked at the artist warily. "Are you concerned about him, or are you concerned about your commission if he's no longer the Pope?"

Michelangelo sat on a slab of marble. "We're both old men, the Pope and I—as you are, Carafa. I think about the future of this building and the future of my family. Should God think it's time to take me, I'm prepared. I assume the Pope thinks as well...that he's concerned for his legacy, and this great church is part of his legacy." He stood. "We should make plans if he is dying. That's all."

"I'll speak to him for you."

"No, I want to go to him myself, but I want a witness. You can be present if you wish."

Carafa reached his hands out and put them on Michelangelo's shoulders, realizing that he wanted to take them to Michelangelo's craggy face. He wanted to draw that face to him and kiss him passionately as he used to when he had first known Michelangelo in Florence. Carafa had convinced himself then that his love for this man was pure because it took place between an eminent sculptor and a man of the Church. He knew all the portions of the Bible that forbade men lying with men, but Carafa felt that applied only to ordinary men.

Michelangelo removed Carafa's hands. "Arrange the meeting," the sculptor said. He then remounted the scaffolding and tugged at the pulleys to draw himself up. He did not look down to see Carafa leave angry at Michelangelo's rebuke. The Jews are not the only ones who need to worry if the Pope dies, the Cardinal thought. With that he hurried back through the streets to get to the palace. Yes, plans needed to be made.

CHAPTER 43

A Decision is Made

Back at their home, Hayyim and Alba sorted through their belongings, deciding what to take and what to give to their friends who were remaining behind. They worked quietly speaking only when they were uncertain about taking or leaving a particular object—the lace tablecloth, the kettles for cooking, or their special goosedown pillows.

"Shall we take these ceramic cups?" She held them up to the light to briefly admire the design and their fragility. What she really wanted to say was that she was concerned about their uncertain future. How does one go off to a strange land? Would they be welcomed in Salonika? And Israel, their one and only dear son, undoubtedly confused about his religion? What was he really feeling? She was afraid that if she spoke these questions aloud, the tears would start to flow, and that would keep her from the work of sorting and packing.

Hayyim sensed her anxiety, answered her quietly, and kissed her on both cheeks. "No, they're likely to break. But take the two down pillows. Who knows when and where will we need to rest our heads?"

"Furniture?"

"I have informed Moses Bascola, and he'll give it to a needy family in the community."

"Are there people who will be ready for us in Salonika when we arrive?"

"Yes." He said these words to reassure his wife, but he indeed was apprehensive. Time was running out. He had already sent a letter by messenger to a rabbi in Salonika but had not heard anything. He knew that both bad weather and bandits could be problematic along the route. Fortunately, they had accumulated enough wealth to have a covered carriage, and had bought another horse so that Hillel need not carry the entire burden of the family.

At midafternoon, when everything had been packed, she watched Hayyim lift the packages and pieces of furniture into the carriage. He was wearing just a loose linen shirt open at the neck and cotton pants held up with a piece of hemp. She could see the sinews of his muscles and the curly hair on his chest as he lifted heavy boxes and placed them in the carriage.

"Hayyim," she called out. "Stop for a moment. You will exhaust yourself and not be able to drive tonight."

"Israel will help with the drive," he said wiping the sweat from his brow with the sleeve of his shirt.

"Are you sure Israel will be ready?"

"Father Bruno promised me." He stepped back, observed his work with satisfaction and turned to see his wife seated by the fire with needlework in hand. She sat with only a long, sheer chemise for the fire was hot. He could see the outline of her breasts, and the sweat running between them.

"The fire, my dear," he said. "Do you really need it?"

"It gives me memories of our life here. If I put it out, it will mean that the life here is already gone, and I'm trying to pospone that moment.

Hayyim took his wife's hand in his. "Come. There's cool water upstairs and I will wash you down." She followed him and they undressed in a room with only a bed and a basin of water, stripped naked, and gently washed each other.

"I'm clean," she said smiling.

He dried her with a piece of linen and led her to the bed. "Let's lie down. We have all the time in the world until nightfall. We'll deal with the books later. It will be for the last time we lie down together in this room." With that she started to weep. He took her in his arms, lifted her body that had grown thinner in recent weeks, and carried her gently to the bed. He slowly rolled her over on her side with her back toward him. She covered tears with her hands. He turned her to face him and kissed her wet cheeks, and they made love with fervor and passion, knowing that they would probably never return to Rome again, and certainly not to this house.

He brushed the hair from her face. "It will be all right. We'll be together in this new life."

Alba turned away from him and remained silent.

Hayyim rose from the bed and said, "Come, we must get ready to go. We'll have something to eat and then depart." They dressed with fresh clothes and hastily stuffed their dirty garments into a muslin sack and ate the chicken and zucchini that Alba had prepared. She took the leftovers and carefully wrapped them in parchment paper, for she knew it would be a while before they would reach an inn that would give them food and shelter.

She removed the crumbs from the table, and threw them to the chickens outside in the courtyard.

"I can't believe we're actually going to leave." She paused and continued throwing crumbs at the animals as they gathered at her feet. "I hope our neighbors take good care of them."

"We are doing what will guarantee safety for our son...and ourselves. You want to live in a ghetto?" Hayyim was carefully looking through his bookshelves deciding on what he should leave and what he should pack in his small carriage. He had left the books for last because he was torn between the space they would take up and how much he needed them for wisdom and comfort. He also hoped that some of the synagogue members would come for them once they found out he was gone.

She shuddered at the word "ghetto." "We're leaving behind some of our dearest friends—your synagogue—people whose lives you saved."

Her husband smiled. "We haven't been called a stubborn, stiff-necked people for no reason. Our friends aren't leaving because they think the Pope needs the services they supply to the community. Ben Shimoni is sure that all will be well with his printing, and maybe it will be, but we cannot take the chance considering what has happened to Israel."

"What do you think will happen to Finzi and DiBelli?"

Hayyim had been stuffing a set of clothing for Israel into a burlap sack. "My guess is that they will be driven from the community."

"And not be turned over to the Christian authorities?"

"No. They won't be turned over to the Christians. I'm sure of that, and I'm sure that they will never live here again."

She sighed. "Perhaps they'll all be better off."

Hayyim tied up the knapsack. "No one is better off with murder on their conscience."

Alba continued to busy herself, sometimes staring for an extra moment at the kettle she was leaving behind. Seeing her stop before the kettle, Hayyim said with a slight smile, "There's not room for the kettle. Come arrange yourself in the carriage. Hillel and Maimonides are getting impatient." Alba smiled as he said the names of his horses—there was great irony in choosing the names of great thinkers for horses who were going to work so hard to get them to Salonika. They stopped in each room and at the front door to touch the mezuzahs then kiss their fingers. Under the light of the full moon, they embraced each other tightly. She picked up her small cloth traveling bag and climbed into the carriage.

* * *

In the meantime, Carafa had hurried back to the Pope from his visit with Michelangelo, determined to get an audience for the artist. Maybe this favor would be returned, Carafa thought. The door to the Pope's chamber was wide open with the two Swiss Guards standing outside. Carafa had never known this chamber door to be open at any time. When he entered the room, he saw Cardinals Justinian and Alfonso kneeling by the side of the bed. Dr. Ludwig knelt between them. Dr. Ludwig looked up at Carafa's stricken face and said, "He's dead. I would certify the death took place about fifteen minutes ago."

Carafa thought that it must have happened at that moment when he was with Michelangelo. Doesn't Satan play strange tricks on us? This is my punishment for my evil and sinful desires, he thought, as he kneeled alongside Justinian and Alfonso and prayed for his friend's salvation in heaven. When they stood and had turned away from the Pope's bed, Carafa hissed, "Why wasn't I notified?"

Justinian answered—a bit too quickly, Carafa thought. "We tried to find you, but we had no idea where you were. We sent messengers scurrying all over the palace." Carafa thought that Justinian knew full well that Carafa had taken over the supervision of St. Peter's ever since the Pope's illness and could have found him there.

"The Pope was lucid in his final moments," Alfonso said. Carafa fell silent. Alfonso then turned to Justinian and said, "Wasn't he, Justinian?" Justinian nodded slowly. Then Alfonso turned to Dr. Ludwig and said, "Wasn't he, Dr. Ludwig?" Dr. Ludwig also nodded, albeit a bit reluctantly. Alfonso offered Carafa a small golden hammer. "We've left the honor to you to tap on his head gently three times to verify the death and to remove his Fisherman's ring."

Carafa took the hammer holding it carefully and noticed that the ring was not on the fourth finger of the Pope's right hand where he usually wore it.

Dr. Ludwig was quick to explain. "It's right here besides his bedside. When his hands became swollen we couldn't put it on anymore, we decided just to leave it near him, in case...in case his health would improve."

Carafa held the hammer in his right hand and seemed to weigh it. "Did he leave any instructions?"

Alfonso spoke again. "Yes, he did. When he saw that you weren't here...mind you he did ask for you...he said that he wanted Justinian to follow him as Pope and that I, because, I'm younger, should follow Justinian. I'm sure you'll wish to abide by the Pope's dying wishes."

Carafa tapped the hammer several times in the palm of his left hand. "That is ridiculous. You know well enough that the cardinals will ultimately decide with the next election."

"Yes," said Justinian. "But they'll want to hear the Pope's dying wishes and that will influence them a great deal, especially when his statement is verified by the good doctor here. We're lucky that the Jew was no longer ministering to the Pope. Some things just work out for the best, don't they?" He was quick to add, "And the Pope didn't suffer much. We're all grateful for that. Aren't we?"

Carafa continued hitting the hammer into the palm of his hand and started to pace. Beads of perspiration appeared on his forehead. He opened his mouth to say something but remained silent. Justinian started to speak but was silenced by Alfonso's quick frown.

"Ludwig," said Carafa. "You were here to hear his last words, weren't you?"

Ludwig hung his head. "I had stepped out for a moment when Justinian and Alfonso asked to be alone with him."

Carafa stopped hitting the hammer in the palm of his hand and faced the three men. "We must plan for an appropriate funeral and burial. Paul was one of the most brilliant Popes we have ever had, and he deserves a tomb equal to Julius. The rest of the cardinals and bishops in the world must know." Almost as an afterthought, he asked, "Where are his sons and why aren't they here?"

"We were caught up in the moment of his death," said Justinian. "You weren't here and we decided to maintain a vigil to let the Pope know we were in continuous prayer."

Carafa again knew that this was a lie—the two cardinals had at their beck and call all sorts of messengers and could have easily located the Pope's sons. Carafa said, "They'll be devastated. I'm sure of that."

Alfonso said, "Only because they will lose their access to riches and lands."

Carafa replied, "Whatever your thoughts of them, they should have been called."

With that Carafa took the golden hammer from Alfonso and tapped it gently on the side of the Pope's head. He called him by the name Alessandro Farnese, his name in the Sacred College. He put the hammer down and then bent over his grayish blue face taking it in his hands and kissing each cheek, brushing away the wetness of his tears with a piece of linen.

* * *

Alba and Hayyim arrived at the monastery with the stars and a full moon to guide their way through the forest. The path they took to the monastery was rarely traveled.

Hayyim was sure that now this monastery would be visited by the condottieri frequently because the Papal Palace knew it had been the home of Father Nicolas. Hayyim remembered the friar's tortured figure over the burning books, the smell of flesh burning, the community's desire to mix the ashes of his clothing with those of its books, and he worried about the other Jews who continued to believe there was a future in Rome.

Hayyim slowed the horses to a walk as they approached the monastery, not wanting to awaken the brothers. In the moonlight, he could see two men waiting under the portico of the building that was open to the elements. Soon he could make out Father Bruno and Israel in their cassocks. Israel carried a small knapsack of brown linen that he held up to his father.

"It just contains some bread and cheese. I entered here with nothing and I'm grateful to leave with these clothes and a little bit of food." He turned to Father Bruno and wrapped his arms around the friar's shoulders. "I can't thank you enough for providing me with this spiritual home, and I want you to know..." He stopped and looked apprehensively at his father. "...I want you to know that if I were not putting you in jeopardy, this would continue to be my spiritual home." Hayyim stiffened but said nothing because he knew that Israel might see life and his religion differently when they were safe in Salonika.

Father Bruno returned the young man's warm hug and said, "You're young yet, Israel. You have been through many difficult times, and you're about to embark on a treacherous journey with your family. You'll see how you feel when you arrive at your new home. Remember we will be thinking of you as we go about our daily chores and prayers. The herb garden will be a special reminder of you...and your family."

Israel said, "You will be in my daily thoughts as well," and climbed into the carriage next to his father.

Hayyim leaned down from his perch on the wagon and gave Israel the reins and bent forward to take Father Bruno's hand in his. "You'll always be in our hearts, and we shall advise you somehow when we have completed our journey." Although it was unusual for women to enter into talks between men, Alba leaned out of the carriage door and uttered her thanks as well. "You've saved my son, and for that I will always be grateful."

Israel clambered up to take a seat next to his mother. She embraced him, took his face in her hands, kissed him on both cheeks, and wiped his tears with the sleeve of her dress. He leaned into her shoulder and rested his head on her chest sobbing so hard that he shook. "It's going to be all right," she said as she rocked him to and fro.

Hayyim clicked his tongue as a signal to his horses, and they took off through the leafy forest where the mist of the Tiber River was rising.

He said, "By morning the fog will have lifted and we'll be well on our way to Salonika."

Just then there was a great pealing of bells that came from the Papal Palace. The horses reared, startled by the sudden noise. Hayyim's steady hands calmed them, and he realized what the pealing of the bells meant. "The Pope is dead. Pope Paul is dead," he murmured.

He clicked his tongue again, and the horses took off to freedom, taking the family to a place that was unknown.

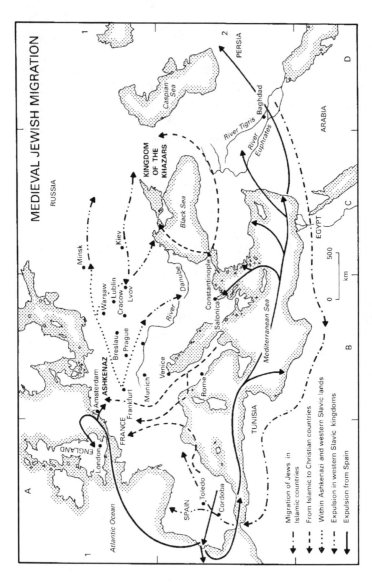

Medieval Jewish Migration

History Timeline . . . Continued

1553 — Convinced that the Talmud attacks Christianity, Pope Julius III burns thousands of volumes of Talmud in *Rome, Bologna, Ferrara,Venice* and *Mantua.*

1555 — Pope Paul IV (Carafa) issues bull,_*cum nimis absurdum,_*bringing religious and economic restrictions to the papal lands, requiring all Jews to live in ghettos and restricting economic relations with Christians to the selling of used clothes. Jews also forced to wear a special cap, forbidden to own real estate, or practice medicine on Christians.

1556 — Responding to persecutions by Pope Paul IV against the Jews of Ancona, Dona Gracia Mendes leads an unsuccessful economic boycott against the port of Ancona, favoring trade with Pisaro, which has accepted the Jewish refugees. The plan fails due to internal divisions in the Jewish community over fear of further persecution.

1559 — Pope Paul IV places the Talmud on the list of banned books, *Index liborum prohibitorum.* Popes Pius IV and Gregory XIII will later permit the printing of the Talmud, but allowing censorship of passages that are deemed insulting to Christianity; therefore, the Talmud is not printed in Italy.

Pope Paul IV permits the printing of the Zohar, book of medieval Jewish mysticism, at the same time he burns 12,000 other books; because he is persuaded that the Zohar contains no anti-Christian statements.

1569 — Pope Pius V expels the Jews from the papal states, with the exception of Ancona and *Rome.*

Bibliography

Carroll, James. Constantine's Sword: The Church and the Jews. Boston: Houghton Mifflin, 2001

Edwards, John.The Jews in Christian Europe, 1400-1700. Routledge: London, 1988.

Friedenwald, Harry. The Jews and Medicine, KTAV Publishing House, Inc. 1944, Vol. 1.

Friedman, Saul S. The Oberammerau Passion Play: A Lance Against Civilization. Carbondale, Illinois: Southern Illinois University Press, 1984

Gitlitz, David M. Secrecey and Deceit: The Religion of the Crypto-Jews. Philadelphia: Jewish Publication Society, 1996.

Halter, Marek. The Book of Abraham. Henry Holt & Co.: New York, 1983.

McCullough, Dearmond. The Reformation: A Common Culture. Viking: New York, 2003.

Manchester, William. A World Lit Only by Fire: The Medieval Mind and the Renaissance. Boston: Little, Brown, 1993.

Murphy, Caroline. The Pope's Daughter: The Extraordinary Life of Felice della Rovere, United Kingdom: Oxford University Press, 2005

Roth, Cecil. The History of the Jews of Italy. Philadelphia: Jewish Publication Society, 1946.

Ruderman, David B. Early Modern Jewry. A New Cultural History, Princeton, New Jersey, Princeton University Press, 2010.

Shulvass, Moses A. The Jews in the World of the Renaissance. Translated by Elvin I Kose. Leiden, Netherlands: E. J. Brill, 1973.

Spitz, Lewis W. The Rise of Modern Europe: The Protestant Reformation 1517-1559. New York: Harper and Row, 1985.

Stow, Kenneth R. The Jews in Rome, Vol 1, 1536-1551.Leiden, Netherlands: E. J. Brill, 1995

Stow, Kenneth R. Taxation, Community and State: The Jews and the Fiscal Foundations of the Early Modern Papal State. Stuttgart: Anton Hiersemann, 1982.

Thomas, Hugh. Rivers of Gold, The Rise of the Spanish Empire from Columbus to Magellan. Random House: New York, 2003.

Wills, Garry. Papal Sin; Structures of Deceit. New York: Doubleday, 2000.

Waagenenaar, Sam. The Pope's Jews. LaSalle, Illinois: Open Court,1974.

Council of Trent," Encyclopedia of REligion. Volume 15, 1987, ed.

Discussion Questions

1. Israel is the young son of Alba and Hayyim Luzzatti who ventured forth to Spain. While there, he converted to Christianity. Do you have any empathy for him in his conversion? What do you think of the community's reaction? His parents' reaction upon his return?

2. What is your analysis of the Pope's behavior?

3. Which of the characters do you see as making the greatest growth in understanding of the events and characters that are around them?

4. If you can place yourself, back in that period, considering the events of the day, at which point in time, if you were a Jew, would you have decided to leave Rome? Can you equate that with the Jews who were reluctant to leave Germany?

5. What did you learn about theological history of the time period? Anything else?

6. Talk about the ending. Were you surprised? Would you have created a different ending?

7. Would you want to learn more about this time period?

8. Were there specific themes in the book that you found interesting?

9. Did any parts of the book make you rethink some of your prejudices, myths, or understandings of history and religion?